MORE

SA... ...S X
George R.R. Martin

His strange pets were an amusing novelty—and they
worshiped him most gratifyingly. But being a god is
a dangerous pastime for a human . . .

TIME SHARDS
Gregory Benford

Sending the future a message is a proud and incredible achievement—if you know what you're saying.

THE VACUUM-PACKED PICNIC
Rick Gauger

Outdoor love-making's a time-honored sport on
Earth—but on the Moon, it calls for a new set of
rules!

THE THAW
Tanith Lee

Flash-frozen at the point of death, they could now be
revived in a world two centuries past their time—but
resurrections aren't always what they seem . . .

★ 1980 Nebula-Award Winner

THE **BEST SCIENCE FICTION** OF THE YEAR
#9

Terry Carr, Editor

A Del Rey Book

BALLANTINE BOOKS • **NEW YORK**

Contents

Introduction

If you're a typical member of the science-fiction audience, you probably read several sf anthologies a year. Maybe you buy them because you like several of the authors represented, or because you've found a given editor's taste is close to yours, or just because you like short stories.

If you buy a best-of-the-year anthology, part of your reason may be an interest in reading a more or less representative sampling of the themes and ideas that are being written about in current science fiction; another motivation might be to find out who some of the up-and-coming new writers are.

Readers who have discovered science fiction only recently often buy anthologies to find out which authors they like, and go on to buy their novels. (I recommend this, by the way; and not just for my own anthologies.)

But whether you're a new sf reader or a long-time fan, chances are you haven't bothered to analyze just how anthologists put their books together, so you may not be getting as much enjoyment from them as you could. By "how anthologists put their books together" I don't mean how they choose the stories—obviously editors buy the ones they consider to be the best—but rather how they decide which stories should go where in a given book: the *structure* of an anthology.

Oh, yes, anthologies are planned products; they're not just thrown together in willy-nilly order. I've discussed this with many editors over the years, and all of them said they arranged their contents according to definite plans. The purpose is always to present each story in an order that will give you maximum enjoyment from it, and thus make the book somewhat more than the simple sum of its parts.

If an anthology has five long stories and seven short ones, for instance, you won't find all the long stories bunched together: for variety of pace, they'll be separated by the shorter tales. If there are three stories about telepathy (or time travel or the far future or whatever), they'll be spaced throughout the book so that you won't become surfeited by a given theme. If there are several "downbeat" stories—grim visions of tomorrow, unhappy endings, etc.—they won't be together either, because these things are best taken in small doses. The same goes for comic stories.

Some things about structuring anthologies are fairly obvious. For instance, the first story in a book is intended as the lead story. And you can expect that the last story will be far from the least in the book, because editors prefer that you finish on a high note.

But just what *is* a lead story? It may be the best in the book, and it will certainly be *one* of the best. It may be the one by the most famous author, placed first to entice you to want to begin reading the book immediately (i.e., to buy it). It may be the one with the best narrative hook, or the most smoothly written one, so that you'll find yourself ten pages into the book even if you only meant to glance at the first page. Ideally, it will be all three of these things.

The final story in an anthology is chosen similarly, except that the fame of the author is less important—if you read the contents page all the way to the end before deciding whether or not to buy a book, you'll already have seen the well-known bylines—and a fast, intriguing beginning isn't as important as a satisfying ending, something you may find yourself thinking about after you've put down the book.

What about the middle of the anthology, those stories between two presumed high points? Are the stories placed there necessarily second-rate? Well, let's hope not, because if an editor has only two outstanding stories to present, then the book is definitely in trouble. Presumably all the stories are at least pretty good, and the "second-rate" ones seem so only in comparison with the very best. And a smart editor will always put at least a couple of the best stories somewhere in the middle in order to jolt your interest along the way. (Sometimes—and this book is an example—the editor's favorite story will appear near the middle.)

The structure of an anthology, then, is analogous to that of a good novel: grab the reader's interest right away, put some excellent stuff along the way, and close out with a satisfying ending.

Of course, all of the foregoing is done on the supposition that you'll read an anthology in order, from front to back. Most readers don't do exactly that—they read the stories of their favorite authors first, *then* go on to read the rest, probably in the order of their appearance just because it's simpler that way. This is natural; and yes, I usually do the same.

But it can't hurt to plan the order of an anthology's contents carefully, and it *will* increase the enjoyment of those readers who go from front to back. You might try doing that as an experiment, if you're not one of those who usually do so.

And even if you can't resist reading Varley, Benford, McIntyre, or Martin first, remember that my contents page recommends otherwise for maximum enjoyment.

Letters of disagreement or whatever can be sent to me at 11037 Broadway Terrace, Oakland, CA 94611.

—TERRY CARR
January 1980

Galatea Galante, the Perfect Popsy

Alfred Bester

Have you noticed that there aren't many robot stories written anymore? In part this is because technology has progressed along other lines: we've had an explosive flowering in the computer sciences, and the possibilities of cloning and bioengineering seem more and more intriguing.

Just as important, though, is the fact that science fiction as a whole has followed a straight-line historical path from the mechanical gimmickry of the twenties and thirties to the more humanistic concerns of present-day sf. Robots were common in early science fiction, but by 1950 writers were more often considering the anomalies of half-human, half-constructed people—androids. By now, androids too have been superceded: we read these days of cyborgs, clones, and people who have been created by genetic manipulation. (Mary Shelley's *Frankenstein* prefigured this trend too. It's almost impossible to overestimate her contribution to science fiction.)

The truth is, sf writers are much like any other kind: they know that most interesting plots arise from the unpredictability of humans. Alfred Bester demonstrates precisely that in his acerbic novelette about a "biodroid"

1

> creator who sets out to produce a perfect
> woman, knowing that she must have a "wild"
> factor to make her complete. He gets more
> than he anticipated.

He was wearing a prefaded jumpsuit, beautifully tailored, the *dernier cri* in the nostalgic 2100s, but really too youthful for his thirty-odd years. Set square on his head was a vintage (circa 1950) English motoring cap with the peak leveled on a line with his brows, masking the light of lunacy in his eyes.

Dead on a slab, he might be called distinguished, even handsome, but alive and active? That would depend on how much demented dedication one could stomach. He was shouldering his way through the crowded aisles of:

*****

THE SATURN CIRCUS
*****

50 PHANTASTIK PHREAKS 50

!!! ALL ALIENS !!!

He was carrying a mini–sound camera that looked like a chrome-and-ebony peppermill, and he was filming the living, crawling, spasming, gibbering monstrosities exhibited in the large showcases and small vitrines, with a murmured running commentary. His voice was pleasant; his remarks were not.

"Ah yes, the *Bellatrix Basilisk*, so the sign assures us. Black-and-yellow bod of a serpent. Looks like a Gila monster head attached. Work of that Tejas tailor who's so nitzy with surgical needle and thread. Peacock coronet on head. Good theater to blindfold the eyes. Conveys the conviction that its glance will kill. Hmmm. Ought to gag the mouth, too. According to myth the Basilisk's breath also kills . . .

"And the *Hyades Hydra*. Like wow. Nine heads, as per revered tradition. Looks like a converted Iguana.

The Mexican again. That seamstress has access to every damn snake and lizard in Central America. She's done a nice join of necks to trunk, got to admit that, but her stitching shows to *my* eye . . .

"*Canopus Cerberus*. Three dog heads. Look like oversized Chihuahuas. Mastiff bod. Rattlesnake tail. Ring of rattlers around the waist. Authentic but clumsy. That Tejas woman ought to know you can't graft snake scales onto hound hide. They look like crud; but at least all three heads are barking . . .

"Well, well, well. Here's the maladroit who claims he's my rival; the Berlin butcher with his zoo castoffs. His latest spectacular, the *Rigel Griffin*. Ta-daaa! Do him justice; it's classic. Eagle head and wings, but they're molting. Lion bod implanted with feathers. They're molting, too. And he's used ostrich claws for the feet. *I* would have generated authentic dragon's feet . . .

"Now *Martian Monoceros*; horse bod, elephant legs, stag's tail. Yes, convincing, but why isn't it howling according to legend? *Mizar Manticora*. Kosher. Kosher. Three rows of teeth. Look like implanted shark's. Lion bod. Scorpion tail. Nice redeyed effect. The *Ares Assida*. Dullsville. Just an ostrich with camel feet, and stumbling all over them, too. No creative spark . . .

"Ah, but I call that poster over the *Sirius Sphinx* brilliant theater. My compliments to the management. It's got to be recorded for posterity:

THE PUBLIC IS RESPECTFULLY
REQUESTED NOT TO GIVE THE
CORRECT ANSWER TO THE
ENIGMA POSED BY
THE SPHINX

"Because if you do, as Oedipus found out, she'll destroy herself out of chagrin. A sore loser. I ought to answer the riddle just to see how they stage it, but no. Theater isn't my shtick. My business is strictly creative genesis . . .

"The Berlin butcher again. *Castor Chimera*. Lion head. Goat's bod. Looks like an Anaconda tail. How the hell did he surgify to get it to vomit those flames? Some sort of catalytic gimmick in the throat, I suppose. It's only a cold corposant fire, quite harmless, but very dramatic, and those fire extinguishers around the showcase are a lovely touch. Damn good theater. Again my compliments to the management . . .

"Ah-ha! Beefcake on the hoof. *Zosma Centaur*. Goodlooking Greek joined to that Shetland pony. Blood must have been a problem. They probably drained both and substituted a neutral surrogate. The Greek looks happy enough; in fact, damn smug. Anyone wondering why only has to see how the pony's hung . . .

"What have we here? *Antares Unicorn*, complete with grafted Narwhal tusk, but not with the virgin who captured it—virgin girls being the only types that can subdue unicorns, legend saith. I thought Narwhals were extinct. They may have bought the tusk from a walking-stick maker. I know virgins are not extinct. I make 'em; purity guaranteed or your money back . . .

"And a *Spica Siren*. Lovely girl. Beautiful! She— But damn my eyes, she's no manufactured freak! That's Sandra, *my* Siren! I can spot my genesis anywhere. What the hell is Sandy doing in this damn disgusting circus, naked in a showcase? This is an outrage!"

He charged the showcase in his rage. He was given to flashes of fury that punctuated his habitual exasperated calm. (His firm conviction was that it was a damned intransigent world because it wasn't run HIS way, which was the RIGHT way.)

He beat and clawed at the supple walls, which yielded but did not break. He cast around wildly for anything destructive, then darted to the Chimera exhibit, grabbed a fire extinguisher, and dashed back to the Siren. Three demoniac blows cracked the plastic, and three more shattered an escape hatch. His fury outdrew the freaks, and a fascinated crowd gathered.

He reached in and seized the smiling Siren. "Sandy, get the hell out. What were you doing there in the first place?"

"Where's your husband?"

"For God's sake!" He pulled off his cap, revealing pale, streaky hair. "Here, cover yourself with this. No, no, girl, downstairs. Use an arm for upstairs, and hide your rear elevation against my back."

"No, I am *not* prudish. I simply will not have my beautiful creation on public display. D'you think I—" He turned fiercely on three Security guards closing in on him and brandished the heavy brass cylinder. "One more step and I let you have it with this. In the eyes. Ever had frozen eyeballs?"

They halted. "Now look, mister, you got no—"

"I am *not* called 'mister.' My degree is 'Dominie,' which means Master Professor. I am addressed as Dominie, Dominie Manwright, and I want to see the owner at once. Immediately. Here. *Sofort! Immediatamente*! Mr. Saturn or Mr. Phreak or whatever!"

"Tell him that Dominie Regis Manwright orders him here now. He'll know my name, or he'd better, by God! Now be off with you. Split. Cut. Vamoose." Manwright glared around at the enthralled spectators. "You turkeys get lost, too. All of you. Go eyeball the other sights. This Siren show is *kaputt*."

As the crowd shuffled back from Manwright's fury, an amused gentleman in highly unlikely 20th century evening dress stepped forward. "I see you understand

Siren, sir. Most impressive." He slung the opera cape off his shoulders and offered it to Sandra. "You must be cold, madame. May I?"

"Thank you," Manwright growled. "Put it on, Sandy. Cover yourself. And thank the man."

"I don't give a damn whether you're cold or not. Cover yourself. I won't have you parading that beautiful body I created. And give me back my cap."

"Women!" Manwright grumbled, yanking the cap down on his ash-blond head. "This is the last time I ever generate one. You slave over them. You use all your expertise to create beauty and implant sense and sensibility, and they all turn out the same. Irrational! A race apart! And where the hell's 50 Phantastik Phreaks 50?"

"At your service, Dominie," the gentleman smiled.

"What? You? The management?"

"Indeed yes."

"In that ridiculous white-tie-and-tails?"

"So sorry, Dominie. The costume is traditional for the role. And by day I'm required to wear hunting dress. It *is* grotesque, I agree, but the public expects it of the ringmaster."

"Hmp! What's your name? I like to know the name of the man I skin alive."

"Corque."

"Cork? As in Ireland?"

"But with a Q U E."

"Cor-kew-ee? Corque?" Manwright's eyes kindled. "Would you by any chance be related to Charles Russell Corque, Syrtus Professor of ETM biology? I'll hold that in your favor."

"Thank you, Dominie. I *am* Charles Russell Corque, Professor of Extra-Terrestrial and Mutation biology at Syrtus University."

"What!"

"Yes."

"In that preposterous costume?"

"Alas, yes."

"Here? On Terra?"

"As you see."

"What a crazy coincidence. It could almost be luck, in which I've never believed. I was going to make that damned tedious trip to Mars just to rap with you."

"And I brought my circus to Terra hoping to meet and consult with you."

"How long have you been here?"

"Two days."

"Then why haven't you called?"

"Setting up a circus show takes time, Dominie. I haven't had a moment to spare."

"This monstrous fakery is really yours?"

"It is."

"You? The celebrated Corque? The greatest researcher into alien life forms that science has ever known? Revered by all your colleagues, including myself . . . Swindling the turkeys with a phony freak show? Incredible, Corque! Unbelievable!"

"But understandable, Manwright. Have you any idea of the cost of ETM research? And the reluctance of grants committees to allocate adequate funds? No, I suppose not. You're in private practice and can charge gigantic fees to support your research, but I'm forced to moonlight and use this circus to raise the money I need."

"Nonsense, Corque. You could have patented one of your brilliant discoveries; that fantastic Jupiter-3 methophyte, for instance. Gourmets call it 'The Ganymede Truffle.' D'you know what an ounce sells for?"

"I know. There *are* discovery rights and royalties. Enormous. But you don't know university contracts, my dear Dominie. By contract, the royalties go to Syrtus where—" Professor Corque's smile soured, "—where they are spent on such studies as Remedial Table Tennis, Demonic Orientation, and The Light Verse of Leopold von Sacher Masoch."

Manwright shook his head in exasperation. "Those damned faculty clowns! I've turned down a dozen university offers, and no wonder. It's an outrage that you should be forced to humiliate yourself and— Listen, Corque, I've been dying for the details on how you discovered that Ganymede methophyte. When will you have some time? I thought— Where are you staying on Terra?"

"The Borealis."

"What? That fleabag?"

"I have to economize for my research."

"Well, you can economize by moving in with me. It won't cost you a cent. I've got plenty of room and I'll put you up for the duration with pleasure. I've generated a housekeeper who'll take good care of you, and rather amuse you, I think. Now do say yes, Corque. We've got a hell of a lot to discuss, and I've got a lot to learn from you."

"I rather think it will be the other way around, my dear Dominie."

"Don't argue. Just pack up, get the hell out of the Borealis, and—"

"What, Sandy?"

"Where?"

"Oh. Yes. I see the ratfink."

"What now, Manwright?"

"Her husband, Corque. I'll trouble you to use restraint on me or he'll become her late husband."

An epicene hove into view; tall, slender, elegant in flesh-colored SkinAll with chest, arms, and legs artfully padded to macho dimensions, as was the ornamented codpiece. Manwright juggled the extinguisher angrily, as though groping for the firing pin of a grenade. He was so intent on the encounter that Corque was able to slip the cylinder out of his hands as the epicene approached, surveyed them, and at last spoke.

"Ah, Manwright."

"Jessamy!" Manwright's tone turned the name into a denunciation.

"Sandra."

"And our impressario."

"Good evening, Mr. Jessamy."

"Manwright, I have a bone to pick with you."

"You? Pick? A bone? With me? Why, you damned pimp, putting your own wife, my magnificent creation, into a damned freak show!" He turned angrily on Professor Corque. "And you bought her, eh?"

"Not guilty, Dominie. I can't supervise everything. Our Freak Foreman made the purchase."

"He did, did he?" Manwright returned to Jessamy. "And how much did you get for her?"

"That is not germane."

"What? That little? You padded procurer, why? Why? God knows, you don't need the money."

"Dr. Manwright—"

"Don't you 'doctor' me. It's Dominie."

"Dominie . . ."

"Speak."

"You sold me a lemon."

"What?"

"You heard me. You sold me a lemon."

"How dare you!"

"I admit I'm a jillionaire."

"Admit it? You broadcast it."

"But nevertheless I resent a rip."

"Rip! I'll kill the man. Don't restrain me, Corque. I'll kill. Look, you damned minty macho, you came to me and contracted for the perfect wife. A Siren, you said. The kind that a man would have to lash himself to the mast to resist, *à la* Ulysses. Well? Didn't you?"

"Yes, I did."

"Ha! Yes you did. And did I or did I not generate a biodroid miracle of beauty, enchantment, and mythological authenticity, guaranteed or your money back?"

"Yes, you did."

"And one week after delivery I discover my Pearl of Perfection sold to the distinguished Charles Russell Corque's obscene freak show and displayed naked in a showcase. My beautiful face and neck! My beautiful back and bottom! My beautiful breasts! My beautiful mons veneris! My beauti—"

"That's what she wanted."

"Did you, Sandy?"

"Shame on you, girl. I know you're vain . . . that was a glitch in my programming . . . but you don't have to flaunt yourself. You're a damned exhibitionist." Back to Jessamy. "But that doesn't excuse your selling her. Why, dammit? Why?"

"She was tearing my sheets."

"What?"

"Your beautiful, enchanting Pearl of Perfection was

tearing my monogrammed silk sheets, woven at incredible cost by brain-damaged nuns. She was tearing them with her mythologically authentic feet. Look at them."

There was no need to look. It was undeniable that the beautiful, enchanting Siren was feathered from the knees down and had delicate pheasant feet.

"So?" Manwright demanded impatiently.

"She was also scratching my ankles."

"Damn you!" Manwright burst out. "You asked for a Siren. You paid for a Siren. You received a Siren."

"With bird feet?"

"Of course with bird feet. Sirens are part bird. Haven't you read your Bulfinch? Aristotle? Sir Thomas Browne? Matter of fact, you're lucky Sandy wasn't poured out bird from the waist down. Ha!"

"Very funny," Jessamy muttered.

"But it wasn't luck," Manwright went on. "No, it was genius. My biodroid genius for creative genesis, and my deep understanding of the sexual appetites."

"Don't be impudent, girl. I have sexual appetites too, but when I guarantee a virgin I— No matter. Take her home, Jessamy. Don't argue or I'll kill you—if I can find that damn brass thing I thought I had. Take Sandra home. I'll refund Professor Corque in full. Got to support his brilliant research. Sandy, trim your talons, for God's sake! Sense and sensibility, girl. Corque, go pack up and move in with me. Here's my card with the address. What the devil are you doing with that silly fire extinguisher?"

"And that's the full schmeer, Charles. I'm sorry I haven't any work in progress to show you, but you can see I'm no tailor or seamstress, cutting up mature animals, human or otherwise, and piecing parts together, like those showbiz monsters in your circus. No, I macrogenerate 'em, pure and whole, out of the basic DNA broth. Mine are all test tube babies . . . Florence flask babies, in fact, which is where I start 'em. Biodroids need womb space like any other animal."

"Fascinating, my dear Reg, and quite overwhelming. But what I can't fathom is your RNA process."

"Ah! The RNA messenger service, eh?"

"Exactly. Now we all know that DNA is the life reservoir . . ."

"All? We all know? Ha! Not bloody likely, even in this day and age. Remind me to show you the abuse I get from the scripture freaks."

"And we know that RNA is the messenger system delivering commands to the developing tissues . . ."

"Right on, Charles. That's where the control lies."

"But how do you control the controls? How do you direct the RNA to deliver specific commands from DNA to embryo, and how do you select the commands?"

"Penthouse."

"Wh-what?"

"Come up to the penthouse and I'll show you."

Manwright led Corque out of the enormous crimson-lit cellar laboratory which was softly glowing with ruby-colored glassware and liquids ("My babies *must* be insulated from light and noise") and up to the main floor of the house. It was decorated with the Dominie's catholic taste; a hodgepodge of Regency, classic Greek, African, and Renaissance. There was even a Pompeiian marble pool inhabited by iridescent manic fish which gazed up at the two men hungrily.

"Hoping we'll fall in," Manwright laughed. "A cross between Piranha and Golden Carp. One of my jokes."

Thence to the second floor, 25 x 100, Manwright's library and study; four walls shelved and crammed with tapes, microfilm, publications, and software, a rolling ladder leaning against each wall, an enormous carpenter's workbench in the center of the room, used as a desk and piled with clutter.

Third floor divided between dining room (front), kitchen and pantry (center), and servants' quarters (rear, overlooking garden).

Fourth floor, enjoying maximum sky and air, bedrooms. There were four, each with its own dressing room and bath, all rather monastic. Manwright regarded sleep as a damned necessity which had to be endured but should never be cosseted into a luxury.

"We all get enough sleep during our nine months in the womb," he had growled to Corque, "and we'll get more than enough after we die. But I'm working on regenerative immortality, off and on. No results yet. Trouble is, tissues get old and cranky and refuse to play ball." He led the professor up a narrow stair to the penthouse.

It was a clear plastic dome, firmly anchored against wind and weather. In the center stood a glimmering mechanical construct. If it resembled anything, it would be a giant collapsing robot waiting for a handyman to straighten it up again. Corque stared at the gallimaufry and then at Manwright.

"Neutrinoscope," the Dominie explained. "My extrapolation of the electron microscope."

"What? Neutrinos? The beta decay process?"

Manwright nodded. "Combined with a cyclotron. I get particular particle selection that way, and acceleration up to 10 Bev. Selection's the crux, Charles. Each genetic molecule in the RNA coil has a specific response to a specific particle bombardment. That way I've been able to identify and isolate somewhere in the neighborhood of ten thousand messenger commands."

"But— But— My dear Reg, this is positively fantastic!"

Manwright nodded again. "Uh-huh. Took me ten years."

"But I had no idea that— Why haven't you published?"

"What?" Manwright snorted in disgust. "Publish? And have every damned quack and campus cretin clowning around with the most sacred and miraculous phenomenon ever generated in our universe? Pah! No way!"

"*You're* into it, Reg."

Manwright drew himself up with hauteur. "*I*, sir, do not clown."

"But Reg—"

"But me no buts, professor. By heaven, if Christ, in whom I've never believed, ever returned to Terra and came to this house, I'd keep it a secret. You know damn well the hell that would break loose if I published. It'd be Golgotha all over again."

While Corque was wondering whether Manwright meant his biodroid techniques, Christ's epiphany, or both, there was a sound of a large object slowly falling upstairs. Manwright's scowl was transformed into a grin. "My housekeeper," he chuckled. "You didn't get the chance to see him when you moved in last night. A treasure."

An imbecile face, attached to a pinhead, poked through the penthouse door. It was followed by a skewed hunchback body with gigantic hands and feet. The mouth, which seemed to wander at will around the face, opened and spoke in a hoarse voice.

"Mahth-ter . . ."

"Yes, Igor?"

"Should I thteal you a brain today, mahth-ter?"

"Thank you, Igor. Not today."

"Then breakfahtht ith therved, mahth-ter."

"Thank you, Igor. This is our distinguished guest, the celebrated Professor Charles Corque. You will make him comfortable and obey him in everything."

"Yeth, mahth-ter. At your thervice, thelebrated Profethor Charlth Corque. Should I thteal you a brain today?"

"Not today, thank you, Igor."

Igor bobbed his head, turned, disappeared, and there was a sound of a large object rapidly falling downstairs. Corque's face was convulsed with suppressed laughter. "What in the world—?"

"A reject," Manwright grinned. "Only one in my career. No, the first of two, if we count Sandy, but I do think Jessamy will keep his Siren. Anyway," he continued, leading Corque downstairs, "this client was absolutely hypnotized by the Frankenstein legend. Came to me and contracted for a faithful servitor, like the Baron's accomplice. Returned five months later, paid like a gent, but said he'd changed his mind. He was now on a Robinson Crusoe gig and wanted a Friday. I made him his Friday but I was stuck with Igor."

"Couldn't you have dissolved him back into the DNA broth?"

"Good God, Charles! No way. Never. I generate life; I don't destroy it. Anyway, Igor's the ideal housekeeper. He does have this brain-stealing hang-up . . . that was part of the original model . . . and I have to lock him in a closet when there's thunder and lightning, but he cooks like a genius."

"I hadn't known that Baron Frankenstein's henchman was a chef."

"To be quite honest, Charles, he wasn't. That was an error in my programming (I *do* glitch now and then) but with a happy ending. When Igor's cooking he thinks he's making monsters."

The card came in on the same tray with the Tomato-Onion Tart (ripe tomatoes, sliced onions, parsley, basil, Gruyère; bake in pastry shell 40 minutes at 375°F.) and Manwright snatched the embossed foil off the salver.

"What's this, Igor? 'Antony Valera—Chairman, Vortex Syndicate—69 Old Slip—CB: 0210-0012-036-216291'?"

"In the waiting room, mahth-ter."

"By God, Charles, a prospective client. Now you may have your chance to watch my genesis from start to finish. Come on!"

"Oh, have a heart, Reg. Let the chairman wait. Igor's monster looks delicious."

"Thank you, thelebrated Profethor Charlth Corque."

"No, no, Igor, the thanks go from me to you."

"Pigs, both of you!" Manwright snorted and dashed for the stairs. Corque rolled his eyes to heaven, grabbed a slice of tart, winked at Igor, and followed, chewing ecstatically.

One would expect the chairman of a syndicate with a seventeen-figure CB telephone number to look like Attila the Hun. Antony Valera looked and dressed like a suave Spanish grandee; he was black and silver, including ribboned peruke. Yet he was very much with it, for as Corque entered, he smiled, bowed, and murmured, "What a happy surprise, Professor Corque. Delighted. I had the pleasure of hearing you speak at the Trivium Charontis convention," and Mr. Valera considerately offered his left palm, Corque's right hand still being busy with the tart.

"He wants an ideal executive secretary," Manwright broke in. He refused to waste time on courtesies. "And I told him that my biodroid talents are damned expensive."

"To which I was about to respond when you most happily entered, Professor Corque, that Vortex is criminally solvent."

"Then it's to be a company contract?"

"No, Dominie, personal," Mr. Valera smiled. "I, too, am criminally solvent."

"Good. I hate doing business with committees. You must know the old saw about camels. Let's discuss your specs and see whether we understand each other. Sex?"

"Female, of course."

"Of course. Physical appearance?"

"You don't take notes?"

"Total recall."

"You *are* lucky. Well then . . . Fair or Titian hair. Medium tall. Endowed with soft grace. Soft voice. Blue eyes. Clear skin. Slender hands. Slender neck. An overall . . . auburn quality."

"Red-gold, eh? Got any particular example of the type in mind?"

"Yes. Botticelli's *Birth of Venus*."

"Ha! Venus on the Half-Shell. Lovely model. Character?"

"What one would expect of a secretary; sterling, faithful, devoted . . . to my work, of course."

"To your work, of course."

"And clever."

"D'you mean clever or intelligent?"

"Aren't they the same?"

"No. Cleverness requires humor. Intelligence does not."

"Then clever. I'll provide the intelligence. She must be able to learn quickly and remember. She must be able to acquire any skill necessary for my work. She must be perceptive and understand the stresses and conflicts that make a chairman's life one constant battle."

"So far you could hire such an executive secretary," Manwright objected. "Why come to me?"

"I haven't finished, Dominie. I want a quality one never finds in ordinary women, no matter what their skills; she must have no private life and be willing to drop everything and be instantly available at all times."

"Available for what?"

"Business luncheons, dinners, last-minute parties, client entertainment, and so forth. She must be chic and fashionable and able to dazzle men. You would not believe how many tough tycoons have been charmed into dubious deals by a seductive secretary."

Manwright looked hard at Valera. "You've left out an important point. How the devil can she be chic and fashionable on a secretary's salary?"

"Oh, I'll provide the money for the wardrobe, the *maquillage*, the beautician, and so forth. She must provide the taste, the charm, the wit, the entertaining conversation."

"Then you want a talker?"

"But only when I want her to talk. Otherwise, mum."

Corque whistled softly. "But you're describing a paragon, my dear sir."

"I would say a miracle, Professor Corque, but Dominie Manwright is celebrated for his miraculous creations, and I'm prepared to pay for one."

"You married?" Manwright shot.

"Five times."

"Then you're a chaser."

"My dear Dominie!"

"And easily landed."

"Really, Manwright, you're extraordinarily blunt. Am I a chaser? Definitely not. Let's say . . . Let's say that I'm attracted . . . occasionally."

"And would you want your executive secretary to be

responsive . . . occasionally? Is that to be programmed?"

"Only unilaterally. If I should happen to desire, I would want a beautiful response, but she is not to make demands." Valera hesitated. "Nevertheless, she will, of course, be faithful to me. Completely faithful."

"These parameters are preposterous," Corque exclaimed indignantly.

"Not at all, Charles, not at all." Manwright grinned sardonically. "Mr. Valera is merely describing what all men desire in a woman, an Aspasia, the captivating *femme galante*, indifferent to morality, who was the adoring mistress and adviser to Pericles of ancient Greece. It's wishful fantasy, of course, but my business is turning fantasy into reality, and I welcome the challenge. This girl may be my *magnum opus*." Again he fired a shot at Valera. "And you'll be bored."

"What?"

"Within six months this adoring, talented, charming, dedicated red-gold slave will bore you to tears."

"But how? Why?"

"Because you've left out the crux of a kept woman's hold over a man."

"Manwright!"

"Don't protest, Valera. We know damn well you're ordering a mistress, and I make no moral judgment, but you've forgotten the drop of acid."

"Dominie, I do protest. I—"

"Just listen. You're contracting for an enchanting mistress, and it's my job to make sure that she remains enchanting. Always! Now there are many sweet confections that require a drop of acid to bring out the full flavor and keep them enjoyable. Your Aspasia will need a drop of acid for the same reason. Otherwise, her perpetual perfection will cloy you in a matter of months."

After a long moment, Valera said slowly, "You know, that's rather astute, Dominie. What would you advise?"

"The acid in any woman who can hold a man; the unexpected, the question mark that makes it impossible to live with them or without them . . . which is why I'm sensible enough to prefer the 'without.' "

"And what would that quality be in my—in my secretary?"

"How the devil can I tell you?" Manwright shouted. "If you knew in advance it wouldn't be unexpected, and anyway *I* won't know. I can't program surprise and adventure with a woman. All I can do is program a deliberate error into the genesis of your perfect Aspasia, and the discovery of that kink will be the captivating drop of acid. Understood?"

"You make it sound like a gamble."

"The irrational is always a gamble."

"Then you're challenging me, Dominie?"

"We're both being challenged. You want the ideal mistress created to your specs; I've got to meet them to your complete satisfaction."

Corque murmured, "And your own, Reg?"

"Certainly my own, Charles. I'm a professional. The job is the boss. Well, Valera? Agreed?"

After a thoughtful pause, Valera nodded. "Agreed, Dominie."

"Splendid. I'll need your Persona Profile from your syndicate."

"Out of the question, Dominie! Persona Profiles are Inviolable Secret. How can I ask Vortex to make an exception?"

"Damn it, can't you understand?" Manwright was infuriated by this intransigence but controlled himself and tried to speak reasonably. "My dear chairman, I'm shaping and conditioning this Aspasia for your exclusive use. She will be the cynosure of all men, so I must make sure that she'll be implanted with an attraction for your qualities and drawn to you alone."

"Surely not all my qualities, Dominie. I have no delusions of perfection."

"Then perhaps to your defects. That will be *your* charming drop of acid, and the two of you can live happily in sin forever after. Come back in twenty-one weeks."

"Why twenty-one specifically?"

"She'll be of age. My biodroids average out at a week of genesis for every physical year of the creation's maturity. One week for a dog; twenty-one weeks for an Aspasia. Good day, Mr. Valera."

After the chairman had left (with offer of a down payment haughtily refused by the Dominie) Manwright cocked an eye at Corque and grinned. "This is going to be a magnificent challenge, Charles. I've never generated a truly contemporary biodroid before. You'll pitch in and help, I hope."

"I'll be honored, Reg." Suddenly Corque returned the grin. "But there's one abstruse reference that I couldn't understand . . ."

"Fear not, you'll learn to decipher me as we go along. What didn't you understand?"

"The old saw about the camel."

Manwright burst out laughing. "What? Never heard it? Penalty of spending too much time on the outer planets, Charles. Question: What is a camel? Answer: A camel is a horse made by a committee." He sobered. "But by God, our gallant girl won't be any camel. She'll be devastating."

"Forgive the question, Reg: too devastating for you to resist?"

"What? That? No way! Never! I've guaranteed and delivered too many virgin myths, deities, naiads, dryads, nymphs, *und so weiter*. I'm seasoned, Charles; tough and hard and impervious to all their lures. But the breasts are going to be a problem," he added absently.

"My dear Reg! Please decipher."

"Her breasts, Charles. Botticelli made 'em too small in his *Venus*. I think I should program 'em fuller, but what size and shape? Like pears? Pomegranates? Melons? It's an aesthetic perplexity."

"Perhaps your deliberate error will solve it."

"Perhaps, but only the Good Lord, in whom I've never believed, can know what her mystery kink will turn out to be. *Selah*! Let's get to work on our perfect mistress, Charles, or, to use an antique expression that's just become a new vogue word, our Perfect Popsy."

The Dominie's program for the Perfect Popsy who was to be trustworthy, loyal, helpful, friendly, courteous, kind, obedient, cheerful, clever, chic, beautiful, busty, entertaining on demand, and always available and faithful, began as follows:

A	12–1	0	0	(scald)
B	12–2	1	1	
C	12–3	2	2	((V.S.O.P.))
D	12–4	3	3	
E	12–5	4	4	
F	12–6	5	5	(¼ dram)
G	12–7	6	6	
H	12–8	7	7	(crimped)
I	12–9	8	8	
J	11–1	9	9	(½ scruple)
K	11–2	(garni)		
L	11–3	#	8–3	
M	11–4	8	11–8–2	
N	11–5	=	8–4	(eau)
O	11–6	$	11–8–3	
P	11–7	%	0–8–4	(MSG)
Q	11–8	φ	12–8–2	
R	11–9	&	12	
S	0–2	★	11–8–4	(only a dash)
T	0–3	+	0–8–3	
U	00–4	■	12–8–3	

Und so weiter for 147 pages. *Und* good luck to the computer software for creative biogenesis, which couldn't possibly interest anyone.

"Anyway, there's no point in reading the program, Charles. Numbers can't paint the picture. I'll just describe the sources I've used for the generation of our Popsy. You may not recognize some of the names, but I assure you that most of them were very real and remarkable celebrities in their time."

"What was your lecture to Igor the other day, Reg? 'A chef is no better than his materials'?"

"Right on, and I'm using the best. Beauty—the Botticelli *Venus* of course, but with Egyptian breasts. I thought of using Pauline Borghese, but there's a queen in a limestone relief from the Ptolemaic period who's the ideal model. Callipygian rear elevation. Maidenhair frontispiece, delicate and fritillary. I— Did you say something, Charles?"

"Not I, Reg."

"You *looked* something. I've decided not to use Aspasia for the virtues."

"But you said that was what Valera wanted."

"So I did, but I was wrong. The real Aspasia was a damned premature Women's Rights activist. Too strong for the chairman's taste."

"And yours?"

"Any man's. So I'm using Egeria instead."

"Egeria? I haven't had a classical education, Reg."

"Egeria, the legendary fountain nymph who was the devoted advisor to King Numa of ancient Rome. She also possessed the gift of prophecy, which might come in handy for Valera. Let's see. Fashion and chic—a famous *couturière* named Coco Chanel. Subtle perceptions—the one and only Jane Austen. Voice and theater sense—Sarah Bernhardt; and she'll add a *soupçon* of lovely Jew."

"What on earth for?"

"It's obvious you haven't met many on the outer planets or you wouldn't ask. Remarkable race, Jews; freethinking, original, creative, obstinate. Impossible to live with or without."

"That's how you described the ideal mistress."

"I did."

"But if your Popsy is obstinate, how can she respond to Valera's desires?"

"Oh, I'm using Lola Montez for that. Apparently she was a tigress in the sex department. Hmmm. Next? Victoria Woodhull for business acumen. La Pasionaria for courage. Hester Bateman—she was the first woman silversmith—for skills. Dorothy Parker for wit. Florence Nightingale for sacrifice. Mata Hari for mystery. What else?"

"Conversation."

"Quite right. Oscar Wilde."

"Oscar Wilde!"

"Why not? He was a brilliant talker; held dinner parties spellbound. I'm giving her dancer's hands, neck and legs, Dolly Madison hostessing, and— I've omitted something . . ."

"Your deliberate mistake."

"Of course. The mystery kink which will catch us all by surprise." Manwright flipped through the software. "It's programmed somewhere around here . . . No, that's Valera's Persona Profile . . ." He shook his head. "Charles, you won't believe the damned intransigent, stubborn, know-it-all, conceited egomania concealed beneath that polished veneer. It's going to be hell imprinting our girl with an attraction-engram for such an impossible man . . . Ah! Here's the unexpected in black and white." Manwright pointed to:

$$R = L \times \sqrt{N}$$

"Wait a minute," Corque said slowly. "That equation looks familiar."

"Ah-ha."

"I think I remember it from one of my boyhood math texts."

"Oh-ho."

"The . . . the most probable distance . . ." Corque was dredging the words up, ". . . from the lamp post after a certain number of . . . of irregular turns is equal to the average length of each track that is—"

"Straight track, Charles," Manwright corrected.

"Right. Each straight track that is walked, times the square root of their number." Corque looked at Manwright with a mixture of wonder and amusement. "Confound you, Reg! That's the solution to the famous 'Drunkard's Walk' problem from the chapter on *The Law of Disorder*. And this is the deliberate uncertainty that you're programming? You're either a madman or a genius."

"A little of both, Charles, a little of both. Our Popsy will walk straight lines within my parameters, but we'll never know when or how she'll hang a right or a left."

"But surely she'll be aiming for Valera?"

"Of course. He's the lamp post. All the same, she'll do some unexpected staggering on the way." Manwright chuckled and sang in an odd, husky voice, *"There's a lamp on a post, there's a lamp on a post, and it sets the night a'glowin'. Boy, girl, boy, girl, boy, boy, girl, girl, but best when flakes is snowin'."*

Regis Manwright's laboratory notes provide a less than dramatic description (to put it politely) of the genesis and embryological development of Galatea Galante, the Perfect Popsy.

Germinal

Day 1: One hundred milliliter Florence flask.
   "   2: Five   "   "   "   "
   "   3: One thousand "   "   "   "
   "   4: Five   "   "   "   "
   "   5: Decanted

(E&A charging TOO DAMN MUCH for flasks!!!)
(Baby nominal. Charles enchanted with her. Too red for my taste. Poured out of the amnion blowing bubbles and talking. Couldn't shut her up. Just another fresh kid with a damn big mouth!)

"Reg, Gally must have a nurse."
"For heaven's sake, Charles! She'll be a year old next week. She'll have outgrown nurses in a month."
"She must have someone to look after her."
"All right. All right." Manwright surrendered. "Igor. She can sleep in his room."
"No, no, no. He's a dear creature, but hardly my idea of a nursemaid."
"I can convince him he made her. He'll be devoted."
"No good, Reg. He isn't child-oriented."
"You want someone child-oriented? Hmmm. Ah. Yes. Got just the right number for you. I generated 'The Old Woman Who Lived in a Shoe' for the Positively Peerless Imitation Plastic company to use in their genuine plastics sales promotion."
"The nursery rhyme woman? 'She had so many children she didn't know what to do'?"
"The same." Manwright punched the CB keyboard. "Seanbhean? This is Regis."

The screen sparkled and cleared. A gypsy crone appeared with begging hand outstretched for alms.

"How's everything going, Seanbhean?"

"*Seanruil aduafar*, Regis."

"Why?"

"*Beiseadh ina ghno e.*"

"What! PPIP gone bankrupt? That's a shocker. So you're out of a job?"

"*Deanfaidh sin!*"

"Well, perhaps I have something for you, Seanbhean. I've just generated—"

"Cut off, Reg," Corque broke in sharply.

Manwright was so startled by Corque's peremptory tone that he obeyed and looked up perplexedly. "Don't think she'll do, Charles?"

"That old hag? Out of the question."

"She isn't old," Manwright protested. "Can't be over twenty-five. I made her look like that according to specs: Seventy-year-old Irish gypsy . . . they call 'em 'tinkers' in Ireland . . . speaking Irish and can handle kid actors who are a pain in the ass. And I delivered, by God."

"As you always do; but still out of the question. Please try someone else."

"Charles, has that damn infant got you enthralled?"

"No."

"Meaning yes," Manwright grinned. "Her first conquest, and she's just out of the flask! Can you imagine what she'll do to men in another twenty weeks? Be at each other's throats. Fighting duels. Ha! I *am* a genius and I don't deny it."

"We need a nurse for Gally, Reg. Someone warm and comforting after the child has endured a session with you."

"I can't think what the man is implying. All right, cradle-snatcher, all right. I'll call Claudia." Manwright punched the CB. "She's warm and maternal and protective. Wish she'd been *my* nanny. Hello? Claudia? It's Regis. Switch on the visual, darling." The screen sparkled and cleared. The magnificent head and face of a black Mountain Gorilla appeared.

"!!" she grunted.

"I'm sorry, love. Been too busy to call. You're looking well. How's that no-good husband of yours?"

"!"

"And the kids?"

"!!!"

"Splendid. Now don't forget, you promised to send them to me so I can surgify them into understanding our kind of speech. Same like you, Claudia, and no charge. And speaking of kids, I've got a new one, a girl, that I'd like you to—"

At this point the stunned Corque collected himself enough to press the cutoff stud. Claudia faded.

"Are you mad?" he demanded.

Manwright was bewildered. "What's wrong, Charles?"

"You actually suggest that terrifying beast for the child's nurse?"

"Beast! She's an angel of mother love. She'll have the brat climbing all over her, kissing and hugging. It's interesting," he reflected with another abrupt gearshift. "I can manipulate the cognition centers, but I can't overcome muscular limitations. I gave Claudia college-level comprehension of spoken and written communications but I couldn't give her human speech. She's still forced to use Mountain, which is hardly a language of ideas. Damn frustrating. For both of us."

"And you actually want her to mother Gally?"

"Certainly. Why not?"

"Your Claudia will frighten the daylights out of the infant."

"Impossible."

"She's hideous."

"Are *you* mad? She's beautiful. Pure. Majestic. And a hell of a lot brighter than your Remedial Table Tennis bums at Syrtus University."

"But she can't talk. She only grunts."

"Talk? Talk? For God's sake, Charles! That damn red Popsy was poured out talking sixteen to the dozen. We can't shut her up. She's filling the house with enough jabber as it is. Be grateful for some silence."

So Claudia, the black Mountain Gorilla, moved into

the Manwright ménage, and Igor was consumed with sullen jealousy.

The first morning that Claudia joined Manwright and Corque at breakfast (while Igor glowered at his massive rival) she printed a message on a pad and handed it to the Dominie.

R DD YU GV G TLT TRG IN YR PRGRM?

"Let's see if I remember your abbreviations, darling. R . . . that's me. Did you give G, for Galatea, of course, toilet . . . trigger? No . . . Oh, training, toilet training, in your program? My God, Claudia, I gave her the best of fifty women. Surely at least one of them must have been toilet trained."

BY DPRS

"By what, Claudia?"

"Buy diapers, Reg."

"Oh. Ah. To be sure. Thank you, Charles. Thank you, Claudia. More coffee, love? It's frustrating . . ." Another abrupt shift of gears. "Muscular dyspraxia again, Charles. Claudia can manage caps in her writing but she can't hack lower case. How many diapers, Claudia?"

1 DZ

"Right. One doz. *Zu Befehl.* Did you bring your kids to play with the baby?"

TO OD

"Too odd for what, dear?"

Claudia looked at Manwright with an expression that might have been exasperation and printed again:

TOO OLD

"Your kids?"

G

"What? Galatea? Too old for your boys? And still in diapers? I'd best see for myself."

One of the top floor bedrooms had been converted into a nursery. The usual biodroid cellar accommodations weren't good enough for Manwright's *magnum opus.* When the Dominie entered with Claudia, the red infant was on the floor, flat on her belly, propped on a pillow, and deep in a book. She looked up and crawled enthusiastically to Claudia.

"Nanny dear, I've found the answer, the old linear shorthand. Just dots and dashes and slashes, and you won't have to bother with cursive abbreviations. It's a simple style and we can practice together." She climbed up on Claudia and kissed her lovingly. "One would think this might have occurred to that egotistical know-it-all whose name escapes me." The infant turned her auburn head. "Why, good morning, Dominie Manwright. What an unpleasant surprise."

"You're right, Claudia," Manwright growled. "She's too damn old for your kids. Diaper her."

"My sphincter will be under control by tomorrow, Dominie," Galatea said sweetly. "Can you say the same for your tongue?"

"Guh!" And Manwright withdrew with what he hoped was impressive dignity.

Of course she shot up like a young bamboo plant and filled the house with joy as she entertained them with her escapades. She taught herself to play Manwright's Regency harpsichord, which was sadly in need of repair. She convinced Igor that it was a monster-in-the-making, and together they refinished and tuned it. The sound of concert-A on the tuning fork droned through the house with agonizing penetration. The others were forced to eat out at the Gastrologue Club because she gave Igor no time for cooking.

She studied linear shorthand with Claudia and then translated it into finger-language. They had glorious raps silently talking to each other until Manwright banned the constant finger waggling, which he denounced as a damned invasion of vision. They simply held hands and talked into each other's palm in their secret code, and Manwright was too proud to ask what they were gossiping about.

"As if I'd get an answer anyway," he growled to Corque.

"D'you think that's her mystery surprise, Reg?"

"Damn if I know. She's unexpected enough as it is. Rotten kid!"

She stole liquid licorice from Igor's sacred pantry and tarred herself; phosphorous from Manwright's sacred laboratory and set herself a'glowin'. She burst into Corque's dark bedroom at three in the morning, howling, "ME METHOPHYTE MOTHER FROM GANNYMEEDY! ALIEN INVADER FROM OUT-SIDE SPACE, YOU KILL ALL MY CHILDERS! NOW ME KILL YOU!"

Corque let out a yell and then couldn't stop laughing for the rest of the day. "The beautiful shock of that adorable apparition, Reg!" Manwright didn't think it was funny.

"That damn child is giving me *real* nightmares," he complained. "I keep dreaming that I'm lost in the Grand Teton mountains, and red Indians are chasing me. Comanches," he added.

She sneaked up into the sacred penthouse and deco-rated the robotlike neutrinoscope with items stolen from Manwright's wardrobe. The construct assumed a ludi-crous resemblance to the Dominie himself. Manwright was indignant but too proud to remove his clothes.

The innocent child fast-talked E&A Chemical deliv-ery—"My daddy forgot to order it. So absent-minded, you know"—into an extra gallon of ethyl alcohol, which she poured into the marble pool and got the pir-anhas drunk and swimming in spasms. Then she jumped in and was discovered floating with her plas-tered pals.

Corque was awed. "Gally doesn't know the meaning of fear, Reg. She's a brave one."

"Pah! Just the Pasionaria in her that *I* pro-grammed."

She stole two hundred meters of virgin magnetic tape from the library with which she fashioned a scarecrow mobile in the garden. The gardener was enraptured. Manwright was infuriated, particularly because art-dealer friends offered huge amounts for the creation.

"But *that's* her charming unexpected, Reg. Gally's a born artist."

"Like hell she is. That's only the Hester Bateman I gave her. No $L \times \sqrt{N}$ yet. And the nightmares are continuing, in sequence. Those damned red Indians have cut me off at the pass."

Claudia took Galatea to her home, where the girl got on famously with Claudia's two sons and brought them to Manwright's house to demonstrate a new dance which she'd devised called the Anthro Hustle. It was performed to a song she'd composed titled "Who Put The Snatch On Gorilla Baby?" which she banged out fortissimo on the harpsichord.

"Bring back the tuning fork," Manwright muttered.

Corque was applauding enthusiastically. "Music's her surprise kink, Reg."

"Call that music!"

Corque took her to his Saturn Circus, where she mesmerized him into letting her try riding bareback and leaping through burning hoops, acting as target for a knife-thrower, trapeze aerobatics, and thrusting her auburn head into a lion's mouth. He couldn't understand how she'd persuaded him to let her take such appalling risks.

"Perhaps cajolery's her mystery quality, Reg," he suggested. "But she did miraculously well. My heart was in my mouth. Gally never turned a hair. Pure aplomb. She's a magnificent creation. You've generated a super-Popsy for Valera."

"Guh."

"Could her unexpected kink be psychic?"

"The Comanches have got me surrounded," Manwright fretted. He seemed strangely disoriented.

What disturbed him most were the daily tutoring sessions with the young lady. Invariably they degenerated into bickering and bitching, with the Dominie usually getting the worst of it.

"When our last session ended in another hassle, we both steamed for the library door," he told Corque. "I said, 'Age before beauty, my dear,' which you must admit was gracious, and started out. That red Popsy snip said, 'Pearls before swine,' and swaggered past me like a gladiator who's wiped an entire arena."

"Brilliant!" Corque laughed. "She *is* witty, Reg. You must admit."

"Oh, you're insanely biased, Charles. That snip's been twisting you through her fingers since the moment she was poured."

"And what about Igor and Claudia and her two boys and the CB repair and the plumber and the electronics and the gardener and the laundry and E&A Chemical and half my circus? All insanely biased?"

"Evidently mine is the only sanity she can't snow. You know the simple psychological truth, Charles; we're always accusing others of our own faults. That red saucebox has the impudence to call me intransigent, stubborn, know-it-all, conceited. Me! Out of her own mouth she damns herself."

"Mightn't the equation work the other way around, Reg?"

"Oh, do try to make sense, Charles. And now that the Grand Teton breastworks are making her top-heavy (I think maybe I was a little too generous with my Egyptian programming) there'll be no living with her vanity. Women take the damn dumbest pride in the thrust of their boozalums."

"Now Reg, you exaggerate. Gally knows we'd all adore her even if she were flatchested."

"All I know is I'm doing a professional job, and I know she has too much ego in her cosmos. She's twice as vain as Sandy, my siren. But next week we start *shlepping* her to parties, openings, talk-ins, dances, concerts, and such to groom her for Valera. *That* ought to take her down a peg . . . The red Indians have got me tied to a stake," he added gloomily.

"Canapés?"

"Ta, evah so. Lahvely pahty, Miz Galante."

"Thank you, Lady Agatha . . . Canapés?"

"Grazie, Signorina."

"Prego, Commendatore . . . Canapés?"

"A dank, meyd'l. Lang leb'n zolt ir."

"Nito far vus, General . . . Hot canapés, dear Professor Corque?"

"Thank you, adorable hostess. Igor's?"

"No. Mine, alas."

"Don't be modest, Gally. They're perfection. And don't be afraid of the Martian consul. He looks ferocious, but he doesn't bite. All Frenchmen are born with that look."

"Canapés, M'sieur Consul?"

"Ah! Mais oui! Merci, Mademoiselle Gallee. Que pensez-vous de lumineux Dominie Manwright?"

"Type très compétent."

"Oui. Romanesque, mais formidablement compétent."

"Quoi? Manwright? Romanesque? Vous me gênez, mon cher Consul."

"Ma foi, oui, romanesque, M'amselle Gallee. C'est justement son cêté romanesque; il a du mal à se trouver une femme."

"Une femme! Ha! Remercie le Ciel de n'être qu'un biodroid!"

"These damn do's are a drag, Charles. Even in one's own home."

"But wasn't she wonderful?"

"And they're making my nightmares worse. A sexy Comanche squaw tore my clothes off last night."

"Mi interesso particolarmente a libri di fanta-scienza, magia-orrare, umorismo, narrativa, attualita, filosofia, sociologia, e cattivo, putrido Dominie Regis Manwright."

"Charles, this is the last literary talk-in I ever attend."

"Did you see how Gally handled those Italian publishers?"

"Yes. Gibes at my expense. She put iron claws on her hands."

"My dear Reg! Gally did no such thing."

"I was referring to that sexy squaw."

"Então agora sabes dançer?"

"Sim. Danço, falo miseravelmente muchas linguas, estudo ciência e flosofia, escrovo uma lamentável poesia, estoiro-me com experiências idiotas, ogrimo como un louco, jogo so boxe como un palhaco— En suma, son a celebra biodroid, Galatea Galante, do Dominie Manwright."

"She was magnificent dancing with that Portuguese prince, Reg. What a lovely couple they made."

"Portuguese pimp, you mean."

"Don't be jealous."

"That squaw's heating the iron claws in a campfire, Charles."

"Didn't you ever fight back, Sandy?"

"Yes, I know, he's a bully; but all bullies are cowards at heart. You should have fought him to a standstill, like me. Did he ever make a pass at you?"

"Uh-huh. Me neither. He's an arrogant egomaniac, too much in love with himself to love anyone else."

"What, Sandy? Me? Give the come-on to that dreadful man? Invite Mr. Impossible? Never! Why did you?"

"And I know how he responded. He didn't even have to lash himself to the mast. Iceberg City. Ah, Mr. Jessamy. So sweet of you to give us your box for the concert. I've just been comparing notes with your darling wife on our common enemy, whose name escapes me.

He's the person who was seated on my right and slept through the Mozart."

"And dreamed that she's torturing me with her burning claws, Charles. All over my bod."

"Man nehme; zwei Teile Selbstgefülligkeit, zwei Teile Selbstsucht, einem Teil Eitelkeit, und einem Teil Esel, mische kräftig, füge etwas Geheimnis hinzu, und man erhält Dominie Regis Manwright."

"Especially my private parts."

"Dominie Manwright's boidroid está al dia en su manera de tratar los neologismos, palabras coloquiales, giros y modismos, clichés y terminos de argot, Señor. Yo soy Galatea Galante, la biodroid."

"Thank you, madame, but I'm not Spanish. I merely admire and imitate the old Castilian style."

"Oh. Scuse me, chorley guy. You tollerday donsk?"

He burst out laughing. "I see that, like myself, you're very much with the classics, madame. Let me think. Yes. The response in that James Joyce litany is 'N.' "

Continuing the passage from *Finnegans Wake*, Galatea asked, "You talkatiff scowegian?"

"Nn."

"You spigotty anglease?"

"Nnn."

"You phonio saxo?"

"Nnnn."

"Clear all so. 'Tis a Jute. Let us swop hats and excheck a few strong verbs weak oach eather yapyazzard."

"Brava, madame!" he applauded. "*Olé! Olé!* I had the easy role; nothing but 'N' for no."

She tilted her auburn head and looked at him strangely, compressing her lips in confusion. "Against my will," she said slowly, "I'm compelled to invite you to a dinner party tonight."

"More classics? The Beatrice and Benedick scene from *Much Ado*?"

"No, it's the Galatea and— I don't know your name."

"Valera. Antony Valera."

"It's the Galatea and Valera scene. Can you come?"

"With delight."

"When this bash is finished I'll give you the address."

"I know it, Galatea."

"My friends call me Gally. How do you know my address? We've never met."

"I contracted with—that is, I'm acquainted with your sponsor, Dominie Manwright, Gally. Tonight? Any particular time?"

"Eight o'clock."

"Dress party?"

"Optional." She shook her head dizzily. "I don't know what's come over me, Valera. But the moment I saw you at this clambake I knew I had to see you again . . . Immediately . . . Intimately . . . I'm possessed!"

The rest of the household was dining in The Gastrologue, and their moods varied.

"Thrown out!" Corque was hurt. "Thrown out without a moment's notice by that ungrateful tyrant!"

"Naturally, Charles," Manwright beamed. "She wants to be alone with Valera. Instant, devoted attraction, as per my brilliant programming. I tell you, I'm a genius."

"She athed me to make month-terth for her to therve, mahth-ter."

"Quite right, Igor. We must all pitch in and promote Valera's romance. He was so turned on meeting her at that bash this afternoon that he sent his check by messenger. Payment in full . . . To protect his claim on my Perfect Popsy, no doubt. Ha!"

"Thrown out! Thrown out by that tyrant!"

"And good riddance to her, Charles. The house will be back to normal as soon as the chairman takes her away."

"But she didn't order a brain, mahth-ter."

"Not to worry, Igor. Tell you what; we'll order *Cervelles de veau au beurre noir,* and if the club doesn't have any calves' brains, you can go out and steal some." He beamed again and bobbed his pale, streaky head. It was as close as Manwright could come to celebrating a triumph.

"Thank you, mahth-ter."

"Evicted!"

The silent Claudia printed: PLAINTAINS FR ME PLS— RENELLOS DE AMARILLO.

At one minute past eight Valera said, "It's fashionable to be a half-hour late, but I— Is it all right to come in?"

Galatea opened the door full. "Oh please! I've been biting my nails for a whole minute."

"Thank you. To tell the truth, I tried to be chic but it didn't take as long as I thought it would to walk up from Old Slip."

"Old Slip? Isn't that where your office is? Were you working overtime, poor drudge?"

"I live there too, Gally. A penthouse on top of the tower."

"Ah, *à la* Alexandre Eiffel?"

"Somewhat, but the syndicate complex is no Tour Eiffel, and I didn't build it. What a fantastic place this is. I've never had more than a peep beyond the waiting room."

"D'you want the full tour?"

"I'd like nothing better."

"You've got it, but drink first. What would you like?"

"What are my options?"

"My dear Valera, I—"

"Tony."

"Thank you. My dear Tony, I share this house with two and a half men and a Mountain Gorilla. We have everything in stock."

"*Stolichnaya,* please. Did you say two and a *half?*"

"Igor, our housekeeper," Galatea explained as she brought a tray with a bucket of ice, a bottle, and heavy glasses. She opened the vodka deftly and began revolving the bottle in the ice. "A biodroid replica of Baron Frankenstein's accomplice."

"Oh yes, I've met that odd thing. The lisping hunchback."

"A dear, dear soul, but only half with it."

"And a Mountain Gorilla?"

"That's Claudia, my beloved Nanny. She's beautiful and wise. This vodka really isn't chilled enough yet, but let's start anyway." She filled the glasses. "Russian style, eh? Knock it back, Tony. Death to the fascist, imperialist invaders from outer space."

"And their Conestoga star-wagons."

They knocked their shots back.

"Gally, what miracle are you wearing?"

"La, sir!" She did a quick kick-turn. "Does it grab you?"

"I'm dazzled."

"If I tell you, promise not to turn me in to the law?"

"I promise."

"I copied it from a Magda."

"Who or what is a Magda? Oh, thank you."

"I'm afraid I filled it too high, but boys like big sandwiches and big drinks. Magda is *the* vogue designer of the year. Down with countertenors."

"May they be heard only in Siberia. Why must I keep it a secret about your copy?"

"Good Lord, Tony! They hang, draw, and quarter you if you pinch a design-original."

"How did you manage?"

"I fell in love with it at one of her openings and memorized it."

"And made it yourself? From memory? You're remarkable!"

"You're exaggerating. Don't you remember complicated stock manipulations?"

"Well . . . yes."

"So with me it's the same damn thing. Oops! That's the tag of a dirty joke. Apologies to the chairman."

"The chairman needs all the dirty jokes he can get for client entertainment. What's this one?"

"Maybe some day, if you coax me nicely."

"Where do you get them? Surely not from straight-laced Dominie Manwright."

"From Claudia's naughty boys. Another shot to the damnation of Blue Laws, and then the guided tour."

Valera was bewildered and delighted by the madness of the Manwright house, and enchanted by the high style with which Galatea flowed through it with equally mad comments. An old song lyric haunted him:

> Hey, diddle-dee-dee,
> I've found the girl for me.
> With raunchy style
> And virgin guile
> She's just the girl for me.

"Never mind the polite compliments, Tony," she said, pulling him down on a couch beside her and refilling his glass. "I'll give you the acid test. Of all things in this house, which would you like most to steal?"

"You."

"I didn't say put the snatch on. Come on, man, steal something."

"I think I spilled my drink."

"My fault. I joggled your arm. Don't mop. So?"

"You're so sudden, Gally. Well—don't laugh—the scarecrow mobile in the garden."

"Oh, I love you for that! I made it; *I, Ich, Moi,* when I was a little kid months ago." She gave him a smacking kiss on the cheek and jumped up. "Like some music?" She turned on the speakers and a soft murmuring drifted through the house.

Valera glanced at his watch. "Your guests must be frightfully chic."

"Oh?"

"You said eight. That was an hour ago. Where's everybody?"

"As a matter of fact they came early."

"I'm the only one who came early."

"That's right."

"You mean I'm . . . ?"

"That's right."

"But you said a dinner party, Gally."

"It's ready any time you are."

"The party is us? Just us?"

"I can call some more people if you're bored with me, Tony."

"You know that's not what I meant."

"No? Then what did you mean?"

"I—" He stopped himself.

"Go ahead," she bullied. "Say it. I dare you."

He capitulated. For perhaps the first time in his suave life he was flustered. In a low voice he said, "I was remembering a tune from twenty years ago."

"Yes? What tune?"

"Hey, diddle-dee-dee / I've found the girl for me / With raunchy style / And virgin guile / She's just the girl for me."

Galatea flushed and began to tremble. Then she took refuge in the hostess role. "Dinner," she said briskly. "Beef stroganoff, potatoes baked with mushrooms, salad, lemon pie, and coffee. *Mouton Rothschild.* No, not in the upstairs dining room, Tony. I've made special arrangements for you. Help me with the table."

Together, in a sort of domestic intimacy, they arranged a gaming table alongside the marble pool, with two painted Venetian chairs. She had already set the table with Spode china and Danish silver, so it needed some careful balancing. Before she began serving she drew the cork from the Bordeaux bottle and poured a little into Valera's goblet.

"Try it, Tony," she said. "I've never been able to decide whether the concept of 'letting a wine breathe' is fact or showoffery. I appeal to your sophistication. Give me the answer."

He tasted and rolled his eyes to heaven. "Superb! It'll be even better after it *has* breathed. You're magnificent with your compliments, Gally. Sit down and try it yourself. I insist." And he filled her glass.

"Wait," she laughed. "The floor show first. I cajoled electronics into bootlegging ultralight into the pool. That's why I wanted our table here. Wait till you see 20 Performing Piranhas 20." She ran to a wall, extinguished the living room lights, and flipped a switch. The pool glowed like lava and the excited fish became a ballet of darting embers. Galatea returned to the table, sat opposite Valera and raised her goblet to him. He smiled back into her face.

"Hey, diddle-dee—" he began and then froze, speechless. He stared. Then he started to his feet so violently that he overturned the table.

"Tony!" She was appalled.

"You goddam bitch!" he shouted. His face was black with rage. "Where's the CB?"

"Tony!"

"Where's the goddam CB? Tell me before I break your goddam neck!"

"Th-that table." She pointed. "B-but I don't understand. What's—"

"You'll understand soon enough." He punched buttons. "By God, you and this whole damn lying house will understand. Rip me? Play me for a patsy?" His fury was a terrifying echo of Manwright at his worst. "Hello Larson. Valera. Don't waste time with visual. Crash mission. Call full Security and comb the city for a son of a bitch named Manwright. Regis Manwright. Yes, that's the pig. I give you a half hour to find him and—"

"B-but I know where he is," Galatea faltered.

"Hold it Larson. You do? Where?"

"The Gastrologue."

"The bastard's in the Gastrologue Club, Larson. Go get him and bring him to his house, which is where I am now. And if you want to get rough with him I'll pay all legals and add a bonus. I'm going to teach that lying pimp and his bitch a lesson they'll remember for the rest of their lives."

The four were herded into Manwright's house at the point of a naked laser which Larson thought advisable in view of the threat of Claudia's mass. They saw a grotesque; Valera and Galatea silhouetted before the glowing pool in the dark room. Valera was holding the weeping girl by her hair, for all the world like a chattel in a slave market.

In this ominous crisis Manwright displayed an aspect

of his character which none had ever seen: a tone of quiet command which took obedience for granted, as if by divine right, and won it through his assurance.

"Mr. Larson, you may pocket that laser now. It was never needed. Valera, you will let Galatea go. No dear, don't move," he added softly. "Stay alongside him. You belong to him, unless he's changed his mind. Have you, Valera?"

"You're goddam right I have," the chairman stormed. "I want no part of this cheap, secondhand trash. Larson, keep that gun handy and get on the CB. I want my check stopped."

"Don't bother, Mr. Larson. The check has not been deposited and will be returned. Why, Valera? Doesn't Galatea meet your exalted standards?"

"Of course she does," Corque burst out. "She's brilliant! She's beautiful! She's perfection! She—"

"I'm handling this, Charles. I repeat: Why, Valera?"

"I don't buy whores at your prices."

"You think Galatea's a whore?"

"Think? I know!"

"You contracted for the perfect mistress who would be faithful and devoted to you."

Galatea let out a moan.

"I'm sorry, my love. You never knew. I'd planned to tell you, but only after I was sure you were genuinely attracted to him. I never had any intention of forcing him on you."

"You wicked men!" she cried. "You're hateful!"

"And now, Valera, you think of a mistress as a whore? Why this sudden eruption of archaic morality?"

"It isn't a question of morality, damn you. It's a question of secondhand goods. I want no part of a shopworn woman."

"Must I stay with him? Does he own me? Am I bought and paid for?"

"No, love. Come to us."

She dashed away from Valera's side and then hesitated. Claudia held out her arms, but Galatea surprised everybody by going to Manwright who took her gently.

"All right, Valera," he said. "Go now and take your

army with you. Your check will be returned first thing in the morning."

"Not until I know who it was."

"Not until who what was?"

"The goddam stud who knocked her up."

"What?"

"She's pregnant, you goddam pimp. The bitch has been sleeping around and I want to know the lover-boy who knocked her up. He's got plenty coming."

After a long pause, Manwright asked, "Are you under a psychiatrist's care, Mr. Valera?"

"Don't be ridiculous."

"No more ridiculous than your slander. What? Galatea pregnant? My lovely, tasteful young lady sleeping around with studs? You're obviously quite mad. Go."

"Mad am I? Ridiculous? You can't see that she's pregnant? Turn her around and look at her face in this ultralight. Look at her!"

After a moment's hesitation, "I'll go through the motions only to get rid of you." Manwright smiled to Galatea as he turned the girl around. "Just a gesture, my love. You'll have your dignity back in a moment and I swear you'll never lose it ag—"

His words were cut off, as by a guillotine. In the ultralight from the glowing pool there was no mistaking the dark pregnancy band across Galatea's face, similar to the banded mask of a raccoon. He took a slow, deep breath and answered the confusion in her eyes by placing a hand over her mouth.

"Go, Valera. This is now a family affair."

"I demand an answer. I won't leave until I know who it was. Your halfwit hunchback, probably. I can picture them in bed; the slobbering idiot and the—"

Manwright's interruption was an explosion. He hurled Galatea into Claudia's arms, pivoted and drove a knee into Larson's groin. He tore the laser away from the convulsed man, whipped Valera across the neck with the barrel, and held the staggering chairman over the edge of the pool.

"The piranhas are starving," he murmured. "Do you go in or get out?"

After the Syndicate had left, not without dire prom-
ises, Manwright turned up the house lights and extinguished the pool ultralight and with that the pregnancy
stigma banding Galatea's face. In a strange way they
were all relieved.

"Not to play the district attorney," he said, "but I
must know how it happened."

"How what happened?" Galatea cried.

"Sweetheart, you *are* pregnant."

"No, no, no!"

"I know it can't be anyone in this house. Claudia,
has she been promiscuous outside?"

NO

"How can you ask such questions!"

"Has Galatea ever been alone with a man in a possibly intimate situation?"

"You're hateful!"

NO

"Reg, we all know that. We've chaperoned Gally every moment outside; you, me, Claudia."

"Not every moment, Charles. It could have happened with this innocent in five minutes."

"But nothing ever happened with a man! Nothing!
Ever!"

"Dear love, you *are* pregnant."

"I can't be."

"You are, undeniably. Charles?"

"Gally, I adore you, no matter what, but Reg is right.
The pregnancy band is undeniable."

"But I'm a virgin."

Manwright turned to Claudia. "Nanny?"

HR MNS HV STOPT

"Her what have stopped?"

Corque sighed. "Her menses, Reg."

"I see."

"I'm a virgin, you wicked, detestable men. A virgin!"

Manwright took her frantic face in his hands. "Sweetheart, no recriminations, no punishments, no coventry,
but I must know where I slipped up. I must know how
it happened. My professional honor is involved. Who
were you with, where and when?"

"I've never been alone with any man, anywhere or anywhen."

"Never?"

"Never . . . except in my dreams."

"Dreams?" Manwright smiled. "All girls have them. That's not what I mean, dear."

Claudia waved her pad to attract his attention.

R MAB U SHD LSN

"Maybe I should listen to what, Claudia?"

LT HR TL U HR DRMS

"Let her tell me her dreams? Why?"

JST LSN

"All right, I'll listen. Tell me about your young dreams, love."

"No. They're private property."

"Claudia wants me to hear them."

"She's the only one I've ever told. I'm ashamed of them."

Claudia fingerwagged, "Tell him, Gally. You don't know how important they may be."

"No!"

"Galatea Galante, are you going to disobey your nanny? I am ordering you to tell your dreams."

"Please, nanny. No. They're erotic."

"I know, dear. That's why they're important. You must tell."

At length, Galatea whispered, "Put out the lights, please."

The fascinated Corque obliged.

In the darkness she began, "They're erotic. Disgusting. I'm so ashamed. They're always the same . . . and I'm always ashamed . . . but I can't stop . . .

"There's a man, a pale man, a moonlight man, and I . . . I want him. I want him to . . . to handle me and ravish me into ecstasy, b-but he doesn't want me . . . so he runs, and I chase him . . . and I catch him. Th-there are some sort of friends who . . . who help me catch him and tie him up. And then they go away and leave me alone with the moonlight man, and I . . . and I do to him what I wanted him to do to me . . ."

They could hear her trembling and rustling in her chair.

Very carefully, Manwright asked, "Who is this moonlight man, Galatea?"

"I don't know."

"But you're drawn to him?"

"Oh, yes. Yes! I always want him."

"Just him alone or are there other men?"

"Only him. He's all I ever want."

"But you don't know who he is?"

"No."

"In the dreams do you know who you are?"

"Me. Just me."

"As you are in real life?"

"Yes, except that I'm dressed different."

"Different? How?"

"Beads and . . . and buckskin with fringe."

They all heard Manwright gasp.

"Perhaps like . . . like a red Indian, Galatea?"

"I . . . I never thought of that. Yes. I'm an Indian, an Indian squaw up in the mountains, and I make love to the paleface every night."

"Oh. My. God." The words were squeezed out of Manwright. "They're no dreams." Suddenly he roared, "Light! Give me light, Charles. Igor! Light!"

The brilliant lights revealed him standing and shaking, moonlight-pale and in shock. "Oh, my God, my God, my God!" He was almost incoherent. "Dear God, what have I created?"

"Mahth-ter!"

"Reg!"

"Don't you understand? Now I know what Claudia suspected, and that's why she made Galatea tell me her dreams."

"B-but they're only dirty dreams," Galatea wailed. "What's the harm?"

"Damn you and damn me! They were *not* dreams. They were reality in disguise. That's the harm. And that's how your dreams lock in with my nightmares, which were reality, too. Christ! I've generated a monster!"

"Now calm yourself, Reg, and do try to make sense."

"I can't. There's no sense in it. There's nothing but that lunatic drop of acid I promised Valera."

"The mystery surprise in her?"

"You kept wondering what it was, Charles. Well, now you know, if you can interpret the evidence."

"What evidence?"

Manwright forced himself into a sort of thunderous control. "I dreamed I was pursued and caught by red Indians, tied up, and ravished by a sexy squaw. I told you. Yes?"

"Yes. Interminably."

"Galatea dreams she's a red Indian squaw, pursuing, capturing, and ravishing a paleface she desires. You heard her?"

"I heard her."

"Did she know about my nightmares?"

"No."

"Did I know about her dreams?"

"No."

"Coincidence?"

"Possibly."

"Would you care to bet on that possibility?"

"No."

"And there you have it. Those 'dreams' were sleep versions or distortions of what was really happening; something which neither of us could face awake." Manwright forced the words out. "Galatea's been coming into my bed every night, and we've been making love."

"Impossible!"

"Is she pregnant?"

"Yes."

"And *I'm* the stud responsible; Valera's lover-boy. My God! My God!"

"Reg, this is outlandish. Claudia, has Gally ever left her bed nights?"

NO

"There, Reg!"

"Damn it, I'm not talking about a conventional, human woman. I didn't generate one. I'm talking about an otherworld creature whose psyche is as physically real as her body, can materialize out of it, accomplish its hidden desires, and amalgamate again . . . an emotional *Doppelgänger,* a counterpart as real as the flesh. You've pestered me about the deliberate unexpected in my programming. Well, here's the R-equals-L-times-the-square-root-of-N. Galatea's a succubus."

"A what?"

"A succubus. A sexy female demon. Perfectly human by day, completely conformist, but with the spectral power to come like a carnal cloud to men in their sleep, nights, and seduce them."

"No!" Galatea cried in despair. "I'm not that. I can't be."

"And she doesn't even know it. She's an unconscious demon. The laugh's on me, Charles," Manwright said ruefully. "By God, when I do goof, it's a beauty. I knock myself out programming the Perfect Popsy with an engram for Valera, and her Drunkard's Walk ruins everything by switching her passion to me."

"It doesn't surprise me, Reg," Corque said. "The two of you are very much alike."

"I'm in no mood for bad jokes, Charles." Manwright waved impatiently. "And then Galatea turns out to be a succubus who doesn't even know it, and has her lustful will of me in our sleep every night."

"No, no! They were dreams. Dreams!"

"Were they? Were they?" Manwright was having difficulty controlling his impatience with her damned intransigence. "How else did you get yourself pregnant, eh? *Enceinte? Gravido?* Knocked up? Don't you dare argue with me, you impudent red snip! You did a seduction number on me. You know," he added judgmatically, "there should have been a smidge of birth control in my programming. Never occurred to me."

He'd returned to his familiar impossible self and Corque relaxed.

"What now, Reg?"

"Oh, I'll marry the saucebox, of course. Can't let a dangerous creature like Galatea out of the house."

"Never!" Galatea shouted. "Never! Marry you, you dreadful, impossible, conceited, bullying, know-it-all, wicked man? Never! If I'm a demon, what are you? Come, Claudia."

The two women swept upstairs.

Manwright watched them leave with a smile. It was the closest he could come to applause. "Now *that's* what I call an exit," he murmured. "Theater is obviously her shtick. My compliments to the management."

"Meaning yourself, of course."

"Who else could I possibly mean, Charles?"

"Gally is absolutely right, Reg. You're an impossible egomaniac, and no woman in her right mind would have anything to do with you."

"Ah, but Galatea's been programmed for the impossible, Charles. On the other hand, has nature programmed all women for all men, no matter how impossible? I've often wondered." He thought for a moment, then, "Ironing board," he added.

"Wh-what?"

"Bed, Charles. The marriage bed. That's nature's ironing board. Smooths out all questions."

"Are you serious about marrying Gally?"

"Certainly, Charles. I'm no Valera. I don't want a relationship with a Popsy, no matter how perfect."

"But do you love her?"

"I love all my creations."

"Don't be sentimental, Reg. Answer the question. Do you love Gally, as a man loves a woman?"

"What? That sexy succubus? That naïve, innocent demon? Love her? A man of my quality? Absurd! No. All I want is the legal right to tie *her* to a stake every night when *I'm* awake. Ha!"

Corque laughed. "I see you do, and I'm very happy for you both; you'll be perfect for each other. But, you know, you'll have to court her."

"What? Court? Woo that impertinent red brat?"

"My dear Reg, can't you grasp that she isn't a child any more? She's a grown young woman with tremendous character and pride."

"Yes, she's had you in her thrall since the moment she was poured," Manwright growled. Then he sighed and accepted defeat. "But I suppose you're right. Igor!"

"Here, mahth-ter."

"Please set up that table again. Fresh service, candles, and see if you can salvage the monsters you created for the dinner. White gloves when you serve."

"Yeth, mahth-ter."

"I see the *Mouton Rothschild*'s been smashed. Another bottle, please. And then my compliments to Ms. Galatea Galante, and will she have the forgiveness to dine, *à deux,* with a most contrite suitor. Present her with a corsage from me . . . something orchidy . . . You know, Charles, this will be a fun necromancy, *alevai,*" he mused. "Man and demon. Our boys will be devils, sorcery says, and the girls witches. But aren't they all?"

Sandkings

George R. R. Martin

Contrary to the suppositions of people who know science fiction primarily through monster movies—including *Alien*—this genre is seldom a vehicle for frightening stories. "Real" science fiction has an extremely wide range of interests, but few of them are as immediately accessible to the general public as is fear; and horrific blobs, shape-changers, and half-seen creatures are easier to present on a movie screen than, say, telepaths.

Still, the terrors of the unknown or unexpected are a legitimate, strong theme, and sf writers do return to it often, producing memorable results. George R. R. Martin does so here, and his story of small, mind-linked alien creatures will raise a goosebump or ten for you.

Not surprisingly, this story has been optioned for a movie.

Simon Kress lived alone in a sprawling manor house among the dry, rocky hills fifty kilometers from the city. So, when he was called away unexpectedly on business, he had no neighbors he could conveniently impose on to take his pets. The carrion hawk was no problem; it roosted in the unused belfry and customarily fed itself anyway. The shambler Kress simply shooed outside and left to fend for itself; the little monster would gorge on slugs and birds and rockjocks. But the fish tank, stocked with genuine Earth piranhas, posed a difficulty. Kress finally just threw a haunch of beef into the huge tank. The piranhas could always eat each other if he were detained longer than expected. They'd done it before. It amused him.

Unfortunately, he was detained *much* longer than expected this time. When he finally returned, all the fish were dead. So was the carrion hawk. The shambler had climbed up to the belfry and eaten it. Simon Kress was vexed.

The next day he flew his skimmer to Asgard, a journey of some two hundred kilometers. Asgard was Baldur's largest city and boasted the oldest and largest starport as well. Kress liked to impress his friends with animals that were unusual, entertaining, and expensive; Asgard was the place to buy them.

This time, though, he had poor luck. Xenopets had closed its doors, t'Etherane the Petseller tried to foist another carrion hawk off on him, and Strange Waters offered nothing more exotic than piranhas, glowsharks, and spider-squids. Kress had had all those; he wanted something new.

Near dusk, he found himself walking down the Rainbow Boulevard, looking for places he had not patronized before. So close to the starport, the street was lined by importers' marts. The big corporate emporiums had impressive long windows, where rare and costly alien artifacts reposed on felt cushions against dark drapes that made the interiors of the stores a mystery. Between them were the junk shops; narrow, nasty little places whose display areas were crammed with all manner of offworld bric-a-brac. Kress tried both kinds of shop, with equal dissatisfaction.

Then he came across a store that was different.

It was quite close to the port. Kress had never been there before. The shop occupied a small, single-story building of moderate size, set between a euphoria bar and a temple-brothel of the Secret Sisterhood. Down this far, the Rainbow Boulevard grew tacky. The shop itself was unusual. Arresting.

The windows were full of mist; now a pale red, now the gray of true fog, now sparkling and golden. The mist swirled and eddied and glowed faintly from within. Kress glimpsed objects in the window—machines, pieces of art, other things he could not recognize—but he could not get a good look at any of them. The mists flowed sensuously around them, displaying a bit of first one thing and then another, then cloaking all. It was intriguing.

As he watched, the mist began to form letters. One word at a time. Kress stood and read.

WO. AND. SHADE. IMPORTERS. ARTIFACTS. ART. LIFEFORMS. AND. MISC.

The letters stopped. Through the fog, Kress saw something moving. That was enough for him, that and the "Lifeforms" in their advertisement. He swept his walking cloak over his shoulder and entered the store.

Inside, Kress felt disoriented. The interior seemed vast, much larger than he would have guessed from the relatively modest frontage. It was dimly lit, peaceful. The ceiling was a starscape, complete with spiral nebulae, very dark and realistic, very nice. The counters all shone faintly, to better display the merchandise within. The aisles were carpeted with ground fog. It came almost to his knees in places, and swirled about his feet as he walked.

"Can I help you?"

She almost seemed to have risen from the fog. Tall and gaunt and pale, she wore a practical gray jumpsuit and a strange little cap that rested well back on her head.

"Are you Wo or Shade?" Kress asked. "Or only sales help?"

"Jala Wo, ready to serve you," she replied. "Shade does not see customers. We have no sales help."

"You have quite a large establishment," Kress said. "Odd that I have never heard of you before."

"We have only just opened this shop on Baldur," the woman said. "We have franchises on a number of other worlds, however. What can I sell you? Art, perhaps?

You have the look of a collector. We have some fine Nor T'alush crystal carvings."

"No," Simon Kress said. "I own all the crystal carvings I desire. I came to see about a pet."

"A lifeform?"

"Yes."

"Alien?"

"Of course."

"We have a mimic in stock. From Celia's World. A clever little simian. Not only will it learn to speak, but eventually it will mimic your voice, inflections, gestures, even facial expressions."

"Cute," said Kress. "And common. I have no use for either, Wo. I want something exotic. Unusual. And not cute. I detest cute animals. At the moment I own a shambler. Imported from Cotho, at no mean expense. From time to time I feed him a litter of unwanted kittens. That is what I think of *cute*. Do I make myself understood?"

Wo smiled enigmatically. "Have you ever owned an animal that worshipped you?" she asked.

Kress grinned. "Oh, now and again. But I don't require worship, Wo. Just entertainment."

"You misunderstand me," Wo said, still wearing her strange smile. "I meant worship literally."

"What are you talking about?"

"I think I have just the thing for you," Wo said. "Follow me."

She led Kress between the radiant counters and down a long, fog-shrouded aisle beneath false starlight. They passed through a wall of mist into another section of the store, and stopped before a large plastic tank. An aquarium, thought Kress.

Wo beckoned. He stepped closer and saw that he was wrong. It was a terrarium. Within lay a miniature desert about two meters square. Pale sand bleached scarlet by wan red light. Rocks: basalt and quartz and granite. In each corner of the tank stood a castle.

Kress blinked, and peered, and corrected himself; actually only three castles stood. The fourth leaned; a crumbled, broken ruin. The other three were crude but intact, carved of stone and sand. Over their battlements and through their rounded porticos, tiny creatures climbed and scrambled. Kress pressed his face against the plastic. "Insects?" he asked.

"No," Wo replied. "A much more complex lifeform. More intelligent as well. Smarter than your shambler by a considerable amount. They are called sandkings."

"Insects," Kress said, drawing back from the tank. "I don't care how complex they are." He frowned. "And kindly don't try to gull me with this talk of intelligence. These things are far too small to have anything but the most rudimentary brains."

"They share hiveminds," Wo said. "Castle minds, in this case. There are only three organisms in the tank, actually. The fourth died. You see how her castle has fallen."

Kress looked back at the tank. "Hiveminds, eh? Interesting." He frowned again. "Still, it is only an oversized ant farm. I'd hoped for something better."

"They fight wars."

"Wars? Hmmm." Kress looked again.

"Note the colors, if you will," Wo told him. She pointed to the creatures that swarmed over the nearest castle. One was scrabbling at the tank wall. Kress studied it. It still looked like an insect to his eyes. Barely as long as his fingernail, six-limbed, with six tiny eyes set all around its body. A wicked set of mandibles clacked visibly, while two long fine antennae wove patterns in the air. Antennae, mandibles, eyes and legs were sooty black, but the dominant color was the burnt orange of its armor plating. "It's an insect," Kress repeated.

"It is not an insect," Wo insisted calmly. "The armored exoskeleton is shed when the sandking grows larger. *If* it grows larger. In a tank this size, it won't." She took Kress by the elbow and led him around the tank to the next castle. "Look at the colors here."

He did. They were different. Here the sandkings had bright-red armor; antennae, mandibles, eyes, and legs were yellow. Kress glanced across the tank. The denizens of the third live castle were off-white, with red trim. "Hmmm," he said.

"They war, as I said," Wo told him. "They even have truces and alliances. It was an alliance that destroyed the fourth castle in this tank. The blacks were getting too numerous, so the others joined forces to destroy them."

Kress remained unconvinced. "Amusing, no doubt. But insects fight wars too."

"Insects do not worship," Wo said.

"Eh?"

Wo smiled and pointed at the castle. Kress stared. A face had been carved into the wall of the highest tower. He recognized it. It was Jala Wo's face. "How . . . ?"

"I projected a holograph of my face into the tank, kept it there for a few days. The face of god, you see? I feed them, I am always close. The sandkings have a rudimentary psionic sense. Proximity telepathy. They sense me, and worship me by using my face to decorate their buildings. All the castles have them, see." They did.

On the castle, the face of Jala Wo was serene and peaceful, and very lifelike. Kress marveled at the workmanship. "How do they do it?"

"The foremost legs double as arms. They even have fingers of a sort: three small, flexible tendrils. And they cooperate well, both in building and in battle. Remember, all the mobiles of one color share a single mind."

"Tell me more," Kress said.

Wo smiled. "The maw lives in the castle. Maw is my name for her. A pun, if you will; the thing is mother and stomach both. Female, large as your fist, immobile. Actually, sandking is a bit of a misnomer. The mobiles are peasants and warriors, the real ruler is a queen. But that analogy is faulty as well. Considered as a whole, each castle is a single hermaphroditic creature."

"What do they eat?"

"The mobiles eat pap, predigested food obtained inside the castle. They get it from the maw after she has worked on it for several days. Their stomachs can't handle anything else, so if the maw dies, they soon die as well. The maw . . . the maw eats anything. You'll have no special expense there. Table scraps will do excellently."

"Live food?" Kress asked.

Wo shrugged. "Each maw eats mobiles from the other castles, yes."

"I am intrigued," he admitted. "If only they weren't so small."

"Yours can be larger. These sandkings are small because their tank is small. They seem to limit their growth to fit available space. If I moved these to a larger tank, they'd start growing again."

"Hmmm. My piranha tank is twice this size, and vacant. It could be cleaned out, filled with sand . . ."

"Wo and Shade would take care of the installation. It would be our pleasure."

"Of course," said Kress, "I would expect four intact castles."

"Certainly," Wo said.

They began to haggle about the price.

Three days later Jala Wo arrived at Simon Kress's estate, with dormant sandkings and a work crew to take charge of the installation. Wo's assistants were aliens unlike any Kress was familiar with; squat, broad bipeds with four arms and bulging, multifaceted eyes. Their skin was thick and leathery, and twisted into horns and spines and protrusions at odd spots upon their bodies. But they were very strong, and good workers. Wo ordered them about in a musical tongue that Kress had never heard.

In a day it was done. They moved his piranha tank to the center of his spacious living room, arranged couches on either side of it for better viewing, scrubbed it clean and filled it two-thirds of the way up with sand and rock. Then they installed a special lighting system, both to provide the dim red illumination the sandkings preferred and to project holographic images into the tank. On top they mounted a sturdy plastic cover, with a feeder mechanism built in. "This way you can feed your sandkings without removing the top of the tank," Wo explained. "You would not want to take any chances on the mobiles escaping."

The cover also included climate control devices, to condense just the right amount of moisture from the air. "You want it dry, but not too dry," Wo said.

Finally one of the four-armed workers climbed into the tank and dug deep pits in the four corners. One of his companions handed the dormant maws over to him, removing them one-by-one from their frosted cryonic traveling cases. They were nothing to look at. Kress decided they resembled nothing so much as a mottled, half-spoiled chunk of raw meat. With a mouth.

The alien buried them, one in each corner of the tank. Then they sealed it all up and took their leave.

"The heat will bring the maws out of dormancy," Wo said. "In less than a week, mobiles will begin to hatch and burrow to the surface. Be certain to give them plenty of food. They will need all their strength until they are well established. I would estimate that you will have castles rising in about three weeks."

"And my face? When will they carve my face?"

"Turn on the hologram after about a month," she advised him. "And be patient. If you have any questions, please call. Wo and Shade are at your service." She bowed and left.

Kress wandered back to the tank and lit a joy stick. The desert was still and empty. He drummed his fingers impatiently against the plastic, and frowned.

On the fourth day, Kress thought he glimpsed motion beneath the sand, subtle subterranean stirrings.

On the fifth day, he saw his first mobile, a lone white.

On the sixth day, he counted a dozen of them, whites and reds and blacks. The oranges were tardy. He cycled through a bowl of half-decayed table scraps. The mobiles sensed it at once, rushed to it, and began to drag pieces back to their respective corners. Each color group was very organized. They did not fight. Kress was a bit disappointed, but he decided to give them time.

The oranges made their appearance on the eighth day. By then the other sandkings had begun to carry small stones and erect crude fortifications. They still did not war. At the moment they were only half the size of those he had seen at Wo and Shade's, but Kress thought they were growing rapidly.

The castles began to rise midway through the second week. Organized battalions of mobiles dragged heavy chunks of sandstone and granite back to their corners, where other mobiles were pushing sand into place with mandibles and tendrils. Kress had purchased a pair of magnifying goggles so he could watch them work, wherever they might go in the tank. He wandered around and around the tall plastic walls, observing. It was fascinating. The castles were a bit plainer than Kress would have liked, but he had an idea about that. The next day he cycled through some obsidian and flakes of colored glass along with the food. Within hours, they had been incorporated into the castle walls.

The black castle was the first completed, followed by the white and red fortresses. The oranges were last, as usual. Kress took his meals into the living room and ate seated on the couch, so he could watch. He expected the first war to break out any hour now.

He was disappointed. Days passed, the castles grew taller and more grand, and Kress seldom left the tank except to attend to his sanitary needs and answer critical business calls. But the sandkings did not war. He was getting upset.

Finally he stopped feeding them.

Two days after the table scraps had ceased to fall from their desert sky, four black mobiles surrounded an orange and dragged it back to their maw. They maimed it first, ripping off its mandibles and antennae and limbs, and carried it through the shadowed main gate of their miniature castle. It never emerged. Within an hour, more than forty orange mobiles marched across the sand and attacked the blacks' corner. They were outnumbered by the blacks that came rushing up from the depths. When the fighting was over, the attackers had been slaughtered. The dead and dying were taken down to feed the black maw.

Kress, delighted, congratulated himself on his genius.

When he put food into the tank the following day, a three-cornered battle broke out over its possession. The whites were the big winners.

After that, war followed war.

Almost a month to the day after Jala Wo had delivered the sandkings, Kress turned on the holographic projector, and his face materialized in the tank. It turned, slowly, around and around, so his gaze fell on all four castles equally. Kress thought it rather a good likeness; it had his impish grin, wide mouth, full cheeks. His blue eyes sparkled, his gray hair was carefully arrayed in a fashionable sidesweep, his eyebrows were thin and sophisticated.

Soon enough, the sandkings set to work. Kress fed them lavishly while his image beamed down at them from their sky. Temporarily, the wars stopped. All activity was directed towards worship.

His face emerged on the castle walls.

At first all four carvings looked alike to him, but as the work continued and Kress studied the reproductions, he began to detect subtle differences in technique and execution. The reds were the most creative, using tiny flakes of slate to put the gray in his hair. The white idol seemed young and mischievous to him, while the face shaped by the blacks—although virtually the same, line for line—struck him as wise and beneficent. The orange sandkings, as ever, were last and least. The wars had not gone well for them, and their castle was sad compared to the others. The image they carved was crude and cartoonish and they seemed to intend to leave it that way. When they stopped work on the face, Kress grew quite piqued with them, but there was really nothing he could do.

When all of the sandkings had finished their Kress-faces, he turned off the holograph and decided that it was time to have a party. His friends would be impressed. He could even stage a war for them, he thought. Humming happily to himself, he began to draw up a guest list.

The party was a wild success.

Kress invited thirty people; a handful of close friends who shared his amusements, a few former lovers, and a collection of business and social rivals who could not afford to ignore his summons. He knew some of them would be discomfited and even offended by his sandkings. He counted on it. Simon Kress customarily considered his parties a failure unless at least one guest walked out in high dudgeon.

On impulse he added Jala Wo's name to his list. "Bring Shade if you like," he added when dictating her invitation.

Her acceptance surprised him just a bit. "Shade, alas, will be unable to attend. He does not go to social functions," Wo added. "As for myself, I look forward to the chance to see how your sandkings are doing."

Kress ordered them up a sumptuous meal. And when at last the conversation had died down, and most of his guests had gotten silly on wine and joy sticks, he shocked them by personally scraping their table leavings into a large bowl. "Come, all of you," he told them. "I want to introduce you to my newest pets." Carrying the bowl, he conducted them into his living room.

The sandkings lived up to his fondest expectations. He had starved them for two days in preparation, and they were in a fighting mood. While the guests ringed the tank, looking through the magnifying glasses Kress had thoughtfully provided, the sandkings waged a glorious battle over the scraps. He counted almost sixty dead mobiles when the struggle was over. The reds and whites, who had recently formed an alliance, emerged with most of the food.

"Kress, you're disgusting," Cath m'Lane told him. She had lived with him for a short time two years before, until her soppy sentimentality almost drove him mad. "I was a fool to come back here. I thought perhaps you'd changed, wanted to apologize." She had never forgiven him for the time his shambler had eaten an excessively cute puppy of which she had been fond. "Don't *ever* invite me here again, Simon." She strode out, accompanied by her current lover and a chorus of laughter.

His other guests were full of questions.

Where did the sandkings come from? they wanted to know. "From Wo and Shade, Importers," he replied, with a polite gesture towards Jala Wo, who had remained quiet and apart through most of the evening.

Why did they decorate their castles with his likeness? "Because I am the source of all good things. Surely you know that?" That brought a round of chuckles.

Will they fight again? "Of course, but not tonight. Don't worry. There will be other parties."

Jad Rakkis, who was an amateur xenologist, began talking about other social insects and the wars they fought. "These sandkings are amusing, but nothing really. You ought to read about Terran soldier ants, for instance."

"Sandkings are not insects," Jala Wo said sharply, but Jad was off and running, and no one paid her the slightest attention. Kress smiled at her and shrugged.

Malada Blane suggested a betting pool the next time they got together to watch a war, and everyone was taken with the idea. An animated discussion about rules and odds ensued. It lasted for almost an hour. Finally the guests began to take their leave.

Jala Wo was the last to depart. "So," Kress said to her when they were alone, "it appears my sandkings are a hit."

"They are doing well," Wo said. "Already they are larger than my own."

"Yes," Kress said, "except for the oranges."

"I had noticed that," Wo replied. "They seem few in number, and their castle is shabby."

"Well, someone must lose," Kress said. "The oranges were late to emerge and get established. They have suffered for it."

"Pardon," said Wo, "but might I ask if you are feeding your sandkings sufficiently?"

Kress shrugged. "They diet from time to time. It makes them fiercer."

She frowned. "There is no need to starve them. Let them war in their own time, for their own reasons. It is their nature, and you will witness conflicts that are delightfully subtle and complex. The constant war brought on by hunger is artless and degrading."

Simon Kress repaid Wo's frown with interest. "You are in my house, Wo, and here I am the judge of what is degrading. I fed the sandkings as you advised, and they did not fight."

"You must have patience."

"No," Kress said. "I am their master and their god, after all. Why should I wait on their impulses? They did not war often enough to suit me. I corrected the situation."

"I see," said Wo. "I will discuss the matter with Shade."

"It is none of your concern, or his," Kress snapped.

"I must bid you good night, then," Wo said with resignation. But as she slipped into her coat to depart, she fixed him with a final disapproving stare. "Look to your faces, Simon Kress," she warned him. "Look to your faces."

Puzzled, he wandered back to the tank and stared at the castles after she had taken her departure. His faces were still there, as ever. Except— He snatched up his magnifying goggles and slipped them on. Even then it was hard to make out. But it seemed to him that the expression on the face of his images had changed slightly, that his smile was somehow twisted so that it seemed a touch malicious. But it was a very subtle change, if it was a change at all. Kress finally put it down to his suggestibility, and resolved not to invite Jala Wo to any more of his gatherings.

Over the next few months, Kress and about a dozen of his favorites got together weekly for what he liked to call his "war games." Now that his initial fascination with the sandkings was past, Kress spent less time around his tank and more on his business affairs and his social life, but he still enjoyed having a few friends over for a war or two. He kept the combatants sharp on a constant edge of hunger. It had severe effects on the orange sandkings, who dwindled visibly until Kress began to wonder if their maw was dead. But the others did well enough.

Sometimes at night, when he could not sleep, Kress would take a bottle of wine into the darkened living room, where the red gloom of his miniature desert was the only light. He would drink and watch for hours, alone. There was usually a fight going on somewhere, and when there was not he could easily start one by dropping in some small morsel of food.

They took to betting on the weekly battles, as Malada Blane had suggested. Kress won a good amount by betting on the whites, who had become the most powerful and numerous colony in the tank, with the grandest castle. One week he slid the corner of the tank top aside, and dropped the food close to the white castle instead of on the central battleground as usual, so the others had to attack the whites in their stronghold to get any food at all. They tried. The whites were brilliant in defense. Kress won a hundred standards from Jad Rakkis.

Rakkis, in fact, lost heavily on the sandkings almost every week. He pretended to a vast knowledge of them and their ways, claiming that he had studied them after the first party, but he had no luck when it came to placing his bets. Kress suspected that Jad's claims were empty boasting. He had tried to study the sandkings a bit himself, in a moment of idle curiosity, tying in to the library to find out what world his pets were native to. But there was no listing for them. He wanted to get in touch with Wo and ask her about it, but he had other concerns, and the matter kept slipping his mind.

Finally, after a month in which his losses totalled more than a thousand standards, Jad Rakkis arrived at the war games carrying a small plastic case under his arm. Inside was a spiderlike thing covered with fine golden hair.

"A sand spider," Rakkis announced. "From Cathaday. I got it this afternoon from t'Etherane the Petseller. Usually they remove the poison sacs, but this one is intact. Are you game, Simon? I want my money back. I'll bet a thousand standards, sand spider against sandkings."

Kress studied the spider in its plastic prison. His sandkings had grown—they were twice as large as Wo's, as she'd predicted—but they were still dwarfed by this thing. It was venomed, and they were not. Still, there were an awful lot of them. Besides, the endless sandking wars had begun to grow tiresome lately. The novelty of the match intrigued him. "Done," Kress said.

"Jad, you are a fool. The sandkings will just keep coming until this ugly creature of yours is dead."

"You are the fool, Simon," Rakkis replied, smiling. "The Cathadayn sand spider customarily feeds on burrowers that hide in nooks and crevices and—well, watch—it will go straight into those castles, and eat the maws."

Kress scowled amid general laughter. He hadn't counted on that. "Get on with it," he said irritably. He went to freshen his drink.

The spider was too large to cycle conveniently through the food chamber. Two of the others helped Rakkis slide the tank top slightly to one side, and Malada Blane handed him up his case. He shook the spider out. It landed lightly on a miniature dune in front of the red castle, and stood confused for a moment, mouth working, legs twitching menacingly.

"Come on," Rakkis urged. They all gathered round the tank. Simon Kress found his magnifiers and slipped them on. If he was going to lose a thousand standards, at least he wanted a good view of the action.

The sandkings had seen the invader. All over the castle, activity had ceased. The small scarlet mobiles were frozen, watching.

The spider began to move towards the dark promise of the gate. On the tower above, Simon Kress's countenance stared down impassively.

At once there was a flurry of activity. The nearest red mobiles formed themselves into two wedges and streamed over the sand towards the spider. More warriors erupted from inside the castle and assembled in a triple line to guard the approach to the underground chamber where the maw lived. Scouts came scuttling over the dunes, recalled to fight.

Battle was joined.

The attacking sandkings washed over the spider. Mandibles snapped shut on legs and abdomen, and clung. Reds raced up the golden legs to the invader's back. They bit and tore. One of them found an eye, and ripped it loose with tiny yellow tendrils. Kress smiled and pointed.

But they were *small*, and they had no venom, and the

spider did not stop. Its legs flicked sandkings off to either side. Its dripping jaws found others, and left them broken and stiffening. Already a dozen of the reds lay dying. The sand spider came on and on. It strode straight through the triple line of guardians before the castle. The lines closed around it, covered it, waging desperate battle. A team of sandkings had bitten off one of the spider's legs, Kress saw. Defenders leapt from atop the towers to land on the twitching, heaving mass.

Lost beneath the sandkings, the spider somehow lurched down into the darkness and vanished.

Jad Rakkis let out a long breath. He looked pale. "Wonderful," someone else said. Malada Blane chuckled deep in her throat.

"Look," said Idi Noreddian, tugging Kress by the arm.

They had been so intent on the struggle in the corner that none of them had noticed the activity elsewhere in the tank. But now the castle was still, the sands empty save for dead red mobiles, and now they saw.

Three armies were drawn up before the red castle. They stood quite still, in perfect array, rank after rank of sandkings, orange and white and black. Waiting to see what emerged from the depths.

Simon Kress smiled. "A *cordon sanitaire*," he said. "And glance at the other castles, if you will, Jad."

Rakkis did, and swore. Teams of mobiles were sealing up the gates with sand and stone. If the spider somehow survived this encounter, it would find no easy entrance at the other castles. "I should have brought four spiders," Jad Rakkis said. "Still, I've won. My spider is down there right now, eating your damned maw."

Kress did not reply. He waited. There was motion in the shadows.

All at once, red mobiles began pouring out of the gate. They took their positions on the castle, and began repairing the damage the spider had wrought. The other armies dissolved and began to retreat to their respective corners.

"Jad," said Simon Kress, "I think you are a bit confused about who is eating who."

The following week Rakkis brought four slim silver snakes. The sandkings dispatched them without much trouble.

Next he tried a large black bird. It ate more than thirty white mobiles, and its thrashing and blundering virtually destroyed that castle, but ultimately its wings grew tired, and the sandkings attacked in force wherever it landed.

After that it was a case of insects, armored beetles not too unlike the sandkings themselves. But stupid, stupid. An allied force of oranges and blacks broke their formation, divided them, and butchered them.

Rakkis began giving Kress promissory notes.

It was around that time that Kress met Cath m'Lane again, one evening when he was dining in Asgard at his favorite restaurant. He stopped at her table briefly and told her about the war games, inviting her to join them. She flushed, then regained control of herself and grew icy. "Someone has to put a stop to you, Simon. I guess it's going to be me," she said. Kress shrugged and enjoyed a lovely meal and thought no more about her threat.

Until a week later, when a small, stout woman arrived at his door and showed him a police wristband. "We've had complaints," she said. "Do you keep a tank full of dangerous insects, Kress?"

"Not insects," he said, furious. "Come, I'll show you."

When she had seen the sandkings, she shook her head. "This will never do. What do you know about these creatures, anyway? Do you know what world they're from? Have they been cleared by the ecological board? Do you have a license for these things? We have a report that they're carnivores, possibly dangerous. We also have a report that they are semi-sentient. Where did you get these creatures, anyway?"

"From Wo and Shade," Kress replied.

"Never heard of them," the woman said. "Probably smuggled them in, knowing our ecologists would never approve them. No, Kress, this won't do. I'm going to confiscate this tank and have it destroyed. And you're going to have to expect a few fines as well."

Kress offered her a hundred standards to forget all about him and his sandkings.

She *tsked*. "Now I'll have to add attempted bribery to the charges against you."

Not until he raised the figure to two thousand standards was she willing to be persuaded. "It's not going to be easy, you know," she said. "There are forms to be altered, records to be wiped. And getting a forged license from the ecologists will be time-consuming. Not to mention dealing with the complainant. What if she calls again?"

"Leave her to me," Kress said. "Leave her to me."

He thought about it for a while. That night he made some calls.

First he got t'Etherane the Petseller. "I want to buy a dog," he said. "A puppy."

The round-faced merchant gawked at him. "A puppy? That is not like you, Simon. Why don't you come in? I have a lovely choice."

"I want a very specific *kind* of puppy," Kress said. "Take notes. I'll describe to you what it must look like."

Afterwards he punched for Idi Noreddian. "Idi," he said, "I want you out here tonight with your holo equipment. I have a notion to record a sandking battle. A present for one of my friends."

The night after they made the recording, Simon Kress stayed up late. He absorbed a controversial new drama in his sensorium, fixed himself a small snack, smoked a joy stick or two, and broke out a bottle of wine. Feeling very happy with himself, he wandered into the living room, glass in hand.

The lights were out. The red glow of the terrarium made the shadows flushed and feverish. He walked over to look at his domain, curious as to how the blacks were doing in the repairs on their castle. The puppy had left it in ruins.

The restoration went well. But as Kress inspected the work through his magnifiers, he chanced to glance closely at the face. It startled him.

He drew back, blinked, took a healthy gulp of wine, and looked again.

The face on the walls was still his. But it was all wrong, all *twisted*. His cheeks were bloated and piggish, his smile was a crooked leer. He looked impossibly malevolent.

Uneasy, he moved around the tank to inspect the other castles. They were each a bit different, but ultimately all the same.

The oranges had left out most of the fine detail, but the result still seemed monstrous, crude: a brutal mouth and mindless eyes.

The reds gave him a satanic, twitching kind of smile. His mouth did odd, unlovely things at its corners.

The whites, his favorites, had carved a cruel idiot god.

Simon Kress flung his wine across the room in rage. "You *dare*," he said under his breath. "Now you won't eat for a week, you damned . . ." His voice was shrill. "I'll teach you." He had an idea. He strode out of the room, returned a moment later with an antique iron throwing-sword in his hand. It was a meter long, and the point was still sharp. Kress smiled, climbed up and moved the tank cover aside just enough to give him working room, opening one corner of the desert. He leaned down, and jabbed the sword at the white castle below him. He waved it back and forth, smashing towers and ramparts and walls. Sand and stone collapsed, burying the scrambling mobiles. A flick of his wrist obliterated the features of the insolent, insulting caricature the sandkings had made of his face. Then he poised the point of the sword above the dark mouth that opened down into the maw's chamber, and thrust with all his strength. He heard a soft, squishing sound, and met resistance. All of the mobiles trembled and collapsed. Satisfied, Kress pulled back.

He watched for a moment, wondering whether he'd killed the maw. The point of the throwing-sword was wet and slimy. But finally the white sandkings began to move again. Feebly, slowly, but they moved.

He was preparing to slide the cover back in place

and move on to a second castle when he felt something crawling on his hand.

He screamed and dropped the sword, and brushed the sandking from his flesh. It fell to the carpet, and he ground it beneath his heel, crushing it thoroughly long after it was dead. It had crunched when he stepped on it. After that, trembling, he hurried to seal the tank up again, and rushed off to shower and inspect himself carefully. He boiled his clothing.

Later, after several fresh glasses of wine, he returned to the living room. He was a bit ashamed of the way the sandking had terrified him. But he was not about to open the tank again. From now on, the cover stayed sealed permanently. Still, he had to punish the others.

Kress decided to lubricate his mental processes with another glass of wine. As he finished it, an inspiration came to him. He went to the tank smiling, and made a few adjustments to the humidity controls.

By the time he fell asleep on the couch, his wine glass still in his hand, the sand castles were melting in the rain.

Kress woke to angry pounding on his door.

He sat up, groggy, his head throbbing. Wine hangovers were always the worst, he thought. He lurched to the entry chamber.

Cath m'Lane was outside. "You monster," she said, her face swollen and puffy and streaked by tears. "I cried all night, damn you. But no more, Simon, no more."

"Easy," he said, holding his head. "I've got a hangover."

She swore and shoved him aside and pushed her way into his house. The shambler came peering round a corner to see what the noise was. She spat at it and stalked into the living room, Kress trailing ineffectually after her. "Hold on," he said, "where do you . . . you can't . . ." He stopped, suddenly horrorstruck. She was carrying a heavy sledgehammer in her left hand. "No," he said.

She went directly to the sandking tank. "You like the

little charmers so much, Simon? Then you can live with them."

"*Cath!*" he shrieked.

Gripping the hammer with both hands, she swung as hard as she could against the side of the tank. The sound of the impact set his head to screaming, and Kress made a low blubbering sound of despair. But the plastic held.

She swung again. This time there was a *crack,* and a network of thin lines sprang into being.

Kress threw himself at her as she drew back her hammer for a third swing. They went down flailing, and rolled. She lost her grip on the hammer and tried to throttle him, but Kress wrenched free and bit her on the arm, drawing blood. They both staggered to their feet, panting.

"You should see yourself, Simon," she said grimly. "Blood dripping from your mouth. You look like one of your pets. How do you like the taste?"

"Get out," he said. He saw the throwing-sword where it had fallen the night before, and snatched it up. "Get out," he repeated, waving the sword for emphasis. "Don't go near that tank again."

She laughed at him. "You wouldn't dare," she said. She bent to pick up her hammer.

Kress shrieked at her, and lunged. Before he quite knew what was happening, the iron blade had gone clear through her abdomen. Cath m'Lane looked at him wonderingly, and down at the sword. Kress fell back whimpering. "I didn't mean . . . I only wanted . . ."

She was transfixed, bleeding, dead, but somehow she did not fall. "You monster," she managed to say, though her mouth was full of blood. And she whirled, impossibly, the sword in her, and swung with her last strength at the tank. The tortured wall shattered, and Cath m'Lane was buried beneath an avalanche of plastic and sand and mud.

Kress made small hysterical noises and scrambled up on the couch.

Sandkings were emerging from the muck on his living room floor. They were crawling across Cath's body.

A few of them ventured tentatively out across the carpet. More followed.

He watched as a column took shape, a living, writhing square of sandkings, bearing something, something slimy and featureless, a piece of raw meat big as a man's head. They began to carry it away from the tank. It pulsed.

That was when Kress broke and ran.

It was late afternoon before he found the courage to return.

He had run to his skimmer and flown to the nearest city, some fifty kilometers away, almost sick with fear. But once safely away, he had found a small restaurant, put down several mugs of coffee and two anti-hangover tabs, eaten a full breakfast, and gradually regained his composure.

It had been a dreadful morning, but dwelling on that would solve nothing. He ordered more coffee and considered his situation with icy rationality.

Cath m'Lane was dead at his hand. Could he report it, plead that it had been an accident? Unlikely. He had run her through, after all, and he had already told that policer to leave her to him. He would have to get rid of the evidence, and hope that she had not told anyone where she was going this morning. That was probable. She could only have gotten his gift late last night. She said that she had cried all night, and she had been alone when she arrived. Very well: he had one body and one skimmer to dispose of.

That left the sandkings. They might prove more of a difficulty. No doubt they had all escaped by now. The thought of them around his house, in his bed and his clothes, infesting his food—it made his flesh crawl. He shuddered and overcame his revulsion. It really shouldn't be too hard to kill them, he reminded himself. He didn't have to account for every mobile. Just the four maws, that was all. He could do that. They were large, as he'd seen. He would find them and kill them.

Simon Kress went shopping before he flew back to his home. He bought a set of skinthins that would cover him from head to foot, several bags of poison pellets for rockjock control, and a spray canister of illegally strong pesticide. He also bought a magnalock towing device.

When he landed, he went about things methodically. First he hooked Cath's skimmer to his own with the magnalock. Searching it, he had his first piece of luck. The crystal chip with Idi Noreddian's holo of the sandking fight was on the front seat. He had worried about that.

When the skimmers were ready, he slipped into his skinthins and went inside for Cath's body.

It wasn't there.

He poked through the fast-drying sand carefully, but there was no doubt of it; the body was gone. Could she have dragged herself away? Unlikely, but Kress searched. A cursory inspection of his house turned up neither the body nor any sign of the sandkings. He did not have time for a more thorough investigation, not with the incriminating skimmer outside his front door. He resolved to try later.

Some seventy kilometers north of Kress's estate was a range of active volcanoes. He flew there, Cath's skimmer in tow. Above the glowering cone of the largest, he released the magnalock and watched it vanish in the lava below.

It was dusk when he returned to his house. That gave him pause. Briefly he considered flying back to the city and spending the night there. He put the thought aside. There was work to do. He wasn't safe yet.

He scattered the poison pellets around the exterior of his house. No one would find that suspicious. He'd always had a rockjock problem. When that task was completed, he primed the canister of pesticide and ventured back inside.

Kress went through the house room by room, turning on lights everywhere he went until he was surrounded by a blaze of artificial illumination. He paused to clean up in the living room, shoveling sand and plastic fragments back into the broken tank. The sandkings were all gone, as he'd feared. The castles were shrunken and distorted, slagged by the watery bombardment Kress had visited upon them, and what little remained was crumbling as it dried.

He frowned and searched on, canister of pest spray strapped across his shoulders.

Down in his deepest wine cellar, he came upon Cath m'Lane's corpse.

It sprawled at the foot of a steep flight of stairs, the limbs twisted as if by a fall. White mobiles were swarming all over it, and as Kress watched, the body moved jerkily across the hard-packed dirt floor.

He laughed, and twisted the illumination up to maximum. In the far corner, a squat little earthen castle and a dark hole were visible between two wine racks. Kress could make out a rough outline of his face on the cellar wall.

The body shifted once again, moving a few centimeters towards the castle. Kress had a sudden vision of the white maw waiting hungrily. It might be able to get Cath's foot in its mouth, but no more. It was too absurd. He laughed again, and started down into the cellar, finger poised on the trigger of the hose that snaked down his right arm. The sandkings—hundreds of them moving as one—deserted the body and formed up battle lines, a field of white between him and their maw.

Suddenly Kress had another inspiration. He smiled and lowered his firing hand. "Cath was always hard to swallow," he said, delighted at his wit. "Especially for one your size. Here, let me give you some help. What are gods for, after all?"

He retreated upstairs, returning shortly with a cleaver. The sandkings, patient, waited and watched while Kress chopped Cath m'Lane into small, easily digestible pieces.

Simon Kress slept in his skinthins that night, the pesticide close at hand, but he did not need it. The whites, sated, remained in the cellar, and he saw no sign of the others.

In the morning he finished clean-up in the living room. After he was through, no trace of the struggle remained except for the broken tank.

He ate a light lunch, and resumed his hunt for the missing sandkings. In full daylight, it was not too difficult. The blacks had located in his rock garden, and built a castle heavy with obsidian and quartz. The reds he found at the bottom of his long-unused swimming pool, which had partially filled with wind-blown sand over the years. He saw mobiles of both colors ranging about his grounds, many of them carrying poison pellets back to their maws. Kress decided his pesticide was unnecessary. No use risking a fight when he could just let the poison do its work. Both maws should be dead by evening.

That left only the burnt-orange sandkings unaccounted for. Kress circled his estate several times, in ever-widening spirals, but found no trace of them. When he began to sweat in his skinthins—it was a hot, dry day—he decided it was not important. If they were out here, they were probably eating the poison pellets along with the reds and blacks.

He crunched several sandkings underfoot, with a certain degree of satisfaction, as he walked back to the house. Inside he removed his skinthins, settled down to a delicious meal, and finally began to relax. Everything was under control. Two of the maws would soon be defunct, the third was safely located where he could dispose of it after it had served his purposes, and he had no doubt that he would find the fourth. As for Cath, all trace of her visit had been obliterated.

His reverie was interrupted when his viewscreen began to blink at him. It was Jad Rakkis, calling to brag about some cannibal worms he was bringing to the war games tonight.

Kress had forgotten about that, but he recovered quickly. "Oh, Jad, my pardons. I neglected to tell you. I grew bored with all that, and got rid of the sandkings. Ugly little things. Sorry, but there'll be no party tonight."

Rakkis was indignant. "But what will I do with my worms?"

"Put them in a basket of fruit and send them to a loved one," Kress said, signing off. Quickly he began calling the others. He did not need anyone arriving at his doorstep now, with the sandkings alive and about the estate.

As he was calling Idi Noreddian, Kress became

aware of an annoying oversight. The screen began to clear, indicating that someone had answered at the other end. Kress flicked off.

Idi arrived on schedule an hour later. She was surprised to find the party cancelled, but perfectly happy to share an evening alone with Kress. He delighted her with his story of Cath's reaction to the holo they had made together. While telling it, he managed to ascertain that she had not mentioned the prank to anyone. He nodded, satisfied, and refilled their wine glasses. Only a trickle was left. "I'll have to get a fresh bottle," he said. "Come with me to my wine cellar, and help me pick out a good vintage. You've always had a better palate than I."

She came along willingly enough, but balked at the top of the stairs when Kress opened the door and gestured for her to precede him. "Where are the lights?" she said. "And that smell—what's that peculiar smell, Simon?"

When he shoved her, she looked briefly startled. She screamed as she tumbled down the stairs. Kress closed the door and began to nail it shut with the boards and air-hammer he had left for that purpose. As he was finishing, he heard Idi groan. "I'm hurt," she called. "Simon, what is this?" Suddenly she squealed, and shortly after that the screaming started.

It did not cease for hours. Kress went to his sensorium and dialed up a saucy comedy to blot it out of his mind.

When he was sure she was dead, Kress flew her skimmer north to his volcanoes and discarded it. The magnalock was proving a good investment.

Odd scrabbling noises were coming from beyond the wine cellar door the next morning when Kress went down to check it out. He listened for several uneasy moments, wondering if Idi Noreddian could possibly have survived and be scratching to get out. It seemed unlikely; it had to be the sandkings. Kress did not like the implications of that. He decided that he would keep the door sealed, at least for the moment, and went outside with a shovel to bury the red and black maws in their own castles.

He found them very much alive.

The black castle was glittering with volcanic glass, and sandkings were all over it, repairing and improving. The highest tower was up to his waist, and on it was a hideous caricature of his face. When he approached, the blacks halted in their labors, and formed up into two threatening phalanxes. Kress glanced behind him and saw others closing off his escape. Startled, he dropped the shovel and sprinted out of the trap, crushing several mobiles beneath his boots.

The red castle was creeping up the walls of the swimming pool. The maw was safely settled in a pit, surrounded by sand and concrete and battlements. The reds crept all over the bottom of the pool. Kress watched them carry a rockjock and a large lizard into the castle. He stepped back from the poolside, horrified, and felt something crunch. Looking down, he saw three mobiles climbing up his leg. He brushed them off and stamped them to death, but others were approaching quickly. They were larger than he remembered. Some were almost as big as his thumb.

He ran. By the time he reached the safety of the house, his heart was racing and he was short of breath. The door closed behind him, and Kress hurried to lock it. His house was supposed to be pest-proof. He'd be safe in here.

A stiff drink steadied his nerve. So poison doesn't faze them, he thought. He should have known. Wo had warned him that the maw could eat anything. He would have to use the pesticide. Kress took another drink for good measure, donned his skinthins, and strapped the canister to his back. He unlocked the door.

Outside, the sandkings were waiting.

Two armies confronted him, allied against the common threat. More than he could have guessed. The damned maws must be breeding like rockjocks. They were everywhere, a creeping sea of them.

Kress brought up the hose and flicked the trigger. A gray mist washed over the nearest rank of sandkings. He moved his hand side to side.

Where the mist fell, the sandkings twitched violently and died in sudden spasms. Kress smiled. They were no match for him. He sprayed in a wide arc before him and stepped forward confidently over a litter of black and red bodies. The armies fell back. Kress advanced, intent on cutting through them to their maws.

All at once the retreat stopped. A thousand sandkings surged toward him.

Kress had been expecting the counterattack. He stood his ground, sweeping his misty sword before him in great looping strokes. They came at him and died. A few got through; he could not spray everywhere at once. He felt them climbing up his legs, sensed their mandibles biting futilely at the reinforced plastic of his skinthins. He ignored them, and kept spraying.

Then he began to feel soft impacts on his head and shoulders.

Kress trembled and spun and looked up above him. The front of his house was alive with sandkings. Blacks and reds, hundreds of them. They were launching themselves into the air, raining down on him. They fell all around him. One landed on his faceplate, its mandibles scraping at his eyes for a terrible second before he plucked it away.

He swung up his hose and sprayed the air, sprayed the house, sprayed until the airborne sandkings were all dead or dying. The mist settled back on him, making him cough. He coughed, and kept spraying. Only when the front of the house was clean did Kress turn his attention back to the ground.

They were all around him, on him, dozens of them scurrying over his body, hundreds of others hurrying to join them. He turned the mist on them. The hose went dead. Kress heard a loud *hiss* and the deadly fog rose in a great cloud from between his shoulders, cloaking him, choking him, making his eyes burn and blur. He felt for the hose, and his hand came away covered with dying sandkings. The hose was severed; they'd eaten it through. He was surrounded by a shroud of pesticide, blinded. He stumbled and screamed, and began to run back to the house, pulling sandkings from his body as he went.

Inside, he sealed the door and collapsed on the carpet, rolling back and forth until he was sure he had crushed them all. The canister was empty by then, hissing feebly. Kress stripped off his skinthins and showered. The hot spray scalded him and left his skin reddened and sensitive, but it made his flesh stop crawling.

He dressed in his heaviest clothing, thick workpants and leathers, after shaking them out nervously. "Damn," he kept muttering, "damn." His throat was dry. After searching the entry hall thoroughly to make certain it was clean, he allowed himself to sit and pour a drink. "Damn," he repeated. His hand shook as he poured, slopping liquor on the carpet.

The alcohol settled him, but it did not wash away the fear. He had a second drink, and went to the window furtively. Sandkings were moving across the thick plastic pane. He shuddered and retreated to his communications console. He had to get help, he thought wildly. He would punch through a call to the authorities, and policers would come out with flamethrowers and . . .

Simon Kress stopped in mid-call, and groaned. He couldn't call in the police. He would have to tell them about the whites in his cellar, and they'd find the bodies there. Perhaps the maw might have finished Cath m'Lane by now, but certainly not Idi Noreddian. He hadn't even cut her up. Besides, there would be bones. No, the police could be called in only as a last resort.

He sat at the console, frowning. His communications equipment filled a whole wall; from here he could reach anyone on Baldur. He had plenty of money, and his cunning; he had always prided himself on his cunning. He would handle this somehow.

Briefly he considered calling Wo, but he soon dismissed the idea. Wo knew too much, and she would ask questions, and he did not trust her. No, he needed someone who would do as he asked *without* questions.

His frown faded, and slowly turned into a smile. Simon Kress had contacts. He put through a call to a number he had not used in a long time.

A woman's face took shape on his viewscreen: white-haired, bland of expression, with a long hook nose. Her voice was brisk and efficient. "Simon," she said. "How is business?"

"Business is fine, Lissandra," Kress replied. "I have a job for you."

"A removal? My price has gone up since last time, Simon. It has been ten years, after all."

"You will be well paid," Kress said. "You know I'm generous. I want you for a bit of pest control."

She smiled a thin smile. "No need to use euphemisms, Simon. The call is shielded."

"No, I'm serious. I have a pest problem. Dangerous pests. Take care of them for me. No questions. Understood?"

"Understood."

"Good. You'll need . . . oh, three or four operatives. Wear heat-resistant skinthins, and equip them with flamethrowers, or lasers, something on that order. Come out to my place. You'll see the problem. Bugs, lots and lots of them. In my rock garden and the old swimming pool you'll find castles. Destroy them, kill everything inside them. Then knock on the door, and I'll show you what else needs to be done. Can you get out here quickly?"

Her face was impassive. "We'll leave within the hour."

Lissandra was true to her word. She arrived in a lean black skimmer with three operatives. Kress watched them from the safety of a second-story window. They were all faceless in dark plastic skinthins. Two of them wore portable flamethrowers, a third carried lasercannon and explosives. Lissandra carried nothing; Kress recognized her by the way she gave orders.

Their skimmer passed low overhead first, checking out the situation. The sandkings went mad. Scarlet and ebony mobiles ran everywhere, frenetic. Kress could see the castle in the rock garden from his vantage point. It stood tall as a man. Its ramparts were crawling with black defenders, and a steady stream of mobiles flowed down into its depths.

Lissandra's skimmer came down next to Kress's and

the operatives vaulted out and unlimbered their weapons. They looked inhuman, deadly.

The black army drew up between them and the castle. The reds— Kress suddenly realized that he could not see the reds. He blinked. Where had they gone?

Lissandra pointed and shouted, and her two flamethrowers spread out and opened up on the black sandkings. Their weapons coughed dully and began to roar, long tongues of blue-and-scarlet fire licking out before them. Sandkings crisped and blackened and died. The operatives began to play the fire back and forth in an efficient, interlocking pattern. They advanced with careful, measured steps.

The black army burned and disintegrated, the mobiles fleeing in a thousand different directions, some back towards the castle, others towards the enemy. None reached the operatives with the flamethrowers. Lissandra's people were very professional.

Then one of them stumbled.

Or seemed to stumble. Kress looked again, and saw that the ground had given way beneath the man. Tunnels, he thought with a tremor of fear; tunnels, pits, traps. The flamer was sunk in sand up to his waist, and suddenly the ground around him seemed to erupt, and he was covered with scarlet sandkings. He dropped the flamethrower and began to claw wildly at his own body. His screams were horrible to hear.

His companion hesitated, then swung and fired. A blast of flame swallowed human and sandkings both. The screaming stopped abruptly. Satisfied, the second flamer turned back to the castle and took another step forward, and recoiled as his foot broke through the ground and vanished up to the ankle. He tried to pull it back and retreat, and the sand all around him gave way. He lost his balance and stumbled, flailing, and the sandkings were everywhere, a boiling mass of them, covering him as he writhed and rolled. His flamethrower was useless and forgotten.

Kress pounded wildly on the window, shouting for attention. "The castle! Get the castle!"

Lissandra, standing back by her skimmer, heard and gestured. Her third operative sighted with the lasercannon and fired. The beam throbbed across the grounds and sliced off the top of the castle. He brought it down sharply, hacking at the sand and stone parapets. Towers fell. Kress's face disintegrated. The laser bit into the ground, searching round and about. The castle crumbled; now it was only a heap of sand. But the black mobiles continued to move. The maw was buried too deeply; they hadn't touched her.

Lissandra gave another order. Her operative discarded the laser, primed an explosive, and darted forward. He leapt over the smoking corpse of the first flamer, landed on solid ground within Kress's rock garden, and heaved. The explosive ball landed square atop the ruins of the black castle. White-hot light seared Kress's eyes, and there was a tremendous gout of sand and rock and mobiles. For a moment dust obscured everything. It was raining sandkings and pieces of sandkings.

Kress saw that the black mobiles were dead and unmoving.

"The pool," he shouted down through the window. "Get the castle in the pool."

Lissandra understood quickly; the ground was littered with motionless blacks, but the reds were pulling back hurriedly and reforming. Her operative stood uncertain, then reached down and pulled out another explosive ball. He took one step forward, but Lissandra called him and he sprinted back in her direction.

It was all so simple then. He reached the skimmer, and Lissandra took him aloft. Kress rushed to another window in another room to watch. They came swooping in just over the pool, and the operative pitched his bombs down at the red castle from the safety of the skimmer. After the fourth run, the castle was unrecognizable, and the sandkings stopped moving.

Lissandra was thorough. She had him bomb each castle several additional times. Then he used the laser-cannon, crisscrossing methodically until it was certain that nothing living could remain intact beneath those small patches of ground.

Finally they came knocking at his door. Kress was grinning manically when he let them in. "Lovely," he said, "lovely."

Lissandra pulled off the mask of her skinthins. "This will cost you, Simon. Two operatives gone, not to mention the danger to my own life."

"Of course," Kress blurted. "You'll be well paid, Lissandra. Whatever you ask, just so you finish the job."

"What remains to be done?"

"You have to clean out my wine cellar," Kress said. "There's another castle down there. And you'll have to do it without explosives. I don't want my house coming down around me."

Lissandra motioned to her operative. "Go outside and get Rajk's flamethrower. It should be intact."

He returned armed, ready, silent. Kress led them down to the wine cellar.

The heavy door was still nailed shut, as he had left it. But it bulged outward slightly, as if warped by some tremendous pressure. That made Kress uneasy, as did the silence that held reign about them. He stood well away from the door as Lissandra's operative removed his nails and planks. "Is that safe in here?" he found himself muttering, pointing at the flamethrower. "I don't want a fire, either, you know."

"I have the laser," Lissandra said. "We'll use that for the kill. The flamethrower probably won't be needed. But I want it here just in case. There are worse things than fire, Simon."

He nodded.

The last plank came free of the cellar door. There was still no sound from below. Lissandra snapped an order, and her underling fell back, took up a position behind her, and leveled the flamethrower square at the door. She slipped her mask back on, hefted the laser, stepped forward, and pulled open the door.

No motion. No sound. It was dark down there.

"Is there a light?" Lissandra asked.

"Just inside the door," Kress said. "On the right hand side. Mind the stairs, they're quite steep."

She stepped into the door, shifted the laser to her left hand, and reached up with her right, fumbling inside for the light panel. Nothing happened. "I feel it," Lissandra said, "but it doesn't seem to . . ."

Then she was screaming, and she stumbled back-

ward. A great white sandking had clamped itself around
her wrist. Blood welled through her skinthins where its
mandibles had sunk in. It was fully as large as her
hand.

Lissandra did a horrible little jig across the room and
began to smash her hand against the nearest wall.
Again and again and again. It landed with a heavy,
meaty thud. Finally the sandking fell away. She whimpered and fell to her knees. "I think my fingers are broken," she said softly. The blood was still flowing freely.
She had dropped the laser near the cellar door.

"I'm not going down there," her operative announced in clear firm tones.

Lissandra looked up at him. "No," she said. "Stand
in the door and flame it all. Cinder it. Do you understand?"

He nodded.

Simon Kress moaned. "My *house*," he said. His
stomach churned. The white sandking had been so
large. How many more were down there? "Don't," he
continued. "Leave it alone. I've changed my mind.
Leave it alone."

Lissandra misunderstood. She held out her hand. It
was covered with blood and greenish-black ichor.
"Your little friend bit clean through my glove, and you
saw what it took to get it off. I don't care about your
house, Simon. Whatever is down there is going to die."

Kress hardly heard her. He thought he could see
movement in the shadows beyond the cellar door. He
imagined a white army bursting forth, all as large as the
sandking that had attacked Lissandra. He saw himself
being lifted by a hundred tiny arms, and dragged down
into the darkness where the maw waited hungrily. He
was afraid. "Don't," he said.

They ignored him.

Kress darted forward, and his shoulder slammed into
the back of Lissandra's operative just as the man was
bracing to fire. The operative grunted, lost his balance,
and pitched forward into the black. Kress listened to
him fall down the stairs. Afterwards there were other
noises; scuttlings and snaps and soft squishing sounds.

Kress swung around to face Lissandra. He was

drenched in cold sweat, but a sickly kind of excitement was on him. It was almost sexual.

Lissandra's calm cold eyes regarded him through her mask. "What are you doing?" she demanded as Kress picked up the laser she had dropped. "*Simon!*"

"Making a peace," he said, giggling. "They won't hurt god, no, not so long as god is good and generous. I was cruel. Starved them. I have to make up for it now, you see."

"You're insane," Lissandra said. It was the last thing she said. Kress burned a hole in her chest big enough to put his arm through. He dragged the body across the floor and rolled it down the cellar stairs. The noises were louder; chitinous clackings and scrapings and echoes that were thick and liquid. Kress nailed up the door once again.

As he fled, he was filled with a deep sense of contentment that coated his fear like a layer of syrup. He suspected it was not his own.

He planned to leave his home, to fly to the city and take a room for a night, or perhaps for a year. Instead Kress started drinking. He was not quite sure why. He drank steadily for hours, and retched it all up violently on his living room carpet. At some point he fell asleep. When he woke, it was pitch dark in the house.

He cowered against the couch. He could hear *noises*. Things were moving in the walls. They were all around him. His hearing was extraordinarily acute. Every little creak was the footstep of a sandking. He closed his eyes and waited, expecting to feel their terrible touch, afraid to move lest he brush against one.

Kress sobbed, and was very still.

After a while, nothing happened.

He opened his eyes again. He trembled. Slowly the shadows began to soften and dissolve. Moonlight was filtering through the high windows. His eyes adjusted.

The living room was empty. Nothing there, nothing, nothing. Only his drunken fears.

Simon Kress steeled himself, and rose, and went to a light.

Nothing there. The room was quiet, deserted.

He listened. Nothing. No sound. Nothing in the walls. It had all been his imagination, his fear.

The memories of Lissandra and the thing in the cellar returned to him unbidden. Shame and anger washed over him. Why had he done that? He could have helped her burn it out, kill it. *Why . . .* he knew why. The maw had done it to him, put fear in him. Wo had said it was psionic, even when it was small. And now it was large, so large. It had feasted on Cath, and Idi, and now it had two more bodies down there. It would keep growing. And it had learned to like the taste of human flesh, he thought.

He began to shake, but he took control of himself again and stopped. It wouldn't hurt him, he was god, the whites had always been his favorites.

He remembered how he had stabbed it with his throwing-sword. That was before Cath came. Damn her anyway.

He couldn't stay here. The maw would grow hungry again. Large as it was, it wouldn't take long. Its appetite would be terrible. What would it do then? He had to get away, back to the safety of the city while it was still contained in his wine cellar. It was only plaster and hard-packed earth down there, and the mobiles could dig and tunnel. When they got free . . . Kress didn't want to think about it.

He went to his bedroom and packed. He took three bags. Just a single change of clothing, that was all he needed; the rest of the space he filled with his valuables, with jewelry and art and other things he could not bear to lose. He did not expect to return.

His shambler followed him down the stairs, staring at him from its baleful glowing eyes. It was gaunt. Kress realized that it had been ages since he had fed it. Normally it could take care of itself, but no doubt the pickings had grown lean of late. When it tried to clutch at his leg, he snarled at it and kicked it away, and it scurried off, offended.

Kress slipped outside, carrying his bags awkwardly, and shut the door behind him.

For a moment he stood pressed against the house, his

heart thudding in his chest. Only a few meters between him and his skimmer. He was afraid to take them. The moonlight was bright, and the front of his house was a scene of carnage. The bodies of Lissandra's two flamers lay where they had fallen, one twisted and burned, the other swollen beneath a mass of dead sandkings. And the mobiles, the black and red mobiles, they were all around him. It was an effort to remember that they were dead. It was almost as if they were simply waiting, as they had waited so often before.

Nonsense, Kress told himself. More drunken fears. He had seen the castles blown apart. They were dead, and the white maw was trapped in his cellar. He took several deep and deliberate breaths, and stepped forward onto the sandkings. They crunched. He ground them into the sand savagely. They did not move.

Kress smiled, and walked slowly across the battle-ground, listening to the sounds, the sounds of safety.

Crunch. Crackle. Crunch.

He lowered his bags to the ground and opened the door to his skimmer.

Something moved from shadow into light. A pale shape on the seat of his skimmer. It was as long as his forearm. Its mandibles clacked together softly, and it looked up at him from six small eyes set all around its body.

Kress wet his pants and backed away slowly.

There was more motion from inside the skimmer. He had left the door open. The sandking emerged and came toward him, cautiously. Others followed. They had been hiding beneath his seats, burrowed into the upholstery. But now they emerged. They formed a ragged ring around the skimmer.

Kress licked his lips, turned, and moved quickly to Lissandra's skimmer.

He stopped before he was halfway there. Things were moving inside that one too. Great maggoty things half-seen by the light of the moon.

Kress whimpered and retreated back towards the house. Near the front door, he looked up.

He counted a dozen long white shapes creeping back and forth across the walls of the building. Four of them were clustered close together near the top of the unused belfry where the carrion hawk had once roosted. They were carving something. A face. A very recognizable face.

Simon Kress shrieked and ran back inside.

A sufficient quantity of drink brought him the easy oblivion he sought. But he woke. Despite everything, he woke. He had a terrific headache, and he smelled, and he was hungry. Oh so very hungry. He had never been so hungry.

Kress knew it was not his *own* stomach hurting.

A white sandking watched him from atop the dresser in his bedroom, its antennae moving faintly. It was as big as the one in the skimmer the night before. He tried not to shrink away. "I'll . . . I'll feed you," he said to it. "I'll feed you." His mouth was horribly dry, sandpaper dry. He licked his lips and fled from the room.

The house was full of sandkings; he had to be careful where he put his feet. They all seemed busy on errands of their own. They were making modifications in his house, burrowing into or out of his walls, carving things. Twice he saw his own likeness staring out at him from unexpected places. The faces were warped, twisted, livid with fear.

He went outside to get the bodies that had been rotting in the yard, hoping to appease the white maw's hunger. They were gone, both of them. Kress remembered how easily the mobiles could carry things many times their own weight.

It was terrible to think that the maw was *still* hungry after all of that.

When Kress reentered the house, a column of sandkings was wending its way down the stairs. Each carried a piece of his shambler. The head seemed to look at him reproachfully as it went by.

Kress emptied his freezers, his cabinets, everything, piling all the food in the house in the center of his kitchen floor. A dozen whites waited to take it away. They avoided the frozen food, leaving it to thaw in a great puddle, but they carried off everything else.

When all the food was gone, Kress felt his own hunger pangs abate just a bit, though he had not eaten a thing. But he knew the respite would be short-lived. Soon the maw would be hungry again. He had to feed it.

Kress knew what to do. He went to his communicator. "Malada," he began casually when the first of his friends answered, "I'm having a small party tonight. I realize this is terribly short notice, but I hope you can make it. I really do."

He called Jad Rakkis next, and then the others. By the time he had finished, nine of them had accepted his invitation. Kress hoped that would be enough.

Kress met his guests outside—the mobiles had cleaned up remarkably quickly, and the grounds looked almost as they had before the battle—and walked them to his front door. He let them enter first. He did not follow.

When four of them had gone through, Kress finally worked up his courage. He closed the door behind his latest guest, ignoring the startled exclamations that soon turned into shrill gibbering, and sprinted for the skimmer the man had arrived in. He slid in safely, thumbed the startplate, and swore. It was programmed to lift only in response to its owner's thumbprint, of course.

Jad Rakkis was the next to arrive. Kress ran to his skimmer as it set down, and seized Rakkis by the arm as he was climbing out. "Get back in, quickly," he said, pushing. "Take me to the city. Hurry, Jad. *Get out of here!*"

But Rakkis only stared at him, and would not move. "Why, what's wrong, Simon? I don't understand. What about your party?"

And then it was too late, because the loose sand all around them was stirring, and the red eyes were staring at them, and the mandibles were clacking. Rakkis made a choking sound, and moved to get back in his skimmer, but a pair of mandibles snapped shut about his ankle, and suddenly he was on his knees. The sand seemed to boil with subterranean activity. Jad thrashed and cried terribly as they tore him apart. Kress could hardly bear to watch.

After that, he did not try to escape again. When it was all over, he cleaned out what remained in his liquor cabinet, and got extremely drunk. It would be the last time he would enjoy that luxury, he knew. The only alcohol remaining in the house was stored down in the wine cellar.

Kress did not touch a bite of food the entire day, but he fell asleep feeling bloated, sated at last, the awful hunger vanquished. His last thoughts before the nightmares took him were on who he could ask out tomorrow.

Morning was hot and dry. Kress opened his eyes to see the white sandking on his dresser again. He shut them again quickly, hoping the dream would leave him. It did not, and he could not go back to sleep, and soon he found himself staring at the thing.

He stared for almost five minutes before the strangeness of it dawned on him; the sandking was not moving.

The mobiles could be preternaturally still, to be sure. He had seen them wait and watch a thousand times. But always there was some motion about them; the mandibles clacked, the legs twitched, the long fine antennae stirred and swayed.

But the sandking on his dresser was completely still.

Kress rose, holding his breath, not daring to hope. Could it be dead? Could something have killed it? He walked across the room.

The eyes were glassy and black. The creature seemed swollen, somehow; as if it were soft and rotting inside, filling up with gas that pushed outward at the plates of white armor.

Kress reached out a trembling hand and touched it.

It was warm; hot even, and growing hotter. But it did not move.

He pulled his hand back, and as he did, a segment of the sandking's white exoskeleton fell away from it. The flesh beneath was the same color, but softer-looking, swollen and feverish. And it almost seemed to throb.

Kress backed away, and ran to the door.

Three more white mobiles lay in his hall. They were all like the one in his bedroom.

He ran down the stairs, jumping over sandkings. None of them moved. The house was full of them, all dead, dying, comatose, whatever. Kress did not care what was wrong with them. Just so they could not move.

He found four of them inside his skimmer. He picked them up one by one, and threw them as far as he could. Damned monsters. He slid back in, on the ruined half-eaten seats, and thumbed the startplate.

Nothing happened.

Kress tried again, and again. Nothing. It wasn't fair. This was *his* skimmer, it ought to start, why wouldn't it lift, he didn't understand.

Finally he got out and checked, expecting the worst. He found it. The sandkings had torn apart his gravity grid. He was trapped. He was still trapped.

Grimly Kress marched back into the house. He went to his gallery and found the antique axe that had hung next to the throwing sword he had used on Cath m'Lane. He set to work. The sandkings did not stir even as he chopped them to pieces. But they splattered when he made the first cut, the bodies almost bursting. Inside was awful; strange half-formed organs, a viscous reddish ooze that looked almost like human blood, and the yellow ichor.

Kress destroyed twenty of them before he realized the futility of what he was doing. The mobiles were nothing, really. Besides, there were so *many* of them. He could work for a day and night and still not kill them all.

He had to go down into the wine cellar and use the axe on the maw.

Resolute, he started down. He got within sight of the door, and stopped.

It was not a door any more. The walls had been eaten away, so the hole was twice the size it had been, and round. A pit, that was all. There was no sign that there had ever been a door nailed shut over that black abyss.

A ghastly choking fetid odor seemed to come from below.

And the walls were wet and bloody and covered with patches of white fungus.

And worst, it was *breathing*.

Kress stood across the room and felt the warm wind wash over him as it exhaled, and he tried not to choke, and when the wind reversed direction, he fled.

Back in the living room, he destroyed three more mobiles, and collapsed. What was *happening*? He didn't understand.

Then he remembered the only person who might understand. Kress went to his communicator again, stepped on a sandking in his haste, and prayed fervently that the device still worked.

When Jala Wo answered, he broke down and told her everything.

She let him talk without interruption, no expression save for a slight frown on her gaunt, pale face. When Kress had finished, she said only, "I ought to leave you there."

Kress began to blubber. "You can't. Help me. I'll pay . . ."

"I ought to," Wo repeated, "but I won't."

"Thank you," Kress said. "Oh, thank . . ."

"Quiet," said Wo. "Listen to me. This is your own doing. Keep your sandkings well, and they are courtly ritual warriors. You turned yours into something else, with starvation and torture. You were their god. You made them what they are. That maw in your cellar is sick, still suffering from the wound you gave it. It is probably insane. Its behavior is . . . unusual.

"You have to get out of there quickly. The mobiles are not dead, Kress. They are dormant. I told you the exoskeleton falls off when they grow larger. Normally, in fact, it falls off much earlier. I have never heard of sandkings growing as large as yours while still in the insectoid stage. It is another result of crippling the white maw, I would say. That does not matter.

"What matters is the metamorphosis your sandkings are now undergoing. As the maw grows, you see, it gets progressively more intelligent. Its psionic powers strengthen, and its mind becomes more sophisticated, more ambitious. The armored mobiles are useful enough when the maw is tiny and only semi-sentient, but now it needs better servants, bodies with more capabilities. Do you understand? The mobiles are all going to give birth to a new breed of sandking. I can't say exactly what it will look like. Each maw designs its own, to fit its perceived needs and desires. But it will be biped, with four arms, and opposable thumbs. It will be able to construct and operate advanced machinery. The individual sandkings will not be sentient. But the maw will be very sentient indeed."

Simon Kress was gaping at Wo's image on the viewscreen. "Your workers," he said, with an effort. "The ones who came out here . . . who installed the tank . . ."

Jala Wo managed a faint smile. "Shade," she said.

"Shade is a sandking," Kress repeated numbly. "And you sold me a tank of . . . of . . . infants, ah . . ."

"Do not be absurd," Wo said. "A first-stage sandking is more like a sperm than an infant. The wars temper and control them in nature. Only one in a hundred reaches second stage. Only one in a thousand achieves the third and final plateau, and becomes like Shade. Adult sandkings are not sentimental about the small maws. There are too many of them, and their mobiles are pests." She sighed. "And all this talk wastes time. That white sandking is going to waken to full sentience soon. It is not going to need you any longer, and it hates you, and it will be very hungry. The transformation is taxing. The maw must eat enormous amounts both before and after. So you have to get out of there. Do you understand?"

"I *can't*," Kress said. "My skimmer is destroyed, and I can't get any of the others to start. I don't know how to reprogram them. Can you come out for me?"

"Yes," said Wo. "Shade and I will leave at once, but it is more than two hundred kilometers from Asgard to you, and there is equipment we will need to deal with the deranged sandking you've created. You cannot wait there. You have two feet. Walk. Go due east, as near as you can determine, as quickly as you can. The land out there is pretty desolate. We can find you easily with an aerial search, and you'll be safely away from the sandkings. Do you understand?"

"Yes," said Simon Kress. "Yes, oh, yes."

They signed off, and he walked quickly towards the door. He was halfway there when he heard the noise; a sound halfway between a pop and a crack.

One of the sandkings had split open. Four tiny hands covered with pinkish-yellow blood came up out of the gap, and began to push the dead skin aside.

Kress began to run.

He had not counted on the heat.

The hills were dry and rocky. Kress ran from the house as quickly as he could, ran until his ribs ached and his breath was coming in gasps. Then he walked, but as soon as he had recovered he began to run again. For almost an hour he ran and walked, ran and walked, beneath the fierce hot sun. He sweated freely, and wished that he had thought to bring some water, and he watched the sky in hopes of seeing Wo and Shade.

He was not made for this. It was too hot, and too dry, and he was in no condition. But he kept himself going with the memory of the way the maw had breathed, and the thought of the wriggling little things that by now were surely crawling all over his house. He hoped Wo and Shade would know how to deal with them.

He had his own plans for Wo and Shade. It was all their fault, Kress had decided, and they would suffer for it. Lissandra was dead, but he knew others in her profession. He would have his revenge. He promised himself that a hundred times as he struggled and sweated his way east.

At least he hoped it was east. He was not that good at directions, and he wasn't certain which way he had run in his initial panic, but since then he had made an effort to bear due east, as Wo had suggested.

When he had been running for several hours, with no sign of rescue, Kress began to grow certain that he had gone wrong.

When several more hours passed, he began to grow afraid. What if Wo and Shade could not find him? He would die out here. He hadn't eaten in two days, he was weak and frightened, his throat was raw for want of water. He couldn't keep going. The sun was sinking now, and he'd be completely lost in the dark. What was wrong? Had the sandkings eaten Wo and Shade? The fear was on him again, filling him, and with it a great thirst and a terrible hunger. But Kress kept going. He stumbled now when he tried to run, and twice he fell. The second time he scraped his hand on a rock, and it came away bloody. He sucked at it as he walked, and worried about infection.

The sun was on the horizon behind him. The ground grew a little cooler, for which Kress was grateful. He decided to walk until last light and settle in for the night. Surely he was far enough from the sandkings to be safe, and Wo and Shade would find him come morning.

When he topped the next rise, he saw the outline of a house in front of him.

It wasn't as big as his own house, but it was big enough. It was habitation, safety. Kress shouted and began to run towards it. Food and drink, he had to have nourishment, he could taste the meal now. He was aching with hunger. He ran down the hill towards the house, waving his arms and shouting to the inhabitants. The light was almost gone now, but he could still make out a half-dozen children playing in the twilight. "Hey there," he shouted. "Help, help."

They came running towards him.

Kress stopped suddenly. "No," he said, "oh, no. Oh, no." He backpedaled, slipped on the sand, got up, and tried to run again. They caught him easily. They were ghastly little things with bulging eyes and dusky-orange skin. He struggled, but it was useless. Small as they were, each of them had four arms, and Kress had only two.

They carried him toward the house. It was a sad, shabby house built of crumbling sand, but the door was quite large, and dark, and it breathed. That was terrible, but it was not the thing that set Simon Kress to screaming. He screamed because of the others, the little orange children who came crawling out from the castle, and watched impassively as he passed.

All of them had his face.

Time Shards

Gregory Benford

Many science-fiction readers find the past as fascinating as the future, for we know that despite innumerable histories, we have almost as little knowledge of day-to-day life centuries ago as we have of how people will live in times to come. If only we could listen in on some of the most commonplace scenes of the Middle Ages, how much we might learn!

Spurred by real-life research first suggested ten years ago by Dr. Richard Woodbridge in the *Proceedings of the I.E.E.E.*, Gregory Benford offers a mordant tale of a man who discovers a very possible method of listening to the past.

It had all gone very well, Brooks told himself. Very well indeed. He hurried along the side corridor, his black dress shoes clicking hollowly on the old tiles. This was one of the oldest and most rundown of the Smithsonian's buildings; too bad they didn't have the money to knock it down. Funding. Everything was a matter of funding.

He pushed open the door of the barnlike workroom and called out, "John? How did you like the ceremony?"

John Hart appeared from behind a vast rack that was filled with fluted pottery. His thin face was twisted in a scowl and he was puffing on a cigarette. "Didn't go."

"John! That's not permitted." Brooks waved at the cigarette. "You of all people should be careful about contamination of—"

"Hell with it." He took a final puff, belched blue, and ground out the cigarette on the floor.

"You really should've watched the dedication of the Vault, you know," Brooks began, adopting a bantering tone. You had to keep a light touch with these research types. "The President was there—she made a very nice speech—"

"I was busy."

"Oh?" Something in Hart's tone put Brooks off his conversational stride. "Well. You'll be glad to hear that I had a little conference with the Board, just before the dedication. They've agreed to continue supporting your work here."

"Um."

"You must admit, they're being very fair." As he talked Brooks threaded amid the rows of pottery, each in a plastic sleeve. This room always made him nervous. There was priceless Chinese porcelain here, Assyrian stoneware, buff-blue Roman glazes, Egyptian earthenware—and Brooks lived in mortal fear that he would trip, fall, and smash some piece of history into shards. "After all, you *did* miss your deadline. You got nothing out of all this"—a sweep of the hand, narrowly missing a green Persian tankard—"for the Vault."

Hart, who was studying a small brownish water jug, looked up abruptly. "What about the wheel recording?"

"Well, there was that, but—"

"The best in the world, dammit!"

"They heard it some time ago. They were very interested."

"You told them what they were hearing?" Hart asked intensely.

"Of course, I—"

"You could hear the hoofbeats of cattle, clear as day."

"They heard. Several commented on it."

"Good." Hart seemed satisfied, but still strangely depressed.

"But you must admit, that isn't what you promised."

Hart said sourly, "Research can't be done to a schedule."

Brooks had been pacing up and down the lanes of pottery. He stopped suddenly, pivoted on one foot, and pointed a finger at Hart. "You said you'd have a *voice*. That was the promise. Back in '98 you said you would have something for the BiMillennium celebration, and—"

"Okay, okay." Hart waved away the other man's words.

"Look—" Brooks strode to a window and jerked up the blinds. From this high up in the Arts and Industries Building the BiMillennial Vault was a flat concrete slab sunk in the Washington mud; it had rained the day before. Now bulldozers scraped piles of gravel and mud into the hole, packing it in before the final encasing shield was to be laid. The Vault itself was already sheathed in sleeves of concrete, shock-resistant and immune to decay. The radio beacons inside were now set. Their radioactive power supply would automatically stir to life exactly a thousand years from now. Periodic bursts of radio waves would announce to the world of the TriMillennium that a message from the distant past awaited whoever dug down to find it. Inside the Vault were artifacts, recordings, everything the Board of Regents of the Smithsonian thought important about their age. The coup of the entire Vault was to have been a message from the First Millennium, the year 1000 A.D. Hart had promised them something far better than a mere written document from that time. He had said he could capture a living voice.

"See that?" Brooks said with sudden energy. "That Vault will outlast everything we know—all those best-selling novels and funny plays and amazing scientific discoveries. They'll all be *dust,* when the Vault's opened."

"Yeah," Hart said.

"Yeah? That's all you can say?"

"Well, sure, I—"

"The Vault was *important*. And I was stupid enough"—he rounded on Hart abruptly, anger flashing across his face—"to chew up some of the only money we had for the Vault to support *you*."

Hart took an involuntary step backward. "You knew it was a gamble."

"I knew." Brooks nodded ruefully. "And we waited, and waited—"

"Well, your waiting is over," Hart said, something hardening in him.

"What?"

"I've got it. A voice."

"You have?" In the stunned silence that followed Hart bent over casually and picked up a dun-colored water jug from the racks. An elaborate, impossibly large-winged orange bird was painted on its side. Hart turned the jug in his hands, hefting its weight.

"Why . . . it's too late for the Vault, of course, but still . . ." Brooks shuffled his feet. "I'm glad the idea paid off. That's great."

"Yeah. Great." Hart smiled sourly. "And you know what it's worth? Just about *this* much—"

He took the jug in one hand and threw it. It struck the far wall with a splintering crash. Shards flew like a covey of frightened birds that scattered through the long ranks of pottery. Each landed with a ceramic tinkling.

"What are you *doing*—" Brooks began, dropping to his knees without thinking to retrieve a fragment of the jug. "That jug was worth—"

"Nothing," Hart said. "It was a fake. Almost everything the Egyptians sent was bogus."

"But why are you . . . you said you succeeded . . ." Brooks was shaken out of his normal role of Undersecretary to the Smithsonian.

"I did. For what it's worth."

"Well . . . show me."

Hart shrugged and beckoned Brooks to follow him. He threaded his way through the inventory of glazed pottery, ignoring the extravagant polished shapes that flared and twisted in elaborate, artful designs, the fruit of millennia of artisans. Glazes of feldspath, lead, tin, ruby salt. Jasperware, soft-paste porcelain, albarelloa festooned with ivy and laurel, flaring lips and serene curved handles. A galaxy of the work of the First Millennium and after, assembled for Hart's search.

"It's on the wheel," Hart said, gesturing.

Brooks walked around the spindle fixed at the center of a horizontal disk. Hart called it a potter's wheel but it was a turntable, really, firmly buffered against the slightest tremor from external sources. A carefully arranged family of absorbers isolated the table from everything but the variable motor seated beneath it. On the turntable was an earthenware pot. It looked unremarkable to Brooks—just a dark red oxidized finish, a thick lip, and a rather crude handle, obviously molded on by a lesser artisan.

"What's its origin?" Brooks said, mostly to break the silence that lay between them.

"Southern England." Hart was logging instructions into the computer terminal nearby. Lights rippled on the staging board.

"How close to the First Mil?"

"Around 1280 A.D., apparently."

"Not really close, then. But interesting."

"Yeah."

Brooks stooped forward. When he peered closer he could see the smooth finish was an illusion. A thin thread ran around the pot, so fine the eye could scarcely make it out. The lines wound in a tight helix. In the center of each delicate line was a fine hint of blue. The jug had been incised with a precise point. Good; that was exactly what Hart had said he sought. It was an ancient, common mode of decoration—incise a seemingly infinite series of rings, as the pot turned beneath the cutting tool. The cutting tip revealed a differently colored dye underneath, a technique called sgraffito, the scratched.

It could never have occurred to the Islamic potters who invented sgraffito that they were, in fact, devising the first phonograph records.

Hart pressed a switch and the turntable began to spin. He watched it for a moment, squinting with concentration. Then he reached down to the side of the turntable housing and swung up the stylus manifold. It came up smoothly and Hart locked it in just above the spinning red surface of the pot.

"Not a particularly striking item, is it?" Brooks said conversationally.

"No."

"Who made it?"

"Near as I can determine, somebody in a co-operative of villages, barely Christian. Still used lots of pagan decorations. Got them scrambled up with the cross motif a lot."

"You've gotten . . . words?"

"Oh, sure. In early English, even."

"I'm surprised crude craftsmen could do such delicate work."

"Luck, some of it. They probably used a pointed wire, a new technique that'd been imported around that time from Saxony."

The computer board hooted a readiness call. Hart walked over to it, thumbed in instructions, and turned to watch the stylus whir in a millimeter closer to the spinning jug. "Damn," Hart said, glancing at the board. "Correlator's giving hash again."

Hart stopped the stylus and worked at the board. Brooks turned nervously and paced, unsure of what his attitude should be toward Hart. Apparently the man had discovered something, but did that excuse his surliness? Brooks glanced out the window, where the last crowds were drifting away from the Vault dedication and strolling down the Mall. There was a reception for the Board of Regents in Georgetown in an hour. Brooks would have to be there early, to see that matters were in order—

"If you'd given me enough money, I could've had a Hewlett-Packard. Wouldn't have to fool with this piece of . . ." Hart's voice trailed off.

Brooks had to keep reminding himself that this foul-tempered, scrawny man was reputed to be a genius. If Hart had not come with the highest of recommendations, Brooks would never have risked valuable Vault funding. Apparently Hart's new method for finding correlations in a noisy signal was a genuine achievement.

The basic idea was quite old, of course. In the 1960s a scientist at the American Museum of Natural History in New York had applied a stylus to a rotating urn and played the signal through an audio pickup. Out came the *wreeee* sound of the original potter's wheel where the urn was made. It had been a Roman urn, made in the era when hand-turned wheels were the best available. The Natural History "recording" was crude, but even that long ago they could pick out a moment when the potter's hand slipped and the rhythm of the *wreeee* faltered.

Hart had read about that urn and seen the possibilities. He developed his new multiple-correlation analysis—a feat of programming, if nothing else—and began searching for pottery that might have acoustic detail in its surface. The sgraffito technique was the natural choice. Potters sometimes used fine wires to incise their wares. Conceivably, anything that moved the incising wire—passing footfalls, even the tiny acoustic push of sound waves—could leave its trace on the surface of the finished pot. Buried among imperfections and noise, eroded by the random bruises of history . . .

"Got it," Hart said, fatigue creeping into his voice.

"Good. Good."

"Yeah. Listen."

The stylus whirred forward. It gently nudged into the jug, near the lip. Hart flipped a switch and studied the rippling, dancing yellow lines on the board oscilloscope. Electronic archaeology. "There."

A high-pitched whining came from the speaker, punctuated by hollow, deep bass thumps.

"Hear that? He's using a foot pump."

"A kick wheel?"

"Right."

"I thought they came later."

"No, the Arabs had them."

There came a *clop clop clop*, getting louder. It sounded oddly disembodied in the silence of the long room.

"What . . . ?"

"Horse. I detected this two weeks ago. Checked it with the equestrian people. They say the horse is unshod, assuming we're listening to it walk on dirt. Farm animal, probably. Plow puller."

"Ah."

The hoofbeats faded. The whine of the kick wheel sang on.

"Here it comes," Hart whispered.

Brooks shuffled slightly. The ranks upon ranks of ancient pottery behind him made him nervous, as though a vast unmoving audience were in the room with them.

Thin, distant: "Alf?"

"Aye." A gruff reply.

"It slumps, sure."

"I be oct, man." A rasping, impatient voice.

"T'art—"

"*Busy*—mark?"

"Ah ha' wearied o' their laws," the thin voice persisted.

"Aye—so all. What mark it?" Restrained impatience.

"Their Christ. He werkes vengement an the alt spirits."

"Hie yer tongue."

"They'll ne hear."

"Wi' 'er Christ 'er're everywhere."

A pause. Then faintly, as though a whisper: "We ha' lodged th' alt spirits."

"Ah? You? Th' rash gazer?"

"I spy stormwrack. A hue an' grie rises by this somer se'sun."

"Fer we?"

"Aye, unless we spake th' *Ave maris stella* 'a theirs."

"Elat. Lat fer that. Hie, I'll do it. Me knees still buckle whon they must."

"I kenned that. So shall I."

"Aye. So shall we all. But wh' of the spirits?"

"They suffer pangs, dark werkes. They are lodged."

"Ah. Where?"

"S'tart."

"'Ere? In me clay?"

"In yer vessels."

"Nay!"

"I chanted 'em in 'fore sunbreak."

"Nay! I fain wad ye not."

whir whir whir

The kick wheel thumps came rhythmically.

"They sigh'd thruu in-t'wixt yer clay. 'S done."

"Fer *what?*"

"These pots—they bear a fineness, aye?"

"Aye."

A rumbling. "—will hie home 'er. Live in yer pots."

"An?"

"Whon time werkes a'thwart 'e Christers, yon spirits of leaf an' bough will, I say, hie an' grie to yer sons, man. To yer *sons'* sons, man."

"Me pots? Carry our kenne?"

"Aye. I investe' thy clay wi' ern'st spirit, so when's ye causes it ta dance, our law say . . ."

whir

A hollow rattle.

"Even this 'ere, as I spin it?"

"Aye. Th' spirits innit. Speak as ye form. The dance, t'will carry yer schop word t' yer sons, yer *sons'* sons' sons."

"While it's spinnin'?"

Brooks felt his pulse thumping in his throat.

"Aye."

"Than't—"

"Speak inta it. To yer sons."

"Ah . . ." Suddenly the voice came louder. "Aye, aye! There! If ye hear me, sons! I be from yer past! The ancient dayes!"

"Tell them wha' ye must."

"Aye. Sons! Blood a' mine! Mark ye! Hie not ta strags in th' house of Lutes. They carry the red pox! An' . . . an', beware th' Kinseps—they bugger all they rule! An', whilst pot-charrin', mix th' fair smelt wi' greeno erst, 'ere ye'll flux it fair speedy. Ne'er leave sheep near a lean-house, ne, 'ey'll snuck down 'an it—"

whir whir thump whir

"What—what happened?" Brooks gasped.

"He must have brushed the incising wire a bit. The

cut continues, but the fine touch was lost. Vibrations as subtle as a voice couldn't register."

Brooks looked around, dazed, for a place to sit. "In . . . incredible."

"I suppose."

Hart seemed haggard, worn.

"They were about to convert to Christianity, weren't they?"

Hart nodded.

"They thought they could seal up the—what? wood spirits?—they worshiped. Pack them away by blessing the clay or something like that. And that the clay would carry a message—to the future!"

"So it did."

"To their sons' sons' sons . . ." Brooks paused. "Why are you so depressed, Hart? This is a great success."

Abruptly Hart laughed. "I'm not, really. Just, well, manic, I guess. We're so funny. So absurd. Think about it, Brooks. All that hooey the potter shouted into his damned pot. What did you make of it?"

"Well . . . gossip, mostly. I can't get over what a long shot this is—that we'd get to hear it."

"Maybe it was a common belief back then. Maybe many tried it—and maybe now I'll find more pots, with just ordinary conversation on them. Who knows?" He laughed again, a slow warm chuckle. "We're all so absurd. Maybe Henry Ford was right—history *is* bunk."

"I don't see why you're carrying on this way, Hart. Granted, the message was . . . obscure. That unintelligible information about making pottery, and—"

"Tips on keeping sheep."

"Yes, and—"

"Useless, right?"

"Well, probably. To us, anyway. The conversation before that was much more interesting."

"Uh huh. Here's a man who is talking to the ages. Sending what he thinks is most important. And he prattles out a lot of garbage."

"Well, true . . ."

"And it *was* important—to him."

"Yes."

Hart walked stiffly to the window. Earthmovers crawled like eyeless insects beneath the wan yellow lamps. Dusk had fallen. Their great awkward scoops pushed mounds of mud into the square hole where the Vault rested.

"Look at that." Hart gestured. "The Vault. Our own monument to our age. Passing on the legacy. You, me, the others—we've spent years on it. Years, and a fortune." He chuckled dryly. "What makes you think we've done any better?"

In the Country of the Blind, No One Can See

Melisa Michaels

We all know that clones wouldn't be "natural" human beings, but would clones themselves agree that they're less human than we are? In fact, are we necessarily right in our assumption?

Melisa Michaels explores this question in a story of adventure on Mars, and gives us an answer that's so logical that you'll wonder why you never considered it.

This is Melisa Michaels's first published story, though she's published poetry and artwork before. She's currently art director of Pennyfarthing Press.

Allyson Hunter lay nestled in protective foam, listening to the howling storm outside. She looked like a fragile china doll packed for shipping. The fragility was deceptive. Pale, perfect skin; wide, sky-blue eyes shaded by dark lashes; pink-tinged, high-boned cheeks—but under the china perfection was something sterner and stronger than china dolls. Her eyes glittered like ice. Her mouth was set in lines of habitual determination. Even the casual elegance of her posture was as dangerous as a coiled spring. She waited.

She couldn't see past the foam to tell how her sisters were, and there was nothing she could do till it melted but wait and listen. At least there was no fire; the pilot must have jettisoned the fuel pods in time. Otherwise the foam would have melted within seconds of impact, to give survivors the best chance of escape. In the absence of fire it took several minutes, to ensure an adequate rest period and decrease the chances of traumatic shock.

Old as the skimmer was, it was still a good craft. There'd been no guarantees either way. If they hadn't gone off-course, if the sandstorm hadn't come up . . . She shivered, listening to the screaming wind. Outside the skimmer's hull the fine red Martian dust raged against metal. Allyson had seen junk craft brought in after a sandstorm. The skimmer would look newly polished, scoured of all paint and identifying markings. Like a huge, winged mirror.

At least it would help the search craft find them. Assuming any pilots dared bring search craft out over the high desert after them. Against the threat of sandstorms, they might not.

The skimmer had been doing fine—the pilot called back to say the radio was out, and to ask if Allyson or her sisters had personal coms that might be affecting the directional finders—but they'd been floating soft and easy in the terraformed Martian atmosphere like a beautiful big blue bird. And then the sandstorm hit.

It must have come out of the east, behind them. One moment they were gliding silently over the Martian plains, and Allyson was about to ask Kim if it didn't look a lot like high desert down there; maybe they were more off course than the pilots realized. . . .

Then the skimmer bucked and dived and she had time for nothing but strapping in, hanging on, and hoping. One of the pilots shouted a warning, but his words were lost in the screaming wind. The pilots fought it as best they could, but they hadn't a chance. Even in a modern craft they couldn't have bucked those winds.

One last stomach-churning dive . . . the wrenching sound of metal against rocks . . . a brief ear-shattering wail as the skimmer's starboard wing ripped off . . . a tumble of red and metal and breaking . . . and the silent, soft crash foam spilled out and built up around Allyson, enveloping her before the skimmer was still.

Since then, only the sound of the wind, and waiting. At first she called to her sisters, but neither they nor the pilots answered. There was nothing more she could do. The skimmer was canted at a weird, awkward angle and it shook now and then with the fury of the winds, but seemed overall steady. They must have landed on rocky ground, but at least not hanging over the edge of a crater or chasm. The pilots were good; if they had any choice in landing places, they'd have taken the best available. But they probably hadn't been able to see through the sand.

If only they or her sisters had answered her calls! She was afraid to call again, now. Her sisters should be protected by the same crash foam that saved her. If it had failed . . . she didn't want to think about that. Safer to think of the pilots, strapped into their cockpit seats. There were a dozen reasons why they might not have answered; they might not have heard her. Or they might be injured. Or it might not have occurred to them that their silence would frighten her.

They thought of her and her sisters more as furniture than people. Cargo. They'd even said that, and then stared at each other with their dark shadowed eyes, and one of them smiled and said with polite indifference, "Excuse me. I mean clones," because they knew she was listening. They knew she had some feelings, anyway. But they still might not think of her now.

"Don't ever forget what you are; no one else will." That was one of the earliest lessons of her childhood. "Nobody will forget for a second; so always be one jump ahead of them. If you're ever to be accepted as people, you'll have to act twice as human as natural-borns; and that only in the ways they respect. No human frailties. Just strengths."

She could almost hear Barbara saying that. And she remembered the first time she'd heard it. Allyson, Kim, and Rebecca were very young; they came in crying from some encounter with the local natural-borns, and listened patiently to that lecture from Barbara. Rebecca cried, "We can't *do* that! You don't know . . ."

But Barbara interrupted, with that soft, sad smile that looked like a mirror of them thirty years from now, and said, "Rebecca. I know exactly what you can do, and what you can't do. And I know how hard it is."

None of them understood, then, how true that was. But later, when they understood genetics, they began to guess. And later still, they knew how much of it was more determination than truth. But they had inherited Barbara's determination, and it stood them in good stead.

It was only by accident of nature, or lab procedure, or some unknown that they were allowed to live at all. When they were scheduled for cerebral death, their EEGs were automatically checked; and they showed the strange, doubled pattern of potential espers.

Even clone espers were needed to guide and communicate with the starships on their long voyages, so they were spared. The process was not yet then sophisticated enough to determine how strong their latent talent was, or they still would have been destroyed; since as it turned out the talent was weak at best.

But they lived. Clones with the same level of talent were now automatically murdered. The testing equipment had been considerably refined. But Allyson and her sisters lived. And Barbara, their donor-sister, the woman whose genes they carried and who fought for the right to raise them as her children once their right to live was established, instilled in them her own fierce horror of the entire cloning industry as it was used today.

Because it led to questions like: why bother protecting endangered species? Just clone some extras. And why not indulge in dangerous, deadly pastimes? Sunjamming and high-diving and race-driving and all the other risk-filled enterprises man's sensation-hungry mind could conjure. It was no more risk than driving a car was a century earlier. If you got mangled, your clones would supply new body parts. If you died, you died. And if you were lucky, you were one whose brain could be transplanted into the body of one of your clones and you'd be immortal!

But your clone wouldn't. He never had a chance. And nobody thought twice about it; they were only clones. Destroy one, make another. No problem. It wasn't as if they were real people.

Allyson and her sisters spent their lives trying to be real people; what they among themselves called natural-borns. And they were reminded, every day in a dozen little ways, that they weren't real people. Everything about them was stamped "clone." Their IDs, their credit cards, even their bodies. At least that was on the soles of their feet, where people couldn't see it all the time. But it was there. And it was like being a carbon copy of a real person; a copy all right for certain functions but not nearly as good as the original.

She should have expected Frank and Todd Lewis's reaction when the three of them came into the little flight office with their request that the brothers fly them and their skimmer to Viking's Rest. Three identical, carbon-copy women; their sky blue eyes identically wary; their faces identically tense; even their clothing and sunburned hair identical—they didn't have to show their IDs to be known for what they were when they traveled together.

They dressed alike as a gesture almost of defiance. Natural-borns never noticed the freckles on Kim's nose; or the way Rebecca's hair stuck up in a little cowlick in back; or that Allyson was always the one who took charge. They just saw three identical women, and called them clones. All interactions were governed by that. If the three of them dressed alike, it was like a shout of pride. They made no effort to conceal what they were; and they expected the reactions they got.

But when Allyson first saw Frank and Todd Lewis she thought, just for a moment, that they were clones, too. Heart in her throat, she stared with wild unexpected hope at their identical faces—and immediately realized she was wrong. They were too comfortable, too confident, too secure. Nothing stamped "clone" could be so self-assured.

She knew at once why their shadowed eyes went narrow with unease when they saw her and her sisters. Still, it hurt. She said, before they could, "You're twins! How fascinating; I've never met identical twins before."

One of them lifted an eyebrow and both of them smiled. It wasn't a friendly smile. If she'd thought she could alleviate their dislike by recognizing its cause, she was mistaken. They were no more pleased she could tell they weren't clones than they would have been if the skimmer could, and no more concerned for her feelings. She wasn't a person. She was just a clone.

She sighed and shifted in the crash foam, trying to get free of a particularly binding safety belt. The wind was definitely abating now, and the foam was receding. In a few moments she would be free to see how the others had fared in the crash.

She was working her way out of the safety harness when the door from the cockpit opened and one of the pilots stepped through. He towered over her seat next to the doorway, his long frame bent a little to keep from bumping his head. There was something wild and terrible in his eyes as he surveyed the cargo hold, but his voice when he spoke was casual and steady. "You all right?"

"I am," she said. He could see past the foam to where her sisters were strapped in their seats. She kept her voice steady and met his eyes as she asked, "Are my sisters alive?"

He glanced at her and then past her, over the foam. "One is." His voice was unexpectedly gentle. There was something like fear or terrible pain in his eyes. "I can't tell about the other. Here, let me help you out of your harness. Then you can check on them. I've got to get my brother out; he's hurt." He bent over the foam to release Allyson's straps, touching her body as indifferently as he would a box of cargo. In that moment she hated him. But it showed only in the darkening of her eyes.

"There's a medikit in the compartment in front," she said.

"I found it." When her straps were loose he stood back, surveying the odd angle of the deck and the melting foam. "What a mess," he said, more to himself than to her.

She was disentangling herself from the straps, trying to stand up, and she spoke without thinking. "You've been in worse."

Those implacable brown eyes returned to her face, impaling her. She stared, oddly frightened. "How would you know?" he asked.

She managed a shrug and a tentative smile. People reacted even worse to espers than to clones. Any sign of talent was always taken for full telepathy. "A guess," she said. "You're a pilot with quite a reputation. You don't get that without a few mishaps along the way."

He watched her a moment longer before he answered. "Yeah." Suddenly all interest in her was gone. "You're right. See to your, um, sisters, okay? If you need the medikit, let me know. I'll be in front; the storm's just about over, and I want to see if we can get out of here and get some signal out for the search planes. I don't suppose this crate has an ADS?"

"Autodirection sender? No, I don't think so."

"It figures." He turned away, but on impulse she caught his arm to stop him.

The words were harder to phrase than she'd expected. But she'd wanted all her life to say them to someone else; and his indifference angered her just enough. "Which one are you? I can't tell you apart." She could, but he had no way of knowing that.

The sardonic twist of his lips showed he knew exactly why she asked. But he said simply, "Todd," and turned away. He was better at insults than she. He didn't bother to ask which one she was. He didn't care.

"Allyson?" With a guilty start, she let Todd go and turned toward the opposite wall where her sisters sat in the melting foam. Rebecca was awake and watching her, her eyes puzzled. "Allyson, are you all right?"

Todd disappeared into the cockpit and Allyson slipped and slid across the foamy floor to Rebecca's side. Near Rebecca, Kim sprawled limp and lifeless in her harness. The side of her head was covered with blood. Half her face was ruined. The other half was still a perfect replica of Allyson's and Rebecca's to the last delicate detail. The one remaining china-blue eye stared in blind consternation at the opposite window, sanded to frosty luminescence by the storm outside.

Allyson set her teeth and forced herself to lift one of the limp white wrists to check for a pulse, but there was really no question. Still, she checked the carotid artery before turning away. Rebecca watched without comprehension.

"I'm okay, Rebecca," Allyson said. "Are you?" Her voice was thin and wavery, like a child's. And her throat hurt.

Rebecca put one hand to her head. "I think so," she said. And then, with sudden realization, "Kim? . . ."

"She's dead," said Allyson. Rebecca closed her eyes, her face pale. Allyson silently released her safety straps. Rebecca was always quicker to tears than Allyson. Her chin trembled. Allyson pushed the straps aside and put her arms around her sister.

"Those damn pilots," said Rebecca.

"It wasn't their fault, Rebecca," said Allyson. "Now, come on. One of them is hurt; we ought to see if we can help."

Rebecca sighed and wiped her eyes. "You're right," she said, rising. She didn't look at Kim. "Okay." She steadied herself against a projecting security bar. "I'm ready; let's go."

They tried the cargo bay first, but that was blocked with dust or some other obstruction, and wouldn't budge. They would have to get out through the cockpit.

Todd and Frank were still inside. Todd had awkwardly covered an abrasion on Frank's temple with spray bandages. They were working on the outside door, which appeared to be drifted shut. They pushed it open an inch or so, and a thin trickle of red dust filled the bottom of the crack.

"Need help?" asked Allyson.

Todd glanced up, startled. The gaunt lines of his face seemed hollowed and pale. The dark eyes searched her, and for a moment she thought she saw something questioning, something pleading in his gaze; then it snicked shut like a door closing and suddenly he was a person and she was furniture again. He shrugged. "Why not?"

Together the four of them wrenched the door open and climbed out over the drift that blocked it. While the others stared in dazed surprise and growing horror at their surroundings, Frank stood by the door, waiting. He kept turning his head from side to side with nervous little gestures like a fox in a cage, his face white, the skin drawn taut over the bones of his cheeks. He didn't say anything, but Allyson realized with a start of unexpected sympathy that he couldn't see.

Beside him, Todd stood with one hand on the door as if for support. He said slowly, "It's a crater, Frank. We're inside the damn thing."

"Inside?" Frank moved his eyes as if he could see, but they were flat and lifeless. "Is it deep? Narrow?"

"Not deep," said Todd, "but too damn narrow. I don't know how visible we are, but I'd say not very. And even if we had an ADS, the signal would bounce off the walls and never get out."

"Oh." Frank thought about it for a moment. "Well, you'd better get busy. Show the clones how to build solar stills; and we'll need shelter. If you bring me whatever electronic equipment you can find, including that damn radio, maybe I can build us some communication equipment."

"We already know how to build stills, Mr. Lewis," Allyson said. "We're Martians, too, you know. Look, why don't you sit down and let my sister have a look at that head wound while your brother and I get the supplies out of the skimmer."

"I'm all right," said Frank.

"My sister's a doctor," said Allyson. "I think you should let her take a look at your injury. Maybe she can't do much, with the equipment at hand, but please let her try." She ignored Todd's startled eyes. Why the hell were people always so surprised Rebecca was a doctor? Todd and Frank were identical twins; surely they wouldn't believe, as so many people did, that because they looked alike the clones were interchangeable.

"Your sister's a doctor?" Frank turned his head again, searching his private darkness, perhaps looking for hope.

"That's right," said Rebecca, "I am. Here, let me help you find a place to sit; I'd really like to take a look at that wound, if you'll let me."

Sunlight glittered off the sanded hull of the skimmer. The air smelled of hot dust and herbs bioformed from Earth varieties for the Martian desert. Allyson reluctantly met Todd's eyes and waited.

He shook himself and glanced from her to Frank and back again. "Sure, let her look at it, Frank." Hope burned like fire in his eyes; Allyson realized with odd disappointment that he wasn't going to comment on the clones' differences. He was wrestling with some personal demon and didn't care about the clones. They were cargo. In a crash, you make use of whatever cargo turns out to be handy.

Even the usual stupid questions would have been better than indifference, she thought, and wondered why it mattered.

"You," Todd said, "could help me get the supplies."

"I have a name," she said, and immediately wished she hadn't.

"Most of us do," he said. Those sardonic eyes raked her again and she blushed.

"Let's go," she said stiffly.

He smiled; a thin, unexpectedly bitter smile; and led her back into the skimmer. While he disconnected the radio and collected what other electronic gear he could find, she sorted through the supplies in the cockpit, piling undamaged goods on an emergency blanket and tossing the useless things aside. They worked in silence, and she was careful to avoid his eyes.

"There's more food and water in back," she said at last. She hesitated, thinking of Kim. She didn't want to face that awful apparition again; but they might be here for days. They couldn't leave her where she was. "And my sister," she said with difficulty. "We'll have to," she swallowed, "bury her."

"I can do that."

She looked up, startled, and met his eyes. They were unexpectedly kind; but there was still a cold, determined barrier there. He held himself apart from her with a fierce, blind rejection that was like a physical pain.

"That's kind of you," she said, "but I can manage."

He shrugged. "Whatever." His expression went flat again; distant and reserved, as if a fog obscured him from her.

She wanted to say, *Clones aren't any different from identical twins, damn you!* But she bit back the words and swallowed a painful lump in her throat. Clones were different. Identical twins were natural-borns. They were identical to each other, but carbon copies of nobody. And they'd never been thought of as organ banks. There was nothing to protect. You could recognize them as people and still not be a murderer; because none of them were slaughtered to provide organ replacement for others.

The tattoo on her foot had branded her soul, but she knew why it had to be there. The first use of clones had been for replacement parts; it was still their main function. Those few who were permitted to live, their cerebrums intact, could not be considered human. What would that say about all those thousands whose cerebrums were destroyed?

It made no difference how many scientific facts people knew; or how much genetics. Every high school student knew that on a genetic basis there was no difference between clones and identical twins. If anything, the twins were stranger; it was perfectly well known what formed clones. You take the nucleus from a cell, put it in an egg from which the nucleus has been removed, and presto! you have the equivalent of a fertilized egg; a diploid cell or zygote, ready to grow and divide and form an embryo.

But it still wasn't known why identical twins sometimes occurred. You take two haploid cells, put them together, and they're a fertilized egg or zygote; but why do the two cells of its first division sometimes separate from one another and develop into two independent embryos? Nobody knew, and it wasn't really important. They were natural-borns, and nobody questioned their right to live.

But clones—people created in the lab, by artificial means—that was different. They were replacement parts. They'd been created for replacement parts, and the first ones permitted to live had been so grateful for the gift of life they'd set the stage for all the discrimination to follow. Of course they didn't demand their rights as people; that would be saying their benefactors were murdering a person every time they destroyed the cerebrum of a cloned embryo.

Allyson smiled thinly, as she always did when she reached that point in her philosophical fury. Maybe it wasn't really much different from abortion. The only real difference was that the cloned embryos were created intentionally for "abortion." And the real question was, would it make any difference to the social attitude if the sex act were somehow involved in the creation of clones?

"What's funny?"

She came back to the present with a start, to find herself staring into Todd's dark, watchful eyes. His face was pale, and there were hard lines of tension around his mouth and eyes.

"Oh, nothing. I was just thinking." For a moment her face, usually rigidly guarded, retained a look of vulnerability or of terrible sorrow; then, as she focused on Todd's hooded gaze, the lines of her expression slowly tautened. The straight, stern set of her lips returned; and the startling intensity of her eyes. "Are you all right, Todd?" she asked. "You look pale."

His own expression hardened. "I'm fine." Their words hung between them like a glittering façade on a broken building; the tone and content bore no relation to their expressions. It was as if four people sat there; two friends speaking, and two wary strangers watching. "While you're in the back," he added in the same friendly tone, "why don't you see if you can find some clear plastic sheeting for the solar stills? I'm gonna get this stuff outside and see what Frank can do with it."

She hesitated. "He may not be able to," she began.

"It'll give him something to do," he said without meeting her eyes. It was quite a concession; he'd explained a behavior, as if she were a normal person with some stake in what happened. But before she could respond he added impatiently, "Go on and find some plastic. We're gonna need all the water we can get."

"Okay," she said. "Hand me the pliers; I'll need them to get into the emergency supplies." Her eyes were as cold and gray as a winter sky.

He kept his hard-shadowed gaze on her as he reached out with the pliers, holding them flat on his palm so she could pick them up without touching him. But she had to look down at his hand to find them, and paused with her hand half-extended, staring.

It wasn't quite a surprise, but it was a shock. She had guessed something was wrong. She hadn't guessed how wrong.

When she didn't accept the pliers he glanced down at them, then looked back at her face, his eyes widened with surprise and something like fear. "Oh," he said, and glanced at his hand again, then drew it back. He made an ineffectual effort to wipe the sticky red stain from the pliers, but it was too late. "It's just a scratch; a little cut. It bled a lot . . ." He paused, watching her. His face was shiny with sweat. But it was early morning, and still chilly outside.

She waited. Her eyes revealed nothing. He offered her the pliers again. "I'm all right," he said. "There's nothing to worry about."

"So you're a hero." The words were as cold as her eyes.

He shrugged. "Think whatever you want to. Just get some plastic from the back, okay?"

"The only human left, so you have to stay in charge, right?" She took the pliers and turned away. "For God's sake don't trust a clone; they're not real people."

"Whatever. If you need help later with your sister back there, let me know."

She whirled on him in a fit of fury. "You won't *touch* her. Do you hear me? You won't so much as *look* at her! I can handle it by myself, or with Rebecca, and I don't want your filthy natural-born hands on her; she can be spared at least that!"

He stared. "Fine." The sardonic, mocking smile was still in his eyes, but fogged or faded as if by a sheet of scratched acrylic between his face and hers. She turned away from his with a bitter feeling of defeat.

When she got outside with the plastic and the rest of

the emergency supplies, Frank was settled happily in the shade of a boulder, fiddling with the electronic equipment Todd brought him. Todd and Rebecca were working on the other side of the skimmer, draping parachutes from the wing and weighting them against wind with rocks and soil. If another sandstorm came up, they'd have to get back in the ruined skimmer; otherwise, the wing would make a good shelter. With a fire under it, they might even manage to stay warm at night.

Todd and Rebecca were doing well enough by themselves. Allyson deposited the plastic and supplies in a heap near the skimmer's door and climbed back into the cockpit. Just in case another sandstorm did come up, it would be a good idea to have Kim's body somewhere else. And in spite of what she'd said in anger to Todd, she didn't think Rebecca would be much help with that. She'd be fine if it were a stranger's body. But not Kim's. Not her sister, with half her face caved in.

Allyson had always been the strongest of them, both physically and emotionally. But even her strength didn't quite match her task. The three of them had always been very close. They had to be; they had no one else. And they were almost identical, so what Allyson had to move was not just the body of her sister, but also the image of herself discolored and distorted by death.

She set about the task reluctantly, but it had to be done. By the time she had Kim's body out the cockpit door tears streaked her cheeks and she was shaking uncontrollably. But she resolutely grasped Kim's wrists and dragged her as far from the skimmer as she could. Only when she was out of sight beyond a low ridge of jutting rocks did she sit down with her head in her hands to cry.

At least, she thought as she piled rocks over the broken body, Kim was free now. She died too far from civilization to be whisked into hospital, taken apart like a mechanical thing, and moved piece by piece to an organ bank or to other people's bodies.

Oh, true, the same thing would happen to anybody who did die within civilization's reach. It wasn't only clones who were viewed as spare parts at the moment of death. Especially on sparsely populated Mars, nobody was "wasted." And that was as it should be. Still, for a clone, the idea of being used as spare parts any time held a peculiar horror.

It seemed oddly fitting that Kim should, instead, have a lonely burial under the rocks and sand of the desert, with only another clone to bid her goodbye. Allyson pushed the last rock into place with a sad satisfaction and settled back on her heels to rest.

Her hands and face were dusty and streaked with tears and sweat. The red dust was everywhere. She could even taste it, along with the sticky salt taste of tears. She wiped her cheeks with the back of her hand and sat for a long time beside her sister's shallow grave, staring with unseeing eyes at the hard red rim of the crater around her. The desert air smelled of dust and pungent herbs. And there was silence, as far as forever. It was a good place to be buried. It might even be a good place to die.

When Allyson returned to the skimmer there was a peculiar light of defiance in her eyes. She set silently about digging holes for solar stills, and when Rebecca and Todd joined her she barely glanced at them.

"I buried Kim," she said.

"We built a shelter," said Todd, as if it were of equal significance. Perhaps it was.

"How's Frank?" she asked without much interest.

He was sitting within hearing distance, but too engrossed in his electronic puzzle to hear what they said. He seemed oddly unconcerned by blindness. Most people in his place would have fought it. He accepted it, and was learning already how to work within its boundaries.

"I'm worried about him," Rebecca said quietly. "The optic nerve is under pressure. If we don't get him to medical facilities in time, it may atrophy—"

"He'll be all right," said Todd.

Allyson looked at Rebecca. " 'Fight when you can win,' " she said. " 'Accept the inevitable when it is.' " She smiled, a sad little smile that twisted her lips and barely touched her glass-blue eyes.

"What's that?" asked Todd. "Sounded like a quote."

He paused in his work and settled back on his heels, watching her. His eyes were sunken, shadowed places in a hollow face. She was startled at the hopelessness there.

"Just something Barbara used to say," she said. "Are you all right?"

"Barbara? Who's that?"

"Our original sister," said Rebecca. "The one we're copies of." She frowned at him. "You do look pale. You could be in shock; you should rest."

He shook his head. "I'm okay."

"He's a hero," said Allyson. Her voice was harsh, her eyes cold. But she caught him when he fell. And was surprised at the answering note of tenderness she felt when he stared up at her with pleading eyes.

"Allyson," he said, and she was so startled she barely heard the rest of what he said. *He knew all along! He could tell them apart!* "For God's sake, tell Frank I'm all right," he whispered before those splendid, pain-wracked, frightened eyes slid shut.

And then she understood. She stared at Rebecca, her own eyes dark like storm clouds. "He *is* a hero." Her voice broke. "Oh, please," she whispered, "will he be all right?"

They carried him to the shelter he had built with Rebecca, and put him on a blanket in the shade. It took them a moment to find the injury; he'd bound it clumsily with spray bandages to slow the bleeding. It was an awful, deadly puncture just below his ribs. Rebecca sent Allyson to get the medikit and water while she tried to make him comfortable and examine the wound.

Allyson knew very little about medicine and, as a rule, cared not at all. She brought the water and kit and sat beside Todd, but her fear was so distracting, Rebecca sent her away again. She wandered out to the rock Frank sat beside with his electronics.

The sun was beginning to encroach on his little island of shade. He heard her coming and lifted his head, blind eyes as private and shadowed as Todd's. "It's Allyson, Frank," she said. "How're you doing?"

"I'm fine," he said. "I always said I could put one of these things together blindfolded. Now I've had a chance to prove it. And I think it's gonna work! It's almost done."

"Then we can call Umbra Landing!"

"If we can get the signal outside this crater." He turned back to his work, his fingers moving among the wires as confidently as if he could see. "How's Todd?"

She stared. "He's," she said, and paused. Frank waited, his shoulders hunched a little against whatever news she might bring him. He knew something was wrong. Todd thought he could keep knowledge of his injury from Frank, but Frank probably knew from the start. All Todd succeeded in doing was keeping it from the clones, who could have helped him. "He'll be all right now. Rebecca's taking care of him." She heard in memory her own terror whispering, *Please, will he be all right?*

They sat in silence for a moment while Frank's busy fingers traced patterns among the wires. "He didn't want to scare me." It wasn't a question, but she answered it anyway.

"No."

Another silence. Then, "D'you do that? It's just like being identical twins, isn't it? D'you find yourself doing stupid things to protect the others?"

She nodded, forgetting he couldn't see her. "Sometimes from dangers that aren't even real."

"Yeah." He put his tools down and rested his hands on the radio. "You know, identical twins are really clones. Accidents of nature, but one of us is a clone of the other. I remember wondering in high school why they were so careful not to use that word when they described the genetic process that caused us."

"For the same reason they're so careful always to use it with us." The sun was hot on her back. She thought about getting up to move into the shade, but it was too much trouble.

"I know that now," he said. "I guess we're just lucky the first identical twins happened a long time before they knew how to do organ transplants."

She picked a branch from a shrub beside her and twisted its leaves in her fingers till the sharp odor of its sap filled the shimmering air. "What will they do when they figure it out?"

He turned a sardonic smile to her, so similar to Todd's it wrenched her heart. "They've figured it out, a long time ago. They don't know what to do."

She sighed. "Is the radio fixed?"

"I think so. You'll have to take it up on the rim, to get a signal out. Is it climbable? It's got to be line-of-sight, so if you can't get it high enough we'll have to wait for a search craft."

"To fly right over us," she said. "I can take it up on the rim. How does it work?"

"Push this," he said, "and pray. Here's the microphone."

She took the awkward bundle in her hands and paused, watching him. "You'll be all right?" The lines of his face were different from Todd's. Not as sharp and distinct.

"I'm fine."

Still she hesitated. "We're all heroes. We keep protecting each other from our own demons, so half the time we don't even see each other's."

"And if we do, we can't touch them."

"No." She closed her eyes. "No, we can't touch them." Abruptly she jumped up, clutching the radio, and ran. He couldn't see her tears, but she wouldn't cry in front of him anyway. She had never in her adult life cried in front of anyone; she wasn't going to start now.

She returned empty-handed through the shimmering heat of the afternoon. The skimmer lay like a broken mirror at the base of the rim. There was no sign of life. Rebecca and the twins must have taken refuge beneath the shade of the wing. Allyson paused to rest on the rocks just above the skimmer, and stared for a long while at the emergency blankets guarding the little shelter under the wing, before heat and thirst finally drove her down the slope.

Her face was streaked with dust, her hands and knees scraped bloody from the rocks. But in the shade of the shelter, only her glittering eyes were visible. "The radio worked," she said. "The forecast's okay, so there should be a rescue craft here by nightfall."

Rebecca handed her a cup of water. Frank lay beside the skimmer next to his brother. None of them spoke. Her eyes still blind from the sun, Allyson couldn't tell if the twins were awake. She accepted the water with trembling hands, squatted just inside the shelter as if prepared for flight, and drank sparingly, watching the darkness where the twins lay.

She was afraid to speak. She rested the cup on her knees and held herself still with a terrible effort. The silence was like a living thing around her. Out in the desert sun, that seemed a blessing. Here it kept her poised, tense, listening. If he were dead they would say it, surely. *Oh, please, will he be all right?*

A pebble scraped in the darkness. Her eyes, dark, burning pits in her sunburned face, were beginning to adjust to the shadows. She waited, staring with a frightened and frightening intensity at the darker shadow that was the twins. Beside her, Rebecca took the forgotten cup from her and sipped from it, looking over its rim at the twins.

Just when Allyson had decided it never would, the shadow moved, separated, became two people. One of them lying with his bandaged head on a folded blanket; the other pushing himself up on one elbow to smile his sardonic, guarded smile at her.

It's one thing to make the decision never to cry in front of anyone. It's quite another to stick to it. She didn't know how she got across the little shelter and into Todd's arms. She was just there. And it was where she belonged.

"So," he said softly. "You're a hero, too."

Re-deem the Time

David Lake

> In a world of increasing complexity, de-
> humanization, and dwindling power sources,
> it seems we must look forward to an era of
> retrenchment, even devolution of technology.
> But if one of us were to find a way to travel
> further and further into the future, what won-
> ders might be discovered?
>
> David Lake, an Australian writer who's pub-
> lished several science-fiction novels in the past
> few years, considered this situation and came
> up with a time-travel story startlingly unlike
> any other.

When Ambrose Livermore designed his Time Machine, he bethought him of the advantages both of mo-
bility and of camouflage, and therefore built his appa-
ratus into the bodywork of a second-hand Volkswagen.
Anyone looking in at the windows, such as an inquisi-
tive traffic policeman, would have taken the thing for
an ordinary 'bug' with a large metal trunk on the back
seat. The large metal trunk contained the workings of
the Time Machine; the front seat and the dashboard
looked almost normal, and the car could still function
as a car.

When all things were ready, one cold afternoon in

1984, Ambrose got into the front seat and drove from his little laboratory in Forminster to a deserted field on a South English hill. A white chalk track led him to the spot he had chosen; further along there was an ancient British hill fort, but not one that was ever visited by tourists. And this gloomy October day there was no one at all to be ruffled by his extraordinary departure. Applying the handbrake, he looked about him; and at last he smiled.

Ambrose did not often smile, for he was a convinced pessimist. He had seen the way the world was going for some time, and in his opinion it was not going well. Energy crisis was followed by energy crisis, and little war by little or not-so-little war, and always the great nations became further locked into their unending arms race. Sooner or later, the big bang was coming; and he wanted out. Luckily, he now had the means for getting out . . .

Briefly, he wished that general time travel were a real possibility. One could then go back to the Good Old Days—say, before 1914. One could *keep* hopping back, living 1913 over and over and over again . . . Only of course the Good Old Days weren't really all that good; one would miss all sorts of modern comforts; and besides, the thing was impossible anyway. Backward time travel was utterly illogical, you could shoot your grandfather and so on. No: his own work had opened up the escape route, the only escape route, the one that led into the *future*. There were no illogicalities involved in that, since everyone travels into the future at all times. The Livermore Accelerator merely speeded up a natural process—speeded it up amazingly, of course, but . . .

But there it was. He would hop forward a century or so, in the hope of evading imminent doom. Surely the crash must come well before that, and by 2100, say, they'd be recovering . . .

Ambrose took a deep breath, and pressed the red lever that projected below the dashboard.

The sensation was bewildering. He had done it before, of course, behind locked doors in the laboratory, but only for a subjective second or two, little jumps of a

couple of hours. Now years were flashing by . . .
Literally flashing! There was a blinding light, and the
ghostly landscape seemed to tremble. Shaken, he
looked at his dials. Not even the end of the century
. . . and yet, that must have been It. The Big Bang,
the War. His forebodings had been entirely right . . .

He steadied himself, his fingers gripping the lever.
The landscape seemed to be rippling and flowing, but
there were no more explosive flashes. As he approached 2100, he eased the red lever towards him,
slowing down, and now he saw things more clearly. The
general outline of the hills and the plain below were not
greatly altered, but at night there were very few lights
showing. Forminster from up here used to be a bright
electric blaze, but now it was no more than a faint flickering glimmer. He smiled grimly. Civilization had been
set back, all right! Probably they were short of power:
you can't get electricity from nothing. But, what luck!
This countryside hadn't been badly hit by bombs or lasers, and there were still small towns or at least villages
dotted about. Yes, he would certainly emerge here and
try his luck . . .

Now for immediate problems. As he slowed to a
crawl, he saw that the surface of this hillside meadow
had dropped by a few centimeters. No worry about
that, it was better than a rise! And a hundred meters
away a wood had sprung up, a sparse copse of beeches
that were rapidly unleaving. It looked deserted, too. A
perfect place to hide the car while he reconnoitered. As
October 2100 ticked away, he pulled the lever firmly
back, and stopped.

The car dropped as though it had just gone over a
bump in a road. It fell those few centimeters, and shuddered to complete stillness. He had done it!

Almost, you might think, nothing had changed, apart
from that wood. The same downs, the same cold cloudy
autumn afternoon. Somewhere in the distance he heard
the baa of a sheep. It was a comfortingly ordinary
sound; even though, come to think of it, there had been
no sheep in these parts in 1984.

Ambrose smiled (that was becoming a new habit).
Then he drove the car deep into the wood.

The village of Ethanton still lay at the foot of the hill. He had driven through it several times in the old days, looking for a safe site for his great evasion: it had then been a crumbling old place, half deserted, its population of course drifting away to Forminster or London, half its cottages converted into desperate would-be tourist-trap tea-rooms. There had been a railway-station a couple of miles off until the economic crisis of 1981; when that had gone, the last flickering vitality had seemed to forsake the place. But now—

Now, to his surprise, Ethanton seemed to be flourishing. There were new cottages along the road. At least, they were new in the sense that they had not been here in the 1980s; otherwise he'd have said they were old. Certainly they were old in style, being mostly of dull red brick with slate roofs, and one even displayed black oak beams and thatch. That one, certainly, had the raw look of recent construction: he peered at it, expecting a sign saying TEAS—but it wasn't there, and indeed the whole front of the house had that shut-in appearance of a genuine cottage. For that matter, there was nothing on this road to suggest tourism: not a single parked car, nor a motorcycle. And the road itself, which led after a dozen kilometers to Formister—it had deteriorated. It was no longer smooth tarmac: it was paved through the village with some lumpy stuff that suggested cobble-stones.

He moved cautiously on into the High Street, and came opposite the Green Dragon Inn. And here he was struck motionless with surprise.

It was not much after four o'clock, and yet there was a small crowd of men milling about the inn, some nursing tankards as they sat on the benches outside. The whole dusky scene was feebly brightened by an oil lamp swinging over the main inn doorway; there was a lamp-post on the pavement nearby, but that was not functioning, and indeed three or four workmen seemed to be doing something to it while the village policeman looked on. The clothes of all these people struck Ambrose as curiously antiquated; one drinker in particular boasted a high collar that might have been in the height of fashion in the 1900s. There were no motorcars anywhere along the street, though there was one odd-looking bicycle leaning against the inn wall, and beyond the lamppost stood a parked horse carriage complete with coachman and harnessed horse.

As Ambrose gazed at the scene, so the scene began to gaze at him. In particular the policeman stiffened, left the workmen at the lamppost, and strode over towards him.

Ambrose braced himself. He had anticipated some difficulties, and now he fingered the gun in his trouser pocket. But that was the last resort. He had done his best to make himself inconspicuous: in a pair of nondescript old trousers and a dark-gray jersey he thought he might not be too unsuitably dressed for England in 2100. And he had to make contact somehow.

The policeman halted directly before him, surveying Ambrose through the half-gloom. Then he touched his fingers to his tall blue helmet.

"Beg pardon, zur," he said, in the broadest of broad bumpkin accents, "but would yew be a stranger in these parrts, zur?" The dialect was more or less appropriate to this county, but almost stagily exaggerated, and in details stagily uncertain, as though the policeman had worked hard to study his role, but still hadn't got it quite right. "Be you a stranger gen'leman, zur?" he repeated.

"Well—yes," stammered Ambrose. "As a matter of fact, I am. I—I was strolling up the hill up there when I had a bit of an accident. Branch of a tree fell on me—nothing serious, but it dazed me, and I don't remember very well—"

Suddenly the policeman's hand shot forward and he seized Ambrose by the shirt collar. Normally when this sort of thing happens, the piece of garment in question is used only for leverage; but strangely now the hand of authority began holding the shirt collar up to the light, and feeling its texture between its large fingers.

"What, what—" spluttered Ambrose.

"Ar, I thought as much!" exclaimed the policeman grimly. "One o' them Anaky fellers, you be. Well, m'lad, you'll come along o' me."

Ambrose clawed for his gun, but the policeman saw

the move and grabbed his wrist. By now the workmen had come up, and they joined in the fun, too. Ambrose was seized by half a dozen heavy hands, he was pulled off his feet, and the next moment the policeman had the gun and was flourishing it, to exclamations of "Ho, yes! One o' *them*, he be! 'Old 'im, me lads—'e's a bleedin' Anaky, 'e is!"

Suddenly there was a new voice. "Now, now, constable: what exactly is going on here?"

Higher Authority had arrived.

Ambrose was marched into a small back room of the Green Dragon, where he was guarded by the policeman, and interrogated by the gentleman who had taken charge of the proceedings.

Dr. Leathey had a trim brown beard, intelligent blue eyes, and a kindly expression; like Ambrose, he seemed in his early thirties. He was dressed very neatly in a dark suit, high collar and tie of pre–World War I vintage. The room where he conducted his investigation was dimly lit by candles and an oil lamp, and boasted in one corner a grandfather clock. There was something about that clock that specially bothered Ambrose, but at present naturally he couldn't give his mind to that.

"So, Mr. Livermore," said Leathey, "you claim loss of memory. That is droll! Loss of memory is no crime whatever, on the contrary, it is extremely virtuous. But I am afraid amnesia will not explain the semi-synthetic texture of your clothing, nor the forbidden make of your automatic pistol. Now really, Mr. Livermore, you had better come clean. If I were to hand you on to the County authorities it might go hard with you, but here in Ethanton *I* am the authorities: I am the JP, the doctor, and the specialist in these matters, and I have certain discretionary powers . . . Come, let us get one thing clear, at least: where do you come from?"

"From—from Forminster," stammered Ambrose.

Leathey and the policeman exchanged glances. Leathey sighed and nodded. "Mr. Livermore, that is practically an admission of guilt, you know."

"Eh?" said Ambrose.

"Come, why pretend? You must know that for the past sixty years that town has been officially rechristened Backminster—for obvious reasons. A shibboleth, Mr. Livermore, a shibboleth! Forminster, indeed! I put it to you, Mr. Livermore—you are a B.A."

"Ph.D, actually," murmured Ambrose. "In Physics."

"Ph.D?" muttered Leathey dubiously. "Oh, well, I suppose that's still permitted; I must look up my annals, but I believe those letters of yours are still within the letter of the law. So—*Dr.* Livermore, I presume? Quite an intellectual. But really, this is surprising! Do you really come from Backminster?"

"Yes," said Ambrose, sulkily. He glanced past Leathey at the grandfather clock, and hated it. "Yes, I did come from—er—Backminster; but that was some time ago."

"Many years ago?"

"Yes."

"Curiouser and curiouser," said Leathey, with a little laugh. Then he seemed to turn serious. "Dr. Livermore, I rather like you. You are an intelligent man, I think, and certainly a gentleman, and that counts for something these days—and of course will count for even more by and by. If you will confess and submit to purgation, you might well become a useful citizen again. You might indeed become a power for good in the land—a perditor, or a chronic healer like myself. Will you submit, Dr. Livermore, and let me help you?"

A disarmed prisoner has very little choice when faced with such a proposition. Ambrose thought for about half a second, and then said yes.

Leathey rose. "Good. I knew you would see reason. But let us continue these conversations in more agreeable surroundings. Simkins," he said, addressing the constable, "I shall take Dr. Livermore to my own house, and I will be answerable for his security till tomorrow."

Then they were escorting him from the inn to the horse carriage, which turned out to be Leathey's private conveyance. As they passed, Ambrose noticed that the workmen, by the light of swinging oil lanterns, were carrying off the lamppost which they had uprooted from the pavement. It wouldn't be much loss, he thought: it was a very old-fashioned looking lamppost. Suddenly, with a kind of horror, it came to him what had been wrong with that grandfather clock in the inn parlour. Its hands had been pointing to somewhere around seven o'clock—several hours wrong; and they had been moving counter-clockwise.

In other words—*backwards*.

As the brougham gathered speed and rattled over the cobblestones, Ambrose leaned toward Leathey, who sat opposite. "What year is this?" he breathed.

"1900," said Leathey calmly. "What year did you think it was?"

Ambrose was too overcome to reply. He slumped back with a groan.

Dr. Leathey was evidently a well-to-do bachelor; his house was large, stone-built, and ivy-covered, and was staffed by several men and maid servants. These people found Ambrose a bedroom, laid him out a nightshirt, and in general saw to his comforts. A valet explained that in the morning, if he wished, he would shave him—"You being, I understand sir, not quite up to handling a razor yourself." Ambrose soon got the point: safety razors did not exist, so he, as a prisoner, could not be trusted with such a lethal weapon as an old cut-throat blade.

The manservant made him change his clothes completely. Luckily, Ambrose was about Leathey's height and build, so an old suit of the master's fitted him quite well. The high starched collar was damnably uncomfortable; but at last he was presentable, and was ushered in to dinner.

He was Leathey's sole guest. "Let's not talk now," said his host, smiling. "Afterwards, sir, afterwards . . ."

It was a very good dinner, of a somewhat old-fashioned English kind. The vegetables and the beef were fresh and succulent, and there was a very good 1904 Burgundy. Leathey made a joke about that.

"Glad the URN don't object to wines of the future, within reason. I suppose you might say four years isn't Blatant. But I like my stuff just a *little* mellow."

Ambrose gazed at him and at the bottle in a sort of stupor. Then suddenly he saw the point, and nearly choked on his roast beef.

"Drink some water," said Leathey kindly. "That's better. You know, Dr. Livermore, you are the strangest Anachronic criminal it has been my lot ever to run across. Mostly they're hardened, bitter, knowing— you're not. And therefore I have good hopes of you. But before we get to the heart of the matter, let me get you to admit one thing. We live well, don't we, we of the Acceptance? Do you see anything wrong with this village, or this house, or this dinner, anything sordid or unwholesome?"

"No—" began Ambrose, "but—"

"There you are, my dear feller. The whole world is coming round to seeing how comfortably one can live this way. As that great old reactionary Talleyrand once said, it's only the *ancien régime* that really understands the *douceur de vie*. You B.A.s are only a tiny minority. The proof of the pudding—ah, talk of the devil! Here it comes now, the pudding. I'm sure you'll like it. It's a genuine old English suet, carefully researched—"

"But it's all insane!" cried Ambrose. Forgetting his manners, he pointed with his fork. "That clock on the sideboard—why is it showing four o'clock and going backwards?"

"My goodness," said Leathey, looking astonished. "You really must have amnesia. Protest is one thing, stark ignorance another. You really don't *know*?"

"No!"

After the meal, Leathey took him to his study, which was fitted with half-empty bookshelves and a huge black wall-safe. Over the safe was hung a painting in a rather academic 18th century style, showing some sort of goddess enfolded in clouds; between that and the safe an oaken scroll bore the florid inscription: "She comes! she comes!" Leathey waved Ambrose to a comfortable armchair, and offered him a cigar.

"No? Cigars will still be all right for quite some time, you know. And separate smoking rooms for gentlemen's houses are not yet compulsory. I do my best to get these things right, you know. All right, now: let's begin . . ."

Ambrose leant forward. "Tell me, *please*: are we really in the year 1900?"

"Of course," smiled Leathey.

"But—but we can't be. Reverse time travel is a stark impossibility—!"

"Time travel?" Leathey's eyebrows shot up; then he laughed. "Ah, I see you're well read, Dr. Livermore." He got up, and took from a shelf near the safe a slim hard-covered volume. "*The Time Machine*," he murmured. "Dear Mr. Wells! We'll only have him for another five years, alas, and then—into the big safe with him! Freud went this year, and *he* was no loss, but one will miss dear old science fiction. Well, *officially*." He brought his head close to Ambrose, and gave a confiding chuckle. "We are acting for the best, you know; but if you join us, there are—compensations. Behind closed doors, with blinds drawn, I can assure you, Dr. Livermore, there's no harm in *us* occasionally reading canceled books. And you can't lick us, you know, so why don't you— Pardon me; you get my meaning, but I believe that's a canceled phrase in this country. I must learn to avoid it."

Ambrose gulped. "I am going mad—"

"No, you *are* mad. I am here to make you sane."

"You are not really living backwards," said Ambrose. "Dammit, you don't take food *out* of your mouths, your carriages don't move in reverse, and yet— Hey, *what was last year*?"

"1901. And next year will be 1899, of course. Today is the 1st of March, and tomorrow will be 28th February, since 1900 is not a leap year."

"Of course!" echoed Ambrose hysterically. "And yet the yellow leaves on the trees show that it's autumn, and— How did this insanity happen? I really do have complete amnesia, you know. In my day time was added, not subtracted—"

"In your day?" said Leathey, frowning. "What are you, Rip Van Winkle? Well, it may help you to emerge from your delusion if I give you a sketch of what has happened since the Treaty—"

"What treaty?"

"There you go again . . . Well, to start with, after the Last War and the Time of Confusion, it became obvious to the surviving civilized peoples of the world that the game was up: the game of Progress, I mean. The earth was in ruins, its minerals exhausted, most of the great cities devastated. If we were to try to go that way again, it would be madness. Besides, we couldn't do it even if we wanted to: there was so little left, almost no fossil fuels, no minerals, no uranium even. We couldn't even keep going at the rate we'd become accustomed to. There was only one thing for it—to return to a simpler way of life. Well, we could do that in one of two ways: by a controlled descent, or by struggle, resistance, and collapse. Luckily, all the leading nations chose control. It was in 2016, by the old Forward Count, that the Treaty was signed by the United Regressive Nations. And forthwith that year was renamed 1984, Backward Count; and the next year 1983, and and so on.

"So we really *are* in 2100," said Ambrose, breathing a sigh of relief.

Leathey fixed him with a severe look. "No, we really are in 1900, Backward Count," he said. "It is only you Blatant Anachronics who call it 2100. And, by God, we are *making* it be 1900! We are removing all the extravagant anachronic wasters of energy—this very day you saw my men getting rid of the last gaslamp in the village—and so it will go on. It is all very carefully programmed, all over the world. One thing makes our plans very easy, of course—we know exactly *when* to forbid each piece of technology, and when to replace it with its functional predecessor. Our Ten Thousand Year Plan will make all Progressive planning of the bad old days look very silly indeed."

"Ten Thou—" began Ambrose, staring. "You're mad! Stark, raving mad! You don't really intend to revert all the way—to the Stone Age!"

"But we do," said Leathey gently. "Metals won't last for ever. And agriculture has to go too, in the end—even with the best of care, at last it destroys the soil. But not to worry. Polished stone is very useful stuff, believe me, and one can learn to hunt . . . By then of course the population should be down to very reasonable limits. Oh, I know there are some heretics even among our Regressive establishment who think we'll be able to call a halt well before that, but they are simply over-optimistic fools."

"There must be a way out," said Ambrose, "there *has* to be—"

"There is no way out." Leathey laughed bitterly now. "Believe me, I know how you feel. I, too—we all have our moments of rebellion. If only, one thinks, if only the Progressives had handled things differently! When the earth was theirs, and the fullness thereof, and the planets were within their grasp! You know, you can pinpoint their fatal error, you can place their ultimate pusillanimity within a few years of the Old Count. It was during the Forward 1970s, when they had reached the Moon, and then—decided that space travel was 'utter bilge,' as one leading light of an earlier time put it. If they had gone on, if they had only gone on *then*—why, we would now have all the metals and minerals of the asteroids, all the wealth of the heavens. Perhaps by now we would have reached the stars . . . and then we could have laughed at the decline of one little planet called Earth. But no: *they* saw no immediate profit in space travel. So they went back, and turned their rockets—not into ploughshares, but into nuclear missiles. Now we haven't the resources to get back into space even if you Anachronics were to take over the world tomorrow. We are tied to Earth for ever—and to the earth, therefore, we must return. Dust to dust."

"But—the *books*," cried Ambrose, waving at the half-empty shelves. "Why are you destroying *knowledge*?"

"Because it's too painful. Why keep reminders of what might have been? It is far, far better to make do with the dwindling literature suitable to our way of life, and not aspire to things that are for ever beyond our reach. We ate of that apple once—now, steadily, we are spitting it out. And in the end we shall return to Paradise."

"A paradise of hunter-gatherers?" said Ambrose sarcastically.

"Why not? That is the *natural* human condition. Hunter-gatherers can be very happy folks, you know—

much happier than agricultural laborers. Hard work is wildly unnatural for humans." Leathey stood up, yawned, and smiled. "Well, so it will be. Back to the womb of the great mindless Mother. In our end is our beginning (I hope that's not a canceled phrase). I'm glad, of course, that the beginning won't come in my time—I would miss all these creature and mental comforts." And he waved at his books. "Now, Dr. Livermore, it's been a hard day, and the little oblivion calls—I suggest you should sleep on what I've been telling you."

The next morning after breakfast Dr. Leathey gave Ambrose a medical examination, paying particular attention to his head. After several minutes, he shrugged.

"Not a trace of the slightest contusion. And yet you still have this complete amnesia?"

"Yes," said Ambrose.

"I am afraid I find it hard to accept your story. Don't try to shield your associates, Dr. Livermore; I know there must be a cell of yours, probably in London. If you confess, I can promise lenient treatment—"

At that moment came an interruption. The maid brought the message that Simkins the policeman was at the door.

"And, sir," she said, her eyes goggling, "he's got a Thing with him sir! I never saw—"

"What sort of Thing, Alice?" said Leathey, getting up.

"A thing on wheels, sir. A sort of an 'orseless carriage . . ."

"Let's go and see it," said Leathey, smiling gently.

"May—may I come too?" stammered Ambrose. He had a frightful presentiment . . .

"I'd rather you did. Perhaps you can throw some light on this Thing."

And so, on the drive before the doctor's house, Ambrose beheld it. It was his rather special Volkswagen all right, with the policeman and several yokels standing by it—and, horror of horrors, one yokel *in* it, in the driver's seat!

Constable Simkins was explaining. "We found this 'ere motor-brougham, sir, up t'wards the Old Camp, in

Half-Acre Wood. Jemmy 'ere knew summat about the things . . ."

Jemmy, from the driver's seat, leaned out and grinned. "Used ter be a chauffer back in old 1910, sir, an' I soon worked the workin's out. Nice little bus she is, too, but mighty queer in some ways. Wot's this little red lever, I want ter know—"

Ambrose screamed, and instantly was clutching the man by the shoulders and upper arms.

"Ah, so it *is* yours," said Leathey, shaking his head. "Naughty, naughty, Dr. Livermore. A Blatant Anachronism if ever there was one, I'm afraid. That model's been forbidden for all of my lifetime, I think."

Ambrose was sweating. "Get—get him out of here!" he choked. "He could do terrible damage . . ."

"All right Jemmy," said Leathey easily, "don't touch anything else. You've done very well up to now. Now, just get out."

As Jemmy emerged, Ambrose leapt. Before anyone could stop him, he was into the front seat of the car, and jamming down the red lever.

The world grew dim.

For quite some (subjective) time, Ambrose was shaking with the remains of his fright, his hand jammed down hard on the red lever. Then as he recovered control of himself, he realized that he was soaring into the future at maximum speed. At this rate, he'd be going on for thousands of years . . . Well, that might not be too bad. Leave that insane Regressive "civilization" well behind.

He eased up on the lever. Where was he now, nearly two thousand years on? It must be quite safe now. Regression would surely have broken down long ago of its own insanity, and the world must be back on the path of moderate progress; chastened no doubt, wisely cautious, climbing slowly but surely . . . That might be a very good world to live in. Now, what did it look like?

Rural: very rural. The village had disappeared. Below him was a flat green, and around that clumps of great trees, broken in one place by a path; along that way in the distance he glimpsed a neat-roofed building, low pitched like a classical villa. Over the trees rose the bare green downs, apparently unchanged except at the old British camp. There the skyline was broken by wooden frameworks. Skeletons of huts? Perhaps they were excavating. Ah, archeology! That, and villas, certainly indicated civilized values. And right below the car's wheels—it was half a meter down, but that wouldn't matter—that green was flat as a lawn. Doubtless this was parkland. A good, safe spot to emerge . . .

He jerked over the red lever, and was falling. The car struck the green surface—

But it struck with a splat. There was a bubbling, a sliding . . .

Suddenly, with horror, he knew it. That greenness was not a lawn, but a weed-covered mere. And he and his Time-car were rapidly sinking into it.

He tore open a door and the stinking water embraced him.

He got out of the pond somehow, and when at last he stood on dry land, people had appeared from the direction of the house, which was not after all a stone-built villa but an erection of wood and thatch, rather sketchily painted. The people were half a dozen barefoot folk dressed in skins, and they jabbered at him in some utterly foreign tongue. Some of the men were fingering long spears. And, as he looked back over the green slime, he saw that his Time Machine had sunk without trace into that weedy womb.

The savage men were in process of taking him prisoner, and he was submitting in listless despair, when a newcomer appeared on the scene. This was an elderly man of a certain presence, escorted by a couple of swordsmen, and dressed in a clean white woollen robe. He stared at Ambrose, then interrogated him in that strange tongue.

Ambrose jabbered helplessly.

"Hospes," said the man suddenly, "profuge aut naufrage squalide, loqueris-ne linguam Latinam . . . ?"

And so Ambrose discovered that Latin was spoken in this age, by some of the people at least. Luckily, he himself had a reading knowledge of Latin, and now he began to make himself brokenly understood. He was also even better able to follow what the wool-draped gentleman was saying. His name was Obliorix, and he was the local magistrate of the tribe, its guide, philosopher, delegate to some federation or other—and protector of the Druids.

"I see that you have met with some accident, stranger," said Obliorix, wrinkling his nose, "and yet, beneath your mire and slime, what extraordinary garments! Braccae might pass, but that is no sort of authorized mantle, and those boots on your feet . . ." He looked grim. "Could it be that you are a Resister of the Will of Chronos? A belated *Christian*?"

A madness came upon Ambrose then. "Domine," he cried, laughing hysterically, "what year is this?"

"Unus ante Christum," said Obliorix seriously. "1 B.C. And therefore, since last year it is decreed by the United Tribes that all Christians shall be put to death, not as misbelievers but as anachronisms. The Druids on the Hill keep their wicker-work cages constantly supplied with logs and oil—you may see them from here— so I fear me, stranger, if you are a Christian, I cannot save you. To the pyre you must go."

"I—I am not a Christian," said Ambrose truthfully but weakly. He was doubled up with helpless laughter. "1 B.C.," he repeated, "1 B.C.!"

"And next year will be 2," said Obliorix. "What is so funny about that? Truly, it will be a relief in future to number the years by addition." He began to smile. "I like you, absurd stranger. Since you are not a Christian, I think I will make you my jester, for laughter begets laughter. What, will you never stop braying?"

And so Ambrose became at first Chief Jester to Obliorix, magistrate of the tribe of the Oblivisces in southern Britannia; but later he went on to greater things. As Ambrosius Aeternus, he grew to be a respected member of the tribe, and on the death of Obliorix he succeeded to the magistracy and the United Tribes delegateship. In 20 B.C. he went as envoy to the Roman Governor of Gaul, who, of course, was gradually unbuilding Roman towns for the great withdrawal that would take place in the 50s. And throughout his long and restful lifetime, Ambrose would from time to time break out into helpless laughter, so that he became known in Britannia as Ambrosius the Merry.

It was an added joke that, when he was able to persuade the Oblivisces to drag a certain weedy pond, the Time Machine proved to be rusted beyond repair, and only good to be beaten into spear points. But for that Ambrose cared nothing; for in any case, what use was a Time Machine which only progressed backwards into history?

And besides, he told himself, he knew what lay in that direction; and he didn't want to get there any faster.

Down & Out on Ellfive Prime

Dean Ing

Despite our current shortages of power and money, it seems likely that we'll continue our push into space, exploring the possibilities of satellite colonies. The logistics of these have already been charted in great detail, right down to schematic diagrams—but do we know everything about the ways people might live in such colonies?

Not really, says Dean Ing, an Oregon-based writer whose novels include *Soft Targets*. People will always surprise us with individual responses to problems . . . and, with a bow to George Orwell, Ing suggests that someone will find a way to beat the system.

Responding to Almquist's control, the little utility tug wafted from the North dock port and made its gentle pirouette. Ellfive Prime Colony seemed to fall away. Two hundred thousand kilometers distant, blue-white Earth swam into view: cradle of mankind, cage for too many. Almquist turned his long body in its cushions and managed an obligatory smile over frown lines. "If that won't make you homesick, Mr. Weston, nothing will."

The fat man grunted, looking not at the planet he

had deserted but at something much nearer. From the widening of Weston's eyes, you could tell it was something big, closing fast. Torin Almquist knew what it was; he eased the tug out, watching his radar, to give Weston the full benefit of it.

When the tip of the great solar mirror swept past, Weston blanched and cried out. For an instant, the view port was filled with cables and the mirror pivot mechanism. Then once again there was nothing but Earth and sharp pinpricks of starlight. Weston turned toward the engineering manager, wattles at his jawline trembling. "Stupid bastard," he grated. "If that'll be your standard joke on new arrivals, you must cause a lot of coronaries."

Abashed, disappointed: "A mirror comes by every fourteen seconds, Mr. Weston. I thought you'd enjoy it. You asked to see the casting facility, and this is where you can see it best. Besides, if you were retired as a heart case, I'd know it." *And the hell with you*, he added silently. Almquist retreated into an impersonal spiel he knew by heart, moving the tug back to gain a panorama of the colony with its yellow legend, L-5′, proud and unnecessary on the hull. He moved the controls gently, the blond hairs on his forearm masking the play of tendons within.

The colony hung below them, a vast shining melon the length of the new Hudson River Bridge and nearly a kilometer thick. Another of its three mirror strips, anchored near the opposite South end cap of Ellfive Prime and spread like curved petals toward the sun, hurtled silently past the view port. Almquist kept talking. ". . . Prime was the second industrial colony in space, dedicated in 2007. These days it's a natural choice for a retirement community. A fixed population of twenty-five hundred—plus a few down-and-out bums hiding here and there. Nowhere near as big a place as Orbital General's new industrial colony out near the asteroid belt."

Almquist droned on, backing the tug farther away. Beyond the South end cap, a tiny mote sparkled in the void, and Weston squinted, watching it. "The first Ellfive was a General Dynamics–Lever Brothers project in close orbit, but it got snuffed by the Chinese in 2012, during the war."

"I was only a cub then," Weston said, relaxing a bit. "This colony took some damage too, didn't it?"

Almquist glanced at Weston, who looked older despite his bland flesh. Well, living Earthside with seven billion people tended to age you. "The month I was born," Almquist nodded, "a nuke was intercepted just off the centerline of Ellfive Prime. Thermal shock knocked a tremendous dimple in the hull; from inside, of course, it looked like a dome poking up through the soil south of center."

Weston clapped pudgy hands, a gesture tagging him as neo-Afrikaner. "That'll be the hill, then. The one with the pines and spruce, near Hilton Prime?"

A nod. "Stress analysts swore they could leave the dimple if they patched the hull around it. Cheapest solution—and for once, a pretty one. When they finished bringing new lunar topsoil and distributing it inside, they saw there was enough dirt on the slope for spruce and ponderosa pine roots. To balance thousands of tons of new processed soil, they built a blister out on the opposite side of the hull and moved some heavy hardware into it."

The fat man's gaze grew condescending as he saw the great metal blister roll into view like a tumor on the hull. "Looks slapdash," he said.

"Not really; they learned from DynLever's mistakes. The first Ellfive colony was a cylinder, heavier than an ellipsoid like ours." Almquist pointed through the view port. "DynLever designed for a low ambient pressure without much nitrogen in the cylinder and raised hell with water transpiration and absorption in a lot of trees they tried to grow around their living quarters. I'm no botanist, but I know Ellfive Prime has an Earthside ecology—the same air you'd breathe in Peru, only cleaner. We don't coddle our grass and trees, and we grow all our crops right in the North end cap below us."

Something new and infinitely pleasing shifted Weston's features. "You used to have an external crop module to feed fifty thousand people, back when this colony was big in manufacturing—"

"Sold it," Almquist put in. "Detached the big rig and towed it out to a belt colony when I was new here. We didn't really need it anymore—"

Weston returned the interruption pointedly: "You didn't let me finish. I put that deal over. OrbGen made a grand sum on it—which is why the wife and I can retire up here. One hand washes the other, eh?"

Almquist said something noncommittal. He had quit wondering why he disliked so many newcomers. He *knew* why. It was a sling-cast irony that he, Ellfive Prime's top technical man, did not have enough rank in OrbGen to be slated for colony retirement. Torin Almquist might last as Civil Projects Manager for another ten years, if he kept a spotless record. Then he would be Earthsided in the crowds and smog and would eat fish cakes for the rest of his life. Unlike his ex-wife, who had left him to teach in a belt colony so that she would never have to return to Earth. And who could blame her? *Shit.*

"I beg your pardon?"

"Sorry; I was thinking. You wanted to see the high-g casting facility? It's that sphere strapped on to the mirror that's swinging toward us. It's moving over two hundred meters per second, a lot faster than the colony floor, being a kilometer and a half out from the spin axis. So at the mirror tip, instead of pulling around one standard g, they're pulling over three g's. Nobody spends more than an hour there. We balance the sphere with storage masses on the other mirror tips."

Restive, only half-interested: "Why? It doesn't look very heavy."

"It isn't," Almquist conceded, "but Ellfive Prime has to be balanced just so if she's going to spin on center. That's why they filled that blister with heavy stored equipment opposite the hill—though a few tons here and there don't matter."

Weston wasn't listening. "I keep seeing something like barn doors flipping around, past the other end, ah, end cap." He pointed. Another brief sparkle. "There," he said.

Almquist's arm tipped the control stick, and the tug slid farther from the colony's axis of rotation. "Stacking mirror cells for shipment," he explained. "We still have slag left over from a nitrogen-rich asteroid they towed here in the old days. Fused into plates, the slag makes good protection against solar flares. With a mirror face, it can do double duty. We're bundling up a pallet load, and a few cargo men are out there in P-suits—pressure suits. They—"

Weston would never know, and have cared less, what Almquist had started to say. The colony manager clapped the fingers of his free hand against the wireless speaker in his left ear. His face stiffened with zealot intensity. Fingers flickering to the console as the tug rolled and accelerated, Almquist began to speak into his throat mike—something about a Code Three. Weston knew something was being kept from him. He didn't like it and said so. Then he said so again.

". . . happened before," Almquist was saying to someone, "but this time you keep him centered, Radar Prime. I'll haul him in myself. Just talk him out of a panic; you know the drill. Please be quiet, Mr. Weston," he added in a too-polite aside.

"Don't patronize me," Weston spat. "Are we in trouble?"

"I'm swinging around the hull; give me a vector," Almquist continued, and Weston felt his body sag under acceleration. "Are you in voice contact?" Pause. "Doesn't he acknowledge? He's on a work-crew-scrambler circuit, but you can patch me in. Do it."

"You're treating me like a child."

"If you don't shut up, Weston, I *will*. Oh, hell, it's easier to humor you." He flicked a toggle, and the cabin speaker responded.

". . . be okay. I have my explosive riveter," said an unfamiliar voice; adult male, thinned and tightened by tension. "Starting to retro-fire now."

Almquist counted aloud at the muffled sharp bursts. "Not too fast, Versky," he cautioned. "You overheat a rivet gun, and the whole load could detonate."

"Jeez, I'm cartwheeling," Versky cut in. "Hang tight, guys." More bursts, now a staccato hammer. Versky's monologue gave no sign that he had heard Almquist, had all the signs of impending panic.

"Versky, listen to me. Take your goddamn finger off the trigger. We have you on radar. Relax. This is Torin Almquist, Versky. I say again—"

But he didn't. Far beyond, streaking out of the ecliptic, a brief nova flashed against the stars. The voice was cut off instantly. Weston saw Almquist's eyes blink hard, and in that moment the manager's face seemed aged by compassion and hopelessness. Then, very quietly: "Radar Prime, what do you have on scope?"

"Nothing but confetti, Mr. Almquist. Going everywhere at once."

"Should I pursue?"

"Your option, sir."

"And your responsibility."

"Yes, sir. No, don't pursue. Sorry."

"Not your fault. I want reports from you and Versky's cargo-team leader with all possible speed." Almquist flicked toggles with delicate savagery, turned his little vessel around, arrowed back to the dock port. Glancing at Weston, he said, "A skilled cargo man named Yves Versky. Experienced man; should've known better. He floated into a mirror support while horsing those slag cells around and got grazed by it. Batted him hell to breakfast." Then, whispering viciously to himself, "God*damn* those big rivet guns. They can't be used like control jets. Versky knew that."

Then, for the first time, Weston realized what he had seen. A man in a pressure suit had just been blown to small pieces before his eyes. It would make a lovely anecdote over sherry, Weston decided.

Even if Almquist had swung past the external hull blister he would have failed to see, through a darkened view port, the two shabby types looking out. Nobody had official business in the blister. The younger man grimaced nervously, heavy cords bunching at his neck. He was half a head taller than his companion. "What d'you think, Zen?"

The other man yielded a lopsided smile. "Sounds good." He unplugged a pocket communicator from the wall and stuffed it into his threadbare coverall, then leaned forward at the view port. His chunky, muscular torso and short legs ill-matched the extraordinary arms that reached halfway to his knees, giving him the look of a tall dwarf. "I think they bought it, Yves."

"What if they didn't?"

Zen swung around, now grinning outright, and regarded Yves Versky through a swatch of brown hair that was seldom cut. "Hey, do like boss Almquist told you: Relax! They *gotta* buy it."

"I don't follow you."

"Then you'd better learn to. Look, if they recover any pieces, they'll find human flesh. How can they know it was a poor rummy's body thawed after six months in deep freeze? And if they *did* decide it's a scam, they'd have to explain how we planted him in your P-suit. And cut him loose from the blister, when only a few people are supposed to have access here; *and* preset the audio tape and the explosive, *and* coaxed a decent performance out of a lunk like you, *and*," he spread his apelike arms wide, his face comically ugly in glee, "nobody can afford to admit there's a scam counterculture on Ellfive Prime. All the way up to Torin Almquist there'd be just too much egg on too many faces. It ain't gonna happen, Versky."

The hulking cargo man found himself infected by the grin, but: "I wonder how long it'll be before *I* see another egg."

Zen snorted, "First time you lug a carton of edible garbage out of Hilton Prime, me lad. Jean Neruda's half-blind; when you put on the right coverall, he won't know he has an extra in his recycling crew, and after two days you won't mind pickin' chicken out of the slop. Just sit tight in your basement hidey-hole when you're off duty for a while. Stay away from crews that might recognize you until your beard grows. And keep your head shaved like I told you."

Versky heaved a long sigh, sweeping a hand over his newly bald scalp. "You'll drop in on me? I need a lot of tips on the scam life. And—and I don't know how to repay you."

"A million ways. I'll think of a few, young fella. And sure, you'll see me—whenever I like."

Versky chuckled at the term *young fella*. He knew Zen might be in his forties, but he seemed younger.

Versky followed his mentor to the air lock into the colony hull. "Well, just don't forget your friend in the garbage business," he urged, fearful of his unknown future.

Zen paused in the conduit that snaked beneath the soil of Ellfive Prime. "Friendship," he half-joked, "varies directly with mutual benefit and inversely with guilt. Put another way," he said, lapsing into scam language as he trotted toward the South end cap, "a friend who's willing to be understood is a joy. One that demands understanding is a pain in the ass."

"You think too much," Versky laughed. They moved softly now, approaching an entry to the hotel basement.

Zen glanced through the spy hole, paused before punching the wall in the requisite place. "Just like you work too much." He flashed his patented gargoyle grin. "Trust me. Give your heart a rest."

Versky, much too tall for his borrowed clothing, inflated his barrel chest in challenge. "Do I *look* like a heart murmur?"

A shrug. "You did to OrbGen's doctors, rot their souls—which is why you were due to be Earthsided next week. Don't lay that on *me*, ol' scam; I'm the one who's reprieved you to a low-g colony, if you'll just stay in low-g areas near the end caps." He opened the door.

Versky saw the hand signal and whispered, "I got it: Wait thirty seconds." He chuckled again. "Sometimes I think you should be running this colony."

Zen slipped through, left the door nearly closed, waited until Versky had moved near the slit. "In some ways," he stage-whispered back, "I do." Wink. Then he scuttled away.

At mid-morning the next day, Almquist arranged the accident report and its supporting documents into a neat sequence across his video console. Slouching behind his desk with folded arms, he regarded the display for a moment before lifting his eyes. "What've I forgot, Emory?"

Emory Reina cocked his head sparrowlike at the display. Almquist gnawed a cuticle, watching the soulful Reina's eyes dart back and forth in sober scrutiny. "It's all there," was Reina's verdict. "The only safety infraction was Versky's, I think."

"You mean the tether he should've worn?"

A nod; Reina started to speak but thought better of it, the furrows dark on his olive face.

"Spit it out, dammit," Almquist goaded. Reina usually thought a lot more than he talked, a trait Almquist valued in his assistant manager.

"I am wondering," the little Brazilian said, "if it was really accidental." Their eyes locked again, held for a long moment. "Ellfive Prime has been orbiting for fifty years. Discounting early casualties throughout the war, the colony has had twenty-seven fatal mishaps among OrbGen employees. Fourteen of them occurred during the last few days of the victim's tour on the colony."

"That's hard data?"

Another nod.

"You're trying to say they're suicides."

"I am trying not to think so." A devout Catholic, Reina spoke hesitantly.

Maybe he's afraid God is listening. I wish I thought He would. "Can't say I'd blame some of them," Almquist said aloud, remembering. "But not Yves Versky. Too young, too much to live for."

"You must account for my pessimism," Reina replied.

"It's what we pay you for," Almquist said, trying in vain to make it airy. "Maybe the insurance people could convince OrbGen to sweeten the Earthside trip for returning people. It might be cheaper in the long run."

Emory Reina's face said that was bloody likely. "After I send a repair crew to fix the drizzle from that rain pipe, I could draft a suggestion from you to the insurance group," was all he said.

"Do that." Almquist turned his attention to the desk console. As Reina padded out of the low Center building into its courtyard, the manager committed the accident report to memory storage, then paused. His fingers twitched nervously over his computer-terminal keyboard. Oh, yes, he'd forgotten something, all right. Conveniently.

In moments, Almquist had queried Prime memory for an accident report ten years past. It was an old story in more ways than one. Philip Elroy Hazen: technical editor, born 14 September 2014, arrived on L-5' for first tour to write modification work orders 8 May 2039. Earthsided on 10 May 2041; a standard two-year tour for those who were skilled enough to qualify. A colony tour did not imply any other bonus: The tour *was* the bonus. It worked out very well for the owning conglomerates that controlled literally everything on their colonies. Almquist's mouth twitched: *well, maybe not literally* . . .

Hazen had wangled a second tour to the colony on 23 February 2045, implying that he'd been plenty good at his work. Fatal injury accident report filed 20 Febbruary 2047.

Uh-*huh;* uh-*huh!* Yes, by God, there was a familiar ring to it: a malf in Hazen's radio while he was suited up, doing one last check on a modification to the casting facility. Flung off the tip of the mirror and—*Jesus, what a freakish way to go*—straight into a mountain of white-hot slag that had radiated like a dying sun near a temporary processing module outside the colony hull. No recovery attempted; why sift ashes?

Phil Hazen; Zen, they'd called him. The guy they used to say needed rollerskates on his hands; but that was envy talking. Almquist had known Zen slightly, and the guy was an absolute terror at sky-bike racing along the zero-g axis of the colony. Built his own tri-wing craft, even gave it a Maltese cross, scarlet polymer wingskin, and a funny name. The *Red Baron* had looked like a joke, just what Zen had counted on. He'd won a year's pay before other sky bikers realized it wasn't a streak of luck.

Hazen had always made his luck. With his sky bike—it was with young seasoned spruce and the foam polymer, fine engineering and better craftsmanship, all disguised to lure the suckers. And all without an engineering degree. Zen had just picked up expertise, never seeming to work at it.

And when his luck ran out, it was—Almquist

checked the display—only days before he was slated for Earthside. Uh-*huh*!

Torin Almquist knew about the shadowy wraiths who somehow dropped from sight on the colony, to be caught later or to die for lack of medical attention or, in a few cases, to find some scam—some special advantage—to keep them hidden on Ellfive Prime. He'd been sure Zen was a survivor, no matter what the accident report said. What was the phrase? *A scam, not a bum*; being on the scam wasn't quite the same. A scam wasn't down and out of resources; he was down and out of sight. Maybe the crafty Zen had engineered another fatality that wasn't fatal.

Almquist hadn't caught anyone matching the description of Zen. Almost, but not quite. He thought about young Yves Versky, whose medical report hadn't been all that bad, then considered Versky's life expectancy on the colony versus his chances Earthside. Versky had been a sharp, hard worker too. Almquist leaned back in his chair again and stared at his display. He had no way of knowing that Reina's rainpipe crew was too late to ward off disaster.

A rain pipe had been leaking long before Grounds Maintenance realized they had a problem. Rain was a simple matter on Ellfive Prime: You built a web of pipes with spray nozzles that ran the length of the colony. From ground level the pipes were nearly invisible, thin lines connected by crosspieces in a great cylindrical net surrounding the colony's zero-g axis. Gravity loading near the axis was so slight that the rain pipes could be anchored lightly.

Yet now and then, a sky biker would pedal foolishly from the zero-g region or would fail to compensate for the gentle rolling movement generated by the air itself. That was when the rain pipes saved somebody's bacon and on rare occasions suffered a kink. At such times, Almquist was tempted to press for the outlawing of sky bikes until the rabid sports association could raise money for a safety net to protect people and pipes alike. But the cost would have been far too great: It would have amounted to a flat prohibition of sky bikes.

The problem had started a month earlier with a mild collision between a sky bike and a crosspiece. The biker got back intact, but the impact popped a kink on the underside of the attached rain pipe. The kink could not be seen from the colony's axis. It might possibly have been spotted from floor level with a good, powerful telescope.

Inspection crews used safety tethers, which loaded the rain pipe just enough to close the crack while the inspector passed. Then the drizzle resumed for as long as the rain continued. Thereafter, the thrice-weekly afternoon rain from that pipe had been lessened in a line running from Ellfive Prime's Hilton Hotel, past the prized hill, over the colony's one shallow lake, to workstaff apartments that stretched from the lake to the North end cap, where crops were grown. Rain was lessened, that is, everywhere but over the pine-covered hill directly below the kink. Total rainfall was unchanged; but the hill got three times its normal moisture, which gradually soaked down through a forty-year accumulation of ponderosa needles and humus, into the soil below.

In this fashion the hill absorbed one hundred thousand kilograms too much water in a month. A little water percolated back to the creek and the lake it fed. Some of it was still soaking down through the humus overburden. And much of it—far too much—was held by the underlying slope soil, which was gradually turning to ooze. The extra mass had already caused a barely detectable shift in the colony's spin axis. Almquist had his best troubleshooter, Lee Shumway, quietly checking the hull for a structural problem near the hull blister.

Suzanne Nagel was a lissome widow whose second passion was for her sky bike. She had been idling along in zero-g, her chain-driven propeller a soft whirr behind her, when something obscured her view of the hill far below. She kept staring at it until she was well beyond the leak, then realized the obstruction was a spray of water. Suzy sprint-pedaled the rest of the way to the end cap, and five minutes later the rains were canceled by Emory Reina.

Thanks to Suzy Nagel's stamina, the slope did not

collapse that day. But working from inspection records, Reina tragically assumed that the leak had been present for perhaps three days instead of a month. The hill needed something—a local vibration, for example—to begin the mud slide that could abruptly displace up to two hundred thousand tons of mass downslope. Which would inevitably bring on the nightmare more feared than meteorites by every colony manager: spinquake. Small meteorites could only damage a colony, but computer simulations had proved that if the spin axis shifted suddenly a spinquake could crack a colony like an egg.

The repair crew was already in place high above when Reina brought his electrabout three-wheeler to a halt near a path that led up to the pines. His belt-comm set allowed direct contact with the crew and instant access to all channels, including his private scrambler to Torin Almquist.

"I can see the kink on your video," Reina told the crew leader, studying his belt-slung video. "Sleeve it and run a pressure check. We can be thankful that a leak that large was not over Hilton Prime," he added, laughing. The retired OrbGen executives who luxuriated in the hotel would have screamed raw murder, of course. And the leak would have been noticed weeks before.

Scanning the dwarf apple trees at the foot of the slope, Reina's gaze moved to the winding footpath. In the forenoon quietude, he could hear distant swimmers cavorting in the slightly reduced gravity of the Hilton pool near the South end cap. But somewhere above him on the hill, a large animal thrashed clumsily through the pines. It wasn't one of the half-tame deer: only maladroit humans made that much commotion on Ellfive Prime. Straining to locate the hiker, Reina saw the leaning trees. He blinked. No trick of eyesight; they were really leaning. Then he saw the long shallow mud slide, no more than a portent of its potential, that covered part of the footpath. For perhaps five seconds, his mind grasping the implication of what he saw, Reina stood perfectly still. His mouth hung open.

In deadly calm, coding the alarm on his scrambler

circuit: "Torin, Emory Reina. I have a Code Three on the hill. And," he swallowed hard, "potential Code One. I say again, Code One; mud slides on the main-path side of the hill. Over." Then Reina began to shout toward the pines.

Code Three was bad enough: a life in danger. Code Two was more serious still, implying an equipment malfunction that could affect many lives. Code One was reserved for colony-wide disaster. Reina's voice shook. He had never called a Code One before.

During the half-minute it took for Almquist to race from a conference to his office, Reina's shouts flushed not one but two men from the hillside. The first, a heavy individual in golf knickers, identified himself testily as Voerster Weston. He stressed that he was not accustomed to peremptory demands from an overall-clad worker. The second man emerged far to Reina's right but kept hidden in a stand of mountain laurel, listening, surmising, sweating.

Reina's was the voice of sweet reason. "If you want to live, Mr. Weston, please lie down where you are. Slowly. The trees below you are leaning outward, and they were not that way yesterday."

"Damnation, I know that much," Weston howled; "that's what I was looking at. Do you know how wet it is up here? I will not lie down on this muck!"

The man in the laurels made a snap decision, cursed, and stood up. "If you don't, two-belly, I'll shoot you here and now," came the voice of Philip Elroy Hazen. Zen had one hand thrust menacingly into a coverall pocket. He was liberally smeared with mud, and his aspect was not pleasant.

"*O demonio*, another one," Reina muttered. The fat man saw himself flanked, believed Zen's implied lie about a weapon, and carefully levered himself down to the blanket of pine needles. At this moment Torin Almquist answered the Mayday.

There was no way to tell how much soil might slide, but through staccato interchanges Emory Reina described the scene better than his video could show it. Almquist was grim. "We're already monitoring an increase in the off-center spin, Emory; not a severe shift, but it could get to be. Affirmative on that potential Code One. I'm sending a full emergency crew to the blister, now that we know where to start."

Reina thought for a moment, glumly pleased that neither man on the slope had moved. "I believe we can save these two by lowering a safety sling from my crew. They are directly overhead. Concur?"

An instant's pause. "Smart, Emory. And you get your butt out of there. Leave the electrabout, man, just *go!*"

"With respect, I cannot. Someone must direct the sling deployment from here."

"It's your bacon. I'll send another crew to you."

"Volunteers only," Reina begged, watching the slope. For the moment it seemed firm. Yet a bulge near cosmetically placed slag boulders suggested a second mass displacement. Reina then explained their predicament to the men on the slope, to ensure their compliance.

"It's worse than that," Zen called down. "There was a dugout over there," he pointed to the base of a boulder, "where a woman was living. She's buried, I'm afraid."

Reina shook his head sadly, using his comm set to his work crew. Over four hundred meters above, men were lashing tether lines from crosspieces to distribute the weight of a sling. Spare tethers could be linked by carabiners to make a lifeline reaching to the colony floor. The exercise was familiar to the crew, but only as a drill until now. And they would be hoisting, not lowering.

Diametrically opposite from the hill, troubleshooters converged on the blister where the colony's long-unused reactor and coolant tanks were stored. Their job was simple—in principle.

The reactor subsystems had been designed as portable elements, furnished with lifting and towing lugs. The whole reactor system weighed nearly ten thousand tons, including coolant tanks. Since the blister originally had been built around the stored reactor elements to balance the hill mass, Almquist needed only to split the blister open to space, then lower the reactor elements on quartz cables. As the mass moved out of the blister and away from the hull, it would increase in apparent weight, balancing the downward flow of mud across the hull. Almquist was lucky in one detail: The reactor was not in line with the great solar-mirror strips. Elements could be lowered a long way while repairs were carried out to redistribute the soil.

Almquist marshaled forces from his office. He heard the colony-wide alarm whoop its signal, watched monitors as the colony staff and two thousand other residents hurried toward safety in end-cap domes. His own P-suit, ungainly and dust-covered, hung in his apartment ten paces away. There was no time to fetch it while he was at his post. *Never again,* he promised himself. He divided his attention among monitors showing the evacuation, the blister team, and the immediate problem above Emory Reina.

Reina was optimistic as the sling snaked down. "South a bit," he urged into his comm set, then raised his voice. "Mr. Weston, a sling is above you, a little north. Climb in and buckle the harness. They will reel you in."

Weston looked around him, the whites of his eyes visible from fifty meters away. He had heard the alarm and remembered only that it meant mortal danger. He saw the sling turning gently on its thin cable as it neared him.

"Now, steady as she goes," Reina said, then, "Stop." The sling collapsed on the turf near the fat man. Reina, fearful that the mud-covered stranger might lose heart, called to assure him that the sling would return.

"I'll take my chances here," Zen called back. The sling could mean capture. The fat man did not understand that any better than Reina did.

Voerster Weston paused halfway into his harness, staring up. Suddenly he was scrambling away from it, tripping in the sling, mindless with the fear of rising into a synthetic sky. Screaming, he fled down the slope. And brought part of it with him.

Reina saw apple trees churning toward him in time to leap atop his electrabout and kept his wits enough to grab branches as the first great wave slid from the slope. He saw Weston disappear in two separate up-heavals, swallowed under the mud slide he had pro-voked. Mauled by hardwood, mired to his knees, Reina spat blood and turf. He hauled one leg free, then the other, pulling at tree limbs. The second man, he saw, had slithered against a thick pine and was now trying to climb it.

Still calm, voice indistinct through his broken jaw, Reina redirected the sling crew. The sling harness bounced upslope near the second man. "Take the sling," Reina bawled.

Now Reina's whole world shuddered. It was a slow, perceptible motion, each displacement of mud worsen-ing the off-center rotation and slight acceleration changes that could bring more mud that could bring worse. . . . Reina forced his mind back to the imme-diate problem. He could not see himself at its focus.

Almquist felt the tremors, saw what had to be done. "Emory, I'm sending your relief crew back. Shum-way's in the blister. They don't have time to cut the blister now; they'll have to blow it open. You have about three minutes to get to firm ground. Then you run like hell to South end cap."

"As soon as this man is in the sling," Reina mum-bled. Zen had already made his decision, seeing the glistening ooze that had buried the fat man.

"Now! Right fucking *now*," Almquist pleaded. "I can't delay it a millisecond. When Shumway blows the blister open it'll be a sudden shake, Emory. You know what that means?"

Reina did. The sharp tremor would probably bring the entire middle of the slope thundering down. Even if the reactor could be lowered in minutes, it would take only seconds for the muck to engulf him. Reina began to pick his way backward across fallen apple trees, wondering why his left arm had an extra bend above the wrist. He kept a running fire of instructions to the rain-pipe crew as Zen untangled the sling harness. Reina struggled toward safety in pain, patience, reluc-tance. And far too slowly.

"He is buckled in," Reina announced. His last words

were, "Haul away." He saw the mud-spattered Zen begin to rise, swinging in a broad arc, and they exchanged "OK" hand signals before Reina gave full attention to his own escape. He had just reached the edge of firm ground when Lee Shumway, moving with incredible speed in a full P-suit, ducked through a blister airlock and triggered the charges.

The colony floor bucked once, throwing Reina off stride. He fell on his fractured ulna, rolled, opened his mouth—perhaps to moan, perhaps to pray. His breath was bottled by mud as he was flung beneath a viscous gray tide that rolled numberless tons of debris over him.

The immense structure groaned, but held. Zen swayed sickeningly as Ellfive Prime shook around him. He saw Reina die, watched helplessly as a retiree home across the valley sagged and collapsed. Below him, a covey of Quetzal birds burst from the treetops like jeweled scissors in flight. As he was drawn higher he could see more trees slide.

The damage worsened; too many people had been too slow. The colony was rattling everything that would rattle. Now it was all rattling louder. Somewhere, a shrill whistle keened as precious air and more precious water vapor rushed toward a hole in the sunlight windows.

When the shouts above him became louder than the carnage below, Zen began to hope. Strong arms reached for his and moments later he was attached to another tether. "I can make it from here," he said, calling his thanks back as he hauled himself toward the end-cap braces.

A crew man with a video comm set thrust it toward Zen as he neared a ladder. "It's for you," he said, noncommittal.

For an instant, an eon, Zen's body froze, though he continued to waft nearer. Then he shrugged and took the comm set as though it were ticking. He saw a remembered face in the video. Wrapping an arm around the ladder, he nodded to the face. "Don Bellows here," he said innocently.

Pause, then a snarl: "You wouldn't believe my mixed emotions when I recognized you on the monitor.

Well, *Mister* Bellows, Adolf Hitler here." Almquist went on, "Or you'll think so damned quick unless you're in my office as fast as your knuckles will carry you."

The crew man was looking away, but he was tense. He knew. Zen cleared his throat for a whine. "I'm scared—"

"You've been dead for ten years, Hazen. How can you be scared? Frazer there will escort you; his instructions are to brain you if he has to. I have sweeping powers right now. Don't con me and don't argue; I need you right here, right now."

By the time Zen reached the terraces with their felled, jumbled crops, the slow shakes had subsided. They seemed to diminish to nothing as he trotted, the rangy Frazer in step behind, to an abandoned electrabout. Damage was everywhere, yet the silence was oppressive. A few electrical fires were kindling in apartments as they moved toward the Colony Center building. Some fires would be out, others out of control, in minutes. The crew man gestured Zen through the courtyard and past two doors. Torin Almquist stood looming over his console display, ignoring huge shards of glass that littered his carpet.

Almquist adjusted a video monitor. "Thanks, Frazer; would you wait in the next room?" The crew man let his face complain of his idleness but complied silently. Without glancing from the monitors, Almquist transfixed the grimy Zen. "If I say the word, you're a dead man. If I say a different word, you go Earthside in manacles. You're still here only because I wanted you here all the time, just in case I ever needed you. Well, I need you now. If you hadn't been dropped into my lap we'd have found you on a Priority One. Never doubt that.

"If I say a third word, you get a special assistant's slot—I can swing that—for as long as I'm here. All I'm waiting for is one word from *you*. If it's a lie, you're dead meat. Will you help Ellfive Prime? Yes or no?"

Zen considered his chances. Not past that longlegged Frazer. They could follow him on monitors for some distance anyhow unless he had a head start. "Given the right conditions," Zen hazarded.

Almquist's head snapped up. "My best friend just died for you, against my better judgment. *Yes or no.*"

"Yes. I owe you nothin', but I owe him somethin'."

Back to the monitors, speaking to Zen: "Lee Shumway's crew has recovered our mass balance, and they can do it again if necessary. I doubt there'll be more mud slides, though; five minutes of spinquakes should've done it all."

Zen moved to watch over the tall man's bare arms. Two crews could be seen from a utility tug monitor, rushing to repair window leaks where water vapor had crystallized in space as glittering fog. The colony's external heat radiator was in massive fragments, and the mirrors were jammed in place. It was going to get hot in Ellfive Prime. "How soon will we get help from other colonies?"

Almquist hesitated. Then, "We won't, unless we fail to cope. OrbGen is afraid some other corporate pirate will claim salvage rights. And when you're on my staff, everything I tell you is privileged data."

"You think the danger is over?"

"Over?" Almquist barked a laugh that threatened to climb out of control. He ticked items off on his fingers. "We're losing water vapor; we have to mask mirrors and repair the radiator, or we fry; half our crops are ruined and food stores may not last; and most residents are hopeless clods who have no idea how to fend for themselves. *Now* d'you see why I diverted searches when I could've taken you twice before?"

Zen's mouth was a cynical curve.

Almquist: "Once when you dragged a kid from the lake filters I could've had you at the emergency room." Zen's eyebrows lifted in surprised agreement. "And once when a waiter realized you were scamming food from the Hilton service elevator."

"That was somebody else, you weren't even close. But okay, you've been a real sweetheart. Why?"

"Because you've learned to live outside the system! Food, shelter, medical help, God knows what else; you have another system that hardly affects mine, and now we're going to teach your tricks to the survivors. This colony is going to make it. You were my experimental group, Zen. You just didn't know it." He rubbed his chin reflectively. "By the way, how many guys are on the scam? Couple of dozen?" An optimist, Torin Almquist picked what he considered a high figure.

A chuckle. "Couple of hundred, you mean." Zen saw slack-jawed disbelief and went on: "They're not all guys. A few growing families. There's Wandering Mary, Maria Polyakova; our only registered nurse, but I found her dugout full of mud this morning. I hope she was sleepin' out."

"Can you enlist their help? If they don't help, this colony can still die. The computer says it will, as things stand now. It'll be close, but we won't make it. How'd you like to take your chances with a salvage crew?"

"Not a chance. But I can't help just standing here swappin' wind with you."

"Right." Eyes bored into Zen's, assessing him. The thieves' argot, the be-damned-to-you gaze, suggested a man who was more than Hazen *had* been. "I'll give you a temporary pass. See you here tomorrow morning; for now, look the whole colony over, and bring a list of problems and solutions as you see 'em."

Zen turned to leave, then looked back. "You're really gonna let me just walk right out." A statement of wonder, and of fact.

"Not without this," Almquist said, scribbling on a plastic chit. He thrust it toward Zen. "Show it to Frazer."

Inspecting the cursive scrawl: "Doesn't look like much."

"*Mas que nada,*" Almquist smiled, then looked quickly away as his face fell. *Better than nothing*; his private joke with Emory Reina. He glanced at the retreating Zen and rubbed his forehead. Grief did funny things to people's heads. To deny a death you won't accept, you invest his character in another man. Not very smart when the other man might betray you for the sheer fun of it. Torin Almquist massaged his temples and called Lee Shumway. They still had casualties to rescue.

Zen fought a sense of unreality as he moved openly in broad daylight. Everyone was lost in his own concerns. Zen hauled one scam from his plastic bubble under the lake surface, half dead in stagnant air after mud from the creek swamped his air exchanger. An entire family of scams, living as servants in the illegal basement they had excavated for a resident, had been crushed when the foundation collapsed.

But he nearly wept to find Wandering Mary safe in a secret conduit, tending to a dozen wounded scams. He took notes as she told him where her curative herbs were planted and how to use them. The old girl flatly refused to leave her charges, her black eyes flashing through wisps of gray hair, and Zen promised to send food.

The luck of Sammy the Touch was holding strong. The crop compost heap that covered his half-acre foam shell seemed to insulate it from ground shock as well. Sammy patted his little round tummy, always a cheerful sign, as he ushered Zen into the bar where, on a good night, thirty scams might be gathered. If Zen was the widest-ranging scam on Ellfive Prime, Sammy the Touch was the most secure.

Zen accepted a glass of potato vodka—Sammy was seldom *that* easy a touch—and allowed a parody of the truth to be drawn from him. He'd offered his services to an assistant engineer, he said, in exchange for unspecified future privileges. Sammy either bought the story or took a lease on it. He responded after some haggling with the promise of a hundred kilos of "medicinal" alcohol and half his supply of bottled methane. Both were produced from compost precisely under the noses of the crop crew, and both were supplied on credit. Sammy also agreed to provision the hidden infirmary of Wandering Mary. Zen hugged the embarrassed Sammy and exited through one of the conduits, promising to pick up the supplies later.

Everywhere he went, Zen realized, the scams were coping better than legal residents. He helped a startlingly handsome middle-aged blonde douse the remains of her smoldering wardrobe. Her apartment complex had knelt into its courtyard and caught fire.

"I'm going to freeze tonight," Suzy Nagel murmured philosophically.

He eyed her skimpy costume and doubted it. Besides, the temperature was slowly climbing, and there wouldn't *be* any night until the solar mirrors could be pivoted again. There were other ways to move the colony to a less reflective position, but he knew Almquist would try the direct solutions first.

Farmer Brown—no one knew his original name— wore his usual stolen agronomycrew coverall as he hawked his pack load of vegetables among residents in the low-rent area. He had not assessed all the damage to his own crops, tucked and espaliered into corners over five square kilometers of the colony. Worried as he was, he had time to hear a convincing story. "Maybe I'm crazy to compete against myself," he told Zen, "but you got a point. If a salvage outfit takes over, it's kay-mag." KMAG: Kiss my ass good-bye. "I'll sell you seeds, even breeding pairs of hamsters, but don't ask me to face the honchos in person. You remember about the vigilantes, ol' scam."

Zen nodded. He gave no thought to the time until a long shadow striped a third of the colony floor. One of the mirrors had been coaxed into pivoting. Christ, he was tired—but why not? It would have been dark long before, on an ordinary day. He sought his sleeping quarters in Jean Neruda's apartment, hoping Neruda wouldn't insist on using Zen's eyesight to fill out receipts. Their arrangement was a comfortable quid pro quo, but please, thought Zen, not tonight!

He found a more immediate problem than receipts. Yves Versky slumped, trembling, in the shambles of Neruda's place, holding a standard emergency oxygen mask over the old man's face. The adjoining office had lost one wall in the spinquake, moments after the recycling crew ran for end-cap domes.

"I had to hole up here," Versky gasped, exhausted. "Didn't know where else to go. Neruda wouldn't leave either. Then the old fool smelled smoke and dumped his goldfish bowl on a live power line. Must've blown half the circuits in his body." Like a spring-wound toy, Versky's movements and voice diminished. "Took me two hours of mouth-to-mouth before he was breathing steady, Zen. Boy, have I got a headache."

Versky fell asleep holding the mask in place. Zen could infer the rest. Neruda, unwilling to leave familiar rooms in his advancing blindness. Versky, unwilling to abandon a life, even that of a half-electrocuted, crotchety old man. Yet Neruda was right to stay put: Earthside awaited the OrbGen employee whose eyes failed.

Zen lowered the inert Versky to the floor, patted the big man's shoulder. More than unremitting care, he had shown stamina and first-aid expertise. Old Neruda awoke once, half-manic, half-just disoriented. Zen nursed him through it with surface awareness. On another level he was cataloguing items for Almquist, for survivors, for Ellfive Prime.

And on the critical level a voice in him jeered, *bullshit: For yourself*. Not because Almquist or Reina had done him any favors, but because Torin Almquist was right. The colony manager could find him eventually; maybe it was better to rejoin the system now, on good terms. Besides, as the only man who could move between the official system and the scam counterculture, he could really wheel and deal. It might cause some hard feelings in the conduits, but . . . Zen sighed, and slept. Poorly.

It was two days before Zen made every contact he needed, two more when Almquist announced that Ellfive Prime would probably make it. The ambient temperature had stabilized. Air and water losses had ceased. They did not have enough stored food to provide three thousand daily calories per person beyond twenty days, but crash courses in multicropping were suddenly popular, and some immature crops could be eaten.

"It'd help if you could coax a few scams into instructing," Almquist urged as he slowed to match Zen's choppy pace. They turned from the damaged crop terraces toward the Center.

"Unnn-likely," Zen intoned. "We still talk about wartime, when vigilantes tried to clean us out. They ushered a couple of nice people out of airlocks, naked, which we think was a little brusque. Leave it alone; it's working."

A nod. "Seems to be. But I have doubts about the maturing rates of your seeds. Why didn't my people know about those hybrid daikon radishes and tomatoes?"

"You were after long-term yield," Zen shrugged. "This hot weather will ripen the stuff faster, too. We've been hiding a dozen short-term crops under your nose, including dandelions better than spinach. Like hamster haunch is better'n rabbit, and a lot quicker to grow."

Almquist could believe the eighteen-day gestation period, but was astonished at the size of the breeding stock. "You realize your one-kilo hamsters could be more pet than protein?"

"Not in our economy," Zen snorted. "It's hard to be sentimental when you're down and out. Or stylish either." He indicated his frayed coverall. "By the time the rag man gets this, it won't yield three meters of dental floss."

Almquist grinned for the first time in many days. What his new assistant had forgotten in polite speech, he made up in the optimism of a young punk. He corrected himself: an *old* punk. "You know what hurts? You're nearly my age and look ten years younger. How?"

It wasn't a specific exercise, Zen explained. It was attitude. "You're careworn," he sniffed. "Beat your brains out for idling plutocrats fifty weeks a year and then wonder why you age faster than I do." Wondering headshake.

They turned toward the Center courtyard. Amused, Almquist said, "You're a plutocrat?"

"Ain't racin' my motors. Look at all the Indians who used to live past a hundred. A Blackfoot busted his ass like I do, maybe ten or twenty weeks a year. They weren't dumb; just scruffy."

Almquist forgot his retort; his desk console was flashing for attention. Zen wandered out of the office, returning with two cups of scam "coffee." Almquist sipped it between calls, wondering if it was really brewed from ground dandelion root, considering how this impudent troll was changing his life, could change it further.

Finally he sat back. "You heard OrbGen's assessment," he sighed. "I'm a Goddamned hero, for now. Don't ask me about next year. If they insist on making poor Emory a sacrificial goat to feed ravening stockholders, I can't help it."

Impassive. "Sure you could. You just let 'em co-opt you." Zen sighed, then released a sad troglodyte's smile. "Like you co-opted me."

"I can unco-opt. Nothing's permanent."

"You said it, bubba."

Almquist took a long breath, then cantilevered a forefinger in warning. "Watch your tongue, Hazen. When I pay your salary, you pay some respect." He saw the sullen look in Zen's eyes and bored in. "Or would you rather go on the scam again and get Earthsided the first chance I get? I haven't *begun* to co-opt you yet," he glowered. "I have to meet with the Colony Council in five minutes—to explain a lot of things, including you. When I get back, I want a map of those conduits the scams built, to the best of your knowledge."

A flood of ice washed through Zen's veins. Staring over the cup of coffee that shook in his hands: "You *know* I can't do that."

Almquist paused in the doorway, his expression smug. "You know the alternative. Think about it," he said, and turned and walked out.

When Torin Almquist returned, his wastebasket was overturned on his desk. A ripe odor wrinkled his nose for him even before he saw what lay atop the wastebasket like an offering on a pedestal: a lavish gift of human excrement. His letter opener, an antique, protruded from the turd. It skewered a plastic chit, Zen's pass. On the chit, in draftsman's neat printing, full CAPS: I THOUGHT ABOUT IT.

Well, you sure couldn't mistake his answer, Almquist reflected as he dumped the offal into his toilet. Trust Zen to make the right decision.

Which way had he gone? Almquist could only guess at the underground warrens built during the past fifty years, but chose not to guess. He also knew better than to mention Zen to the Colony Council. The manager felt a twinge of guilt at the choice, truly no choice at all, that he had forced on Zen—but there was no other way.

If Zen knew the whole truth, he might get careless, and a low profile was vital for the scams. The setup benefited all of Ellfive Prime. Who could say when the colony might once more need the counterculture and its primitive ways?

And that meant Zen had to disappear again, genuinely down and out of reach. If Almquist himself didn't know exactly where the scams hid, he couldn't tell OrbGen even under drugs. And he didn't intend to tell. Sooner or later OrbGen would schedule Torin Almquist for permanent Earthside rotation, and when that day came he might need help in his own disappearance. *That* would be the time to ferret out a secret conduit, to contact Zen. The scams could use an engineering manager who knew the official system inside out.

Almquist grinned to himself and brewed a cup of dandelion coffee. Best to get used to the stuff now, he reasoned; it would be a staple after he retired, down and out on Ellfive Prime.

The Exit Door Leads In

Philip K. Dick

In recent years, our schools have come to realize that what students need to learn isn't just tensor calculus or the wellsprings of John Milton's art, but also practical knowledge about how to function in the world that awaits them after graduation. The result has been a major, and controversial, shift in teaching methods.

Philip K. Dick offers a darkly satiric story about a future world with demands on the individual that transcend anything we know today . . . and about the education of one young man adrift in that world.

Bob Bibleman had the impression that robots wouldn't look you in the eye. And when one had been in the vicinity small valuable objects disappeared. A robot's idea of order was to stack everything into one pile. Nonetheless, Bibleman had to order lunch from robots, since vending ranked too low on the wage scale to attract humans.

"A hamburger, fries, strawberry shake and—" Bibleman paused, reading the printout. "Make that a supreme double cheeseburger, fries, a chocolate malt—"

"Wait a minute," the robot said. "I'm already working on the burger. You want to buy into this week's contest while you're waiting?"

"I don't get the royal cheeseburger," Bibleman said.

"That's right."

It was hell living in the twenty-first century. Information transfer had reached the velocity of light. Bibleman's older brother had once fed a ten-word plot outline into a robot fiction machine, changed his mind as to the outcome, and found that the novel was already in print. He had had to program a sequel in order to make his correction.

"What's the prize structure in the contest?" Bibleman asked.

At once the printout posted all the odds, from first prize down to last. Naturally, the robot blanked out the display before Bibleman could read it.

"What is first prize?" Bibleman said.

"I can't tell you that," the robot said. From its slot came a hamburger, french fries and a strawberry shake. "That'll be one thousand dollars in cash."

"Give me a hint," Bibleman said as he paid.

"It's everywhere and nowhere. It's existed since the seventeenth century. Originally it was invisible. Then it became royal. You can't get in unless you're smart, although cheating helps and so does being rich. What does the word 'heavy' suggest to you?"

"Profound."

"No, the literal meaning."

"Mass." Bibleman pondered. "What is this, a contest to see who can figure out what the prize is? I give up."

"Pay the six dollars," the robot said, "to cover our costs, and you'll receive an—"

"Gravity," Bibleman broke in. "Sir Isaac Newton. The Royal College of England. Am I right?"

"Right," the robot said. "Six dollars entitles you to a chance to go to college—a statistical chance, at the posted odds. What's six dollars? Pratfare."

Bibleman handed over a six-dollar coin.

"You win," the robot said. "You get to go to college. You beat the odds, which were two trillion to one against. Let me be the first to congratulate you. If I had a hand I'd shake hands with you. This will change your life. This has been your lucky day."

"It's a setup," Bibleman said, feeling a rush of anxiety.

"You're right," the robot said, and it looked Bibleman right in the eye. "It's also mandatory that you accept your prize. The college is a military college located in Buttfuck, Egypt, so to speak. But that's no problem; you'll be taken there. Go home and start packing."

"Can't I eat my hamburger and drink—"

"I'd suggest you start packing right away."

Behind Bibleman a man and woman had lined up; reflexively he got out of their way, trying to hold on to his tray of food, feeling dizzy.

"A char-broiled steak sandwich," the man said, "onion rings, root beer and that's it."

The robot said, "Care to buy into the contest? Terrific prizes." It flashed the odds on its display panel.

When Bob Bibleman unlocked the door of his one-room apartment his telephone was on. It was looking for him.

"There you are," the telephone said.

"I'm not going to do it," Bibleman said.

"Sure you are," the phone said. "Do you know who this is? Read over your certificate, your first-prize legal form. You hold the rank of shavetail. I'm Major Casals. You're under my jurisdiction. If I tell you to piss purple you'll piss purple. How soon can you be on a transplan rocket? Do you have friends you want to say goodbye to? A sweetheart, perhaps? Your mother?"

"Am I coming back?" Bibleman said with anger. "I mean, who are we fighting, this college? For that matter, what college is it? Who is on the faculty? Is it a liberal-arts college or does it specialize in the hard sciences? Is it government sponsored? Does it offer—"

"Just calm down," Major Casals said quietly.

Bibleman seated himself. He discovered that his hands were shaking. To himself he thought, I was born in the wrong century. A hundred years ago this wouldn't have happened and a hundred years from now it will be illegal. What I need is a lawyer.

His life had been a quiet one. He had, over the years, advanced to the modest position of floating-home salesman. For a man twenty-two years old that wasn't bad. He almost owned his one-room apartment; that is, he rented with an option to buy. It was a small life, as lives went; he did not ask too much and he did not complain—normally—at what he received. Although he did not understand the tax structure that cut through his income, he accepted it; he accepted a modified state of penury the same way he accepted it when a girl would not go to bed with him. In a sense this defined him; this was his measure. He submitted to what he did not like, and he regarded this attitude as a virtue. Most people in authority over him considered him a good person. As to those over whom *he* had authority, that was a class with zero members. His boss at Cloud Nine Homes told him what to do and his customers, really, told him what to do. The government told everyone what to do, or so he assumed. He had very few dealings with the government. That was neither a virtue nor a vice; it was simply good luck.

Once he had experienced vague dreams. They had to do with giving to the poor. In high school he had read Charles Dickens and a vivid idea of the oppressed had fixed itself in his mind to the point where he could see them: all those who did not have a one-room apartment and a job and a high-school education. Certain vague place names had floated through his head, gleaned from TV, places like India where heavy-duty machinery swept up the dying. Once a teaching machine had told him, *You have a good heart*. That amazed him—not that a machine would say so, but that it would say it to him. A girl had told him the same thing. He marveled at this. Vast forces colluding to tell him that he was not a bad person! It was a mystery and a delight.

But those days had passed. He no longer read novels, and the girl had been transferred to Frankfurt. Now he had been set up by a robot, a cheap machine, to shovel shit in the boonies, dragooned by a mechanical scam that was probably pulling citizens off the streets in record numbers. This was not a college he was going to; he had won nothing. He had won a stint at some kind of forced-labor camp, most likely. The exit door leads in, he thought to himself. Which is to say, when they want you they already have you; all they need is the paper work. And a computer can process the forms at the touch of a key. The H key for hell and the S key for slave, he thought. And the Y key for you.

Don't forget your toothbrush, he thought. You may need it.

On the phone screen Major Casals regarded him, as if silently estimating the chances that Bob Bibleman might bolt. Two trillion to one I will, Bibleman thought. But the one will win, as in the contest; I'll do what I'm told.

"Please," Bibleman said, "let me ask you one thing, and give me an honest answer."

"Of course," Major Casals said.

"If I hadn't gone up to that Earl's Senior robot and—"

"We'd have gotten you anyhow," Major Casals said.

"Okay," Bibleman said, nodding. "Thanks. It makes me feel better. I don't have to tell myself stupid stuff like, If only I hadn't felt like a hamburger and fries. If only—" He broke off. "I'd better pack."

Major Casals said, "We've been running an evaluation on you for several months. You're overly endowed for the kind of work you do. And undereducated. You need more education. You're *entitled* to more education."

Astonished, Bibleman said, "You're talking about it as if it's a genuine college!"

"It is. It's the finest in the system. It isn't advertised; something like this can't be. No one selects it; the college selects you. Those were not joke odds that you saw posted. You can't really imagine being admitted to the finest college in the system by this method, can you, Mr. Bibleman? You have a lot to learn."

"How long will I be at the college?" Bibleman said.

Major Casals said, "Until you have learned."

They gave him a physical, a haircut, a uniform and a place to bunk down, and many psychological tests. Bibleman suspected that the true purpose of the tests was to determine if he were a latent homosexual, and then he suspected that his suspicions indicated that he *was* a latent homosexual, so he abandoned the suspicions and supposed instead that they were sly intelligence and aptitude tests, and he informed himself that he was showing both: intelligence and aptitude. He also informed himself that he looked great in his uniform, even though it was the same uniform that everyone else wore. That is why they call it a uniform, he reminded himself as he sat on the edge of his bunk reading his orientation pamphlets.

The first pamphlet pointed out that it was a great honor to be admitted to the College. That was its name—the one word. How strange, he thought, puzzled. It's like naming your cat Cat and your dog Dog. This is my mother, Mrs. Mother, and my father, Mr. Father. Are these people working right? he wondered. It had been a phobia of his for years that someday he would fall into the hands of madmen—in particular madmen who seemed sane up until the last moment. To Bibleman this was the essence of horror.

As he sat scrutinizing the pamphlets a red-haired girl, wearing the College uniform, came over and seated herself beside him. She seemed perplexed.

"Maybe you can help me," she said. "What is a syllabus? It says here that we'll be given a syllabus. This place is screwing up my head."

Bibleman said, "We've been dragooned off the streets to shovel shit."

"You think so?"

"I know so."

"Can't we just leave?"

"You leave first," Bibleman said. "And I'll wait and see what happens to you."

The girl laughed. "I guess you don't know what a syllabus is."

"Sure I do. It's an abstract of courses or topics."

"Yes, and pigs can whistle."

He regarded her. The girl regarded him.

"We're going to be here forever," the girl said.

Her name, she told him, was Mary Lorne. She was, he decided, pretty, wistful, afraid and putting up a good front. Together they joined the other new students for a showing of a recent Herbie the Hyena cartoon which Bibleman had seen; it was the episode in which Herbie attempted to assassinate the Russian monk Rasputin. In his usual fashion Herbie the Hyena poisoned his victim, shot him, blew him up six times, stabbed him, tied him up with chains and sank him in the Volga, tore him apart with wild horses and finally shot him to the moon strapped to a rocket. The cartoon bored Bibleman. He did not give a damn about Herbie the Hyena or Russian history and he wondered if this was a sample of the College's level of pedagogy. He could imagine Herbie the Hyena illustrating Heisenberg's indeterminacy principle. Herbie—in Bibleman's mind—chased after a subatomic particle fruitlessly, the particle bobbing up at random here and there . . . Herbie making wild swings at it with a hammer; then a whole flock of subatomic particles jeering at Herbie, who was doomed as always to fuck up.

"What are you thinking?" Mary whispered to him.

The cartoon ended; the hall lights came on. There stood Major Casals on the stage, larger than on the phone. The fun is over, Bibleman said to himself. He could not imagine Major Casals chasing subatomic particles fruitlessly with wild swings of a sledgehammer. He felt himself grow cold and grim and a little afraid.

The lecture had to do with classified information. Behind Major Casals a giant hologram lit up with a schematic diagram of a homeostatic drilling rig. Within the hologram the rig rotated so that they could see it from all angles. Different stages of the rig's interior glowed in various colors.

"I asked what you were thinking," Mary whispered.

"We have to listen," Bibleman said quietly.

Mary said, equally quietly, "It finds titanium ore on its own. Big deal. Titanium is the ninth most abundant element in the crust of the planet. I'd be impressed if it could seek out and mine pure wurtzite, which is found only at Potosi, Bolivia; Butte, Montana; and Goldfield, Nevada."

"Why is that?" Bibleman said.

"Because," Mary said, "wurtzite is unstable at temperatures below one thousand degrees centigrade. And further—" She broke off. Major Casals had ceased talking and was looking at her.

"Would you repeat that for all of us, young woman?" Major Casals said.

Standing, Mary said, "Wurtzite is unstable at temperatures below one thousand degrees centigrade." Her voice was steady.

Immediately the hologram behind Major Casals switched to a readout of data on zinc-sulfide minerals.

"I don't see 'wurtzite' listed," Major Casals said.

"It's given on the chart in its inverted form," Mary said, her arms folded. "Which is sphalerite. Correctly, it is ZnS, of the sulfide group of the AX type. It's related to greenockite."

"Sit down," Major Casals said. The readout within the hologram now showed the characteristics of greenockite.

As she seated herself, Mary said, "I'm right. They don't have a homeostatic drilling rig for wurtzite because there is no—"

"Your name is?" Major Casals said, pen and pad poised.

"Mary Wurtz." Her voice was totally without emotion. "My father was Charles-Adolphe Wurtz."

"The discoverer of wurtzite?" Major Casals said uncertainly; his pen wavered.

"That's right," Mary said. Turning toward Bibleman she winked.

"Thank you for the information," Major Casals said.

He made a motion and the hologram now showed a flying buttress and, in comparison to it, a normal buttress.

"My point," Major Casals said, "is simply that certain information such as architectural principles of longstanding—"

"Most architectural principles are longstanding," Mary said.

Major Casals paused.

"Otherwise they'd serve no purpose," Mary said.

"Why not?" Major Casals said, and then he colored. Several uniformed students laughed.

"Information of that type," Major Casals continued, "is not classified. But a good deal of what you will be learning is classified. This is why the College is under military charter. To reveal or transmit or make public classified information given you during your schooling here falls under the jurisdiction of the military. For a breech of these statutes you would be tried by a military tribunal."

The students murmured. To himself, Bibleman thought, banged, ganged and then some. No one spoke. Even the girl beside him was silent. A complicated expression had crossed her face, however; a deeply introverted look, somber and—he thought—unusually mature. It made her seem older, no longer a girl. It made him wonder just how old she really was. It was as if in her features a thousand years had surfaced before him as he scrutinized her and pondered—and as she scrutinized and pondered the officer on the stage and the great information hologram behind him. What is she thinking? he wondered. Is she going to say something more? How can she be not afraid to speak up? We've been told we are under military law.

Major Casals said, "I am going to give you an instance of a strictly classified cluster of data. It deals with the Panther Engine." Behind him the hologram, surprisingly, became blank.

"Sir," one of the students said, "the hologram isn't showing anything."

"This is not an area that will be dealt with in your studies here," Major Casals said. "The Panther Engine is a two-rotor system, opposed rotors serving a common main shaft. Its main advantage is a total lack of centrifugal torque in the housing. A cam chain is thrown between the opposed rotors, which permits the main-shaft to reverse itself without hysteresis."

Behind him the big hologram remained blank. Strange, Bibleman thought. An eerie sensation: information without information, as if the computer has gone blind.

Major Casals said, "The College is forbidden to release any information about the Panther Engine. It cannot be programmed to do otherwise. In fact it knows nothing about the Panther Engine; it is programmed to destroy any information it receives in that sector."

Raising his hand a student said, "So even if someone fed information into the College about the Panther—"

"It would eject the data," Major Casals said.

"Is this a unique situation?" another student asked.

"No," Major Casals said.

"Then there're a number of areas we can't get print-outs for," a student murmured.

"Nothing of importance," Major Casals said. "At least as far as your studies are concerned."

The students were silent.

"The subjects which you will study," Major Casals said, "will be assigned to you, based on your aptitude and personality profiles. I'll call off your names and you will come forward for your allocation of topic assignment. The College itself has made the final decision for each of you, so you can be sure no error has been made."

What if I get proctology? Bibleman asked himself. In panic he thought, Or podiatry. Or herpetology. Or suppose the College in its infinite computeroid wisdom decides to ram into me all the information in the universe pertaining to or resembling herpes labialis . . . or things even worse. If there is anything worse.

"What you want," Mary said, as the names were read alphabetically, "is a program that'll earn you a living. You have to be practical. I know what I'll get; I know where my strong point lies. It'll be chemistry."

His name was called; rising, he walked up the aisle to Major Casals. They looked at each other, and then Casals handed him an unsealed envelope.

Stiffly, Bibleman returned to his seat.

"You want me to open it?" Mary said.

Wordlessly, Bibleman passed the envelope to her. She opened it and studied the printout.

"Can I earn a living with it?" he said.

She smiled. "Yes, it's a high-paying field. Almost as good as—well, let's just say that the colony planets are really in need of this. You could go to work anywhere."

Looking over her shoulder he saw the words on the page.

COSMOLOGY COSMOGONY PRE-SOCRATICS

"Pre-Socratic philosophy," Mary said. "Almost as good as structural engineering." She passed him the paper. "I shouldn't kid you. No, it's not really something you can make a living at, unless you teach . . . but maybe it interests you. Does it interest you?"

"No," he said, shortly.

"I wonder why the College picked it, then," Mary said.

"What the hell," he said, "is cosmogony?"

"How the universe came into being. Aren't you interested in how the universe—" She paused, eyeing him. "You certainly won't be asking for printouts of any classified material," she said meditatively. "Maybe that's it," she murmured, to herself. "They won't have to watchdog you."

"I can be trusted with classified material," he said.

"Can you? Do you know yourself? But you'll be getting into that when the College bombards you with early Greek thought. 'Know thyself.' Apollo's motto at Delphi. It sums up half of Greek philosophy."

Bibleman said, "I'm not going up before a military tribunal for making public classified military material." He thought, then, about the Panther Engine and he realized, fully realized, that a really grim message had been spelled out in that little lecture by Major Casals. "I wonder what Herbie the Hyena's motto is," he said.

" 'I am determined to prove a villain,' " Mary said. " 'And hate the idle pleasures of these days. Plots have I laid.' " She reached out to touch him on the arm. "Remember? The Herbie the Hyena cartoon version of *Richard the Third*."

"Mary Lorne," Major Casals said, reading off the list.

"Excuse me." She went up, returned with her envelope, smiling. "Leprology," she said to Bibleman.

"The study and treatment of leprosy. I'm kidding; it's chemistry."

"You'll be studying classified material," Bibleman said.

"Yes," she said. "I know."

On the first day of his study program Bob Bibleman set his College input-output terminal on AUDIO and punched the proper key for his coded course.

"Thales of Miletus," the terminal said. "The founder of the Ionian school of natural philosophy."

"What did he teach?" Bibleman said.

"That the world floated on water, was sustained by water and originated in water."

"That's really stupid," Bibleman said.

The College terminal said, "Thales based this on the discovery of fossil fish far inland, even at high altitudes. So it is not as stupid as it sounds." It showed on its holo-screen a great deal of written information, no part of which struck Bibleman as very interesting. Anyhow he had requested AUDIO. "It is generally considered that Thales was the first rational man in history," the terminal said.

"What about Ikhnaton?" Bibleman said.

"He was strange."

"Moses?"

"Likewise strange."

"Hammurabi?"

"How do you spell that?"

"I'm not sure. I've just heard the name."

"Then we will discuss Anaximander," the College terminal said. "And, in a cursory initial survey, Anaximenes, Xenophanes, Parmenides, Melissus—wait a minute; I forgot Heraclitus and Cratylus. And we will study Empedocles, Anaxagoras, Zeno—"

"Christ," Bibleman said.

"That's another program," the College terminal said.

"Just continue," Bibleman said.

"Are you taking notes?"

"That's my business."

"You seem to be in a state of conflict."

Bibleman said, "What happens to me if I flunk out of the College?"

"You go to jail."

"I'll take notes."

"Since you are so driven—"

"What?"

"Since you are so full of conflict, you should find Empedocles interesting. He was the first dialectical philosopher. Empedocles believed that the basis of reality was an antithetical conflict between the forces of Love and Strife. Under Love the whole cosmos is a duly proportioned mixture, called a krasis. This krasis is a spherical deity, a single perfect mind which spends all its time—"

"Is there any practical application to any of this?" Bibleman interrupted.

"The two antithetical forces of Love and Strife resemble the Taoist elements of Yang and Yin with their perpetual interaction from which all change takes place."

"Practical application."

"Twin mutually opposed constituents." On the holoscreen a schematic diagram, very complex, formed. "The two-rotor Panther Engine."

"What?" Bibleman said, sitting upright in his seat. He made out the large words PANTHER HYDRODRIVE SYSTEM TOP SECRET above the schematic comprising the readout. Instantly he pressed the PRINT key; the machinery of the terminal whirred and three sheets of paper slid down into the retrieve slot.

They overlooked it, Bibleman realized, this entry in the College's memory banks relating to the Panther Engine. Somehow the cross-referencing got lost. No one thought of pre-Socratic philosophy—who would expect an entry on an engine, a modern-day top-secret engine, under the category PHILOSOPHY, PRE-SOCRATIC subheading EMPEDOCLES?

I've got it in my hands, he said to himself as he swiftly lifted out the three sheets of paper. He folded them up and stuck them into the notebook the College had provided.

I've hit it, he thought. Right off the bat. Where the

hell am I going to put these schematics? Can't hide them in my locker. And then he thought, Have I committed a crime already, by asking for a written printout?

"Empedocles," the terminal was saying, "believed in four elements as being perpetually rearranged: earth, water, air and fire. These elements eternally—"

Click. Bibleman had shut the terminal down. The holoscreen faded to opaque gray.

Too much learning doth make a man slow, he thought as he got to his feet and started from the cubicle. Fast of wit but slow of foot. Where the hell am I going to hide the schematics? he asked himself again as he walked rapidly down the hall toward the ascent tube. Well, he realized, they don't know I have them; I can take my time. The thing to do is hide them at a random place, he decided, as the tube carried him to the surface. And even if they find them they won't be able to trace them back to me, not unless they go to the trouble of dusting for fingerprints.

This could be worth billions of dollars, he said to himself. A great joy filled him and then came the fear. He discovered that he was trembling. Will they ever be pissed, he said to himself. When they find out, *I* won't be pissing purple; *they'll* be pissing purple. The College itself will, when it discovers its error.

And the error, he thought, is on its part, not mine. The College fucked up and that's too bad.

In the dorm where his bunk was located he found a laundry room maintained by a silent robot staff, and when no robot was watching he hid the three pages of schematics near the bottom of a huge pile of bed sheets. As high as the ceiling, this pile. They won't get down to the schematics this year. I have plenty of time to decide what to do.

Looking at his watch he saw that the afternoon had almost come to an end. At five o'clock he would be seated in the cafeteria eating dinner with Mary.

She met him a little after five o'clock; her face showed signs of fatigue.

"How'd it go?" she said to him as they stood in line with their trays.

"Fine," Bibleman said.

"Did you get to Zeno? I always liked Zeno; he proved that motion is impossible. So I guess I'm still in my mother's womb. You look strange." She eyed him.

"Just sick of listening to how the earth rests on the back of a giant turtle."

"Or is suspended on a long string," Mary said. Together they made their way among the other students to an empty table. "You're not eating much."

"Feeling like eating," Bibleman said as he drank his cup of coffee, "is what got me here in the first place."

"You could flunk out."

"And go to jail."

Mary said, "The College is programmed to say that. Much of it is probably just threats. Talk loudly and carry a small stick, so to speak."

"I have it," Bibleman said.

"You have what?" She ceased eating and regarded him.

He said, "The Panther Engine."

Gazing at him, the girl was silent.

"The schematics," he said.

"Lower your goddamn voice."

"They missed a citation in the memory storage. Now that I have them I don't know what to do. Just start walking, probably. And hope no one stops me."

"They don't know? The College didn't self-monitor?"

"I have no reason to think it's aware of what it did."

"Jesus Christ," Mary said softly. "On your first day. You had better do a lot of slow, careful thinking."

"I can destroy them," he said.

"Or sell them."

He said, "I looked them over. There's an analysis on the final page. The Panther—"

"Just say *it*," Mary said.

"It can be used as a hydroelectric turbine and cut costs in half. I couldn't understand the technical language but I did figure out that. Cheap power source. Very cheap."

"So everyone would benefit."

He nodded.

"They really screwed up," Mary said. "What was it Casals told us? 'Even if someone fed data into the College about the—about it, the College would eject the data.'" She began eating slowly, meditatively. "And they're withholding it from the public. It must be industry pressure. Nice."

"What should I do?" Bibleman said.

"I can't tell you that."

"What I was thinking is that I could take the schematics to one of the colony planets where the authorities have less control. I could find an independent firm and make a deal with them. The government wouldn't know how—"

"They'd figure out where the schematics came from," Mary said. "They'd trace it back to you."

"Then I better burn them."

Mary said, "You have a very difficult decision to make. On the one hand you have classified information in your possession which you obtained illegally. On the other—"

"I didn't obtain it illegally. The College screwed up."

Calmly, she continued. "You broke the law, military law, when you asked for a written transcript. You should have reported the breach of security as soon as you discovered it. They would have rewarded you. Major Casals would have said nice things to you."

"I'm scared," Bibleman said, and he felt the fear moving around inside him, shifting about and growing; as he held his plastic coffee cup it shook, and some of the coffee spilled onto his uniform.

Mary, with a paper napkin, dabbed at the coffee stain.

"It won't come off," she said.

"Symbolism," Bibleman said. "Lady Macbeth. I always wanted to have a dog named Spot so I could say, 'Out, out, damned Spot.'"

"I am not going to tell you what to do," Mary said. "This is a decision that you will make alone. It isn't ethical for you even to discuss it with me; that could be considered conspiracy and put us both in prison."

"Prison," he echoed.

"You have it within your—Christ, I was going to say, 'You have it within your power to provide a cheap power source to human civilization.' " She laughed and shook her head. "I guess this scares me, too. Do what you think is right. If you think it's right to publish the schematics—"

"I never thought of that. Just publish them. Some magazine or newspaper. A slave printing construct could print it and distribute it all over the solar system in fifteen minutes." All I have to do, he realized, is pay the fee and then feed in the three pages of schematics. As simple as that. And then spend the rest of my life in jail or anyhow in court. Maybe the adjudication would go in my favor. There are precedents in history where vital classified material—military classified material—was stolen and published, and not only was the person found innocent but we now realize that he was a hero; he served the welfare of the human race itself, and risked his life.

Aproaching their table, two armed military security guards closed in on Bob Bibleman; he stared at them, not believing what he saw but thinking, *Believe it*.

"Student Bibleman?" one of them said.

"It's on my uniform," Bibleman said.

"Hold out your hands, Student Bibleman." The larger of the two security guards snapped handcuffs on him.

Mary said nothing; she continued slowly eating.

In Major Casals' office Bibleman waited, grasping the fact that he was being—as the technical term had it—"detained." He felt glum. He wondered what they would do. He wondered if he had been set up. He wondered what he would do if he were charged. He wondered why it was taking so long. And then he wondered what it was all about really and he wondered whether he would understand the grand issues if he continued with his courses in COSMOLOGY COSMOGONY PRESOCRATICS.

Entering the office, Major Casals said briskly, "Sorry to keep you waiting."

"Can these handcuffs be removed?" Bibleman said.

They hurt his wrists; they had been clapped on to him as tightly as possible. His bone structure ached.

"We couldn't find the schematics," Casals said, seating himself behind his desk.

"What schematics?"

"For the Panther Engine."

"There aren't supposed to be any schematics for the Panther Engine. You told us that in orientation."

"Did you program your terminal for that deliberately? Or did it just happen to come up?"

"My terminal programmed itself to talk about water," Bibleman said. "The universe is composed of water."

"It automatically notified security when you asked for a written transcript. All written transcripts are monitored."

"Fuck you," Bibleman said.

Major Casals said, "I tell you what. We're only interested in getting the schematics back; we're not interested in putting you in the slam. Return them and you won't be tried."

"Return what?" Bibleman said, but he knew it was a waste of time.

"Can I think it over?"

"Yes."

"Can I go? I feel like going to sleep. I'm tired. I feel like having these cuffs off."

Removing the cuffs, Major Casals said, "We made an agreement, with all of you, an agreement between the College and the students, about classified material. You entered into that agreement."

"Freely?" Bibleman said.

"Well, no. But the agreement was known to you. When you discovered the schematics for the Panther Engine encoded in the College's memory and available to anyone who happened for any reason, any reason whatsoever, to ask for a practical application of pre-Socratic—"

"I was as surprised as hell," Bibleman said. "I still am."

"Loyalty is an ethical principle. I'll tell you what; I'll waive the punishment factor and put it on the basis of loyalty to the College. A responsible person obeys laws and agreements entered into. Return the schematics and you can continue your courses here at the College. In fact we'll give you permission to select what subjects you want; they won't be assigned to you. I think you're good college material. Think it over and report back to me tomorrow morning, between eight and nine, here in my office. Don't talk to anyone; don't try to discuss it. You'll be watched. Don't try to leave the grounds. Okay?"

"Okay," Bibleman said, woodenly.

He dreamed that night that he had died. In his dream vast spaces stretched out, and his father was coming toward him, very slowly, out of a dark glade and into the sunlight. His father seemed glad to see him, and Bibleman felt his father's love.

When he awoke, the feeling of being loved by his father remained. As he put on his uniform he thought about his father and how rarely, in actual life, he had gotten that love. It made him feel lonely, now, his father being dead and his mother as well. Killed in a nuclear-power accident along with a whole lot of other people.

They say someone important to you waits for you on the other side, he thought. Maybe by the time I die Major Casals will be dead and he will be waiting for me, to greet me gladly. Major Casals and my father combined as one.

What am I going to do? he asked himself. They have waived the punitive aspects; it's reduced to essentials, a matter of loyalty. Am I a loyal person? Do I qualify?

The hell with it, he said to himself. He looked at his watch. Eight-thirty. My father would be proud of me, he thought. For what I am going to do.

Going into the laundry room he scoped out the situation. No robots in sight. He dug down in the pile of bed sheets, found the pages of schematics, took them out, looked them over and headed for the tube that would take him to Major Casals' office.

"You have them," Casals said, as Bibleman entered.

Bibleman handed the three sheets of paper over to him.

"And you made no other copies?" Casals asked.

"No."

"You give me your word of honor?"

"Yes," Bibleman said.

"You are herewith expelled from the College," Major Casals said.

"What?" Bibleman said.

Casals pressed a button on his desk. "Come in."

The door opened and Mary Lorne stood there.

"I do not represent the College," Major Casals said to Bibleman. "You were set up."

"I am the College," Mary said.

Major Casals said, "Sit down, Bibleman. She will explain it to you before you leave."

"I failed?" Bibleman said.

"You failed me," Mary said. "The purpose of the test was to teach you to stand on your own feet even if it meant challenging authority. The covert message of institutions is, 'Submit to that which you psychologically construe as an authority.' A good school trains the whole person; it isn't a matter of data and information; I was trying to make you morally and psychologically complete. But a person can't be commanded to disobey. You can't order someone to rebel. All I could do was give you a model, an example."

Bibleman thought — when she talked back to Casals at the initial orientation. He felt numb.

"The Panther Engine is worthless," Mary said, "as a technological artifact. This is a standard test we use on each student, no matter what study course he is assigned."

"They *all* got a readout on the Panther Engine?" Bibleman said with disbelief. He stared at the girl.

"They will, one by one. Yours came very quickly. First you are told that it is classified; you are told the penalty for releasing classified information; then you are leaked the information. It is hoped that you will make it public or at least try to make it public."

Major Casals said, "You saw on the third page of the printout that the engine supplied an economical source of hydroelectric power. That was important. You knew that the public would benefit if the engine design was released."

"And legal penalties were waived," Mary said. "So what you did was not done out of fear."

"Loyalty," Bibleman said. "I did it out of loyalty."

"To what?" Mary said.

He was silent; he could not think.

"To a holo-screen?" Major Casals said.

"To you," Bibleman said.

Major Casals said, "I am someone who insulted you and derided you. Someone who treated you like dirt. I told you that if I ordered you to piss purple you—"

"Okay," Bibleman said. "Enough."

"Goodbye," Mary said.

"What?" Bibleman said, startled.

"You're leaving. You're going back to your life and job, what you had before we picked you."

Bibleman said, "I'd like another chance."

"But," Mary said, "you know how the test works, now. So it can never be given to you again. You know what is really wanted from you by the College. I'm sorry."

"I'm sorry, too," Major Casals said.

Bibleman said nothing.

Holding out her hand, Mary said, "Shake?"

Blindly, Bibleman shook hands with her. Major Casals only stared at him blankly; he did not offer his hand. He seemed to be engrossed in some other topic, perhaps some other person. Another student was on his mind, perhaps. Bibleman could not tell.

Three nights later, as he wandered aimlessly through the mixture of lights and darkness of the city, Bob Bibleman saw ahead of him a robot food vendor at its eternal post. A teenage boy was in the process of buying a taco and an apple turnover. Bob Bibleman lined up behind the boy and stood waiting, his hands in his pockets, no thoughts coming to him, only a dull feeling, a sense of emptiness. As if the inattention which he had seen on Casals' face had taken him over, he thought to himself. He felt like an object, an object among objects, like the robot vendor. Something which, as he well knew, did not look you directly in the eye.

"What'll it be, sir?" the robot asked.

Bibleman said, "Fries, a cheeseburger and a strawberry shake. Are there any contests?"

After a pause the robot said, "Not for you, Mr. Bibleman."

"Okay," he said, and stood waiting.

The food came, on its little throwaway plastic tray, in its little throwaway cartons.

"I'm not paying," Bibleman said, and walked away.

The robot called after him, "Nine hundred dollars, Mr. Bibleman. You're breaking the law."

He turned, got out his wallet.

"Thank you, Mr. Bibleman," the robot said. "I am very proud of you."

Options

John Varley

If we had one purely sociological change in the seventies, it was the feminist movement with its challenges to "traditional" gender-roles. John Varley, probably the major new sf writer of that decade, wrote many stories about a future in which sex changes are commonplace and categorization-by-sex is outmoded—but perhaps this change seemed too facile. What of the transition period, when such changes wouldn't be the norm and people would have to wonder about the advisability of upsetting thousands of years of tradition?

In "Options," a logical and moving novelette, Varley comes to grips with such questions. The answers aren't easy, but you'll remember them long after you've finished reading the story.

Cleo hated breakfast.

Her energy level was lowest in the morning, but not so the children's. There was always some school crisis, something that had to be located at the last minute, some argument that had to be settled.

This morning it was a bowl of cereal spilled in Lilli's lap. Cleo hadn't seen it happen; her attention had been diverted momentarily by Feather, her youngest.

And of course it had to happen *after* Lilli was dressed.

"Mom, this was the *last* outfit I *had*."

"Well, if you wouldn't use them so hard they might last more than three days, and if you didn't . . ." She stopped before she lost her temper. "Just take it off and go as you are."

"But Mom, nobody goes to school naked. *No*body. Give me some money and I'll stop at the store on—"

Cleo raised her voice, something she tried never to do. "Child, I know there are kids in your class whose parents can't afford to buy clothes at all."

"All right, so the poor kids don't—"

"That's enough. You're late already. Get going."

Lilli stalked from the room. Cleo heard the door slam.

Through it all Jules was an island of calm at the other end of the table, his nose in his newspad, sipping his second cup of coffee. Cleo glanced at her own bacon and eggs cooling on the plate, poured herself a first cup of coffee, then had to get up and help Paul find his other shoe.

By then Feather was wet again, so she put her on the table and peeled off the sopping diaper.

"Hey, listen to this," Jules said. " 'The City Council today passed without objection an ordinance requiring—' "

"Jules, aren't you a little behind schedule?"

He glanced at his thumbnail. "You're right. Thanks." He finished his coffee, folded his newspad and tucked it under his arm, bent over to kiss her, then frowned.

"You really ought to eat more, honey," he said, indicating the untouched eggs. "Eating for two, you know. 'By, now."

"Good-by," Cleo said, through clenched teeth. "And if I hear that 'eating for two' business again, I'll . . ." But he was gone.

She had time to scorch her lip on the coffee, then was out the door, hurrying to catch the train.

There were seats on the sun car, but of course Feather was with her and the UV wasn't good for her tender skin. After a longing look at the passengers reclining with the dark cups strapped over their eyes—and a rueful glance down at her own pale skin—Cleo boarded the next car and found a seat by a large man wearing a hardhat. She settled down in the cushions, adjusted the straps on the carrier slung in front of her, and let Feather have a nipple. She unfolded her newspad and spread it out in her lap.

"Cute," the man said. "How old is he?"

"She," Cleo said, without looking up. "Eleven days." And five hours and thirty-six minutes . . .

She shifted in the seat, pointedly turning her shoulder to him, and made a show of activating her newspad and scanning the day's contents. She did not glance up as the train left the underground tunnel and emerged on the gently rolling, airless plain of Mendeleev. There was little enough out there to interest her, considering she made the forty-minute commute run to Hartman crater twice a day. They had discussed moving to Hartman, but Jules liked living in King City near his work, and of course the kids would have missed all their school friends.

There wasn't much in the news storage that morning. She queried when the red light flashed for an update. The pad printed some routine city business. Three sentences into the story she punched the reject key.

There was an Invasion Centennial parade listed for 1900 hours that evening. Parades bored her, and so did the Centennial. If you've heard one speech about how liberation of Earth is just around the corner if we all pull together, you've heard them all. Semantic content zero, bullshit quotient high.

She glanced wistfully at sports, noting that the J Sector jumpball team was doing poorly in the intracity tournament without her. Cleo's small stature and powerful legs had served her well as a starting sprint-wing in her playing days, but it just didn't seem possible to make practices any more.

As a last resort, she called up the articles, digests, and analysis listings, the newspad's *Sunday Supplement* and Op-Ed department. A title caught her eye, and she punched it up.

Changing: The Revolution in Roles
(Or, Who Do You Fuck, and Who Fucks You?)

Twenty years ago, when cheap and easy sex changes first became available to the general public, it was seen as the beginning of a revolution that would change the shape of human society in ways impossible to foresee. Sexual equality is one thing, the sociologists pointed out, but certain residual inequities—based on biological imperatives or on upbringing, depending on your politics—have proved impossible to weed out. Changing was going to end all that. Men and women would be able to see what it was like from the other side of the barrier that divides humanity. How could sex roles survive that?

Ten years later the answer was obvious. Changing had appealed to only a tiny minority. It was soon seen as a harmless aberration, practiced by only 1 per cent of the population. Everyone promptly forgot about the tumbling of barriers.

But in the intervening ten years a quieter revolution has been building. Almost unnoticed on the broad scale because it is an invisible phenomenon (how do you know the next woman you meet was not a man last week?), changing has been gaining growing, matter-of-fact acceptance among the children of the generation that rejected it. The chances are now better than even that you know someone who has had at least one sex change. The chances are better than one out of fifteen that you yourself have changed; if you are under twenty, the chance is one in three.

The article went on to describe the underground society which was springing up around changing. Changers tended to band together, frequenting their own taprooms, staging their own social events, remaining aloof from the larger society which many of them saw as outmoded and irrelevant. Changers tended to marry other changers. They divided the childbearing equally, each preferring to mother only one child. The author viewed this tendency with alarm, since it went against the socially approved custom of large families. Changers retorted that the time for that was past, pointing out that Luna had been tamed long ago. They quoted statistics proving that at present rates of expansion, Luna's population would be in the billions in an amazingly short time.

There were interviews with changers, and psychological profiles. Cleo read that the males had originally been the heaviest users of the new technology, stating sexual reasons for their decision, and the change had often been permanent. Today, the changer was slightly more likely to have been born female, and to give social reasons, the most common of which was pressure to bear children. But the modern changer committed him/herself to neither role. The average time between changes in an individual was two years, and declining.

Cleo read the whole article, then thought about using some of the reading references at the end. Not that much of it was really new to her. She had been aware of changing, without thinking about it much. The idea had never attracted her, and Jules was against it. But for some reason it had struck a chord this morning.

Feather had gone to sleep. Cleo carefully pulled the blanket down around the child's face, then wiped milk from her nipple. She folded her newspad and stowed it in her purse, then rested her chin on her palm and looked out the window for the rest of the trip.

Cleo was chief on-site architect for the new Food Systems, Inc., plantation that was going down in Hartman. As such, she was in charge of three junior architects, five construction bosses, and an army of drafters and workers. It was a big project, the biggest Cleo had ever handled.

She liked her work, but the best part had always been being there on the site when things were happening, actually supervising construction instead of running a desk. That had been difficult in the last months of carrying Feather, but at least there were maternity pressure suits. It was even harder now.

She had been through it all before, with Lilli and Paul. Everybody works. That had been the rule for a century, since the Invasion. There was no labor to spare for baby-sitters, so having children meant the mother or father must do the same job they had been doing before, but do it while taking care of the child. In practice, it was usually the mother, since she had the milk.

Cleo had tried leaving Feather with one of the women in the office, but each had her own work to do, and not unreasonably felt Cleo should bear the burden of her own offspring. And Feather never seemed to respond well to another person. Cleo would return from her visit to the site to find the child had been crying the whole time, disrupting everyone's work. She had taken Feather in a crawler a few times, but it wasn't the same.

That morning was taken up with a meeting. Cleo and the other section chiefs sat around the big table for three hours, discussing ways of dealing with the cost overrun, then broke for lunch only to return to the problem in the afternoon. Cleo's back was aching and she had a headache she couldn't shake, so Feather chose that day to be cranky. After ten minutes of increasingly hostile looks, Cleo had to retire to the booth with Leah Farnham, the accountant, and her three-year-old son, Eddie. The two of them followed the proceedings through earphones while trying to cope with their children and make their remarks through throat mikes. Half the people at the conference table either had to turn around when she spoke, or ignore her, and Cleo was hesitant to force them to that choice. As a result, she chose her remarks with extreme care. More often, she said nothing.

There was something at the core of the world of business that refused to adjust to children in the board room, while appearing to make every effort to accommodate the working mother. Cleo brooded about it, not for the first time.

But what did she want? Honestly, she could not see what else could be done. It certainly wasn't fair to disrupt the entire meeting with a crying baby. She wished she knew the answer. Those were her friends out there, yet her feeling of alienation was intense, staring through the glass wall that Eddie was smudging with his dirty fingers.

Luckily, Feather was a perfect angel on the trip home. She gurgled and smiled toothlessly at a woman who had stopped to admire her, and Cleo warmed to the infant for the first time that day. She spent the trip playing hand games with her, surrounded by the approving smiles of other passengers.

"Jules, I read the most interesting article on the pad this morning." There, it was out, anyway. She had decided the direct approach would be best.

"Hmm?"

"It was about changing. It's getting more and more popular."

"Is that so?" He did not look up from his book.

Jules and Cleo were in the habit of sitting up in bed for a few hours after the children were asleep. They spurned the video programs that were designed to lull workers after a hard day, preferring to use the time to catch up on reading, or to talk if either of them had anything to say. Over the last few years, they had read more and talked less.

Cleo reached over Feather's crib and got a packet of dopesticks. She flicked one to light with her thumbnail, drew on it, and exhaled a cloud of lavender smoke. She drew her legs up under her and leaned back against the wall.

"I just thought we might talk about it. That's all."

Jules put his book down. "All right. But what's to talk about? We're not into that."

She shrugged and picked at a cuticle. "I know. We did talk about it, way back. I just wondered if you still felt the same, I guess." She offered him the stick and he took a drag.

"As far as I know, I do," he said easily. "It's not something I spend a great deal of thought on. What's the matter?" He looked at her suspiciously. "You weren't having any thoughts in that direction, were you?"

"Well, no, not exactly. No. But you really ought to

read the article. More people are doing it. I just thought we ought to be aware of it."

"Yeah, I've heard that," Jules conceded. He laced his hands behind his head. "No way to tell unless you've worked with them and suddenly one day they've got a new set of equipment." He laughed. "First time it was sort of hard for me to get used to. Now I hardly think about it."

"Me, either."

"They don't cause any problem," Jules said with an air of finality. "Live and let live."

"Yeah." Cleo smoked in silence for a time and let Jules get back to his reading, but she still felt uncomfortable. "Jules?"

"What is it now?"

"Don't you ever wonder what it would be like?"

He sighed and closed his book, then turned to face her.

"I don't quite understand you tonight," he said.

"Well, maybe I don't either, but we could talk—"

"Listen. Have you thought about what it would do to the kids? I mean, even if I was willing to seriously consider it, which I'm not."

"I talked to Lilli about that. Just theoretically, you understand. She said she has two teachers who change, and one of her best friends used to be a boy. There's quite a few kids at school who've changed. She takes it in stride."

"Yes, but she's older. What about Paul? What would it do to his concept of himself as a young man? I'll tell you, Cleo, in the back of my mind I keep thinking this business is a little sick. I feel it would have a bad effect on the children."

"Not according to—"

"Cleo, Cleo. Let's not get into an argument. Number one, I have no intention of getting a change, now or in the future. Two, if only one of us was changed, it would sure play hell with our sex life, wouldn't it? And three, I like you too much as you are." He leaned over and began to kiss her.

She was more than a little annoyed, but said nothing

as his kisses became more intense. It was a damnably effective way of shutting off debate. And she could not stay angry: she was responding in spite of herself, easily, naturally.

It was as good as it always was with Jules. The ceiling, so familiar, once again became a calming blankness that absorbed her thoughts.

No, she had no complaints about being female, no sexual dissatisfactions. It was nothing as simple as that.

Afterward she lay on her side with her legs drawn up, her knees together. She faced Jules, who absently stroked her leg with one hand. Her eyes were closed, but she was not sleepy. She was savoring the warmth she cherished so much after sex; the slipperiness between her legs, holding his semen inside.

She felt the bed move as he shifted his weight.

"You did make it, didn't you?"

She opened one eye enough to squint at him.

"Of course I did. I always do. You know I never have any trouble in that direction."

He relaxed back onto the pillow. "I'm sorry for . . . well, for springing on you like that."

"It's okay. It was nice."

"I had just thought you might have been . . . faking it. I'm not sure why I would think that."

She opened the other eye and patted him gently on the cheek.

"Jules, I'd never be that protective of your poor ego. If you don't satisfy me, I promise you'll be the second to know."

He chuckled, then turned on his side to kiss her.

"Good night, babe."

"G'night."

She loved him. He loved her. Their sex life was good—with the slight mental reservation that he always seemed to initiate it—and she was happy with her body.

So why was she still awake three hours later?

Shopping took a few hours on the vidphone Saturday morning. Cleo bought the household necessities for delivery that afternoon, then left the house to do the shopping she fancied: going from store to store, looking at things she didn't really need.

Feather was with Jules on Saturdays. She savored a quiet lunch alone at a table in the park plaza, then found herself walking down Brazil Avenue in the heart of the medical district. On impulse, she stepped into the New Heredity Body Salon.

It was only after she was inside that she admitted to herself she had spent most of the morning arranging for the impulse.

She was on edge as she was taken down a hallway to a consulting room, and had to force a smile for the handsome young man behind the desk. She sat, put her packages on the floor, and folded her hands in her lap. He asked what he could do for her.

"I'm not actually here for any work," she said. "I wanted to look into the costs, and maybe learn a little more about the procedures involved in changing."

He nodded understandingly, and got up.

"There's no charge for the initial consultation," he said. "We're happy to answer your questions. By the way, I'm Marion, spelled with an 'O' this month." He smiled at her and motioned for her to follow him. He stood her in front of a full-length mirror mounted on the wall.

"I know it's hard to make that first step. It was hard for me, and I do it for a living. So we've arranged this demonstration that won't cost you anything, either in money or worry. It's a nonthreatening way to see some of what it's all about, but it might startle you a little, so be prepared." He touched a button in the wall beside the mirror, and Cleo saw her clothes fade away. She realized it was not really a mirror, but a holographic screen linked to a computer.

The computer introduced changes in the image. In thirty seconds she faced a male stranger. There was no doubt the face was her own, but it was more angular, perhaps a little larger in its underlying bony structure. The skin on the stranger's jaw was rough, as if it needed shaving.

The rest of the body was as she might expect, though

overly muscled for her tastes. She did little more than glance at the penis; somehow that didn't seem to matter so much. She spent more time studying the hair on the chest, the tiny nipples, and the ridges that had appeared on the hands and feet. The image mimicked her every movement.

"Why all the brawn?" she asked Marion. "If you're trying to sell me on this, you've taken the wrong approach."

Marion punched some more buttons. "I didn't choose this image," he explained. "The computer takes what it sees, and extrapolates. You're more muscular than the average woman. You probably exercise. This is what a comparable amount of training would have produced with male hormones to fix nitrogen in the muscles. But we're not bound by that."

The image lost about eight kilos of mass, mostly in the shoulders and thighs. Cleo felt a little more comfortable, but still missed the smoothness she was accustomed to seeing in her mirror.

She turned from the display and went back to her chair. Marion sat across from her and folded his hands on the desk.

"Basically, what we do is produce a cloned body from one of your own cells. Through a process called Y-Recombinant Viral Substitution we remove one of your X chromosomes and replace it with a Y.

"The clone is forced to maturity in the usual way, which takes about six months. After that, it's just a simple non-rejection-hazard brain transplant. You walk in as a woman, and leave an hour later as a man. Easy as that."

Cleo said nothing, wondering again what she was doing here.

"From there we can modify the body. We can make you taller or shorter, rearrange your face, virtually anything you like." He raised his eyebrows, then smiled ruefully and spread his hands.

"All right, Ms. King," he said. "I'm not trying to pressure you. You'll need to think about it. In the meantime, there's a process that would cost you very little, and might be just the thing to let you test the waters. Am I right in thinking your husband opposes this?"

She nodded, and he looked sympathetic.

"Not uncommon, not uncommon at all," he assured her. "It brings out castration fears in men who didn't even suspect they had them. Of course, we do nothing of the sort. His male body would be kept in a tank, ready for him to move back whenever he wanted to."

Cleo shifted in her chair. "What was this process you were talking about?"

"Just a bit of minor surgery. It can be done in ten minutes, and corrected in the same time before you even leave the office if you find you don't care for it. It's a good way to get husbands thinking about changing; sort of a signal you can send him. You've heard of the androgenous look. It's in all the fashion tapes. Many women, especially if they have large breasts like you do, find it an interesting change."

"You say it's cheap? And reversible?"

"All our processes are reversible. Changing the size or shapes of breasts is our most common body operation."

Cleo sat on the examining table while the attendant gave her a quick physical.

"I don't know if Marion realized you're nursing," the woman said. "Are you sure this is what you want?"

How the hell should I know? Cleo thought. She wished the feeling of confusion and uncertainty would pass.

"Just do it."

Jules hated it.

He didn't yell or slam doors or storm out of the house; that had never been his style. He voiced his objections coldly and quietly at the dinner table, after saying practically nothing since she walked in the door.

"I just would like to know why you thought you should do this without even talking to me about it. I don't demand that you *ask* me, just discuss it with me."

Cleo felt miserable, but was determined not to let it show. She held Feather in her arm, the bottle in her other hand, and ignored the food cooling on her plate. She was hungry but at least she was not eating for two.

"Jules, I'd ask you before I rearranged the furniture. We both own this apartment. I'd ask you before I put Lilli or Paul in another school. We share the responsibility for their upbringing. But I don't ask you when I put on lipstick or cut my hair. It's my body."

"I like it, Mom," Lilli said. "You look like me."

Cleo smiled at her, reached over and tousled her hair.

"What do you like?" Paul asked, around a mouthful of food.

"See?" said Cleo. "It's not that important."

"I don't see how you can say that. And I said you didn't have to ask me. I just would . . . you should have . . . I should have *known*."

"It was an impulse, Jules."

"An impulse. An *impulse*." For the first time, he raised his voice, and Cleo knew how upset he really was. Lilli and Paul fell silent, and even Feather squirmed.

But Cleo liked it. Oh, not forever and ever: as an interesting change. It gave her a feeling of freedom to be that much in control of her body, to be able to decide how large she wished her breasts to be. Did it have anything to do with changing? She really didn't think so. She didn't feel the least bit like a man.

And what was a breast, anyway? It was anything from a nipple sitting flush with the rib cage to a mammoth hunk of fat and milk gland. Cleo realized Jules was suffering from the more-is-better syndrome, thinking of Cleo's action as the removal of her breasts, as if they had to be large to exist at all. What she had actually done was reduce their size.

No more was said at the table, but Cleo knew it was for the children's sake. As soon as they got into bed, she could feel the tension again.

"I can't understand why you did it *now*. What about Feather?"

"What about her?"

"Well, do you expect me to nurse her?"

Cleo finally got angry. "Damn it, that's *exactly* what

I expect you to do. Don't tell me you don't know what I'm talking about. You think it's all fun and games, having to carry a child around all day because she needs the milk in your breasts?"

"You never complained before."

"I . . ." She stopped. He was right, of course. It amazed even Cleo that this had all come up so suddenly, but here it was, and she had to deal with it. *They* had to deal with it.

"That's because it isn't an awful thing. It's great to nourish another human being at your breast. I loved every minute of it with Lilli. Sometimes it was a headache, having her there all the time, but it was worth it. The same with Paul." She sighed. "The same with Feather, too, most of the time. You hardly think about it."

"Then why the revolt now? With no warning?"

"It's not a revolt, honey. Do you see it as that? I just . . . I'd like you to try it. Take Feather for a few months. Take her to work like I do. Then you'd . . . you'd see a little of what I go through." She rolled on her side and playfully punched his arm, trying to lighten it in some way. "You might even like it. It feels real good."

He snorted. "I'd feel silly."

She jumped from the bed and paced toward the living room, then turned, more angry than ever. "Silly? Nursing is silly? Breasts are silly? Then why the hell do you wonder why I did what I did?"

"Being a *man* is what makes it silly," he retorted. "It doesn't look right. I almost laugh every time I see a man with breasts. The hormones mess up your system, I heard, and—"

"That's *not true!* Not any more. You can lactate—"

"—and besides, it's my body, as you pointed out. I'll do with it what pleases me."

She sat on the edge of the bed with her back to him. He reached out and stroked her, but she moved away.

"All right," she said. "I was just suggesting it. I thought you might like to try it. *I'm* not going to nurse her. She goes on the bottle from now on."

"If that's the way it has to be."

"It is. I want you to start taking Feather to work with you. Since she's going to be a bottle baby, it hardly matters which of us cares for her. I think you owe it to me, since I carried the burden alone with Lilli and Paul."

"All right."

She got into bed and pulled the covers up around her, her back to him. She didn't want him to see how close she was to tears.

But the feeling passed. The tension drained from her, and she felt good. She thought she had won a victory, and it was worth the cost. Jules would not stay angry at her.

She fell asleep easily, but woke up several times during the night as Jules tossed and turned.

He did adjust to it. It was impossible for him to say so all at once, but after a week without love-making he admitted grudgingly that she looked good. He began to touch her in the mornings and when they kissed after getting home from work. Jules had always admired her slim muscularity, her athlete's arms and legs. The slim chest looked so natural on her, it fit the rest of her so well that he began to wonder what all the fuss had been about.

One night while they were clearing the dinner dishes, Jules touched her nipples for the first time in a week. He asked her if it felt any different.

"There is very little feeling anywhere but the nipples," she pointed out, "no matter how big a woman is. You know that."

"Yeah, I guess I do."

She knew they would make love that night and determined it would be on her terms.

She spent a long time in the bathroom, letting him get settled with his book, then came out and took it away. She got on top of him and pressed close, kissing and tickling his nipples with her fingers.

She was aggressive and insistent. At first he seemed reluctant, but soon he was responding as she pressed her lips hard against his, forcing his head back into the pillow.

"I love you," he said, and raised his head to kiss her nose. "Are you ready?"

"I'm ready." He put his arms around her and held her close, then rolled over and hovered above her.

"Jules. *Jules.* Stop it." She squirmed onto her side, her legs held firmly together.

"What's wrong?"

"I want to be on top tonight."

"Oh. All right." He turned over again and reclined passively as she repositioned herself. Her heart was pounding. There had been no reason to think he would object—they had made love in any and all positions, but basically the exotic ones were a change of pace from the "natural" one with her on her back. Tonight she had wanted to feel in control.

"Open your legs, darling," she said, with a smile. He did, but didn't return the smile. She raised herself on her hands and knees and prepared for the tricky insertion.

"Cleo."

"What is it? This will take a little effort, but I think I can make it worth your while, so if you'd just—"

"Cleo, what the hell is the purpose of this?"

She stopped dead and let her head sag between her shoulders.

"What's the matter? Are you feeling silly with your feet in the air?"

"Maybe. Is that what you wanted?"

"Jules, humiliating you was the farthest thing from my mind."

"Then what *was* on your mind? It's not like we've never done it this way before. It's—"

"Only when *you* chose to do so. It's always your decision."

"It's not degrading to be on the bottom."

"Then why were you feeling silly?"

He didn't answer, and she wearily lifted herself away from him, sitting on her knees at his feet. She waited, but he didn't seem to want to talk about it.

"I've never complained about that position," she ventured. "I don't *have* any complaints about it. It works pretty well." Still he said nothing. "All right. I wanted to see what it looked like from up there. I was tired of looking at the ceiling. I was curious."

"And *that's* why I felt *silly*. I never minded you being on top before, have I? But before . . . well, it's never been in the context of the last couple weeks. I *know* what's on your mind."

"And you feel threatened by it. By the fact that I'm curious about changing, that I want to know what it's like to take charge. You know I can't—and wouldn't if I could—force a change on you."

"But your curiosity is wrecking our marriage."

She felt like crying again, but didn't let it show except for a trembling of her lower lip. She didn't want him to try and soothe her; that was all too likely to work, and she would find herself on her back with her legs in the air. She looked down at the bed and nodded slowly, then got up. She went to the mirror and took the brush, began running it through her hair.

"What are you doing now? Can't we talk about this?"

"I don't feel much like talking right now." She leaned forward and examined her face as she brushed, then dabbed at the corners of her eyes with a tissue. "I'm going out. I'm still curious."

He said nothing as she started for the door.

"I may be a little late."

The place was called Oophyte. The capital "O" had a plus sign hanging from it, and an arrow in the upper right side. The sign was built so that the symbols revolved; one moment the plus was inside and the arrow out, the next moment the reverse.

Cleo moved in a pleasant haze across the crowded dance floor, pausing now and then to draw on her dope-stick. The air in the room was thick with lavender smoke, illuminated by flashing blue lights. She danced when the mood took her. The music was so loud that she didn't have to think about it; the noise gripped her bones and animated her arms and legs. She glided through a forest of naked skin, feeling the occasional roughness of a paper suit and, rarely, expensive cotton clothing. It was like moving underwater, like wading through molasses.

She saw him across the floor and began moving in his direction. He took no notice of her for some time, though she danced right in front of him. Few of the dancers had partners in more than the transitory sense. Some were celebrating life, others were displaying themselves, but all were looking for partners, so eventually he realized she had been there an unusual length of time. He was easily as stoned as she was.

She told him what she wanted.

"Sure. Where do you want to go? Your place?"

She took him down the hall in back and touched her credit bracelet to the lock on one of the doors. The room was simple, but clean.

He looked a lot like her phantom twin in the mirror, she noted with one part of her mind. It was probably why she had chosen him. She embraced him and lowered him gently to the bed.

"Do you want to exchange names?" he asked. The grin on his face kept getting sillier as she toyed with him.

"I don't care. Mostly I think I want to use you."

"Use away. My name's Saffron."

"I'm Cleopatra. Would you get on your back, please?"

He did, and they did. It was hot in the little room, but neither of them minded it. It was healthy exertion, the physical sensations were great, and when Cleo was through she had learned nothing. She collapsed on top of him. He did not seem surprised when tears began falling on his shoulder.

"I'm sorry," she said, sitting up and getting ready to leave.

"Don't go," he said, putting his hand on her shoulder. "Now that you've got that out of your system, maybe we can make love."

She didn't want to smile, but she had to, then she was crying harder, putting her face to his chest and feeling the warmth of his arms around her and the hair tickling her nose. She realized what she was doing, and tried to pull away.

"For God's sake, don't be ashamed that you need someone to cry on."

"It's weak. I . . . I just didn't want to be weak."

"We're all weak."

She gave up struggling and nestled there until the tears stopped. She sniffed, wiped her nose, and faced him.

"What's it like? Can you tell me?" She was about to explain what she meant, but he seemed to understand.

"It's like . . . nothing special."

"You were born female, weren't you? I mean, you . . . I thought I might be able to tell."

"It's no longer important how I was born. I've been both. It's still me, on the inside. You understand?"

"I'm not sure I do."

They were quiet for a long time. Cleo thought of a thousand things to say, questions to ask, but could do nothing.

"You've been coming to a decision, haven't you?" he said, at last. "Are you any closer after tonight?"

"I'm not sure."

"It's not going to solve any problems, you know. It might even create some."

She pulled away from him and got up. She shook her hair and wished for a comb.

"Thank you, Cleopatra," he said.

"Oh. Uh, thank you . . ." She had forgotten his name. She smiled again to cover her embarrassment, and shut the door behind her.

"Hello?"

"Yes. This is Cleopatra King. I had a consultation with one of your staff. I believe it was ten days ago."

"Yes, Ms. King. I have your file. What can I do for you?"

She took a deep breath. "I want you to start the clone. I left a tissue sample."

"Very well, Ms. King. Did you have any instructions concerning the chromosome donor?"

"Do you need consent?"

"Not as long as there's a sample in the bank."

"Use my husband, Jules La Rhin. Security number 4454390."

"Very good. We'll be in contact with you."

Cleo hung up the phone and rested her forehead against the cool metal. She should never get this stoned, she realized. What had she done?

But it was not final. It would be six months before she had to decide if she would ever use the clone. Damn Jules. Why did he have to make such a big thing of it?

Jules did *not* make a big thing of it when she told him what she had done. He took it quietly and calmly, as if he had been expecting it.

"You know I won't follow you in this?"

"I know you feel that way. I'm interested to see if you change your mind."

"Don't count on it. I want to see if you change yours."

"I haven't *made up* my mind. But I'm giving myself the option."

"All I ask is that you bear in mind what this could do to our relationship. I love you, Cleo. I don't think that will ever change. But if you walk into this house as a man, I don't think I'll be able to see you as the person I've always loved."

"You could if you were a woman."

"But I won't be."

"And I'll be the same person I always was." But would she be? What the hell was *wrong?* What had Jules ever done that he should deserve this? She made up her mind never to go through with it, and they made love that night and it was very, very good.

But somehow she never got around to calling the vivarium and telling them to abort the clone. She made the decision not to go through with it a dozen times over the next six months, and never had the clone destroyed.

Their relationship in bed became uneasy as time passed. At first, it was good. Jules made no objections when she initiated sex, and was willing to do it any way she preferred. Once that was accomplished she no longer cared whether she was on top or underneath. The important thing had been having the option of making love when she wanted to, the way she wanted to.

"That's what this is all about," she told him one night, in a moment of clarity when everything seemed to make sense except his refusal to see things from her side. "It's the option I want. I'm not unhappy being female. I don't like the feeling that there's *anything* I *can't* be. I want to know how much of me is hormones, how much is genetics, how much is upbringing. I want to know if I feel more secure being aggressive as a man, because I sure don't, most of the time, as a woman. Or do men feel the same insecurities I feel? Would Cleo the man feel free to cry? I don't know any of those things."

"But you said it yourself. You'll still be the same person."

They began to drift apart in small ways. A few weeks after her outing to the Oophyte she returned home one Sunday afternoon to find him in bed with a woman. It was not like him to do it like that; their custom had been to bring lovers home and introduce them, to keep it friendly and open. Cleo was amused, because she saw it as his way of getting back at her for her trip to the encounter bar.

So she was the perfect hostess, joining them in bed, which seemed to disconcert Jules. The woman's name was Harriet, and Cleo found herself liking her. She was a changer—something Jules had not known or he certainly would not have chosen her to make Cleo feel bad. Harriet was uncomfortable when she realized why she was there. Cleo managed to put her at ease by making love to her, something that surprised Cleo a little and Jules considerably, since she had never done it before.

Cleo enjoyed it; she found Harriet's smooth body to be a whole new world. And she felt she had neatly turned the tables on Jules, making him confront once more the idea of his wife in the man's role.

The worst part was the children. They had discussed the possible impending change with Lilli and Paul.

Lilli could not see what all the fuss was about; it was a part of her life, something that was all around her which she took for granted as something she herself would do when she was old enough. But when she began picking up the concern from her father, she drew subtly closer to her mother. Cleo was tremendously relieved. She didn't think she could have held to it in the face of Lilli's displeasure. Lilli was her first born, and though she hated to admit it and did her best not to play favorites, her darling. She had taken a year's leave from her job at appalling expense to the household budget so she could devote all her time to her infant daughter. She often wished she could somehow return to those simpler days, when motherhood had been her whole life.

Feather, of course, was not consulted. Jules had assumed the responsibility for her nurture without complaint, and seemed to be enjoying it. It was fine with Cleo, though it maddened her that he was so willing about taking over the mothering role without being willing to try it as a female. Cleo loved Feather as much as the other two, but sometimes had trouble recalling why they had decided to have her. She felt she had gotten the procreation impulse out of her system with Paul, and yet there Feather was.

Paul was the problem.

Things could get tense when Paul expressed doubts about how he would feel if his mother were to become a man. Jules's face would darken, and he might not speak for days. When he did speak, often in the middle of the night when neither of them could sleep, it would be in a verbal explosion that was as close to violence as she had ever seen him.

It frightened her, because she was by no means sure of herself when it came to Paul. Would it hurt him? Jules spoke of gender identity crises, of the need for stable role models, and finally, in naked honesty, of the fear that his son would grow up to be somehow less than a man.

Cleo didn't know, but cried herself to sleep over it many nights. They had read articles about it and found that psychologists were divided. Traditionalists made much of the importance of sex roles, while changers felt sex roles were important only to those who were trapped in them; with the breaking of the sexual barrier, the concept of roles vanished.

The day finally came when the clone body was ready. Cleo still did not know what she should do.

"Are you feeling comfortable now? Just nod if you can't talk."

"Wha . . ."

"Relax. It's all over. You'll be feeling like walking in a few minutes. We'll have someone take you home. You may feel drunk for a while, but there's no drugs in your system."

"Wha' . . . happen?"

"It's over. Just relax."

Cleo did, curling up in a ball. Eventually he began to laugh.

Drunk was not the word for it. He sprawled on the bed, trying on pronouns for size. It was all so funny. *He* was on *his* back with *his* hands in *his* lap. He giggled and rolled back and forth, over and over, fell on the floor in hysterics.

He raised his head.

"Is that you, Jules?"

"Yes, it's me." He helped Cleo back onto the bed, then sat on the edge, not too near, but not unreachably far away. "How do you feel?"

He snorted. "Drunker 'n a skunk." He narrowed his eyes, forced them to focus on Jules. "You must call me Leo now. Cleo is a woman's name. You shouldn't have called me Cleo then."

"All right. I didn't call you Cleo, though."

"You didn't? Are you *sure?*"

"I'm very sure it's something I wouldn't have said."

"Oh. Okay." He lifted his head and looked confused for a moment. "You know what? I'm gonna be sick."

Leo felt much better an hour later. He sat in the living room with Jules, both of them on the big pillows that were the only furniture.

They spoke of inconsequential matters for a time, punctuated by long silences. Leo was no more used to the sound of his new voice than Jules was.

"Well," Jules said, finally, slapping his hands on his knees and standing up. "I really don't know what your plans are from here. Did you want to go out tonight? Find a woman, see what it's like?"

Leo shook his head. "I tried that out as soon as I got home," he said. "The male orgasm, I mean."

"What was it like?"

He laughed. "Certainly you know that by now."

"No, I meant, after being a woman—"

"I know what you mean." He shrugged. "The erection is interesting. So much larger than what I'm used to. Otherwise . . ." He frowned for a moment. "A lot the same. Some different. More localized. Messier."

"Um." Jules looked away, studying the electric fireplace as if seeing it for the first time. "Had you planned to move out? It isn't necessary, you know. We could move people around. I can go in with Paul, or we could move him in with me in . . . in our old room. You could have his." He turned away from Leo, and put his hand to his face.

Leo ached to get up and comfort him, but felt it would be exactly the wrong thing to do. He let Jules get himself under control.

"If you'll have me, I'd like to continue sleeping with you."

Jules said nothing, and didn't turn around.

"Jules, I'm perfectly willing to do whatever will make you most comfortable. There doesn't have to be any sex. Or I'd be happy to do what I used to do when I was in late pregnancy. You wouldn't have to do anything at all."

"No sex," he said.

"Fine, fine. Jules, I'm getting awfully tired. Are you ready to sleep?"

There was a long pause, then he turned and nodded.

They lay quietly, side by side, not touching. The lights were out; Leo could barely see the outline of Jules's body.

After a long time, Jules turned on his side.

"Cleo, are you in there? Do you still love me?"

"I'm here," she said. "I love you. I always will."

Jules jumped when Leo touched him, but made no objection. He began to cry, and Leo held him close. They fell asleep in each other's arms.

The Oophyte was as full and noisy as ever. It gave Leo a headache.

He did not like the place any more than Cleo had, but it was the only place he knew to find sex partners quickly and easily, with no emotional entanglements and no long process of seduction. Everyone there was available; all one needed to do was ask. They used each other for sexual calisthenics just one step removed from masturbation, cheerfully admitted the fact, and took the position that if you didn't approve, what were you doing there? There were plenty of other places for romance and relationships.

Leo didn't normally approve of it—not for himself, though he cared not at all what other people did for amusement. He preferred to know someone he bedded.

But he was here tonight to learn. He felt he needed the practice. He did not buy the argument that he would know just what to do because he had been a woman and knew what they liked. He needed to know how people reacted to him as a male.

Things went well. He approached three women and was accepted each time. The first was a mess—so *that's* what they meant by too soon!—and she was rather indignant about it until he explained his situation. After that she was helpful and supportive.

He was about to leave when he was propositioned by a woman who said her name was Lynx. He was tired, but decided to go with her.

Ten frustrating minutes later she sat up and moved away from him. "What are you here for, if that's all the interest you can muster? And don't tell me it's my fault."

"I'm sorry," he said. "I forgot. I thought I could . . . well, I didn't realize I had to be really interested before I could perform."

"Perform? That's a funny way to put it."

"I'm sorry." He told her what the problem was, how many times he had made love in the last two hours. She sat on the edge of the bed and ran her hands through her hair, frustrated and irritable.

"Well, it's not the end of the world. There's plenty more out there. But you could give a girl a warning. You didn't have to say yes back there."

"I know. It's my fault. I'll have to learn to judge my capacity, I guess. It's just that I'm used to being *able* to, even if I'm not particularly—"

Lynx laughed. "What am I saying? Listen to me. Honey, I used to have the same problem myself. *Weeks* of not getting it up. And I know it hurts."

"Well," Leo said, "I know what you're feeling like, too. It's no fun."

Lynx shrugged. "In other circumstances, yeah. But like I said, the woods are full of 'em tonight. I won't have any problem." She put her hand on his cheek and pouted at him. "Hey, I didn't hurt your poor male ego, did I?"

Leo thought about it, probed around for bruises, and found none.

"No."

She laughed. "I didn't think so. Because you don't have one. Enjoy it, Leo. A male ego is something that has to be grown carefully, when you're young. People have to keep pointing out what you have to do to be a man, so you can recognize failure when you can't 'perform.' How come you used that word?"

"I don't know. I guess I was just thinking of it that way."

"Trying to be a quote *man* unquote. Leo, you don't have enough emotional investment in it. And you're *lucky*. It took me over a year to shake mine. Don't be a man. Be a male human, instead. The switchover's a lot easier that way."

"I'm not sure what you mean."

She patted his knee. "Trust me. Do you see me getting all upset because I wasn't sexy enough to turn you on, or some such garbage? No. I wasn't brought up to worry that way. But reverse it. If I'd done to you what you just did to me, wouldn't something like that have occurred to you?"

"I think it would. Though I've always been pretty secure in that area."

"The most secure of us are whimpering children beneath it, at least some of the time. You understand that I got upset because you said yes when you weren't ready? And that's *all* I was upset about? It was impolite, Leo. A male human shouldn't do that to a female human. With a man and a woman, it's different. The poor fellow's got a lot of junk in his head, and so does the woman, so they shouldn't be held responsible for the tricks their egos play on them."

Leo laughed. "I don't know if you're making sense at all. But I like the sound if it. 'Male human.' Maybe I'll see the difference one day."

Some of the expected problems never developed.

Paul barely noticed the change. Leo had prepared himself for a traumatic struggle with his son, and it never came. If it changed Paul's life at all, it was in the fact that he could now refer to his maternal parent as Leo instead of mother.

Strangely enough, it was Lilli who had the most trouble at first. Leo was hurt by it, tried not to show it, and did everything he could to let her adjust gradually. Finally she came to him one day about a week after the change. She said she had been silly, and wanted to know if she could get a change, too, since one of her best friends was getting one. Leo talked her into remaining female until after the onset of puberty. He told her he thought she might enjoy it.

Leo and Jules circled each other like two tigers in a cage, unsure if a fight was necessary but ready to start clawing out eyes if it came to it. Leo didn't like the analogy; if he had still been a female tiger, he would have felt sure of the outcome. But he had no wish to engage in a dominance struggle with Jules.

They shared an apartment, a family, and a bed. They

were elaborately polite, but touched each other only rarely, and Leo always felt he should apologize when they did. Jules would not meet his eyes; their gazes would touch, then rebound like two cork balls with identical static charges.

But eventually Jules accepted Leo. He was "that guy who's always around" in Jules's mind. Leo didn't care for that, but saw it as progress. In a few more days Jules began to discover that he liked Leo. They began to share things, to talk more. The subject of their previous relationship was taboo for a while. It was as if Jules wanted to know Leo from scratch, not acknowledging there had ever been a Cleo who had once been his wife.

It wasn't that simple; Leo would not let it be. Jules sometimes sounded like he was mourning the passing of a loved one when he hesitantly began talking about the hurt inside him. He was able to talk freely to Leo, and it was in a slightly different manner from the way he had talked to Cleo. He poured out his soul. It was astonishing to Leo that there were so many bruises on it, so many defenses and insecurities. There was buried hostility which Jules had never felt free to tell a woman.

Leo let him go on, but when Jules started a sentence with, "I could never tell this to Cleo," or, "Now that she's gone," Leo would go to him, take his hand, and force him to look.

"I'm Cleo," he would say. "I'm right here, and I love you."

They started doing things together. Jules took him to places Cleo had never been. They went out drinking together and had a wonderful time getting sloshed. Before, it had always been dinner with a few drinks or dopesticks, then a show or concert. Now they might come home at 0200, harmonizing loud enough to get thrown in jail. Jules admitted he hadn't had so much fun since his college days.

Socializing was a problem. Few of their old friends were changers, and neither of them wanted to face the complications of going to a party as a couple. They couldn't make friends among changers, because Jules correctly saw he would be seen as an outsider.

So they saw a lot of men. Leo had thought he knew all of Jules's close friends, but found he had been wrong. He saw a side of Jules he had never seen before: more relaxed in ways, some of his guardedness gone, but with other defenses in place. Leo sometimes felt like a spy, looking in on a stratum of society he had always known was there, but had never been able to penetrate. If Cleo had walked into the group its structure would have changed subtly; she would have created a new milieu by her presence, like light destroying the atom it was meant to observe.

After his initial outing to the Oophyte, Leo remained celibate for a long time. He did not want to have sex casually; he wanted to love Jules. As far as he knew, Jules was abstaining, too.

But they found an acceptable alternative in double-dating. They shopped around together for a while, taking out different women and having a lot of fun without getting into sex, until each settled on a woman he could have a relationship with. Jules was with Diane, a woman he had known at work for many years. Leo went out with Harriet.

The four of them had great times together. Leo loved being a pal to Jules, but would not let it remain simply that. He took to reminding Jules that he could do this with Cleo, too. What Leo wanted to emphasize was that he could be a companion, a buddy, a confidant no matter which sex he was. He wanted to combine the best of being a woman and being a man, be both things for Jules, fulfill all his needs. But it hurt to think that Jules would not do the same for him.

"Well, hello, Leo. I didn't expect to see you today."

"Can I come in, Harriet?"

She held the door open for him.

"Can I get you anything? Oh, yeah, before you go any further, that 'Harriet' business is finished. I changed my name today. It's Joule from now on. That's spelled j-o-u-l-e."

"Okay, Joule. Nothing for me, thanks." He sat on her couch.

Leo was not surprised at the new name. Changers

had a tendency to get away from "name" names. Some did as Cleo had done by choosing a gender equivalent or a similar sound. Others ignored gender connotations and used the one they had always used. But most eventually chose a neutral word, according to personal preference.

"Jules, Julia," he muttered.

"What was that?" Joule's brow wrinkled slightly. "Did you come here for mothering? Things going badly?"

Leo slumped down and contemplated his folded hands.

"I don't know. I guess I'm depressed. How long has it been now? Five months? I've learned a lot, but I'm not sure just what it is. I feel like I've grown. I see the world . . . well, I see things differently, yes. But I'm still basically the same person."

"In the sense that you're the same person at thirty-three as you were at ten?"

Leo squirmed. "Okay. Yeah, I've changed. But it's not any kind of reversal. Nothing turned topsy-turvy. It's an expansion. It's not a new viewpoint. It's like filling something up, moving out into unused spaces. Becoming . . ." His hands groped in the air, then fell back into his lap. "It's like a completion."

Joule smiled. "And you're disappointed? What more could you ask?"

Leo didn't want to get into that just yet. "Listen to this, and see if you agree. I always saw male and female—whatever that is, and I don't know if the two *really* exist other than physically and don't think it's important anyway. . . . I saw those qualities as separate. Later, I thought of them like Siamese twins in everybody's head. But the twins were usually fighting, trying to cut each other off. One would beat the other down, maim it, throw it in a cell, and never feed it, but they were always connected and the beaten-down one would make the winner pay for the victory.

"So I wanted to try and patch things up between them. I thought I'd just introduce them to each other and try to referee, but they got along a lot better than I expected. In fact, they turned into one whole person, and found they could be very happy together. I can't tell them apart any more. Does that make any sense?"

Joule moved over to sit beside him.

"It's a good analogy, in its way. I feel something like that, but I don't think about it any more. So what's the problem? You just told me you feel whole now."

Leo's face contorted. "Yes. I do. And if I am, what does that make Jules?" He began to cry, and Joule let him get it out, just holding his hand. She thought he'd better face it alone, this time. When he had calmed down, she began to speak quietly.

"Leo, Jules is happy as he is. I think he could be much happier, but there's no way for us to show him that without having him do something that he fears so much. It's possible that he will do it someday, after more time to get used to it. And it's possible that he'll hate it and run screaming back to his manhood. Sometimes the maimed twin can't be rehabilitated."

She sighed heavily, and got up to pace the room.

"There's going to be a lot of this in the coming years," she said. "A lot of broken hearts. We're not really very much like them, you know. We get along better. We're not angels, but we may be the most civilized, considerate group the race has yet produced. There are fools and bastards among us, just like the one-sexers, but I think we tend to be a little less foolish, and a little less cruel. I think changing is here to stay.

"And what you've got to realize is that you're lucky. And so is Jules. It could have been much worse. I know of several broken homes just among my own friends. There's going to be many more before society has assimilated this. But your love for Jules and his for you has held you together. He's made a tremendous adjustment, maybe as big as the one you made. He *likes* you. In either sex. Okay, so you don't make love to him as Leo. You may never reach that point."

"We did. Last night." Leo shifted on the couch. "I . . . I got mad. I told him if he wanted to see Cleo, he had to learn to relate to me, because I'm *me*, dammit."

"I think that might have been a mistake."

Leo looked away from her. "I'm starting to think so, too."

"But I think the two of you can patch it up, if there's any damage. You've come through a lot together."

"I didn't mean to force anything on him, I just got mad."

"And maybe you *should* have. It might have been just the thing. You'll have to wait and see."

Leo wiped his eyes and stood up.

"Thanks, Harr . . . sorry. Joule. You've helped me. I . . . uh, I may not be seeing you as often for a while."

"I understand. Let's stay friends, okay?" She kissed him, and he hurried away.

She was sitting on a pillow facing the door when he came home from work, her legs crossed, elbow resting on her knee with a dopestick in her hand. She smiled at him.

"Well, you're home early. What happened?"

"I stayed home from work." She nearly choked, trying not to laugh. He threw his coat to the closet and hurried into the kitchen. She heard something being stirred, then the sound of glass shattering. He burst through the doorway.

"Cleo!"

"Darling, you look so handsome with your mouth hanging open."

He shut it, but still seemed unable to move. She went to him, feeling tingling excitement in her loins like the return of an old friend. She put her arms around him, and he nearly crushed her. She loved it.

He drew back slightly and couldn't seem to get enough of her face, his eyes roaming every detail.

"How long will you stay this way?" he asked. "Do you have any idea?"

"I don't know. Why?"

He smiled, a little sheepishly. "I hope you won't take this wrong. I'm so *happy* to see you. Maybe I shouldn't say it . . . but no, I think I'd better. I like Leo. I think I'll miss him, a little."

She nodded. "I'm not hurt. How could I be?" She drew away and led him to a pillow. "Sit down, Jules. We have to have a talk." His knees gave way under him and he sat, looking up expectantly.

"Leo isn't gone and don't you ever think that for a minute. He's right here." She thumped her chest and looked at him defiantly. "He'll always be here. He'll never go away."

"I'm sorry, Cleo, I—"

"No, don't talk yet. It was my own fault, but I didn't know any better. I never should have called myself Leo. It gave you an easy out. You didn't have to face Cleo being a male. I'm changing all that. My name is Nile. N-i-l-e. I won't answer to anything else."

"All right. It's a nice name."

"I thought of calling myself Lion. For Leo the lion. But I decided to be who I always was, the queen of the Nile, Cleopatra. For old time's sake."

He said nothing, but his eyes showed his appreciation.

"What you have to understand is that they're both gone, in a sense. You'll never be with Cleo again. I look like her now. I resemble her inside, too, like an adult resembles the child. I have a tremendous amount in common with what she was. But I'm not her."

He nodded. She sat beside him and took his hand.

"Jules, this isn't going to be easy. There are things I want to do, people I want to meet. We're not going to be able to share the same friends. We could drift apart because of it. I'm going to have to fight resentment because you'll be holding me back. You won't let me explore your female side like I want to. You're going to resent me because I'll be trying to force you into something you think is wrong for you. But I want to try and make it work."

He let out his breath. "God, Cl . . . Nile. I've never been so scared in my life. I thought you were leading up to leaving me."

She squeezed his hand. "Not if I can help it. I want each of us to try and accept the other as they are. For me, that includes being male whenever I feel like it. It's all the same to me, but I know it's going to be hard for *you*."

They embraced, and Jules wiped his tears on her shoulder, then faced her again.

"I'll do anything and everything in my power, up to—"

She put her finger to her lips. "I know. I accept you that way. But I'll keep trying to convince you."

In Trophonius's Cave

James P. Girard

> Our desires to revisit the past aren't always
> due to curiosity or the search for lost treasures.
> The motivation could be something as simple
> as wishing to go back and share our adult
> knowledge with our young selves ("If I'd
> known then what I know now . . ."). So it is
> with the time traveler in this quietly moving
> story by James P. Girard.
>
> Girard has been a science-fiction reader
> since junior high school, but he's primarily a
> "mainstream" writer. He earned writing
> degrees from the University of Kansas and
> Johns Hopkins University, has taught writing at
> the college level, and is currently copy chief on
> the Wichita *Eagle*; his novella *Changing All
> Those Changes* was published by Ishmael
> Reed's Yardbird Wing Editions. He has also
> sold sf stories to *Fantasy and Science Fiction*,
> *Penthouse*, and *New Dimensions*.

The wire slipped off again, stinging the back of Max
Kufus's hand, and he jerked backward with a grunt and
then said, "Shit!" and sat back heavily on the shed's
dirt floor, catching himself on one hand. He wiped the
other across his forehead, then reached out absent-

mindedly for the bottle standing on the busted chair
against the wall, and took a swallow.

His hand was slippery with sweat, where he'd wiped
his forehead, and he took care not to drop the bottle.
He'd left one of the heavy wooden doors open, for light
as well as air, but it was still dark and close in the shed.
When he'd begun, a little after noon, there'd been a
wind, and clouds had been racing overhead, but it was
still now, and he knew that the clouds had bunched up
overhead, even without seeing them.

He stared at the bicycle wheel a minute, thinking of
saying the hell with it, then reminded himself of how
he'd feel tomorrow, when he'd be completely sober, if
he let himself give up. It had been bad enough when
he'd busted it, what with Dougie going around all day
trying to pretend it didn't really matter to him, though
he'd finally managed to put the guilt out of his mind—
something he'd had a lot of practice at over the years.
He sighed and put it away again, letting himself remember instead the moments he'd already spent enjoying
Dougie's reaction when he found the spokes repaired,
his own rare moment of self-congratulation. Over the
years he'd come to know which disappointments hurt
the most; this would be one, if he let it. He rocked forward onto his feet again, nearly losing his balance, and
came to rest in a squat, fumbling at the bent spoke.

The other one had been fairly easy because the little
metal socket had still been in the rim and there'd been
enough wire to work with. So he'd been able to thread
it and then nip the end enough to keep the wire from
pulling back out. It looked like it ought to be soldered
or something; it probably wasn't the way they'd do it at
a bike shop. But it looked like the wheel would ride
straight enough for the time being, especially if he could
fix the other busted spoke. Maybe by the time it came
loose again, he'd be able to figure out something better,
or he'd have enough money to get it done right or to
get a new wheel or even a new bike for the kid. He
smiled and took another swallow of whisky; that was an
old joke.

The problem with the remaining spoke was that the
socket had pulled out along with the spoke and gotten

lost, leaving only the hole in the rim—too much hole and not enough wire, so that no matter how he contrived to twist the end, it slipped out again. What he really needed was something to replace the socket with.

He laid the wheel down on its axle and rose stiffly to his feet, then picked his way gingerly through old paint buckets and odd lengths of wood, laid edgewise, getting close enough to the shelf holding the nail and screw jars to reach over and lift out the one he wanted, hooking two fingers inside the dusty rim. He carried it to the chair and poured out an assortment of oddball bits of metal beside the whisky bottle.

He frowned and pushed the stuff around with one finger, hunched over to peer at it in the half-light, but nothing suggested itself. There were some little *L*-shaped braces he'd once used to make a bookshelf for Georgette, a few rusty springs, some old brackets from the windowshades that had once hung in the kitchen, where the window now was unadorned, and a lot of other odd metal things whose uses were long lost to memory. He sighed and scooped the stuff back into the jar, along with dust from the chair, then left the jar sitting where it was and turned back to the bicycle wheel, beginning to feel defeated.

He had always been good at figuring things out, at thinking of ways to do things that most people wouldn't have thought of. One year in school, they'd put him in a special class with all the gifted kids. But he hadn't been like them; he hadn't cared enough about it, and so he hadn't made good grades. Anyway, he'd known, as everyone else had, that he was only going to wind up working at the processing plant, like his old man. Being able to figure out different ways of doing things didn't count for much there.

If he could have figured out how to kick the booze, that would have been worth something to him at one time, but it had had him stumped, just like this damned bicycle wheel. He shrugged and took another drink.

Suppose his bigself showed up right now and told him to go on the wagon, even gave him some good reason for doing so? It was a fantasy he'd enjoyed for a while after the bigselves started coming around, as if it

might somehow be a way out, although it was mostly
little kids who got visited. Anyway, it hadn't taken him
long to reason it out: If his bigself came back with that
kind of advice, it would mean he hadn't kicked the
habit, up ahead in the future, and was trying to go back
and change things. And why should he take the advice
from himself, 30 years older, that he wouldn't take
from himself now? The thing to do would be to go back
to when he was 17, when he'd started drinking, and
give himself a good kick in the ass—except that there
hadn't been any visits until two years ago, that anybody
knew about. So it probably wasn't possible.

He stared at the far corner of the shed, not seeing it,
thinking that a kick in the ass probably wouldn't be
necessary; all he'd have to do would be to show himself
where he was going to end up. You know what they call
me? he'd say. Old Max, the alky, that's you, 30 years
ahead. He remembered vividly the first time he'd heard
it, down at the gas station when he was filling the car,
from somebody talking in a normal tone of voice, not
bothering to whisper, as if it wouldn't matter to him.

He shook his head sharply and grabbed the wheel,
putting that too out of his mind. He spread his feet a
bit, to brace himself, and got a better grip on the pliers.
It looked like this job was going to boil down to brute
force more than anything else—and strength had never
been something he was long on.

Dougie Kufus walked home as slowly as he could,
feeling the gray sky like a weight on the top of his head,
pushing him into the earth. He didn't want to go home,
but there was nowhere else he wanted to go either—
especially not back to the schoolground, where the
other kids were. And he couldn't just stand still; it'd get
dark and some grown-up would come around and make
him go home anyway. So he walked slowly, as if each
step were the last.

Already he was thinking how it was going to be tomorrow in school—and not just tomorrow, but the
whole rest of the seventh grade. He'd never in a million
years figured on Jeff getting a visit from his bigself.
They'd talked about it sometimes, imagining, but he'd

always thought of it as one of those things that just happened to the kids on the other side of town, like stereoviewers and kiddicomputers and other expensive things. But now it was as if Jeff was one of those other kids, as if he'd changed somehow. What if all the other kids got visited, all over town, and he was the only one left? Suddenly he felt sure that was how it was going to be, that that was the way it was supposed to be for some-one like him, Old Max's kid, the drunk's kid. Really, when he thought about it, Jeff had always been different from him: he had a mother, for one thing, and his father didn't drink much, even though he didn't work much either, and he was kind of mean; at least, he didn't get drunk all over town, so that the police had to bring him home sometimes, like Pop.

He kicked a rock hard, wanting it to smash against something, but it just skipped out into the street and bounced a couple of times and stopped. Maybe Jeff had just been fooling him all the time, pretending to be his friend; maybe everybody had been doing that, pretending he was just like them when really everybody knew that he was the only one different. He stopped for a moment, feeling desolate, on the verge of believing it, then shrugged and started walking again, thinking: maybe it's better to be that way. But it didn't make him feel any better.

When he got home the door was standing open even though it looked like it was going to rain, and he half expected to find Pop passed out on the couch or in the bedroom, but he wasn't anywhere around. Dougie went into the kitchen, feeling vaguely hungry, but all he could find was a package of the chipped beef Pop made gravy with sometimes. He tore it open and ate the thin slices one at a time, taking little bites to make it last longer, then went into the living room and flicked on the TV, throwing himself down on the armchair, sitting sideways against the sag so he'd be more or less upright.

The news was on, which he was supposed to watch for social studies, but he couldn't keep his mind on it. He wondered what Jeff's bigself had said. He hadn't asked because it was usually a secret and it wasn't polite to ask, though he'd wanted to. Jeff had told him that it happened while he was alone, while his mom and dad were out partying the night before. Everyone said that's how it always was—that the bigselves always showed up when you were by yourself because they couldn't stay very long, for some reason, and they didn't want to be interrupted. Jeff said his bigself had said he'd remembered that night because it was his parents' anniversary and they'd decided he was old enough to stay home by himself without a sitter. Jeff had said that was funny because they'd let him stay by himself a couple of times before, but he guessed his bigself must have forgotten about that.

It had never really occurred to Dougie before that the bigselves would have to remember when to show up, but it made sense, so they didn't have to waste time finding their littleselves or having to talk to a bunch of other people. He tried to think of when he'd go back and visit himself if he was a bigself now. It could be just about any night, he guessed, since he never knew whether Pop was going to be around or not. He frowned. If he had to figure out a time to visit himself, even just last week, he couldn't do it for sure. He was by himself a lot, but he wasn't sure exactly which days it had been. He tried to think back further, to some memorable time when he'd been all alone, but he couldn't remember the exact date of any particular time.

He leaned forward in the chair. That meant his bigself couldn't have visited him, up to now, because, if he couldn't remember a time for a visit, even last week, how was his bigself going to remember a time, 30 years from now?

He got up and walked distractedly into the kitchen, not with any purpose, just walking and thinking. Suppose he made a time for his bigself to visit—a time and a place he'd be sure to remember even if he had to scratch it on his skin. He stopped, his eyes growing suddenly wide. Whenever he did, it might be the time his bigself came, if he was ever going to come, and he could do it right now, tonight.

He put one thumb in his mouth and chewed at the nail, making a fist. It couldn't be here; Pop might show up anytime. He stared at the graying kitchen window, not seeing it, running down possibilities in his mind, then suddenly thought of the place where he and Jeff had made a hideout once, over on the far side of town, out past the houses along the river. But it was a long way away—a long way to ride a bike, let alone walk. He winced, remembering what had happened to the bike, and then realized for the first time that he was staring out the kitchen window at the shed, where the bike was, and he noticed that the big door was open and there was a light on inside.

He stood still for a moment, his lips pursed, wondering what to do about it. If he just slipped out the front door, he could be gone before Pop even knew he'd come home; on the other hand, Pop might be able to get the old car started. He probably wouldn't be willing to take Dougie where he really wanted to go, but he could tell Pop he had to go downtown for something, and that would get him halfway; he could figure it out from there.

He nodded to himself abruptly and headed out the back door and across the yard to the shed.

Pop was slumped against one wall, asleep, a pair of pliers in his hand and an empty whisky bottle lying beside him. Dougie's bike was sitting upsidedown, balanced on the seat and handlebars, and the back wheel was off, lying at an angle in front of Pop. The tire and the deflated tube were hanging on the end of a shelf just above the busted chair.

Dougie stepped on into the shed, keeping quiet for the moment, and examined the wheel. One of the busted spokes looked like it had been fixed, but one was still disconnected. He licked his lips, then grabbed the wheel and slid it into the prongs of the bike frame, giving it a slight spin. It still wobbled from side to side but not nearly as badly as before; the one spoke seemed to make a lot of difference. It looked like it would turn, at least, without rubbing against the frame. He glanced around at the scattered parts. He'd never put a bike tire on from scratch, but he'd seen it done. He reached down and eased the pliers out of Pop's hand.

It was nearly dark outside by the time he finished,

and it was growing windy again. Getting the tire onto the rim had had him baffled for a while until he'd figured out how to use a screwdriver to hold it down in one place while he forced it in the rest of the way around with the plier handle. Then he'd had to work on the axle nuts a long time to get the wheel centered enough not to rub. And when that was done, he'd realized that the disconnected spoke, which he'd tried to bend back out of the way, was going to come loose eventually and catch on the frame. So he'd gripped it with the pliers, down near the hub, and twisted it back and forth until it broke off. That left nothing but airing the tire, and he'd have to walk it down to the gas station to do that.

As he was wheeling it out, he glanced back at Pop and thought for a second that he ought to wake him up and make him go in the house and get in bed, but he didn't want to have to explain what he was up to or make up something. So he went on, closing the door behind him, in case it started raining.

Something loud woke Max up, and he struggled briefly, not recognizing the hot, dark place he awoke in, thinking it might be a jail cell. But then lightning struck again outside; thunder rattled the shed's roof, showing him where he was and reminding him of what he had been doing.

But the bike was gone, and the wheel with it—even the tire and tube. He licked his lips and looked around for the whisky bottle, found it lying empty beside the chair. The inside of his mouth was dry, and he needed something for it, but the rest of him was wet; sweat made his body itch all over.

He rose clumsily to all fours, then to his feet, and looked at his watch but couldn't read it in the dark. He pushed through the heavy door, surprised to find a cool wind blowing outside, and twisted his wrist to catch the little light there was. It was only 7:20, though it looked dark enough to be 9 or 10 because of the clouds packed overhead. The scraggly backyard was dry and dust-patched. So it hadn't rained yet. He stretched his neck and scratched it, feeling the sweat drying quickly in the wind.

He supposed Dougie had come and found the bike half-fixed and had gone ahead and put it together and then gone for a ride. That made Max feel good, not only because he'd apparently fixed the bike enough to make it rideable but also because Dougie had been able to put it together by himself. Evidence that Dougie could take care of himself always made Max feel a little less guilty about things.

In the kitchen he checked the icebox for something to eat or drink but found neither. He thought about going after a bottle, but he wasn't sure the car would start, and it looked like it was going to rain like hell anytime. Anyway, he didn't have to have it, no matter what people thought.

He went into the living room, where the TV was on, and threw himself down on the sofa without bothering to turn on any lights. There was a nice breeze coming in the window at the far end of the room, and he really felt, as he did now and then, that he could get along without booze without too much effort. If he didn't go after a bottle the rest of the evening, then pretty soon it would be too late, and he'd have to wait until morning, and then it would be broad daylight, and he might be able to make himself go the whole day without a drink, and what he could do for one day he could do for one more, and so on, and he might never take another drink. He propped his hands behind his head, feeling generally optimistic about himself, although he knew that this was only a game he played with himself from time to time. He still had a few hours before the liquor stores closed, and he might fall asleep and spend the whole night without another drink—and that would be a plus, of sorts—though there was no real chance that he'd be able to make it through the day tomorrow or that he'd even think about doing so, once it was morning. But it was nice to halfway believe in the possibility for a while, when it didn't seem threatening, and he was feeling good anyway about Dougie's bike.

Thinking of that, he twisted his neck slightly and looked toward the front door, where he expected to see

Dougie momentarily. He was pretty sure the kid had sense enough to come in out of the rain, unlike his old man.

He frowned, realizing for the first time that Dougie hadn't bothered to wake him up and make him go to bed, as he usually did. He shrugged. The kid had probably been excited about his bike and in a hurry to take a ride before it got too dark. It wasn't like him to leave the TV on, either, come to think of it.

Max looked at the TV again, thinking for a moment it was a scene from a movie he'd seen somewhere, but then realizing it was one of the new shows, he wondered momentarily whether it might be one of the R-rated ones they were showing now but then remembered they were only showing them after 9 p.m. The window lightened briefly and thunder banged outside, and he frowned again, hoping Dougie would get back soon.

The tire still wobbled enough to make him concentrate on keeping his balance, but after a couple of blocks he had the hang of it, and he began to feel good. There was a little bit of breeze coming up behind him now, drying the sweat he'd worked up in the shed and walking the bike to the gas station, and he was happy to be riding again, going as fast as he dared down the broad street running between bars and used-car lots toward the nice side of town, where streetlamps were just beginning to glow faintly ahead of him, reminding him of why he was taking the ride. As he thought of it, his stomach gave a quick jerk from excitement. He wondered if his bigself might even be waiting for him when he got there, and he rose a little on the pedals, sending the bike shooting on ahead a little faster.

It wasn't until he'd had to turn off the big road into the darker neighborhood streets leading toward the river that he began to feel less confident. What if his bigself didn't show up? Would it mean he wasn't coming? Or would it just mean that he'd have to remember the time and place until he was the bigself, so he could go back? He sat back on the seat, noticing that his legs were growing tired, and let the bike coast a little, just pedaling every now and then when he had to swing out to pass a parked car. There was no traffic here, and the houses blocked the wind that had been blowing down the big boulevard. So there was no sound except his breathing and the crunch of his tires over occasional pebbles, and now and then an unseen dog in some backyard complaining of his passage.

If he did come back and visit himself when he got to be a bigself, then wouldn't he remember being visited when he was a littleself? He remembered now that they'd talked about that in science class one day—it had something to do with what they called a paradox— but he couldn't remember now what the teacher had said about it, and he wished he could. Because if the only bigselves who went back were the ones who re- membered being visited, then that's how they'd remem- ber the time and place—it wouldn't take any special remembering, like he was planning on.

But if it was just the bigselves who remembered being visited . . . why should they bother to go back? In that case, it wouldn't change anything. But if they didn't go back, how could they remember being visited? So it had to be the ones who didn't remember being visited, who wanted to change things by going back. But did that mean that all the kids who were being vis- ited now wouldn't bother to go back when they got to be bigselves? Because, really, if things were changed, then by the time they got to be bigselves, they'd be dif- ferent bigselves from the ones who visited them in the first place . . .

He shook his head, feeling slightly nauseous. It just kept going around and around in his mind, like one of those dreams that kept repeating and waking you up all night long, so that it seemed like you never got any sleep.

The important thing, he thought, forcing himself to grab onto the thought, was that things had to change— that's what it was all about; that's why the bigselves started coming in the first place, to make things change. So, if his bigself showed up tonight, that would be great. But if he didn't, it would just mean that Dougie would have to plan on coming back himself eventually and that he'd have this time and place to do it.

He leaned forward again, pedaling steadily, anxious now to get beyond the neat, dark houses that made him feel small and alone. He had been this way in daylight, and he knew kids who lived in this part of town, but nothing looked familiar in the dark. He saw faces at the bright windows now and then and realized that none of them could see him passing by outside, and it made him feel as if he were somehow beyond their reach, for good or ill, as if he were a ghost.

By the time he reached the gravel stretch leading to the riverbank, he was tired and winded and confused and even a little scared; it was darker out beyond the houses, and there was a strong wind behind him now, seeming to stand between him and the town, as if he couldn't turn back, and the insect sounds made it seem like a long way from anywhere.

The wobbly tire made it too hard to fight the bike through the gravel. So he got off and pushed it, breathing hard, and it took him a while to find the path in the darkness. When he did, it seemed as if the bank were steeper than he remembered, so that it was scary going down toward the narrow level path just above the dark water, and then the place where the big concrete pipe ran out of the earth—their old hideout—looked like a black pit, so that he stood for a moment working up his courage, remembering for the first time tales of snakes and wild animals.

When he did finally enter, leaving his bike on the path, he was surprised to find himself walking in a narrow stream of water. It had never really occurred to him before to wonder what the pipe was for; he had sort of vaguely supposed it was to keep the river from overflowing by taking in water when it rose that high. Now it occurred to him that there might be some danger in hanging around in it, although he planned to stick close to the end, and he figured he could get out quick enough if he had to.

Once he got a few feet inside, it didn't seem so dark anymore, thanks to the gray light filtering in from the opening. It was hot, though, and none of the wind seemed to get in. He began to itch and jerk after a few minutes, but he couldn't tell if it was from nighttime insects or sweat. After some experimentation he found a way to half sit and half lie with his knees arched over the stream, his back against one slope of the pipe.

Once he had gotten used to the heat and the darkness, the silence began to bother him, so that he kept still and listened hard for outside noises. But then he began to think he heard faint sounds from farther inside the pipe, and that worried him a lot until he decided it must just be the echoes of his own small sounds, and he even sang a couple of songs, in a low voice, to prove it to himself but stopped that when the echo began to seem kind of scary.

Finally, he decided to concentrate on listening for the sound of footsteps from outside, but he listened for a long time and nothing happened—although now and then there was a flash of light which might have been distant lightning or passing headlights on the road above—and he grew bored and even began to feel a little silly about the whole thing.

He thought of Pop and felt guilty for having left him on the floor of the shed, and he thought maybe he'd better be starting back soon because, anyway, he was beginning to feel kind of sleepy and the pipe was uncomfortable. But it was going to be an awful long ride back, and he thought he'd better rest awhile before he started. So he laid his head back against the arching concrete and closed his eyes for a moment.

He was cold and wet, and when he woke up he thought at first he might have peed on himself in his sleep, but then he felt the wind from the window and saw the strip of water running clear from the window to the couch, and he shivered and sat up, feeling dizzy. There was a kind of flapping light from somewhere, making it hard to focus on things, and it took him a moment to realize it came from the TV, where a test pattern was rolling over and over.

He got up and turned it off, feeling stiff and sore, then went and closed the window. He was on his way down the hall to his bedroom when he remembered about Dougie, and so he looked in the kid's room just to make sure, but he couldn't tell whether there was anyone in the bed or not, and so he turned on the hall light, which showed him clearly that the bed was empty.

Confused, he went on to his own bedroom, half expecting to find him there, but it was empty too. He sat down on the edge of his bed and began untying one shoe, as if he might just go ahead and go to sleep, but then he realized that he couldn't do that; the kid might be in some kind of trouble.

That thought woke him up. Where could Dougie be, in the middle of the night? He turned on the bedroom light and checked his watch, then shook his head, perplexed. It was after 1 A.M., and it looked like it must have been raining like hell outside. He stood up uncertainly and began to wander through the rest of the little house, thinking Dougie might be there somewhere, after all, but he wasn't in the kitchen or the bathroom, and that was it.

Max stood in the middle of the dark kitchen and licked his lips, wishing to hell he had a bottle. What could have happened? Maybe the spoke busted again, and the kid was out in the middle of nowhere, walking his bike home. Or maybe he'd just had to hole up somewhere for a long time because of the rain. He nodded, trying to decide that that must be it. But the time worried him. It was awful goddamn late; he couldn't quite convince himself that Dougie wouldn't have tried to make it home before now, rain or no rain.

He was beginning to feel a little scared, and he decided he'd better do what he could, which was get in the car and take a swing around the area. He patted his pants pocket, out of habit, to make sure the keys were there and then went out the back door to where the car was parked beside the shed.

He'd left the window open, as usual, and the whole front seat was soaked. So he went back in the house and hunted up an old ragged army blanket to put over it. But then when he tried to start the car, it didn't even turn over. There was just a kind of clicking sound, and then even that died away.

He sat for a moment in the dark front seat, feeling helpless. As if on cue, it started raining again, big drops coming nearly straight down that struck the window ledge and splattered his face, making him blink. He put his face in his hands and then lifted his eyes slowly to look over his fingertips at the dark windshield, where water ran in wavy lines. He felt certain now that something very bad had happened to Dougie while he had slept on the sofa, oblivious to a storm that splashed water clear across the living room. Maybe there'd been a flood or a tornado; how would he have known?

He fought his way out of the car, filled with the old ache of anger at himself, as if it were a pain that was with him always, but that he only noticed when he was most vulnerable. He went back into the kitchen, not bothering to close the door behind him, and then to the front hall, where he searched in vain for his raincoat, finally settling instead for an old brown leather jacket. He started out the front door, then turned back to the closet and rummaged again for a moment, coming up at last with a wadded white sailor's cap which he jammed onto his head, letting the brim sag all around. Thus equipped, he plunged out the door and into the rain, heading toward the gas station at the corner and the big boulevard that led downtown.

"Dougie? Hey, Dougie, wake up."

He was lost for a moment, forgetting where he had been, but then it came back to him and he sat up straight, straining to see in the darkness. He looked first at the gray circle of the pipe's end, but then realized the voice had come from the other direction. Looking that way, open-mouthed, he could barely make out the form of someone sitting a few feet further into the pipe's interior.

"Don't be scared, Dougie. I come here on purpose, to tell you something."

He nodded, unable for the moment to say anything. He noticed that it was colder and that his legs were wet, and he thought the water must have risen while he slept.

"You gotta get out of here, Dougie. It ain't safe. Don't you know this is a drainage pipe? All that rainwater's gonna be rushin' down here before you know it."

The voice sounded older than he'd expected. He twisted his head a little to one side, but there was no way he could make out the face.

"Are you my bigself?" he blurted suddenly, surprising himself.

There was a silence, and then the voice said, "Uhh . . . yeah. Yeah, that's right. I figured you knew that already. That's why you come here, isn't it? Course it is. Since I'm you, I knew that already, you see?"

Dougie caught a faint, familiar smell and frowned.

"Are you drinking whisky?" he asked.

There was another brief silence.

"Uhh . . . well, I did have a drink before I come down here, Dougie. Lots of folks have a drink now and then and it don't mean nothin'. I mean, don't let it worry you none, that you're gonna have a drink every now and then, like anyone else, when you get to be big."

Dougie nodded, feeling some of his initial elation fade.

"You're not rich, are you?" he asked.

His bigself chuckled.

"No, not exactly. No, I don't think you could say I was rich." His voice changed suddenly, the way Pop's did sometimes when he tried to make himself be serious. "But, now, that don't mean I ain't happy, does it? You don't have to be rich to be happy with your life, Dougie. I mean . . ." But then he seemed to run down, as if he couldn't think of anything more to say about it.

"You're just like Pop," Dougie said, and it was an accusation.

This time the silence went on a little longer. When the bigself spoke again, his voice had softened, become matter-of-fact.

"Yeah, you're right, Dougie. I guess that's what I really come to tell you, besides gettin' out of this pipe. I'm an alky, just like your old man . . . just like our old man . . . and that means you're an alky, too, up ahead. But, see, things can change. That's why us bigselves come back, ain't it? Here's the thing, Dougie: You got this sickness in you, just like your old man,

that makes you an alcoholic if you let it. It's genetic
. . . inherited . . . they found that out for sure up
ahead. And the only way you can ever lick it is just
never to start, never to take that first drink. 'Cause
once you do, it's got you. You see what I mean? That's
what I come to tell, and it's up to you to take it or leave
it. I don't know what you can make out of your life—I
don't say you're gonna get rich if you don't drink—but
I do know you can keep from ending up like me, for
sure. That's entirely up to you."

Dougie nodded, feeling a little ashamed, and beginning to feel intensely grateful to his bigself, who had
somehow managed to come back and tell him this.

"How . . . ?" he started to ask, but the bigself cut
him off.

"Listen, Dougie, I wasn't kiddin' about that rainwater. You gotta clear out of here, for sure, the sooner the
better."

Dougie half stood, getting control of his stiff legs on
the slanting pipe and trying to keep his feet out of the
water. He started to turn away, toward the outside, but
then looked back.

"What about you?" he asked.

It looked as though the bigself shrugged.

"Don't sweat it. They're gonna jerk me back anytime
now. I'm gonna be just fine." There was a sharp clink-
ing sound, and Dougie realized that the bigself had
picked up a bottle. He turned again toward the opening.

"Say, Dougie," the bigself said. "One more thing, I
just happened to remember. You don't know it, but
your old man's out lookin' for you tonight. He got worried when he woke up and you weren't around anywhere. And the thing is, if you don't go find him and
get him home, he's gonna get sick and be in the hospital
a long time. Let's see . . . if you head straight back
out to the highway and then toward home, you oughta
run into him."

"I will," Dougie said. "I'll find him. Thanks a lot."

The figure of the bigself gave him a little wave, and
Dougie turned and headed out, nearly stumbling over
his bike on the path outside. He wrestled it up the

slope and then along the gravel stretch to where the pavement began, then jumped on and pedaled hard into the cold wind, feeling an occasional heavy raindrop against his face and arms.

Max Kufus took another big swallow, which made his eyes water, and then giggled, lying back against the curve of the pipe. When he put his ear against the concrete, he thought he could hear the roar of a lot of water coming up fast.

That had been a good one, all right, that business about the drinking, and he'd just thought it up on the spur of the moment. If he'd scared the kid enough to keep him off the sauce for good, that would be a big bonus. Things were working out even better than he'd planned.

He took another swallow and then coughed for a time. It had been a long time since he'd had anything to drink, and he hated to guzzle it this way, but he wanted to make sure he got it all down. When they pulled his body back, it had to look like he'd just fallen off the wagon and gotten himself drowned by accident.

That way, with luck, they wouldn't bother to go back and check on him, and they'd never find out he hadn't visited his own younger self, and they'd never know that Dougie was alive this time around, and so no government agent would be sent back to "rectify" things.

Shit, he'd even saved himself a round of pneumonia, it looked like, and a hell of a lot of hospital bills. It looked like a bargain all the way around, from where he sat. He held the bottle out toward the darkness, toasting it, and then took as big a swallow as he could stand.

Fireflood

Vonda N. McIntyre

> We return to the subject of bioengineering—
> but this time purely for function, not at all for
> beauty. Question: What place in the world is
> left for a squat, ugly woman who was con-
> structed for barehanded digging underground,
> once her specific abilities are no longer
> needed?
>
> Vonda McIntyre's scientific training was in
> biology and genetics, which she has put to
> good use in stories and novels such as *Dream-
> snake*, winner of both the Nebula Award and
> the Hugo Award in 1979.

Dark moved slowly along the bottom of a wide, swift
river, pushing against its current. The clean water made
long bubbling strokes over her armor, and round stones
scraped against her belly scales. She could live here,
hidden in rapids or pools, surfacing every few hours to
replenish her internal supplies of oxygen, looking little
different from a huge boulder. In time she could even
change the color of her armor to conform perfectly to
the lighter, grayer rock of this region. But she was moving on; she would not stay in the river long enough to
alter her rust-red hue.

Vibrations warned her of rapids. She took more care

with her hand- and footholds, though her own mass was
her main anchor. Stones rumbling gradually downstream did not afford much purchase for her claws. The
turbulence was treacherous and exciting. But now she
had to work harder to progress, and the riverbed shifted
more easily beneath her. As the water grew swifter it
also became more shallow, and when she sensed a number of huge boulders around her, she turned her back to
the flow and reared up above the surface to breathe.

The force of the current sent water spraying up over
her back, forming a curtain that helped conceal her.
She breathed deeply, pumping air through her storage
lungs, forcing herself not to exceed her body's most
efficient absorption rate. However anxious she was to get
underwater again, she would do herself no good if she
used more oxygen than she stored during the stop.

Dark's armor, though impenetrable and insensitive to
pain, detected other sensations. She was constantly
aware of the small point of heat—call it that, she had
no more accurate word—in the center of her spinal
ridge. It was a radio transceiver. Though she could
choose not to hear its incoming messages, it sent out a
permanent beacon of her presence that she could not
stop. It was meant to bring aid to her in emergencies,
but she did not want to be found. She wanted to escape.

Before she had properly caught her breath, she
sensed the approach of a helicopter, high above and
quite far away. She did not see it: the spray of water
glittered before her shortsighted eyes. She did not hear
it: the rush of the river drowned out all other sounds.
But she had more than one sense that had as yet no
name.

She let herself sink beneath the water. An observer
would have had to watch a single boulder among many
to see what had happened. If the searchers had not
homed in on the transmitter she could still get away.

She turned upstream again and forged ahead toward
the river's source.

If she was very lucky, the helicopter was flying a pattern and had not actually spotted her transmitter at all.
That was a possibility, for while it did not quite have
the specificity of a laser, it worked on a narrow beam.

It was, after all, designed to send messages via satellite.

But the signal did not pass through water and even as the searchers could not detect her, she could not see or feel them through the rough silver surface of the river. Trusting her luck, she continued on.

The country was very different from where she had trained. Though she was much more comfortable underground than underwater, this land was not ideal for digging. She could survive as well beneath liquid, and travel was certainly quicker. If she could not get to the surface to breathe, the time it would take her to stop and extract oxygen directly was about the same. But the character of water was far too constant for her taste. Its action was predictable and its range of temperature was trivial compared to what she could stand. She preferred to go underground, where excitement spiced the exploration. For, though she was slow, methodical, and nearly indestructible, she *was* an explorer. It was just that now she had nowhere to explore.

She wondered if any of her friends had made it this far. She and six others had decided, in secret, to flee. But they offered each other only moral support; each had gone out alone. Twenty more of her kind still remained scattered in their reserve, waiting for assignments that would never come and pretending they had not been abandoned.

Though it was not yet evening, the light faded around her and left the river bottom gray and black. Dark slowly and cautiously lifted her eyes above the water. Her eyes peered darkly from beneath her armor. They were deep blue, almost black, the only thing of beauty about her: the only thing of beauty about her after or before her transformation from a creature who could pass for human to one who could not. Even now she was not sorry to have volunteered for the change. It did not further isolate her; she had always been alone. She had also been useless. In her new life, she had some worth.

The riverbed had cut between tall, thick trees that shut out much of the sunlight. Dark did not know for certain if they would interfere with the radio signal as well. She had not been designed to work among lush vegetation and she had never studied how her body might interact with it. But she did not believe it would be safe for her to take a quiet stroll among the giant cedars. She tried to get her bearings with sun time and body memory. Her ability to detect magnetic fields was worthless here on Earth; that sense was designed for more delicate signals. She closed it off as she might shut her eyes to a blinding light.

Dark submerged again and followed the river upward, keeping to its main branch. As she passed the tributaries that ran and rushed to join the primary channel the river became no more than a stream itself, and Dark was protected only by thin ripples.

She peered out again.

The pass across the ridge lay only a little ahead and above her, just beyond the spring that created the river. To Dark's left lay a wide field of scree, where a cliff and hillside had collapsed. The river flowed around the pile, having been displaced by tons of broken stone. The rubble stretched on quite a way, at least as far as the pass and, if she were lucky, all the way through. It was ideal. Sinking barely underwater, she moved across the current. Beneath her feet she felt the stones change from rounded and water-worn to sharp and freshly broken. She reached the edge of the slope, where the shattered rock projected into the river. On the downstream side she nudged away a few large stones, set herself, and burrowed quickly into the shards.

The fractured crystalline matrix disrupted her echo perception. She kept expecting to meet a wall of solid rock that would push her out and expose her, but the good conditions existed all the way through the pass. Then, on the other side, when she chanced a peek out into the world, she found that the texture of the ground changed abruptly on this side of the ridge. When the broken stone ended, she did not have to seek out another river. She dug straight from the scree into the earth.

In the cool dry darkness, she traveled more slowly but more safely than in the river. Underground there was no chance of the radio signal's escaping to give her away. She knew exactly where the surface was all the time. It, unlike the interface of water and air, did not constantly change. Barring the collapse of a hillside, little could unearth her. A landslide was possible, but her sonar could detect the faults and weaknesses in earth and rock that might create a danger.

She wanted to rest, but she was anxious to reach the flyers' sanctuary as quickly as she could. She did not have much farther to go. Every bit of distance might make a difference, for she would be safe only after she got inside the boundaries . . . She could be safe there from normal people: what the flyers would do when she arrived she could not say.

Dark's vision ranged much farther through the spectrum than it had when she was human. In daytime she saw colors, but at night and underground she used infrared, which translated to distinguishable and distinctive shades of black. They were supposed to look like colors, but she saw them all as black. They told her what sort of land she was passing through and a great deal about what grew above. Nevertheless, when the sun went down she broke through thick turf and peered around at the forest. The moon had not yet risen, and a nearby stream was almost as dark as ice. The fir trees kept the same deep tone as in bright sunlight. Still, all the colors were black.

Dark breathed deeply of the cold air. It was stuffy underground, though she had not had to switch to reducing her own oxygen. That was for deeper down, in altogether more difficult regions.

The air smelled of moss and ferns, evergreen trees, and weathered stone. But under it all was the sulfurous volcano, and the sweet delicate fragrance of flyers.

Sinking down into the earth once more, Dark traveled on.

The closer Dark got to the volcano, the more jumbled and erratic grew the strata. Lava flows and land movement, glaciers and erosion had scarred and unsettled and twisted the surface and all that lay beneath it. Deep underground Dark encountered a tilted slab of granite, too hard for her to dig through quickly. She followed it upward, hoping it would twist and fold back down again. But it did not, and she broke through topsoil into the chill silence of a wilderness night. Dirt and pebbles fell away from her shoulder armor. From the edge of the outcropping she looked out, in infrared, over her destination.

The view excited her. The tree-covered slope dropped to tumbled masses of blackened logs that formed the first barrier against intrusion into the flyers' land. Beyond, at the base of the volcano, solidified lava created another wasteland. The molten rock had flowed from the crater down the flank of the mountain; near the bottom it broke into two branches which ran, one to each side, until both ended like true rivers, in the sea. The northern shore was very close, and the pale nighttime waves lapped gently on the dim cool beach. To the south the lava had crept through a longer sweep of forest, burning the trees in its path and toppling those beyond its heat, for a much longer distance to the ocean. The wide solid flood and the impenetrable wooden jumble formed a natural barricade. The flyers were exiled to their peninsula, but they stayed there by choice. The humans had no way of containing them short of killing them. They could take back their wings or chain them to the ground or imprison them, but they wished to isolate the flyers, not murder them. And murder it would be if they denied the creatures flight.

The basalt streams glowed with heat retained from the day, and the volcano itself was a softly radiant cone, sparkling here and there where upwellings of magma approached the surface. The steam rising from the crater shone brightly, and among its clouds shadows soared in spirals along the edges of the column. One of the shadows dived dangerously toward the ground, risking destruction, but at the last moment it pulled up short to soar skyward again. Another followed, another, and Dark realized they were playing a game. Entranced, she hunched on the ridge and watched the flyers play. They did not notice her. No doubt they could see better than she, but their eyes would be too dazzled by the heat's luminous blackness to notice an earthbound creature's armor-shielded warmth.

Sound and light burst upon her like explosions. Clearing the ridge that had concealed it, a helicopter leaned into the air and ploughed toward her. Until this moment she had not seen or heard or sensed it. It must have been grounded, waiting for her. Its searchlights caught and blinded her for a moment, till she shook herself free in an almost automatic reaction and slid across the bare rock to the earth beyond. As she plunged toward the trees the machine roared over her, its backwash blasting up a cloud of dirt and leaves and pebbles. The copter screamed upward, straining to miss treetops. As it turned to chase her down again, Dark scuttled into the woods.

She had been careless. Her fascination with the volcano and the flyers had betrayed her, for her stillness must have convinced the humans that she was asleep or incapacitated.

Wondering if it would do any good, she burrowed into the earth. She felt the helicopter land, and then the lighter vibrations of footsteps. The humans could find her by the same technique, amplifying the sounds of her digging. From now on they did not even need her beacon.

She reached a boundary between bedrock and earth and followed its lessened resistance. Pausing for a moment, she heard both movement and its echoes. She felt trapped between sounds, from above and below. She started digging, pushing herself until her work drowned out all other noises. She did not stop again.

The humans could move faster down the steep terrain than she could. She was afraid they would get far enough ahead of her to dig a trench and head her off. If they had enough equipment or construction explosives, they could surround her, or simply kill her with the shock waves of a shaped charge.

She dug violently, pushing herself forward, feeling the debris of her progress slide over her shoulder armor and across her back, filling in the tunnel as quickly as she made it. The roots of living trees, springy and thick, reached down to slow her. She had to dig between and sometimes through them. Their malleable consistency made them harder to penetrate than solid rock, and more frustrating. Dark's powerful claws could shatter stone, but they tangled in the roots and she was forced to shred the tough fibers a few strands at a time. She tired fast, and she was using oxygen far more quickly than she could take it in underground.

Dark slashed out angrily at a thick root. It crumbled completely in a powdery dust of charcoal. Dark's momentum, meeting no resistance, twisted her sideways in her narrow tunnel. She was trapped. The footsteps of the humans caught nearly up to her, and then, inexplicably, stopped. Scrabbling frantically with her feet and one clawed hand, her left front limb wedged uselessly beneath her, she managed to loosen and shift the dirt in the small enclosed space. Finally, expecting the humans to start blasting toward her at any moment, she freed herself.

Despite the ache in her left shoulder, deep under her armor, she increased her pace tremendously. She was beneath the dead trees now, and the dry porous earth contained only the roots of trees that had burned from top to deep underground, or roots riddled with insects and decay. Above her, above ground, the treetrunks lay in an impassable tangle, and that must be why the humans had paused. They could not trench her now.

Gauging her distance to the basalt flow by the pattern of returning echoes, Dark tunneled through the last few lengths of earth. She wanted to go under the stone barrier and come up on the other side in safety. But the echoes proved that she could not. The basalt was much thicker than she had hoped. It was not a single flow but many, filling a deep-cleft valley the gods only knew how far down. She could not go under and she did not have time or strength right now to go through.

It was not the naked sheet of stone that would keep the humans from her, but the intangible barrier of the flyers' boundary. That was what she had to reach. Digging hard, using the last of her stored oxygen, Dark burst up through the earth at the edge of the lava flow and scrambled out onto the hard surface. Never graceful at the best of times, she was slow and unwieldy on land. She lumbered forward, panting, her claws clacking on the rock and scraping great marks across it.

Behind her the humans shouted, as their detectors went off so loudly even Dark could hear them, and as the humans saw Dark for themselves, some for the first time.

They were very close. They had almost worked their way through the jammed treetrunks, and once they reached solid ground again they could overtake her. She scrambled on, feeling the weight of her armor as she never did underground. Its edges dragged along the basalt, gouging it deeply.

Two flyers landed as softly as wind, as milkweed floss, as pollen grains. Dark heard only the rustle of their wings, and when she looked up from the fissured gray rock, they stood before her, barring her way.

She was nearly safe: she was just on the boundary, and once she was over it the humans could not follow. The delicate flyers could not stand up against her if she chose to proceed, but they did not move to let her pass. She stopped.

Like her, the flyers had huge eyes, to extend the spectrum of their vision. Armored brow ridges and transparent shields protected Dark's eyes and almost hid them. The flyers' eyes were protected, too, but with thick black lashes that veiled and revealed them.

"What do you want, little one?" one of the flyers said. Its voice was deep and soft, and it wrapped its body in iridescent black wings.

"Your help," Dark said. "Sanctuary." Behind her, the humans stopped too. She did not know if they still had the legal right to take her. Their steel net scraped along the ground, and they moved hesitantly closer. The black flyer glared, and the human noises ceased. Dark inched forward, but the flyers did not retreat at all.

"Why have you come?" The black flyer's voice withheld all emotion, warmth, or welcome.

"To talk to you," Dark said. "My people need your help."

The raven-winged flyer did not move, except to blink its luminous eyes. But its blue-feathered companion peered at Dark closely, moved a step one way, a step the other, and ruffled the plumage of its wings. The blue flyer's movements were as quick and sharp as those of a bird itself.

"We have no help to offer you," the black flyer said.

"Let me in, let me talk to you." Her claws ground against stone as she moved nervously. She could not flee, and she did not want to fight. She could crush the humans or the flyers, but she had not been chosen for her capacity for violence. Her pursuers knew that perfectly well.

Again the nets scraped behind her as the humans moved forward.

"We've only come for her," one of them said. "She's a fugitive—we don't want to involve you in any unpleasantness." The powerful searchlight he carried swept over Dark's back, transfixing the flyers, who turned their faces away. The harsh white illumination washed out the iridescent highlights of the black feathers but brightened the other's wings to the brilliant color of a Stellar's jay.

"Turn out your lights," the jay said, in a voice as brash and demanding as any real bluejay's. "It's dawn—you can see well enough."

The human hesitated, swung the light away, and turned it off. He motioned to the helicopter and its lights faded. As the jay had said, it was dawn, misty and gray and eerie. The flyers faced Dark's adversaries again.

"We have no more resources than you," the raven flyer said. "How do you expect us to help you? We have ourselves. We have our land. You have the same."

"Land!" Dark said bitterly. "Have you ever seen my land? It's nothing but piles of rotting stone and pits full of rusty water—" She stopped; she had not meant to lose her temper. But she was hunched on the border of captivity, straining toward sanctuary and about to be refused.

"Send her out so we can take her without violating your boundaries. Don't let her cause you a lot of trouble."

"A little late for such caution," Jay said. "Redwing, if we bow to their threats now, what will they do next time? We should let her in."

"So the diggers can do to our refuge what they did to their own? Pits, and rusting water—"

"It was like that when we came!" Dark cried, shocked and hurt. "We make tunnels, yes, but we don't destroy! Please hear what I've got to say. Then, if you ask me to go . . . I'll obey." She made the promise reluctantly, for she knew that once she had lived near the volcano, she would need great will to leave. "I give my word." Her voice quivered with strain. The humans muttered behind her; a few steps inside the boundary, a few moments inside and then out—who, besides Dark, would accuse them of entering the flyers' territory at all?

Jay and Redwing glared at each other, but suddenly Jay laughed sharply and turned away. He stepped back and swept one wingtip along the ground, waving Dark into his land. "Come in, little one," he said.

Hesitantly, afraid he would change his mind, Dark moved forward. Then, in a single moment, after her long journey, she was safe.

"We have no reason to trust it!" Redwing said.

"Nor any reason not to, since we could just as well be mashed flat between stone and armor. We do have reason not to help the humans."

"You'll have to send her back," the leader of the humans said. He was angry; he stood glowering at the very edge of the border, perhaps a bit over. "Laws will take her, if we don't now. It will just cost you a lot more in trouble."

"Take your threats and your noisy machine and get out of here," Jay said.

"You *will* be sorry, flyer," the humans' leader said.

Dark did not really believe they would go until the last one boarded the helicopter and its roar increased, it climbed into the air, and it clattered off into the brightening gray morning.

"Thank you," Dark said.

"I had ulterior motives," Jay said.

Redwing stood back, looking at Jay but not at Dark. "We'll have to call a council."

"I know. You go ahead. I'll talk to her and meet you when we convene."

"I think we will regret this," Redwing said. "I think we are closer to the humans than to the diggers." The black flyer leaped into the air, wings outspread to reveal their brilliant scarlet underside, and soared away.

Jay laid his soft hand on Dark's shoulder plate to lead her from the lava to volcanic soil. His skin felt frail, and very warm: Dark's metabolism was slower than it had been, while the flyers' chemistry had been considerably speeded up. Dark was ugly and clumsy next to him. She thought of digging down and vanishing but that would be ill-mannered. Besides, she had never been near a flyer before. Curiosity overcame her. Glancing surreptitiously sideways, beneath the edge of her armor, she saw that he was peeking at her, too. Their gazes met; they looked away, both embarrassed. Then Dark stopped and faced him. She settled back to regard him directly.

"This is what I look like," she said. "My name is Dark and I know I'm ugly, but I could do the job I was made for, if they'd let me."

"I think your strength compensates for your appearance," the flyer said. "I'm Jay." Dark was unreasonably pleased that she had guessed right about his name.

"You never answered Redwing's question," Jay said. "Why come *here?* The strip mines——"

"What could you know of strip mines?"

"Other people lived near them before they were given over to you."

"So you think we should stay there!"

Jay replied to her abrupt anger in a gentle tone. "I was going to say, this place is nicer than the strip mines, true, but a lot of places nicer than the strip mines are more isolated than we are. You could have found a hidden place to live."

"I'm sorry," Dark said. "I thought——"

"I know. Never mind."

"No one else like me got this far, did they?"

Jay shook his head.

"Six of us escaped," Dark said. "We hoped more than one would reach you. Perhaps I'm just the first, though."

"That could be."

"I came to ask you to join us," Dark said.

Jay looked at her sharply, his thick flaring eyebrows raised in surprise. He veiled his eyes for a moment with the translucent avian membranes, then let them slowly retract.

"Join you? In . . . your preserve?" He was polite enough to call it this time by its official name. Though she had expressed herself badly, Dark felt some hope.

"I misspoke myself," she said. "I came—the others and I decided to come—to ask you to join us politically. Or at least to support us."

"To get you a better home. That seems only fair."

"That isn't quite what we're hoping for. Or rather it is, but not the way you mean."

Jay hesitated again. "I see. You want . . . what you were made for."

Dark wanted to nod; she missed the shorthand of the language of the human body, and she found she was unable to read Jay's. She had been two years out of contact with normal humans; or perhaps it was that Jay was a flyer, and his people had made adjustments of their own.

"Yes. We were made to be explorers. It's a useless economy, to keep us on earth. We could even pay our own way after a while."

Dark watched him closely, but could not tell what he thought. His face remained expressionless; he did not move toward her or away. Then he sighed deeply. That, Dark understood.

"Digger—" She flinched, but inwardly, the only way she could. He had not seemed the type to mock her. "—the projects are over. They changed their minds. There will be no exploring or colonizing, at least not by you and me. And what difference does it make? We have a peaceful life and everything we need. You've been badly used but that could be changed."

"Maybe," Dark said, doubting his words. The flyers were beautiful, her people were ugly, and as far as the humans were concerned that made every difference. "But we had a purpose, and now it's gone. Are you happy, living here with nothing to do?"

"We're content. You people are all ready, but we

aren't. We'd have to go through as much change again as we already have."

"What's so bad about that? You've gone this far. You volunteered for it. Why not finish?"

"Because it isn't necessary."

"I don't understand," Dark said. "You could have a whole new living world. You have even more to gain than we do, that's why we thought you'd help us." Dark's planned occupation was the exploration of dead worlds or newly formed ones, the places of extremes where no other life could exist. But Jay's people were colonists; they had been destined for a world that was being made over for them, even as they were being suited for what it would become.

"The terraforming is only beginning," Jay said. "If we wait until it's complete—"

"But that won't be for generations."

Jay shrugged. "We know."

"You'll never see it!" Dark cried. "You'll be dead and dust before it changes enough for people like you are now to live on it."

"We're virus-changed, not constructed," Jay said. "We breed true. Our grandchildren may want another world, and the humans may be willing to help them go. But we intend to stay here." He blinked slowly, dreamily. "Yes, we *are* happy. And we don't have to work for the humans."

"I don't care who I work for, as long as I can be something better than a deformed creature," Dark said angrily. "This world gives my people nothing and because of that we're dying."

"Come now," Jay said tolerantly.

"We're dying!" Dark stopped and rocked back on the edge of her shell so she could more nearly look him in the eye. "You have beauty all around you and in you, and when the humans see you they admire you. But they're afraid of us! Maybe they've forgotten that we started out human or maybe they never considered us human at all. It doesn't matter. I don't care! But we can't be anything, if we don't have any purpose. All we ask is that you help us make ourselves heard, because they'll listen to you. They love you. They almost worship you!" She paused, surprised by her own outburst.

"Worship us!" Jay said. "They shoot us out of the sky, like eagles."

He looked away from her. His gaze sought out clouds, the direction of the sun, for all she knew the eddies of the wind. Dark thought she sensed something, a call or a cry at the very edge of one of her new perceptions. She reached for it, but it eluded her. It was not meant for her.

"Wait for me at sunset," Jay said, his voice remote. He spread his huge furled wings and sprang upward, the muscles bunching in his short, powerful legs. Dark watched him soar into the sky, a graceful dark blue shape against the cloud-patterned gold and scarlet dawn.

Dark knew she had not convinced him. When he was nothing but a speck she eased herself down again and lumbered up the flank of the volcano. She could feel it beneath her feet. Its long rumbles pulsed through her, at a far lower frequency than she ever could have heard as a human. It promised heat and danger; it excited her. She had experienced no extremes, of either heat or cold, pressure or vacuum, for far too many months.

The ground felt hollow beneath Dark's claws: passages lay beneath her, and lava beaten to a froth by the violence of its formation and frozen by exposure into spongy rock. She found a crevice that would leave no trace of her passing and slid into it. She began to dig, slowly at first, then faster, dirt and pulverized stone flying over her shoulders. In a moment the earth closed in around her.

Dark paused to rest. Having reached the gas-formed tunnels, she no longer had to dig her way through the substance of the mountain. She relaxed in the twisted passage, enjoying the brilliance of the heat and the occasional shining puff of air that came to her from the magma. She could analyze the gases by taste: that was another talent the humans had given her. Vapors toxic to them were merely interesting scents to her. If necessary she could metabolize some gases; the ability would have been necessary in many of the places she had expected to see, where sunlight was too dim to convert, where life had vanished or never evolved and there were no organic chemicals. On the outer planets, in the asteroids, even on Mars, her energy would have come from a tenuous atmosphere, from ice, even from the dust. Out there the challenging extremes would be cold and emptiness, unless she discovered hot, living veins in dying planets. Perhaps now no one would ever look for such activity on the surface of an alien world. Dark had dreamed of the planets of a different star, but she might never get a chance even to see the moon.

Dark sought a living vein in a living world: she moved toward the volcano's central core. Her people had been designed to resist conditions far more severe than the narrow range tolerated by normals, but she did not know if she could survive this great a temperature. Nor did she care. The rising heat drew her toward a heightened state of consciousness that wiped away caution and even fear. The rock walls glowed in the infrared, and as she dug at them, the chips flew like sparks. At last, with nothing but a thin plate of stone between her and the caldera, she hesitated. She was not afraid for her life. It was almost as if she were afraid she *would* survive: afraid the volcano, like all else, would finally disappoint her.

She lashed out with her armored hand and shattered the fragile wall. Steam and vapor poured through the opening, flowing past her. Before she stopped normal breathing she chanced a quick, shallow mouthful and savored the taste and smell, then moved forward to look directly into the crater.

Whatever she had imagined dissolved in the reality. She was halfway up the crater, dazzled from above by light and from below by heat. She had been underground a long time and it was almost exactly noon. Sunlight beat down through clouds of steam, and the gases and sounds of molten rock reached up to her. The currents swirled, hot and hotter, and in the earth's wound a flood of fire burned.

She could feel as well as see the heat, and it pleased her intensely that she would die if she remained where she was. Internal oxygen sustained her: a few deep breaths of the mountain's uncooled exhalations and she would die.

She wanted to stay. She did not want to return to the surface and the probability of rejection. She did not want to return to her people's exile.

Yet she had a duty toward them, and she had not yet completed it. She backed into the tunnel, turned around, and crawled away, hoping someday she could return.

Dark made her way back to the surface, coming out through the same fissure so the land would not change. She shook the dirt off her armor and looked around, blinking, waiting for her eyes to reaccustom themselves to the day. As she rested, colors resolved out of the afterimage dazzle of infrared: the blue sky first, then the deep green trees, the yellow of a scatter of wildflowers. Finally, squinting, she made out dark specks against the crystal clarity of the sky. The flyers soared in small groups or solo, now and again two coming together in lengthy graceful couplings, their wings brushing tips. She watched them, surprised and a little ashamed to be aroused despite herself. For her kind, intercourse was more difficult and more pedestrian. Dark had known how it would be when she volunteered; there was no secret about it. Like most of the other volunteers, she had always been a solitary person. She seldom missed what she had so seldom had, but watching the flyers she felt a long pang of envy. They were so beautiful, and they took everything so for granted.

The winged dance went on for hours, until the sun, reddening, touched mountains in the west. Dark continued to watch, unable to look away, in awe of the flyers' aerial and sexual stamina. Yet she resented their extended play, as well; they had forgotten that an earthbound creature waited for them.

The several pairs of coupled flyers suddenly broke apart, as if on signal, and the whole group of them scattered. A moment later Dark sensed the approach of the humans' plane.

It was too high to hear, but she knew it was there. It circled slowly. Sitting still, not troubling now to conceal the radio-beacon in her spine, Dark perceived it spiraling in, with her as its focus. The plane descended; it was a point, then a silver shape reflecting scarlet sunset. It did not come too close; it did nothing immediately threatening. But it had driven the flyers out of Dark's sight. She hunkered down on the stone promontory, waiting.

Dark heard only the sudden rush of air against outstretched wings as Jay landed nearby. His approach had been completely silent, and intent as she was on the search plane, she had not seen him. She turned her attention from the sky to Jay, and took a few steps toward him. But then she stopped, shamed once more by her clumsiness compared to the way he moved. The flyers were not tall, and even for their height their legs were quite short. Perhaps they had been modified that way. Still, Jay did not lumber. He strode. As he neared her he furled his wings over his back, folding them one bit at a time, ruffling them to smooth the feathers, folding a bit more. He reminded her not so much of a bird, as of a spectacular butterfly perched in the wind, flicking his wings open and closed. When he stopped before her his wings stilled, each bright-blue feather perfectly placed, framing him from behind. Unconcealed this time by the wings, his body was naked. Flyers wore no clothes: Dark was startled that they had nothing to conceal. Apparently they were as intricately engineered as her own people.

Jay did not speak for so long that Dark, growing uncomfortable, reared back and looked into the sky. The search plane still circled loudly.

"Are they allowed to do that?" she said.

"We have no quick way of stopping them. We can protest. No doubt someone already has."

"I could send them a message," she said grumpily. That, after all, was what the beacon was for, though the message would not contain the sort of information anyone had ever planned for her to send.

"We've finished our meeting," Jay said.

"Oh. Is that what you call it?"

Dark expected a smile or a joke, but Jay spoke quite seriously.

"That's how we confer, here."

"Confer—!" She dropped back to the ground, her claws digging in. "You met without letting me speak? You told me to wait for you at sunset!"

"I spoke for you," Jay said softly.

"I came here to speak for myself. And I came here to speak for my kind. I trusted you—"

"It was the only way," he said. "We only gather in the sky."

Dark held down an angry retort. "And what is the answer?"

Jay sat abruptly on the hard earth, as if he could no longer support the weight of his wings on his delicate legs. He drew his knees to his chest and wrapped his arms around them.

"I'm sorry." The words burst out in a sigh, a moan.

"Call them," Dark said. "Fly after them, find them, make them come and speak to *me*. I will not be refused by people who won't even face me."

"It won't help," Jay said miserably. "I spoke for you as well as I could, but when I saw I would fail I tried to bring them here. I begged them. They wouldn't come."

"They wouldn't come . . ." She had risked her life only to have her life dismissed as nothing. "I don't understand," she whispered.

Jay reached out and touched her hand: it still could function as a hand, despite her armor and her claws. Jay's hand, too, was clawed, but it was delicate and fineboned, and veins showed blue through the translucent skin. Dark pulled back the all too solid mass of her arm.

"Don't you, little one?" Jay said, sadly. "I was so different, before I was a flyer—"

"So was I," Dark said.

"But you're strong, and you're ready. You could go tomorrow with no more changes and no more pain. I have another stage to go through. If I did it, and then they decided not to send us after all—Dark, I would never be able to fly again. Not in this gravity. There are too many changes. They'd thicken my skin, and regress

me again so my wings weren't feathered but scaled—
they'd shield my eyes and reconstruct my face for the
filters."

"It isn't the flying that troubles you," Dark said.

"It is. The risk's too great."

"No. What troubles you is that when you were finished, you wouldn't be beautiful anymore. You'd be
ugly, like me."

"That's unfair."

"Is it? Is that why all your people flock around me
so willingly to hear what I have to say?"

Jay stood slowly and his wings unfolded above him:
Dark thought he was going to sail away off the side of
the mountain, leaving her to speak her insults to the
clouds and the stones. But, instead, he spread his beautiful black-tipped blue wings, stretched them in the air,
and curved them around over Dark so they brushed the
ridge of her spine. She shivered.

"I'm sorry," he said. "We have grown used to being
beautiful. Even I have. They shouldn't have decided to
make us in stages, they should have done it all at once.
But they didn't, and now it's hard for us, being reminded of how we were."

Dark stared at Jay, searching for the remnants of
how he had been until he became a flyer, understanding, finally, the reasons he had decided to become
something other than human. Before, she had only perceived his brilliant plumage, his luminous eyes, and the
artificial delicacy of his bones. Now she saw his original proportions, the disguised coarseness of his features, and she saw what he must have looked like.

Perhaps he had not actually been deformed, as Dark
had been. But he had never been handsome, or even so
much as plain. She gazed at him closely. Neither of
them blinked: that must be harder for him, Dark
thought. Her eyes were shielded, his were only fringed
with long, thick, dark eyelashes.

His eyes were too close together. That was something
the virus-forming would not have been able to cure.

"I see," she said. "You can't help us, because we
might succeed."

"Don't hate us," he said.

She turned away, her armor scraping on rock. "What do you care, if a creature as repellent as I hates you?"

"I care," Jay said very quietly.

Dark knew she was being unfair, to him if not to his kind, but she had no sympathy left. She wanted to hide herself somewhere and cry.

"When are the humans coming for me?"

"They come when they please," he said. "But I made the others promise one thing. They won't ask you to leave till morning. And if we can't find you, then— there's time for you to get away, if you hurry."

Dark spun around, more quickly than she thought herself able to. Her armor struck sparks, but they glowed only briefly and died.

"Where should I go? Somewhere no one at all will ever see me? Underground, all alone, forever?" She thought of the mountain and its perils, but it meant nothing now. "No," she said. "I'll wait for them."

"But you don't know what they might do! I told you what they've done to us—"

"I hardly think they'll shoot me out of the sky."

"Don't joke about it! They'll destroy anything, the things they love and the things they fear . . ."

"I don't care anymore," Dark said. "Go away, flyer. Go away to your games, and to your illusions of beauty."

He glared at her, turned, and sprang into the air. She did not watch him go, but pulled herself completely inside the shadows of her armor to wait.

Sometime during the night she drifted off to sleep. She dreamed of the fireflood: she could feel its heat and hear its roar.

When she awoke, the rising sun blazed directly into her eyes, and the steel blades of a helicopter cut the dawn. She tried and failed to blot out the sound of the humans' machine. She began to shiver, with uncertainty or with fear.

Dark crept slowly down the side of the mountain, toward the border where the humans would land. The flyers would not have to tell her to leave. She wondered if she were protecting herself, or them, from humiliation.

Something touched her and she started, drawing herself tightly into her armor.

"Dark, it's only me."

She peered out. Jay stood over her with his wings curved around them both.

"You can't hide me," she said.

"I know. We should have, but it's too late." He looked gaunt and exhausted. "I tried, Dark, I did try."

On the humans' side of the lava flow, the machine landed and sent up a fine spray of dust and rock particles. People climbed out, carrying weapons and nets. Dark did not hesitate.

"I have to go." She raised her armor up off the ground and started away.

"You're stronger than we are," Jay said. "The humans can't come and get you and we can't force you to leave."

"I know." The invisible boundary was almost at her feet; she moved reluctantly but steadily toward it.

"Why are you doing this?" Jay cried.

Dark did not answer.

She felt Jay's wingtip brush the edge of her armor as he walked alongside her. She stopped and glanced up at him.

"I'm coming with you," he said. "Till you get home. Till you're safe."

"It's no more safe for you. You can't leave your preserve."

"Nor could you."

"Jay, go back."

"I'll not lose another friend to the humans."

Dark touched the boundary. As if they were afraid she would still try to escape them, the humans rushed toward her and flung the net over her, pulling in its edges so it caught beneath her armor. They jostled the flyer away from her side.

"This isn't necessary," she said. "I'll come with you."

"Sorry," one finally said, in a grudging tone. "It's necessary."

"Her word's good," Jay said. "Otherwise she never would have come out to you at all."

"What happened to the others?" Dark asked.

One human shrugged.

"Captured," another said.

"And then?"

"Returned to the sanctuary."

Dark had no reason not to believe them, simply because they had no reason to spare her feelings if any of her friends were dead.

"You see, Jay, there's no need for you to come."

"You can't trust them! They'll lie to you for your cooperation and then kill you when I've left you with no witness."

That could be true; still, she lumbered toward the helicopter, more hindered than helped by the humans' tugging on the steel cables. The blades circled rhythmically over her.

Jay followed, but the humans barred his way.

"I'm going with her," he said.

She glanced back. Somehow, strangely, he looked even more delicate and frail among the normal humans than he had when she compared him to her own massive self.

"Don't come any farther, flyer."

He pushed past them. One took his wrist and he pulled away. Two of the humans grabbed him by the shoulders and pushed him over the border as he struggled. His wings opened out above the turmoil, flailing, as Jay fought to keep his balance. A blue feather fluttered free and spiraled to the ground.

Dragging her own captors with her, pulling them by the net-lines as they struggled and failed to keep her on their side, Dark scuttled toward Jay and broke through the group of humans. The flyer lay crumpled on the ground, one wing caught awkwardly beneath him, the other curved over and around him in defense. The humans sprang away from him, and from Dark.

"Jay," she said. "Jay . . ."

When he rose, Dark feared his wing was crushed. He winced when he lifted it, and his plumage was in disarray, but, glaring at the humans, he extended and flexed it and she saw to her great relief that he was all right. He glanced down at her and his gaze softened. Dark reached up toward him, and their clawed hands touched.

One of the humans snickered. Embarrassed, Dark jerked her hand away.

"There's nothing you can do," she said. "Stay here."

The net jerked tighter around her, but she resisted it.

"We can't waste any more time," the leader of her captors said. "Come on, now, it's time to go."

They succeeded in dragging her halfway around, and a few steps toward the helicopter, only because she permitted it.

"If you won't let me come with her, I'll follow," Jay said. "That machine can't outpace me."

"We can't control anyone outside your preserve." Strangely, the human sounded concerned. "You know the kind of thing that can happen. Flyer, stay inside your boundaries."

"You pay no heed to boundaries!" Jay cried, as they pulled and pushed Dark the last few paces back into their own territory. She moved slowly, at her own speed, ignoring them.

"Stay here, Jay," she said. "Stay here, or you'll leave me with guilt as well as failure."

Dark did not hear him, if he answered. She reached the copter, and steeled herself against the discomfort of its noise and unshielded electrical fields. She managed to clamber up into the cargo hold before they could subject her to the humiliation of being hoisted and shoved.

She looked out through the open door. It was as if the rest of the world were silent, for she could hear and sense nothing but the clamor immediately around her. On the lava ridge, Jay stood still, his shoulders slumped. Suddenly his wings flared out, rose, descended, and he soared into the air. Awestruck once more, Dark watched through the mesh of the net. Jay sailed in a huge circle and glided into the warm updraft of the volcano.

The rotors moved faster, blurring and nearly disappearing. The machine rose with a slight forward lurch, laboring under the weight of the hunting party and

Dark as well. At the same time, Jay spiraled upward through the glowing steam. Dark tried to turn away, but she could not. He was too beautiful.

The distance between them grew greater, until all Dark could see was a spark of bright blue appearing, then vanishing, among the columns of steam.

As the helicopter swung round, she thought she saw the spiral of Jay's flight widen, as if he were ignoring the threats the humans had made and cared nothing for warnings, as if he were drifting gently toward the boundaries of his refuge, gradually making up his mind to cross them and follow.

Don't leave your sanctuary, Jay, Dark thought. You don't belong out here.

But then, just before the machine cut off her view, he veered away from the mountain and in one great soaring arc passed over the boundary and into the humans' world.

No More Pencils, No More Books

John Morressy

Everyone knows that education in the United States has deteriorated to a depressing degree in recent decades. Books such as *The Blackboard Jungle* and *Why Johnny Can't Read* warned us of the problem over twenty years ago, and recent tests of university students have shown that nearly half of them are semiliterate at best. (English *teachers* in New York City fared only slightly better when they were tested.)

An important cause is the fact that when government budgets must be trimmed, school funds are among the first to suffer. Considering the state of our economy, therefore, can we expect better than John Morressy's tense evocation of tomorrow's schools?

Morressy is a teacher at Franklin Pierce College and the author of more than half a dozen science-fiction novels, including *Under a Calculating Star* and *Frostworld and Dreamfire*.

It wasn't first-timer's shakes. Colby was long past that. All the same, he felt the lightness in his belly and the tightness in his throat, and the creeping feeling that everyone else in the car knew just where he was going on this gloomy Monday morning.

He leaned back, took a deep breath, and directed his gaze out the window of the silent, rocking train, trying to keep his nerves calm. They were well into the city now, speeding along behind the protective fence, just above ground level. Colby's eyes flicked automatically from burned-out window to window, from one rubble heap to the next, searching out danger signs. He saw nothing. The light rain was falling steadily, and he guessed that the rubble rats had stayed in shelter. They'll all be in school today, keeping dry, he thought. Just my luck.

The train climbed, moved smoothly along, safely above roof level for the next two miles, then slowed for the main transfer point. Colby took his bag and moved out with the others, not too fast and not too slow, trying to damp his rising excitement.

Even at this early hour, most of the passengers were heading for the eight-car Business District and Midtown shuttles, where there were almost as many guards as riders. Colby headed for the special shuttle marked Inner City No. 3. The gateman checked his identification, took a quick look in his bag, and passed him through without a word. The inside guard gave Colby a just-perceptible smile and said, "Good luck, buddy."

"Thanks," Colby replied. His voice was hoarse, but he did not want to clear his throat in the guard's hearing.

The shuttle was a small electric with seats for twelve. It carried no guard. Colby was alone in it for a few minutes before a tall husky man entered and took the seat behind him. The newcomer gave Colby a quick glance but said nothing. Two more men entered. They stretched out as comfortably as the seats permitted, folded their arms, and went to sleep. Colby tried to do the same. He could not sleep. He kept thinking of the school at Greenbelt, where he could be right now. It was not too late; they would still have to take him back.

This was a bad way to be thinking, he knew. A man made his decisions and then he stuck with them. The

move to Inner City No. 3 was a free choice, made with
full knowledge of the gains and losses entailed. A little
tougher, perhaps, especially in the beginning, but he'd
been trained for it. And, here, he could count on support. There was nothing to worry about.

With nine men aboard, the shuttle pulled out of the
station, down the ramp to the street. The ride was silent
and surprisingly smooth. At one bumpy stretch Colby
took a quick look outside and saw a pile of burned-out
cars, real old-style gassers, in a tumbled roadside heap.
They had probably been set up as a barrier during the
night and thrust aside by an early patrol. He closed his
eyes again. A loud thump brought him upright as something heavy crashed on the roof of the shuttle. None of
the others stirred. He leaned back, shut his eyes, and
kept them shut until the ride was over.

He was feeling better, more confident, when the shuttle pulled into the learning compound. The others filed
out, mumbling a word now and then but generally silent, and he trailed along. At the first checkpoint he
was given a locker number and sent down a short corridor. He changed quickly, relieved himself, and drank
two glasses of water to moisten his throat.

A wiry little man entered the locker room and called
Colby's name. When Colby replied, the man approached and held out his hand.

"I'm Ed Mills. I'm the assistant principal here," he
said.

"Glad to meet you, Mr. Mills."

"Sorry I wasn't able to get together with you sooner,
Colby. Things have been hectic here. If you have any
questions about routine or schedules, or any of the op-
erations, I'll try to answer them. Any questions at all,
I'm here to help."

"Mr. Oakland explained things pretty well, sir. I've
read all the orientation material he gave me. I've memorized the ground plan and the schedules."

"That's good. And you're familiar with the monitor
we use?"

"I've logged sixty hours on the M-6 and eighty hours
on the M-6A, sir."

"Good, good," Mills said, obviously pleased. "I have to remember that I'm dealing with an experienced teacher."

"This is my first Inner City hitch, sir."

"It's not as bad as some people like to make it sound. We've got a tight ship here, Colby, and a good crew. You'll meet them later. Now, do you have any questions? The kids will be finished with breakfast and morning medication in five minutes. You'd better be in place when they get out."

"No questions, sir. I'll head for my room."

"Remember one thing, Colby, and you'll be all right. Once you're behind that monitor, you're the boss. Never forget it, and never let them forget it. If something has to be done, do it. We'll back you up." Mills extended his hand once again. "Good luck, Colby."

Colby settled into place behind his monitor. Everything he needed to run a class was there at his fingertips, all the information before his eyes. He set the classroom lights high, dimmed his own, turned on the speakers, and waited for his class to enter. At precisely 8:30 the access door slid back and they began to saunter in. A few stared at him, others elaborately ignored him. The PSMs shuffled unaware to their places. When every student was at his proper console, still half asleep and sluggish from breakfast and his medication, Colby switched on the morning sports readout. The class settled down, and the room was quiet.

Second and third periods went by without an incident. Inner City wasn't supposed to be this quiet, Colby knew. He began to wonder what was going on. Perhaps one of the pill men had taken pity on the new teacher and overdosed everyone. He had heard of that being done. Or maybe the kids had a surprise planned for him.

The morning continued to go so well that Colby let his vigilance slip. He made the mistake of keeping his eyes on the monitor screen for too long. When he looked up, a fist was coming straight for his face.

He didn't flinch. He had been warned of this trick. The fist slammed into the plexine barrier and slowed, impact absorbed harmlessly. It stopped six inches from Colby's face. The kid looked at him with eyes cold as stones.

Colby stayed cool. He let the kid curse him out for a few seconds; then he cut the incoming speaker and let the kid stand there working his mouth without a sound coming through to the teacher's side.

That was a point for Colby. When he turned the speaker on again, he found that some of the others in the classroom were applauding, whistling, and stamping their feet to show approval. One of the PSMs struggled to his feet and went into a slow lurching dance. A kid in the front row began to spar playfully with the one who had thrown the punch at Colby.

Colby let them go on for a time to work off some of the morning's pent-up energy. So far, no harm was being done. But the playful mood did not last long. When he saw knives, Colby knew that things had gone far enough. He hit two switches, fast. His amplified voice boomed into the room, cutting through the uproar.

"I'm locked on both of you. You use the knives, I use the stinger," he said.

The kids studied each other and then him. Colby kept his finger lightly resting on the white button. Slowly, with the greatest disdain they could pack into each movement, they put away the knives. They slouched to their places and slumped into the consoles.

Colby ran a quick readout of names. One thing he had learned was to get the names of the troublemakers right away. The one who had thrown the punch was Santos. The other one, the boxer, was Turner.

Santos sat glaring at him. Colby lowered his eyes to study the monitor screen. When he looked up, Santos's eyes were still fixed on him.

The kid was a hard case, he thought. Hell, they were all hard cases here. Even the PSMs, the quiet ones who spent most of the day nodding and staring into space, were dangerous when they came out of their fog. This wasn't a Greenbelt prep school, where kids smiled at the teacher and carried their own reader deck. This was Inner City No. 3, where kids carried weapons. If they smiled, it was a sure sign they were getting ready to use them. No teacher could afford to forget that.

Colby switched to the speaker on Santos's console and said, "What's the matter, Santos? Your reader broken?"

"Not yet, general."

"Then get to work."

"Up yours, general."

"Get to work, Santos."

Santos pulled off his boot. Still looking straight at Colby, he brought the steel-tipped heel down hard on the reader screen. Those screens were made of a plexine tougher than the barrier that divided teachers from their classes, but Santos was not trying to break the reader, he was out for Colby. Colby knew it, and knew that he had to react. He locked the stinger on Santos.

"Hit the reader once more and you get stung," he said.

Santos brought the boot heel down, and Colby tapped the white button. Santos straightened like an icicle, then slumped in his seat. The boot dropped from his twitching fingers.

The room was very still. Colby ran a quick individual scan of all consoles. The PSMs, still deep under from their morning's dosage, were vegetables. The others all had their readers on, and some were making a pretense of following the bright images that capered across the screen in the day's reading assignment.

Colby felt better, with a sense that he was in control now. These kids had seen that a greenie could use the stinger as well as any I.C. old-timer.

They stayed put after that. Seeing someone stung always took the fight out of them for a time. The room was relatively peaceful for the remainder of the fifth period.

The bell rang at 11:30, the signal for shouts and stomping. Even a few of the PSMs showed signs of life. It was lunchtime for class 3-12A, and for Colby as well. He watched them file out, keeping his eyes on the corridor cameras to make sure the lanes remained clear and the traffic flowed smoothly. Once he saw the cafeteria doors locked behind class 3-12A, Colby was on his own, free until 12:15.

Colby took the teachers' passage to the dining room. It was shorter and faster than using the corridors, and he had to show his pass at only two checkpoints.

He was looking around the room for a place to sit when a stocky black man at the center table beckoned to him, saying, "Over here, buddy. Time you got to meet your colleagues."

Five men sat at the table. There was one empty place, and Colby settled into it, looked around the ring of faces, and said, "Thanks. My name's Tom Colby."

The others were all in their late twenties or early thirties. They were burly men, Colby's size or bigger. Their presence seemed to crowd the room. All were clean-shaven, with close-cropped hair, and all wore standard light-blue teaching fatigues like Colby's. They moved with the smooth easy grace of athletes.

"I'm Howard," said the man who had called him. He looked to be the oldest of the group, as well as the biggest. He wore senior instructor's stripes with seven hitch marks. Pointing to the man at his left, Howard went around the table clockwise. "This is Lehman, Wood, Bakersfield, and Hunter."

From across the table, Wood asked, "You're Young's replacement, aren't you?"

"That's right," Colby replied.

"Yeah, I saw you in the shuttle this morning. Wondered who you were."

Bakersfield laughed and shook his head. "Lucky you, Colby. You got Santos and his whole zoo to keep you busy."

"It's not bad so far. Most of the class are on permanent medication."

"The ones who aren't can kill you. You used the stinger this morning. I picked up the static on the monitor."

"Santos was pushing pretty hard. I gave him a touch of it."

"That was smart," Howard said. "Most new guys wait too long before they use the stinger. They lose the initiative. I'd tell every new teacher to use it the first day."

"You're not new at this, are you, Colby?" Wood asked. "I heard that Young's replacement was coming from another school."

"I taught at Greenbelt No. 31 for two years," Colby said.

"You moved here from a Greenbelt school . . . what the hell did you do, Colby, lose your mind?"

"Just got greedy," Colby said blandly, and they laughed at his answer. He smiled and said, "What I really mean is, I needed extra money. Greenbelt schools are nice easy places to teach, sure, but it takes a long time and a lot of payoffs to get anywhere. My wife's going to have a baby in the fall, and we're hurting for money, so I volunteered for an I.C. hitch."

"You won't get rich here, buddy," said Lehman, and Wood added, "No, but you might get hurt."

Colby enumerated on his fingers as he said, "Inner City Teaching Corps means a pay differential, promotion preference, early retirement, total medical, full insurance . . . that's pretty good."

"It has to be. The work is rotten."

"What about endorsements, Colby? From what I hear, you can pick up a lot of endorsement money in the greenbelts," Bakersfield said.

"Not until you're there a while. I was starving."

Bakersfield raised an eyebrow and looked at him in disbelief. "Starving? At Greenbelt No. 31?"

"Well, all right, not starving, but I just couldn't get out of the hole. They'd only run a twelve-period day, but every teacher has to supervise a student activity, and everyone has a weekend study group. There's no money for that until you get to supervisory level. I couldn't hold down a part-time job, and my wife couldn't get any kind of work at all. There's nothing out there that isn't sewed up. I'm still paying off the people I had to bribe to get the job in the first place."

"Things sure have changed. When my father was in school, there was a shortage of teachers. Never had to bribe people to get an interview in those days," Howard said.

Bakersfield laughed. "You still don't—if it's an interview for Inner City No. 3."

"So now you're here. Think you can handle this rat-pack after all that time in Greenbelt?" Wood asked.

"I went back and took the full course at Quantico. Four months ICTC Basic, eight weeks advanced. Came out first in my class."

"Young was pretty good, too, but they got him," Wood said.

"How?"

Howard answered. "Somebody waited for him in the teachers' passage. Caught him off-guard and put a knife into him. Seventeen times."

"How'd they get into the corridor?"

"Nobody knows. So don't get careless between checkpoints."

"Maybe nobody can prove it yet, but it was Santos," said Wood. "I covered that class last week, while they were looking for a replacement, and I could see it right away. The kid's dangerous."

"Santos is a hard case," Colby said. "He didn't give me much choice about using the stinger."

Wood went on as if he had not heard. "He's like a steel brick: hard as hell and all sharp edges. And he's smart, too, don't let him fool you. Everybody else in that class is a moron, but Santos has brains. He should be on permanent medication. Keep him doped up and the whole school will be better off."

"He'll be getting out soon, won't he?" Bakersfield asked.

"End of next term, if he doesn't screw up again," Howard said. "He's just waiting out a diploma so he'll be eligible for unemployment benefits. That's the only reason any of these kids are here."

"Kids? Santos is as old as you are, Howard."

"They shouldn't give that class a new guy. Santos will eat Colby alive," said Wood.

Without looking up from his coffee cup, Colby said evenly, "I'll handle Santos. Nobody has to worry about me."

Hunter, silent until now, looked around the table and said irritably, "Why the hell are we talking about Santos? It's lunchtime. You're getting me sick. Who watched the playoff last night?"

Lunch kept everyone calm for a time, and the seventh and eighth periods passed with nothing more than a few minor scuffles. Colby cooled them with a warning. The kids looked at Santos, still appearing groggy from the morning's jolt, and decided to stay in their consoles and watch the science cartoons.

Today's ninth and tenth periods were set aside for a sex-education hollie, a weekly routine at all I.C. schools. Everyone from the superintendent on down knew that I.C. kids needed sex education as much as they needed classes in vandalism, but the life-sized, full-color holographic projections kept them quiet. There was some ethical objection to the practice, mostly from local preachers and neolibertarians, but the pious warning tacked on the end of each hollie served to satisfy everyone else. The sex hollies gave the teachers a chance to catch their breath and get through the afternoon, and that was all anyone really cared about.

Urging and threats were unnecessary now. Every student was in his console before the bell rang. Colby activated the hollie matrix, dimmed the lights, and turned the class over to his automatic monitors. Ten minutes into the period, his intercom buzzed. It was Howard.

"How's it going, Colby?"

"Everybody's studious all of a sudden."

"They always are. We take our break these two periods. You go as soon as Wood gets back. He'll lock his monitor into yours when he leaves, and you reverse it when it's your turn."

"Right. Where do I go, the dining room?"

"That's where most of us head. Be careful in the passage."

"I hear you, Howard. Thanks."

Ninth period flowed unnoticed into the tenth. At 2:40, Colby's intercom buzzed once again, this time with a message from Wood, who was leaving on his break. As they spoke, the backup monitor flashed the diagram of Wood's class.

Colby scanned both monitors quickly, then sat back

to await Wood's return. At 2:45, restless, he arose, scanned the monitors again, and then did a visual check of his room.

Santos and two others were missing. They showed on the monitor, but their consoles were empty. There was no way of telling how long they had been gone.

Colby grabbed the intercom and hit the all-channels override. "Three students missing from 3-12A. They've found a way to bypass the monitor. I'm going to check the passage."

"Don't go in that passage alone!" Howard's voice thundered.

"Wood's on his break. He could need help," Colby said, cutting the switch before Howard could respond.

The lights in the passage were out. Colby flashed his handbeam in both directions, saw nothing, and headed for the dining room. Just beyond the first checkpoint, his light caught the cluster of struggling forms.

"Hang on, Wood!" he shouted.

Wood went down before he could reach him, and the three turned to face Colby. Two had knives, the third carried a club, and Colby had only the flashlight. He kept it to one side, at arm's length, aimed into their eyes, and moved in on them.

The passage was narrow. They had no way to surround him, and if two came at him simultaneously, they would only crowd each other. Santos fell back, and the other knife wielder, one hand before him to shield his eyes from the light, came forward to close with Colby.

He was eager, but not very good. Colby dodged his thrust and kicked hard at his kneecap. The kid screamed and went down. One more kick and he was out. Santos and the other one hesitated. Colby snatched up the fallen knife and moved in on them. Santos threw his knife down and both kids turned to run. Howard and Bakersfield were waiting for them.

The hollie ended with the standard warning, which drew the customary catcalls and whistling. Colby raised the lights. Two minutes later, the bell rang to end tenth period. The kids, all laughing and grinning except for the PSMs, filed out for dinner. If anyone noticed that

Santos and the others were missing, he gave no sign of it.

Colby kept an eye on both monitors, his and Wood's, until the cafeteria doors closed behind their classes. When he entered the passage to the dining room, he noticed that the lights were working again.

Wood and Howard came in halfway through the period. Wood had a bandage on his hand and a bruise on his forehead, but he flashed Colby a big grin. Howard only nodded. They brought their trays to Colby's table.

"Thanks, Colby," said Wood. "They had me boxed in. If you hadn't come along, I would have gotten what Young got."

Colby shrugged off his gratitude. "It could have been me in that corridor, and if it was, you'd have come in to help. That's what ICTC is all about, isn't it?"

"All the same, you saved my skin. How'd you know they were there?"

"Dumb luck. I just happened to do a visual check, and they were missing. I can't figure out how they did it, though."

"I told you Santos was smart, didn't I? He figured out a way to override all the monitors in his console. He also managed to unscramble the locks on the faculty-access doors. He could've caused a hell of a lot of trouble."

"Sure could. What'll they do with him?"

"Permanent socializing medication, as of right now. This was his tenth offense, so it's automatic—no appeal," said Wood contentedly.

Howard added, "They'll keep him on here for another two years. Student stipend's only half what he'd get on unemployment. So that hits him in the pocket, where it really hurts."

"What about the others?"

"I recommended the same thing." Howard bit off a piece of roll, sipped his coffee, and off-handedly asked, "You didn't hear me say anything about not going into the passage, did you, Colby?"

Colby glanced at him quickly, but Howard was looking away. Colby looked to Wood for guidance. Wood closed his eyes and shook his head once, slowly.

"Not go in . . . ? Gee, I don't recall hearing that," Colby said.

Howard turned to him and nodded, as if Colby had given the proper response. "I figured you didn't hear. I guess your intercom's out of order."

"I guess so," Colby said.

Howard emptied his coffee cup and set it down. "That's good," he said. "If you disobeyed a direct order, I'd have to report it, and that would look bad, this being your first day and all. I want you to have a nice clean record, Colby. We want you to stick around."

"I don't know, Howard. I hear that all these Greenbelt guys are soft," said Wood. He looked from one to the other, then broke into a grin and began to laugh.

"I heard that, too, but this one's learning fast," Howard said. "He'll make a good teacher some day."

The Vacuum-packed Picnic

Rick Gauger

Given the (still) dominant opinion that new frontiers will be best explored and developed by men, we can assume our first lunar colony will be predominantly womanless—a situation that's likely to lead to desperate, even ludicrous, courting of the few women who will show up there. And on an all-male world, locker room jokes may become so common that they'll come to be taken seriously, much to everyone's regret.

Rick Gauger's tale of such an occurrence has the ring of inevitability. It's funny, but in the frightening way that jokes are when they're considered with the cold logic of space.

Rick Gauger is a former army officer (Vietnam) now in his late thirties. "The Vacuum-packed Picnic" was his first sale, though he has more stories forthcoming in *Analog* and *Destinies.*

As she approached my table across the pilots' crowded ready room with her teacup in her hand, I felt an urge coming over me. I had this urge to bite her—on the smooth, ivory neck, which emerged from the heavy aluminum collar ring of her close-fitting pilot's vacuum suit. Maybe it was the way she jangled all those pockets, tubes, clipboards, and electronic terminals as she made her way through the mob toward me. The typical space pilot's swagger—but female. Maybe it was the merry brown eyes and the humorous twist of her lips as she sat down in front of me.

"You're Captain Suarez, aren't you?"

"Yeah. My friends call me—"

"Pancho. Right?"

"Right. I hope you're one of my friends," I said, my figurative tail wagging furiously. Worst case of vibes I'd ever had. It seemed to be mutual. She studied me amusedly while her tea cooled.

I said, "Surely we've never met before. I know I'm pretty absent-minded, but . . ."

"Your friend Arunis Pittman told me about you. I met him on the polar sky station. He thought I should look you up when I got to West Limb. He said you would probably offer to keep me amused. You were highly recommended."

"Old Arunis! Damn! How is he?"

"He's fine. He said I should ask you whether you're still keeping the CO_2 high in your spacecraft life-support system, instead of doing the regulation aerobic exercises, the way you're supposed to."

"Damn again! How could he know about that? I'll bet he's trying to warn me that the agency is monitoring my life-support system again. I appreciate that. Thanks, Captain . . . er . . ."

"Cramblitt. I prefer Stacy, however." After a pause she asked, "Well, are you?"

"Not anymore. I don't want to be grounded again. I'll do my exercises like a good boy—"

"I don't mean that," she said. "I mean are you going to amuse me? This is the first time I've been on the moon. I don't have anything to do until the passenger shuttle begins its preflight countdown tomorrow night."

An opening big enough to drive a truck into. I had to think of something, immediately, that would capture her imagination. She tucked an errant strand of glossy black hair into her chignon as my mind raced.

"A picnic. How would you like to go on a picnic?

With me," I said, blurting out the first idiocy that came into my mind. "If you like, I'll take you to one of my favorite spots. It's not far, just a short walk from the base."

Her reaction was everything I could have hoped for. Her delicate mouth dropped open a little. "You're kidding. An *outdoor* picnic?"

"Why, sure," I lied. "It's a new recreation we have come up with here on the moon. Gets us away from the madding crowd. A great view, the hills, some nice rock colors. Perfect time of the month for it, too." Bridges were flaming behind me. *Why do I do these things?* "Of course you'd probably rather not go to the trouble. You're probably too tired, right?"

She had broken into excited smiles and twinkles. "Oh, no! I wouldn't miss this for anything!" she exclaimed. "A picnic on the moon! That's fantastic! Arunis was right about you, Pancho."

"Aw," I mumbled, standing up and giving her the boyish grin. "Just leave it all to me. Meet me at Hatch Seven-Charlie—anyone can tell you where it is—at ten hours tomorrow. Put on your vacuum suit and bring a fully charged backpack. I'll take care of the rest. I have to make a hopper run now. See you then."

Her smile followed me across the ready room as I made my way to the hopper dock. I waved goodbye before turning into the corridor. Male residents of the base who happened to be in the ready room watched all this enviously. They didn't see the grimace that appeared on my face as soon as I was out of sight. I had really jumped into it with both feet this time.

The business I had handed her about a picnic wasn't one-hundred-percent baloney. No one had ever really been on a picnic on the moon before, but the West Limb intellectual elite (my pals and I) had been discussing the idea for quite a while. We regarded our project as a noble pioneering effort, an expansion of man's capability in the space environment, but, mainly, as a way to get some privacy with our female colleagues. The base at West Limb hadn't yet become the luxurious suburb that it is today. In those days it was more like a big locker room on the moon, a crowded, noisy set of tunnels and domes, which reeked of old socks and new paint. We all lived in this warren like a bunch of crazy monks and nuns. The transients were bananas from months of isolation in the boonies, while the permanent party was crackers from never being able to get away from each other. Life was rough on the old high frontier, yes sir.

Unfortunately, plans for outings *à deux* hadn't gotten past the bullshit stage yet. One of my friends had analyzed the problem of picnic-site selection. Using lots of stolen computer time, he had determined which areas on the lunar surface around West Limb could be inhabited by a man—and a woman—for a reasonable length of time in a standard vacuum-survival tent. Of course, the idea was to obtain a comfortable shirt-sleeves-or-less habitat.

You know what survival tents are. They're what's inside those emergency boxes you see everywhere on the moon. Buggies have to carry one per passenger; so do the rocket hoppers. You've undoubtedly got several small ones under the bed in your hotel room. Solo prospectors and other outdoor workers use them regularly when they can't get to any other pressurized shelter. They climb into a tent, seal the opening, and inflate it with their reserve air. The tents blow up into a transparent plastic dome. Once the dome is pressurized, you can take off your vacuum suit and relax a bit. The old-timers say they're for leaks, whether you get one or have to take one. That's a joke.

Anyway, the most important parameter of my friend's analysis was the temperature inside the tent. Sunshine was everything. Anyone exposing his ass to the direct rays coming through the plastic would be rapidly rump-roasted. Complete lunar nighttime would be a glacial and gloomy experience, to say the least. No, what we wanted was a cheerful, sunshiny, picnicky sort of experience, with lots of scenery, close to, but not in sight of, the base or any of the main trails. A flat, shady spot on a slope facing a sunlit landscape, with an illuminated boulder nearby to reflect warmth toward the picnickers, would be ideal.

The computer in my friend's office, properly (and

illegally) stroked, coughed up a number of map over-
lays, one for each standard day in the lunar month,
showing where such sites might be looked for in the
area around West Limb. It was a brilliant piece of applied astronomy.

That afternoon my rocket hopper was scheduled to
haul a load of hung-over engineers back to Polar Solar
from their monthly spree at Grimaldi, and we had to
make a lot of local trips, too. I let my copilot do all the
flying while I studied one of those maps. Each time we
boosted out of the West Limb hopper pad, I compared
the map with the territory (or is it lunitory?) round
about. By quitting time I had selected a promising rock
field a short distance north of the base. It all seemed so
safe and easy.

That night I cashed in on the accumulated favors
that people on the base owed me. I got the next day off
and a free recharge of my vacuum-suit backpack, and I
borrowed two one-man vacuum-survival tents. I arranged for an airtight case packed with cold chicken,
potato salad, cole slaw, some vegetables, a fresh loaf of
French bread with real butter, lemonade, and two bottles of Boordy Vineyards' *vin gris*. West Limb may
have been a real sty in those days, but the pigs ate and
drank well.

The cafeteria manager had heard rumors. He drew
me into a corner of the kitchen, looked around carefully,
and leered at me.

"Suarez," he said confidentially, "what are you up
to? I mean, really?"

"Porkner," I said, "a gentleman, who is entrusted—"

"No, I mean, really. No shit. Is it—"

"You got it. It's a technical operation. Something
new," I said, leering back at him.

I made my escape while he was oh-ho-ho-ing at me.
It doesn't do to antagonize the cafeteria manager, or to
tell him anything, either. I went to bed early that evening. Lucky for me, it was my turn in the shower.

Stacy Cramblitt was waiting for me at the hatch
when I got there at ten hours. All the running around
and plotting I had done had seemed a little sordid to
me, I guess. But the way she looked, standing there,

cool and amused, in her tailor-made, fluorescent-pink pilot's vacuum suit, made my conscience clear up right away.

"Everything set?" she asked.

"Not quite yet," I said, putting my load of survival tents, blankets, and the food case into the airlock. For once there wasn't anyone in the corridor near the hatch. I held her by the arms and drew her close to me.

"I'm setting your suit radio on my private channel," I said. She looked at my face as I clicked the knob on her chest module. A delicate perfume rose from her collar ring.

"You have nice eyes," she said. "Now you're blushing."

"Nonsense. After you."

We stepped into the airlock and went through the rest of the suit-checkout procedure. I locked us through to the outside. The sun was glaring in the west. The structures scattered on the surface extended inky shadows across the rutted, pockmarked ground. As we walked, Stacy's helmet swiveled. She was taking in the torn-up ground, the glinting litter of aluminum scraps and shards, the awkward tangle of antenna towers and guy wires, and the humped and ugly buildings.

"It's not very pretty," I said.

"The human race takes its mess with it everywhere it goes," she said.

"Better here than on the earth," I said. "Besides, it's not all like this. This is a little zit on the face of a whole world. We're just a short walk from the real moon, where no one has ever set foot. Give it a chance." I took hold of one of her gloved hands.

"Okay," she said, looking at me. I couldn't see her face through her mirrored sun visor, but I felt her squeeze my hand.

We must have been an odd sight as we hiked out of view over the first ridge north of the base. There were undoubtedly a hundred people peeking at us from the windows of the base buildings. I was lugging the rolled-up tents and the food case. Stacy had a blanket over each shoulder. One of the blankets was a garish plaid;

the other was white with green and orange stripes and the words FUERZAS ARMADAS DE MEXICO printed on it.

An hour later we were crossing the vast, boulder-strewn slopes of Hevelius Crater, overlooking the flat Oceanus to our right. I noted that our feet were in the shade, but the tallest boulders reflected a lot of sunlight onto the ground. We could see well enough to pick our way along, and my blackbody thermometer registered in the middle teens. The map supplied by my computer-pushing pal was proving remarkably reliable.

"You know, it's not just all gray, black, and white," Stacy said. "I can see all kinds of subtle colors. Look at that greenish streak in the rocks over there. See it?"

"I sure do. You've really got good eyes. Most people can't see these things until they've been on the moon for a year or more. Most don't care. There's a lot of beauty here. It just doesn't smack you in the eye the way it does back on Earth. God didn't make this scenery for clods. You have to have some talent and sensitivity." I was laying it on a bit thick, but it wasn't *all* crap.

Stacy was having a good time in the low gravity, bouncing around me as I went striding along. She kicked up a big cloud of dust in front of us.

"Look at that," she said. "That dust settled so quickly that I could almost hear the thump it made on the ground. I've logged a lot of hours in space, but this is the first time I've ever been on my feet like this on another world. Do you ever get used to the strangeness?"

"Not really," I answered. "I never really get completely used to it. I'm always finding new things to look at." I stopped suddenly and stooped to look at the ground. "Look here."

As she bent over, I pointed out a circular pattern in the dust. In the center of the circle was a tiny grain of shiny glass. Hairlike lines and concentric arcs radiated from the center of the pattern. The lines looked as if someone had drawn them in the dust with a fine needle. The entire formation was about the size of a dime.

"What *is* it?" Stacy asked.

"I call them dust flowers," I said. "Don't touch it, it'll fall apart if you do. A friend of mine thinks they're micrometeorite craters. Where the glass is in the middle is where the micrometeorite struck, and the pattern around it was formed by shock waves traveling in the dust. My friend says they can form only on this kind of fine-dust surface. He's writing a paper about it."

"What do *you* think they are?"

"I think they're dust flowers. We'll probably find more of them if we look around carefully."

"I'd hate to step on something that's maybe been waiting here for millions of years."

"Let's keep our eyes open."

We started off again, passing among shattered heaps of rocks and skirting around the lesser craters.

Stacy said, "You know, it seems odd to me that there should be so much fine dust on the ground around here. I thought the lunar soil wasn't supposed to be differentiated—no wind or water to sort it out into particles of varying sizes, and so forth."

"That's right," I said. "Somebody's not following the rules."

We marched along in silence. I kept looking for an open spot to pitch the tents in. After a while Stacy and I emerged, so to speak, from a forest of boulders into a clearing. The scene was extraordinary, really. It was like a natural Stonehenge, with a circle of rough columns surrounding a sort of terrace in the hillside. The circle was open to the east, and we could see far out over the flatlands. A nearly full Earth hung low over the razor horizon. I almost expected to see a sail on that dappled, oceanlike expanse and surf rolling in on the beach several kilometers below us.

Stacy was superimpressed. She just stood there and said, "Glorious. Glorious. It really is." She turned to me. "No one else has ever been here, have they?"

"Don't see any footprints, do you? I've been saving it for someone special." *Someday God is going to punish me,* I thought.

"Let's get out of these suits and have some lunch," I said. "I'm starving."

I untied the roll of survival tents and laid them out on the ground, arranging them so that their door openings faced each other. The openings in tents of the kind I had are round, surrounded by a complicated, flexible gasket. You can seal up a single tent with its own door, or double up two tents by pressing their door gaskets together. The gaskets are supposed to interlock tightly when the tents are filled with air.

I held up the entrance of one of the tents to allow Stacy to crawl in, dragging the food case and the blankets. Then I crawled into it. Crouching on my knees, I carefully sealed the two tents together.

"That looks airtight," I said. "Let's see what happens when I let the air out of one of these reserve bottles. If it doesn't hold, we'll have to call it off and go back to the base."

"That would be miserable," Stacy said, poking me playfully in the backside.

I opened the valve on the air bottle. The tents stirred like living things, then ballooned into a pair of dome shapes.

"It's like being inside a waterbed mattress," Stacy remarked.

"Or two jellyfish kissing," I answered, watching the other tent through the transparent plastic walls of our tent.

Stacy began to spread the blankets on the tent floor. "Why did we bring two tents?" she asked.

"For storage. When we take our suits off, it'll be like having two extra people in here."

"So long as they don't want any lunch. Did you notice what's happening to the blankets?" she asked, holding up a ripped-off handful. "Looks like vacuum and sunlight aren't good for wool."

"They were getting pretty worn out anyway."

"How's the inflation going?" she said.

"Looks okay so far," I answered. The two tents, joined at their doorways, had become rigid. The air temperature had leveled off at twenty-five degrees centigrade, and the air pressure was holding steady at an alpine two hundred thirteen millibars.

"Can we take off our suits now?"

"Let me go first," I said. Cautiously I rotated the locking ring on my suit collar. Nothing happened. So I removed my helmet. The air in the tent felt fine. On my cheeks I could feel the cheery warmth of the nearest boulders.

"It's great," I said, disconnecting my backpack hoses. Soon we were both shucking ourselves out of our vacuum suits.

In her long johns, Stacy looked like a tax-free million. She removed her inner gloves and socks and sat, twiddling her toes at me and smiling. I gathered up our suits, helmets, and boots and passed them through the now-rigid doorway into the other tent. That made enough room in our tent for us to spread out the blankets. I kept my backpack with us and shoved Stacy's through the doorway into the other tent with the rest of our gear.

"All righty," I said, unlatching the food container, "luncheon is served at noon, under the stars. We have chicken, cold, and French bread, hot. We have slaw, tomatoes, and chilis. Have a glass of this good rosé, my dear Captain Cramblitt." I poured some wine into our glasses. Then I dished up big platefuls of everything. We sprawled comfortably together on the blankets, leaning on my backpack.

"Pancho, this is delicious," Stacy mumbled through a mouthful of Porkner's warm bread.

"Yep. My compliments to Cookie, and I'm so glad he's not here now," I joked.

After two hours I was feeling pleasantly tight around the middle. Stacy was pouring refills for us from our second bottle. The atmosphere in the tent was tropical. The brilliant earth, blazing cobalt, turquoise, and white, shone down on us. We lay, hips touching, Stacy's head on my shoulder.

I raised my glass to the home planet. "Here's to everybody who happens to be looking at us right now. Here's looking at them." My speech was only a little slurred.

"They can't see us," Stacy whispered, finishing her wine. "We're in the new-moon phase right now."

I turned to her and said, "Well, here's looking at you, anyway," and, what the hell, I kissed her on the mouth. She kissed me back, clutching at my neck.

"Guess what we're having for dessert," she whispered

into my ear, sending goose bumps along my arms and down my back.

Well, I never kiss and tell, but I will say that Stacy and I peeled each other out of our remaining clothing in rapid fashion. I threw the food box and our long johns into the other tent with the other stuff. Infrared from the ground and the surrounding boulders shone on our naked bodies, but it was nothing compared to the glow that was in the tent already. Her breasts flushing dark rose, Stacy spread herself on the blankets and held her arms out to me.

Now you're not going to believe this, but I hesitated at this point. I was, after all, an old space hand, and the open doorway leading to the other tent had been troubling me. There was no reason to worry about it, but open hatches of any kind sort of hover in my mind's eye until I get up and close them. Most of us out here are like that.

"Don't go away," I said, rising to my knees. I found the tent's door, a flat disk of flexible, transparent plastic, rolled up in a corner. I unrolled it and pressed its gasket into place around the circumference of the doorway between the two tents.

"Now I can give you the attention you deserve," I said, and I embraced her. Stacy snuggled in my arms and gave me a wet kiss. I really had my hands full.

While Stacy was tickling me behind the ear, we were interrupted by a strange noise. It sounded like a sudden release of steam. The total silence of the lunar mountainside had seeped into our unconscious during the afternoon, and this uncanny sound made us leap off the floor. There was one second of panicky thrashing as we disentangled our arms and legs. I crouched like a cornered alley cat, glaring around at the motionless landscape outside the tent. I didn't see anything. Then I noticed Stacy was staring goggle-eyed at the entrance of our tent.

"Holy Mother of God," I moaned. The other tent, the one with our stuff in it, had become detached from the tent we were in. The two door gaskets had separated, the air had escaped, and now the other tent was lying collapsed over our suits, our helmets, our boots, our underwear, the food container, Stacy's backpack, the dirty dishes. All of it was out there in the clean, fresh vacuum. We were left buck-naked in the tent, with nothing but the blankets and my backpack.

Stacy gulped for several seconds. "Well," she finally said in a small voice, "now we won't have to wash the dishes."

There was only one reason we weren't already dead of explosive decompression: I had sealed the door of our tent after getting rid of the last of our clothes. I could see my vacuum suit and helmet less than a meter away through the transparent plastic of the tent. I studied Stacy's backpack. A little red tag was sticking out of the air-regulator compartment. For some reason, the safety on her air bottle had blown, allowing the bottle to vent freely in the sealed tent. The excess pressure had blown the door gaskets of the two tents apart. The storage tent lost its pressure suddenly; if it hadn't had all our equipment in it, it probably would have flown away like a released balloon. Our own tent was holding air just fine, although the plastic door was bulging outward unnervingly.

I dragged my backpack toward me and looked at the readouts. Four hours, at the most, of reserve air and CO_2 absorption. The arm's length of vacuum that separated us from the radios in our helmets might as well have been millions of kilometers. Our ass was really in a sling, and my face must've shown it as I looked up from the backpack.

Stacy covered my hand with hers. As calm and beautiful as an angel, she said to me, "Don't be afraid, Pancho."

Guilt replaced terror in my wretched soul. "N-no," I said. "We're not dead yet, are we?"

"Although we might as well disregard the chances of anybody finding us out here by accident," she said firmly.

Oh, yes. And my own stupid fault, too.

"Well, I shouldn't have pressured you into bringing me out here," she said.

"Don't say that, Stacy. I always think I know what I'm doing." *Don't I ever!* By this time she was holding me, stroking me. There I was, lower than a crater's bottom, and *she* was trying to comfort *me*.

The sky over our heads was black, black. The stars were waiting to see what I could come up with. "Whatever we do, we'll have to do it soon," I quavered. "Any suggestions?"

"Only two. The first one is, we say the hell with it, hope for rescue, and have a good, but short, time."

"I'm not up to it."

"Forget it. The other idea is to open the entrance of our tent and try to grab one of the helmets before the decompression kills us."

"Now I'm *really* not up to it."

"Nothing to it. You get the helmet and reseal the door. I let out all the air from your backpack reserve bottle to repressurize our tent. One, two, three. Then we radio for help."

"I could never reclose the door gasket fast enough."

"We could wrap ourselves in strips of blanket, mummy-style, really tight, to prevent embolism."

"Darling, it sounds like a brave way to commit suicide. If we can't think of anything else, we'll try it, all right?"

"Okay," she said, crestfallen.

"Besides, the blankets are falling apart," I said, holding one up. The blankets had become so dried out and flimsy that they were turning to shreds as we moved around in the tent.

There was a long silence. We sat huddled, arms around each other, like a pair of monkeys in a thunderstorm. Stacy had been doing her best to encourage me. Her proposal, to chance letting the air out of our tent, was a long shot, but it was basically practical. Definitely worth a try. But I couldn't face it right away. She was a better man than I was.

Stacy started to droop a little. I hugged her more tightly, and she straightened up again. Damn it! I visualized the path we had walked from West Limb. Just a short walk, if we didn't stop for sightseeing and fooling around. Between the rocks, the ground was smoother than usual for the moon, like a beach made of fine ash instead of sand. We could do it barefooted. I was beginning to have a thought.

"Stacy—"

She responded with a loud sniff. Then she said, "I'm sorry. I thought I was being brave. It's just such a damn rotten break—"

"I should be shot for getting you into this," I said. "When we get back to the base, you should turn me in for disciplinary action."

"I d-definitely will. Corrupting my morals—" By this time tears were running down my face, too.

"Listen, Stacy, there's another thing we can do. We can try to walk back to the base. We could stand the tent on its edge and roll it along from the inside. We'll just leave all our stuff here. There's enough air in my backpack for us to make it if we start now."

She thought about it for a moment. "Why not?" she said, finally. "Even if the tent rips and we depressurize, we won't be any worse off than we are now, will we?"

"Nope."

"Let's do it," she said, jumping up and pulling me to my feet.

I lifted up my backpack and hung it on my back, tucking the dangling air and coolant hoses under one of the shoulder straps. Stacy helped me adjust the harness to fit my naked torso.

Stooping, we both pushed against the wall on one side of the tent, trying to tip it over. The plastic felt icy cold against my hands.

"Try to shuffle your feet toward the edge of the floor," I said. The tent slowly rolled onto its side, the scraps of blanket sliding downward as the tent floor tilted upward. The rim of the tent flattened on the ground. It was like standing inside a huge flat tire. The floor of the tent was now a wall to my right. Since it was no longer resting on the ground, it was bulging outward almost as much as the dome roof on my left side. The floor was made of the same kind of transparent plastic as the dome was. I tapped on it to knock off the dust that stuck to its outside surface. Very little dust actually fell off, but at least we could see through the material.

"Okay," I said. "Luckily, we're already facing the way we want to go. Stacy, stay close behind me. The idea is to step along carefully and make the tent roll like a wheel on its edge."

"I hope we don't have to make any sharp turns."

We took a tentative step. As I put my weight on the plastic that curved up in front of me, it stretched until my foot was on the ground. Alarming stress wrinkles developed in the dome and floor. Abruptly the tent lurched forward. Stacy fell against me from behind. We both staggered, but we managed to keep the tent upright.

"What happened?" I asked Stacy over my shoulder.

"When I picked up my foot, the tent rolled forward and pushed me into you," she said. "If we want the tent to roll smoothly, I've got to take my trailing foot off the ground at the same time you put your leading foot down on the plastic. We'll have to march in step. I'll have to hold on to your backpack."

"Jesus Christ! All right, forward, march. Left, right, left, right, left, right . . ."

And so it went. The tent rolled along like a big wheel, wobbling this way and that, but never quite falling over. Whenever we came to one of the huge boulders, we would walk a little to one side of the edge of the dome, forcing the tent to curve its path in that direction. Occasionally we had to stop and put the tent into reverse. Generally, I followed the footprints we had made on our way to the picnic site, but, as we came to more open country, I started taking shortcuts. I carefully avoided the rims of any craters more than a few meters across. I didn't care to find out whether we could develop enough traction to climb up out of one of them.

Things went better than I'd hoped. We moved steadily downhill, with me still counting cadence until Stacy yelled at me to shut up.

On and on we trundled the tent, my arches flattening in little craters, sharp little rocks jabbing my soles. As we tramped out of the dust area into coarser soil, I started worrying about puncturing the tent. There wasn't a single damn thing I could do about it at all.

Stacy was cussing under her breath with pain as she marched behind me.

The blankets had turned to scraps and fuzz by this time, sliding down to the lowest part of the tent as it rotated. I attempted to walk on the stuff, but the effort threw Stacy and me out of step.

"Even if we had our boots with us," I said, "we probably couldn't wear them in this tent. The cleats would hurt the tent worse than the ground outside does."

"Yeah," said Stacy. "Let's keep moving."

I didn't have a watch, but we must have gone on that way about three hours. We left the boulders behind us, and the air grew chilly in the tent. If the ground hadn't been warm, we would have had trouble with frostbite. The pocked fields of the moon were around us. It seemed as if we were making our way down the sides of an endless ash heap. My bare skin cringed away from the sharp stars overhead.

"At least it's a nice cloudy day," Stacy said.

"What?"

"On Earth. We can see where we're going."

"Oh."

I wondered whether we could jump the tent over an obstacle if we had to. I was taking bigger chances, leading us into unfamiliar ground, trying to make our return to West Limb along a more nearly straight line than the route we had taken to reach the place where we had our picnic.

As we got closer to the base, the sloping side of Hevelius trended more to the west. The sun began to peep among the undulating hills on our right horizon. When we came to the first long strip of sunlight shining directly on the ground, it was like stepping on a hot griddle.

"Yow! Back up, quick!"

"Is your foot burnt?" Stacy asked.

"No, thank God."

"Will the tent plastic be able to stand the heat?"

"Oh, sure. It's designed for use on hotter surfaces than this. But we'll need to protect our feet with something."

We allowed the tent to topple over. Then we sat down for a breather.

"How far do we still have to go?" Stacy asked me as we bound our bruised and blistered feet with strips of disintegrating blanket.

"Less than a kilometer. The base is right around the corner of that ridge." Good thing, too. I had taken advantage of our halt to inspect the condition of our tent. The plastic was frosty and scratched and was obviously starting to wear out.

After tying up our makeshift booties, we got the tent up and rolling again. The remaining distance had to be covered more slowly than we had been proceeding. We were forced to go from one patch of shade to another. Crossing the strips of sunlight was hell. I felt like I was being roasted in a bonfire. At each stopping place in the shade I tried to plan the next sunlight crossing so we could as much as possible avoid running over rocks. The tent plastic was beginning to make little crackling noises with each step we took. I kept slogging away on my throbbing feet. Whatever was bad for me was worse for Stacy, I knew.

At last, the base buildings came in sight. I never thought I could be so happy to see that dump as I was just then. "Stacy!" I cried. "You see that? We're almost there!"

I couldn't see her behind me, but I could feel her leaning heavily on my backpack.

"Don't stop now, honey. We're getting there," I said, doggedly pacing on. There were no more sunlit places to cross. I had to consider the problem of how to get inside the buildings. The quickest thing to do would be to head for the buggy hatch, the only airlock big enough to allow us to roll the tent inside without collapsing it first.

I explained all this to Stacy while we approached the buildings. "Fortunately, it'll be easy to get somebody to cycle the airlock for us," I said. "The trail to the buggy hatch runs right under the picture window of the staff bar and lounge. My instincts tell me it must be about Happy Hour now. The bar will be full of people. It'll be easy to attract their attention——"

Stacy came to an abrupt halt, jerking on my back-pack so hard that I almost fell.

"What did you say?" she said thickly.

"Huh?"

"You expect me to walk in front of the West Limb Base staff bar and lounge during Happy Hour on Friday night *stark-naked*?"

"Stacy," I said, turning to face her, "we're lucky to be *alive*, and—"

She burst into tears. "I can't. I won't!"

She had been carrying me through an ordeal so har-rowing that it still gives me the creeps just thinking about it. We were sunburned salmon-pink; our feet were bleeding; we were in deadly danger just standing there. She had bolstered my morale and kept me from despair. This was the first crack in her bravery and her sense of humor I had seen during the whole awful thing. Some other short-tempered son of a bitch might have raised his voice at that point, but not I.

I held her close, then looked her up and down. My hands ran up her back, caressed her hair, fondled her breasts, rubbed against her downy belly. I almost wasn't aware of what I was doing.

"Stacy, Stacy, darling," I choked. "You'll be the most beautiful thing any of them has ever seen, you know." Just then my left ear popped. It had always been the sensitive one. The air pressure in the tent was falling. We had finally sprung a leak!

Stacy felt it, too. She grabbed the straps of my back-pack and whirled me around. "Go, Pancho!" she shouted. "The hatch!"

I stifled the impulse to bolt. "Double time!" I barked. "Leftrightleftrightleftright!"

We were lucky again. Though fog was forming in the tent, I could see that the buggy hatch stood wide open. This was in violation of base safety directives, but I'll be eternally grateful to whoever was responsible. With me in front and Stacy clinging behind, we bustled across the open space in front of the window.

I caught a glimpse of round eyes, open mouths, and hands holding drinks in suspended animation. Porkner happened to be tending the bar that night. He later told me that it was the only dead silence he had ever heard in that place.

Stacy and I ran into the airlock so fast that I got a black eye colliding with the inside door. Icepicks in my ears, heart slamming, I pounded at the airlock controls through the tent plastic. I managed to hit the EMERGENCY CLOSE button; the outer door clanged down. The tent folded around us as the airlock roared itself full of that wonderful air.

I staggered against the wall, fighting the tent. Stacy sat down hard on the floor. We were both gasping for air. I was about to say we had made it, or words to that effect, when I became aware of the sound of trampling feet and the murmur of voices from behind the inner door. The Happy Hour stampede had arrived.

Stacy ripped the plastic door off the entrance of the tent and stepped out. She said through clenched teeth, "I'll kill the first bastard who—"

"Hey! Suarez! You all right?" It was Porkner's voice, coming over the airlock speaker. He had won the footrace down the corridor from the bar to the buggy hatch. I jumped out of the tent and palmed the lens of the TV camera that surveilled the airlock.

"Yeah, Suarez," said another voice, "you need any help in there?" Muffled laughter. Stacy glared at the door.

"We're all right," I said into the intercom grille. "We, uh, we need some clothes."

"Already taken care of," Porkner's voice answered. "We've got a red light on the airlock panel out here. We'll have to open the hatch by hand. Stand by."

Stacy and I stood to one side. After much talk and clanking, the hatch opened a crack, and Porkner's arm came through, proffering a couple of white tablecloths. Blessed be the name of Porkner, and I'll never malign his spaghetti again.

Stacy and I emerged discreetly togaed, to the plaudits of the multitude, and entered the dusty buggy bay. Stacy was escorted to her quarters, and I had to answer a lot of questions. There were some sly remarks about my, ah, alleged physical state, which had not gone unnoticed as we sprinted past the picture window. I always say that it's up to us pioneers to point the way forward, as it were.

As for my relationship with Captain Cramblitt, her goodbye kiss at the shuttle pad the next day seemed promising. The next time I saw her, she asked me whether I wanted to go skiing. We were on the north polar icecap of Mars at the time, but that's another story.

The Thaw

Tanith Lee

Most of us think that cryonics—freezing bodies at death so that they may be thawed out at some future time when medical science has advanced so much that they can be brought back to life—is an invention of the sixties. Not true, as far as the concept goes: Neil R. Jones first proposed this notion in "The Jameson Satellite," published in *Amazing Stories* for July 1931. R. C. W. Ettinger, the father of cryonics, acknowledges that he got the idea from reading Jones's story as a teenager.

The validity of cryonics remains to be proven, of course, and even if the techniques prove workable someday, will the results necessarily be happy ones? Tanith Lee offers a story of cryonic rebirth suggesting that one's ancestors might not be entirely welcome in a new world—might, in fact, prove very dangerous.

Ladies first, they said.

That was O.K. Then they put a histotrace on the lady in question, and called me.

"No thanks," I said.

"Listen," they said, "you're a generative blood-line descendant of Carla Brice. Aren't you interested, for God's sake? This is a unique moment, a unique experience. She's going to need support, understanding. A contact. Come on. Don't be frigid about it."

"I guess Carla is more frigid than I'm ever likely to be."

They laughed, to keep up the informalities. Then they mentioned the Institute grant I'd receive, just for hanging around and being supportive. To a quasi-unemployed artist, that was temptation and a half. They also reminded me that on this initial bout there wouldn't be much publicity, so later, if I wanted to capitalize as an eyewitness, and providing good old Carla was willing—I had a sudden vision of getting very rich, very quick, and with the minimum of effort, and I succumbed ungracefully.

Which accurately demonstrates my three strongest qualities: laziness, optimism, and blind stupidity. Which in turn sums up the whole story, more or less. And that's probably why I was told to write it down for the archives of the human race. I can't think of a better way to depress and wreck the hopes of frenzied, shackled, bleating humanity.

But to return to Carla. She was, I believe, my great-great-great-great-great grandmother. Give or take a great. Absolute accuracy isn't one of my talents, either. The relevant part is, however, that at thirty-three, Carla had developed the rare heart complaint valu—val—well, she'd developed it. She had a few months, or less, and so she opted, along with seventy other people that year, to undergo Cryogenic Suspension till a cure could be found. Cry Sus had been getting progressively more popular, ever since the 1980s. Remember? It's the freezing method of holding a body in refrigerated stasis, indefinitely preserving thereby flesh, bones, organs and the rest, perfect and pristine, in a frosty crystal box. (Just stick a tray of water in the freezer and see for yourself.) It may not strike you as cozy any more, but that's hardly surprising. In 1993, seventy-one persons, of whom four-or-five-or-six-great granny Carla was one, saw it as the only feasible alternative to death. In the following two hundred years, four thousand others copied their example. They froze their malignancies, their unreliable hearts, and their corroding tissues, and as the light faded from their snowed-over eyes, they must have dreamed of waking up in the fabulous future.

Funny thing about the future. Each next second is the future. And now it's the present. And now it's the past.

Those all-together four thousand and ninety-one who deposited their physiognomies in the cold-storage compartments of the world were looking forward to the future. And here it was. And we were it.

And smack in the middle of this future, which I naïvely called Now, was I, Tacey Brice, a rotten little unskilled artist, painting gimcrack flying saucers for the spacines. There was a big flying saucer sighting boom that year of 2193. Either you recollect that, or you don't. Nearly as big as the historic boom between the 1930s and '90s. Psychologists had told us it was our human inadequacy, searching all over for a father-mother figure to replace God. Besides, we were getting desperate. We'd penetrated our solar system to a limited extent, but without meeting anybody on the way.

That's another weird thing. When you read the speculativia of the 1900s, you can see just how much they expected of us. It was going to be all or nothing. Either the world would become a miracle of rare device with plastisteel igloos balanced on the stratosphere and metal giblets, or we'd have gone out in a blast of radiation. Neither of which had happened. We'd had problems, of course. Over two hundred years, problems occur. There had been the Fission Tragedy, and the World Flood of '14. There'd been the huge pollution clear-ups complete with the rationing that entailed, and one pretty nasty pandemic. They had set us back, that's obvious. But not halted us. So we reached 2193 mostly unscathed, with a whizz-bang technology not quite as whizz, or bang, as prophesied. A place where doors opened when they saw who you were, and with a colony on Mars, but where they hadn't solved the unemployment problem or the geriatric problem. Up in the ether there were about six hundred buzz-whuzzes headed out into nowhere, bleeping information about earth. But we hadn't landed on Alpha Centauri yet. And if the waste-disposal jammed, brother, it jammed. What I'm trying to say (superfluously, because you're ahead of me), is that their future, those four thousand and ninety-one, their future which was our present, wasn't as spectacular as they'd trusted or feared. Excepting the Salenic Vena-derivative drugs, which had rendered most of the diseases of the 1900s and the 2000s obsolete.

And suddenly, one day, someone had a notion.

"Hey, guys," this someone suggested, "you recall all those sealed frosty boxes the medic centers have? You know, with the onice carcinomas and valu-diddums in 'em? Well, don't you think it'd be grand to defrost the lot of them and pump 'em full of health?"

"Crazy," said everybody else, and wet themselves with enthusiasm.

After that, they got the thing organized on a global scale. And first off, not wanting to chance any public mishaps, they intended to unfreeze a single frost box, in relative privacy. Perhaps they put all the names in a hat. Whatever, they picked Carla Brice, or Brr-Ice, if you liked that Newsies' tablotape pun.

And since Carla Brr-Ice might feel a touch extra chilly, coming back to life two hundred years after she's cryonized out of it, they dredged up a blood-line descendant to hold her cold old thirty-three-year hand. And that was Tacey Brr-Ice. Me.

The room below was pink, but the cold pink of strawberry ice cream. There were forty doctors of every gender prowling about in it and round the crystal slab. It put me in mind of a pack of wolves with a carcass they couldn't quite decide when to eat. But then, I was having a nervous attack, up on the spectator gallery where they'd sat me. The countdown had begun two days ago, and I'd been ushered in at noon today. For an hour now, the crystal had been clear. I could see a sort of blob in it, which gradually resolved into a naked woman. Straight off, even with her lying there stiff as a board and utterly defenseless, I could tell she was the sort of lady who scared me dizzy. She was large and well-shaped, with a mane of dark-red hair. She was the type that goes outdoor swimming at all seasons, skis, shoots rapids in a canoe, becomes the co-ordinator of a moon colony. The type that bites. Valu-diddums had got her, but nothing else could have done. Not child, beast, nor man. Certainly not another woman. Oh my. And this was my multiple-great granny that I was about to offer the hand of reassurance.

Another hour, and some dial and click mechanisms down in the strawberry ice room started to dicker. The wolves flew in for the kill. A dead lioness, that was Carla. Then the box rattled and there was a yell. I couldn't see for scrabbling medics.

"What happened?"

The young medic detailed to sit on the spec gallery with me sighed.

"I'd say she's opened her eyes."

The young medic was black as space and beautiful as the stars therein. But he didn't give a damn about me. You could see he was in love with Carla the lioness. I was simply a pain he had to put up with for two or three hours, while he stared at the goddess beneath.

But now the medics had drawn off. I thought of the Sleeping Beauty story, and Snow White. Her eyes were open indeed. Coppery brown to tone with the mane. She didn't appear dazed. She appeared contemptuous. Precisely as I'd anticipated. Then the crystal box lid began to rise.

"Jesus," I said.

"Strange you should say that," said the black medic. His own wonderful eyes fixed on Carla, he'd waxed profound and enigmatic. "The manner in which we all still use these outdated religious expletives: *God, Christ, Hell,* long after we've ceased to credit their religious basis as such. The successful completion of this experiment in life-suspense and restoration has a bearing on the same matter," he murmured, his inch-long lashes brushing the plastase pane. "You've read of the controversy regarding this process? It was seen at one era as an infringement of religious faith."

"Oh, yes?"

I kept on staring at him. Infinitely preferable to

Carla, with her open eyes, and the solitary bending medic with the supadermic.

"The idea of the soul," said the medic on the gallery. "The immortal part which survives death. But what befalls a soul trapped for years, centuries, in a living yet statically frozen body? In a physical limbo, a living death. You see the problem this would pose for the religious?"

"I—uh—"

"But, of course, today . . ." he spread his hands. "There is no such barrier to lucid thought. The life force, we now know, resides purely in the brain, and thereafter in the motor nerves, the spinal cord, and attendant reflexive centers. There is no *soul*."

Then he shut up and nearly swooned away, and I realized Carla had met his eye.

I looked, and she was sitting, part reclined against some medic's arm. The medic was telling her where she was and what year it was and how, by this evening, the valu-diddums would be no more than a bad dream, and then she could go out into the amazing new world with her loving descendant, who she could observe up there on the gallery.

She did spare a glance for me. It lasted about .09 of a mini-instant. I tried to unglue my mouth and flash her a warming welcoming grin, but before I could manage it, she was back to studying the black medic.

At that moment somebody came and whipped me away for celebratory alcohol, and two hours later, when I'd celebrated rather too much, they took me up a plushy corridor to meet Carla, skin to skin.

Actually, she was dressed on this occasion. She'd had a shower and a couple of post-defrosting tests and some shots and the anti-valu-diddums stuff. Her hair was smouldering like a fire in a forest. She wore the shiny smock medical centers insisted that you wore, but on her it was like a designer original. She'd even had a tan frozen in with her, or maybe it was my dazzled eyes that made her seem all bronzed and glowing. Nobody could look that good, that *healthy*, after two hundred years on ice. And if they did, they shouldn't. Her room was crammed with flowers and bottles of scent and exotic light paintings, courtesy of the Institute. And then they trundled me in.

Not astoundingly, she gazed at me with bored amusement. Like she'd come to the dregs at the bottom of the wine.

"This is Tacey," somebody said, making free with my forename.

Carla spoke, in a voice of maroon velvet.

"Hallo, er, Tacey." Patently, my cognomen was a big mistake. Never mind, she'd overlook it for now. "I gather we are related."

I was drunk, but it wasn't helping.

"I'm your gr—yes, we are, but—" I intelligently blurted. The "but" was going to be a prologue to some nauseating, placatory, crawler's drivel about her gorgeousness and youth. It wasn't necessary, not even to let her know how scared I was. She could tell that easily, plus how I'd shrunk to a shadow in her high-voltage glare. Before I could complete my hiccupping sycophancy, anyway, the medic in charge said: "Tacey is your link, Mz Brice, with civilization as it currently is."

Carla couldn't resist it. She raised one manicured eyebrow, frozen exquisite for two centuries. If Tacey was the link, civilization could take a walk.

"My apartment," I went on blurting, "it's medium, but—"

What was I going to say now? About how all my grant from the Institute I would willingly spend on gowns and perfumes and skis and automatic rifles, or whatever Carla wanted. How I'd move out and she could have the apartment to herself. (She wouldn't like the spacine murals on the walls.)

"It's just a bri—a bridge," I managed. "Till you get acclimatosed—atized."

She watched me as I made a fool of myself, or rather, displayed my true foolishness. Finally I comprehended the message in her copper eyes: Don't bother. That was all: Don't bother. You're a failure, Carla's copper irises informed me, as if I didn't know. Don't make excuses. You can alter nothing. I expect nothing from you. I will stay while I must in your ineffectual vicinity, and you may fly round me and scorch your wings if you like. When I am ready, I shall leave immediately, searing over your sky like a meteor. You can offer no aid, no interest, no grain I cannot garner for myself.

"How kind of Tacey," Carla's voice said. "Come, darling, and let me kiss you."

Somehow, I'd imagined her still as very cold from the frosty box, but she was blood heat. Ashamed, I let her brush my cheek with her meteoric lips. Perhaps I'd burn.

"I'd say this calls for a toast," said the medic in charge. "But just rose-juice for Mz Brice, I'm afraid, at present."

Carla smiled at him, and I hallucinated a rose-bush, thorns too, eviscerated by her teeth. Lions drink blood, not roses.

I got home paralyzed and floundered about trying to change things. In the middle of attempting to re-spray-paint over a wall, I sank on a pillow and slept. Next day I was angry, the way you can only be angry over something against which you are powerless. So damn it. Let her arrive and see space-shuttles, motherships, and whirly bug-eyed monsters all across the plastase. And don't pull the ready-cook out of the alcove to clean the feed-pipes behind it that I hadn't seen for three years. Or dig the plant out of the cooled-water dispenser. Or buy any new garments, blinds, rugs, sheets. And don't conceal the Wage-Increment checks when they skitter down the chute. Or prop up the better spacines I'd illustrated, on the table where she won't miss them.

I visited her one more time during the month she stayed at the Institute. I didn't have the courage not to take her anything, although I knew that whatever I offered would be wrong. Actually, I had an impulse to blow my first grant check and my W-I together and buy her a little antique stiletto of Toledo steel. It was blatantly meant to commit murder with, and as I handed it to her I'd bow and say, "For you, Carla. I just know you can find a use for it." But naturally I didn't have the bravura. I bought her a flagon of expensive scent she didn't need and was rewarded by seeing her put it on a shelf with three other identically packaged flagons, each twice the size of mine. She was wearing a recline-robe of amber silk, and I almost reached for sunglasses. We didn't say much. I tottered from her room, sun-burned and peeling. And that night I painted another flying saucer on the wall.

The day she left the Institute, they sent a mobile for me. I was supposed to collect and ride to the apartment with Carla, to make her feel homey. I felt sick.

Before I met her, though, the medic in charge wafted me into his office.

"We're lucky," he said. "Mz Brice is a most inde-pendent lady. Her readjustment has been, in fact, re-markable. None of the traumas or rebuttals we've been anxious about. I doubt if most of the other subjects to be revived from Cryogenesis will demonstrate the equivalent rate of success."

"They're really reviving them, then?" I inquired lamely. I was glad to be in here, putting off my fourth congress with inadequacy.

"A month from today. Dependent on the ultimately positive results of our post-resuscitation analysis of Mz Brice. But, as I intimated, I hardly predict any hitch there."

"And how long," I swallowed, "how long do you think Carla will want to stay with me?"

"Well, she seems to have formed quite an attachment for you, Tacey. It's a great compliment, you know, from a woman like that. A proud, volatile spirit. But she needs an anchor for a while. We all need our an-chors. Probably, her proximity will benefit you, in re-turn. Don't you agree?"

I didn't answer, and he concluded I was over-whelmed. He started to describe to me that glorious scheduled event, the global link-up, when every single cryogone was to be revived, as simultaneously with each other as they could arrange it. The process would be going out on five channels of the Spatials, visible to us all. Technology triumphant yet again, bringing us a minute or two of transcendental catharsis. I thought about the beautiful black medic and his words on reli-gion. And this is how we replaced it, presumably (when we weren't saucer-sighting), shedding tears sentimentally over four thousand and ninety idiots fumbling out of the deep-freeze.

"One last, small warning," the medic in charge added. "You may notice—or you may not, I can't be positive—the occasional lapse in the behavioral patterns of Mz Brice."

There was a fantasy for me. Carla, *lapsed*.

"In what way?" I asked, miserably enjoying the unlikelihood.

"Mere items. A mood, an aberration—a brief disorientation even. These are to be expected in a woman reclaimed by life after two hundred years, and in a world she is no longer familiar with. As I explained, I looked for much worse and far greater quantity. The odd personality slip is inevitable. You mustn't be alarmed. At such moments the most steadying influence on Mz Brice will be a non-Institutional normalcy of surroundings. And the presence of yourself."

I nearly laughed.

I would have, if the door hadn't opened, and if Carla, in mock red-lynx fur, hadn't stalked into the room.

I didn't even try to create chatter. Alone in the mobile, with the auto driving us along the cool concrete highways, there wasn't any requirement to pretend for the benefit of others. Carla reckoned I was a schmoil, and I duly schmoiled. Mind you, now and again, she put out a silk paw and gave me a playful tap. Like when she asked me where I got my hair *done*. But I just told her about the ready-set parlors and she quit. Then again, she asked a couple of less abstract questions. Did libraries still exist, that was one. The second one was if I slept well.

I went along with everything in a dank stupor. I think I was half kidding myself it was going to be over soon. Then the mobile drove into the auto-lift of my apartment block, the gates gaped and we got out. As my door recognized me and split wide, it abruptly hit me that Carla and I were going to be hand in glove for some while. A month at least, while the Institute computed its final tests. Maybe more, if Carla had my lazy streak somewhere in her bronze and permasteel frame.

She strode into my apartment and stood flaming among the flying saucers and the wine-ringed furniture. The fake-fur looked as if she'd shot it herself. She was a head taller than I was ever going to be. And then she startled me, about the only way she could right then.

"I'm tired, Tacey," said Carla.

No wise-cracks, no vitriol, no stare from Olympus.

She glided to the bedroom. O.K. I'd allocated the bed as hers, the couch as mine. She paused, gold digit on the panel that I'd pre-set to respond to her finger.

"Will you forgive me?" she wondered aloud.

Her voice was soporific. I yawned.

"Sure, Carla."

She stayed behind the closed panels for hours. The day reddened over the city, colors as usual heightened by the weather control that operates a quarter of a mile up. I slumped here and there, unable to eat or rest or read or doodle. I was finding out what it was going to be like, having an apartment and knowing it wasn't mine any more. Even through a door, Carla dominated.

Around 19, I knocked. No reply.

Intimidated, I slunk off. I wouldn't play the septophones, even with the ear-pieces only, even with the volume way down. Might wake Granny. You see, if you could wake her from two hundred years in the freezer, you could certainly wake her after eight hours on a dormadais.

At twenty-four midnight, she still hadn't come out.

Coward, I knocked again, and feebly called: "Night, Carla. See you tomorrow."

On the couch I had nightmares, or nightcarlas to be explicit. Some were very realistic, like the one where the trust bonds Carla's estate had left for her hadn't accumulated after all and she was destitute, and going to remain with me for ever and ever. Or there were the comic-strip ones where the fake red-lynx got under the cover and bit me. Or the surreal ones where Carla came floating towards me, clad only in her smouldering hair, and everything caught fire from it, and I kept saying, "Please, Carla, don't set the rug alight. Please, Carla, don't set the couch alight." In the end there was merely a dream where Carla bent over me, hissing something like an anaconda—if they do hiss. She wanted me to stay asleep, apparently, and for some reason I was fighting her, though I was almost comatose. The strange thing in this dream was that Carla's eyes had altered from copper to a brilliant topaz yellow, like the lynx's.

It must have been about four in the morning that I woke up. I think it was the washer unit that woke me. Or it could have been the septophones. Or the waste-disposal. Or the drier. Or any of the several gadgets a modern apartment was equipped with. Because they were all on. It sounded like a madhouse. Looked like one. All the lights were on, too. In the middle of chaos: Carla. She was quite naked, the way I'd seen her at the first, but she had the sort of nakedness that seems like clothes, clean-cut, firm and flawless. The sort that makes me want to hide inside a stone. She was reminiscent of a sorceress in the midst of her sorcery, the erupting mechanisms sprawling round her in the fierce light. I had a silly thought: *Carla's going nova.* Then she turned and saw me. My mouth felt as if it had been security-sealed, but I got out, "You O.K., Carla?"

"I am, darling. Go back to sleep now."

That's the last thing I remember till 10 A.M. the next day.

I wondered initially if Carla and the gadgets had been an additional dream. But when I checked the energy-meter I discovered they hadn't. I was plodding to the ready-cook when Carla emerged from the bedroom in her amber reclinerobe.

She didn't say a word. She just relaxed at the counter and let me be her slave. I got ready to prepare her the large breakfast she outlined. Then I ran her bath. When the water-meter shut off half through, Carla suggested I put in the extra tags to ensure the tub was filled right up.

As she bathed, I sat at the counter and had another nervous attack.

Of course, Carla was predictably curious. Back in 1993, many of our gadgets hadn't been invented, or at least not developed to their present standard. Why not get up in the night and turn everything on? Why did it have to seem sinister? Maybe my sleeping through it practically non-stop was the thing that troubled me. All right. So Carla was a hypnotist. Come to consider, should I run a histotrace myself, in an attempt to learn what Carla was—had been?

But let's face it, what really upset me was the low on the energy-meter, the water-meter taking a third of my week's water tags in one morning. And Carla luxuriously wallowing, leaving me to foot the bill.

Could I say anything? No. I knew she'd immobilize me before I'd begun.

When she came from the bathroom, I asked her did she want to go out. She said no, but I could visit the library, if I would, and pick up this book and tape list she'd called through to them. I checked the call-meter. That was down, too.

"I intend to act the hermit for a while, Tacey," Carla murmured behind me as I guiltily flinched away from the meter. "I don't want to get involved in a furor of publicity. I gather the news of my successful revival will have been leaked today. The tablotapes will be sporting it. But I understand, by the news publishing codes of the '80s, that unless I approach the Newsies voluntarily, they are not permitted to approach me."

"Yes, that's right." I gazed pleadingly into the air. "I guess you wouldn't ever reconsider that, Carla? It could mean a lot of money. That is, not for you to contact the Newsies. But if you'd all—allow me to on your beh—half."

She chuckled like a lioness with her throat full of gazelle. The hair rose on my neck as she slunk closer. When her big, warm, elegant hand curved over my skull, I shuddered.

"No, Tacey. I don't think I'd care for that. I don't need the cash. My estate investments, I hear, are flourishing."

"I was thinking of m—I was thinking of me, Carla. I cou—could use the tags."

The hand slid from my head and batted me lightly. Somehow, I was glad I hadn't given her the Toledo knife after all.

"No, I don't think so. I think it will do you much more good to continue as you are. Now, run along to the library, darling."

I went mainly because I was glad to get away from her. To utter the spineless whining I had had drained entirely my thin reserves of courage. I was shaking when I reached the auto-lift. I had a wild plan of leaving town, and leaving my apartment with Carla in it, and going to ground. It was more than just inadequacy now. Hunter and hunted. And as I crept through the long grass, her fiery breath was on my heels.

I collected the twenty books and the fifty tapes and paid for the loan. I took them back to the apartment and laid them before my astonishing amber granny. I was too scared even to hide. Much too scared to disobey.

I sat on the sun-patio, though it was the weather control day for rain. Through the plastase panels I heard the tapes educating Carla on every aspect of contemporary life; social, political, economic, geographical, and carnal.

When she summoned me, I fixed lunch. Later, drinks and supper.

Then I was too nervous to go to sleep. I passed out in the bathroom, sitting in the shower cubicle. Had nightcarlas. Carla eating salad. Didn't wake up till 10 A.M. Checked. All meters down again.

When I trod on smashed plastase I thought it was sugar. Then I saw the cooled-water dispenser was in ninety-five bits. Where the plant had been, there was only soil and condensation and trailing roots.

I looked, and everywhere beheld torn-off leaves and tiny clots of earth. There was a leaf by Carla's bedroom. I knocked and my heart knocked to keep my hand company.

But Carla wasn't interested in breakfast, wasn't hungry.

I knew why not. She'd eaten my plant.

You can take a bet I meant to call up the Institute right away. Somehow, I didn't. For one thing, I didn't want to call from the apartment and risk Carla catching me at it. For another, I didn't want to go out and leave her, in case she did something worse. Then again, I was terrified to linger in her vicinity. A *lapse,* the medic in charge had postulated. It was certainly that. Had she done anything like it at the Institute? Somehow I had the idea she hadn't. She'd saved it for me. Out of playful malice.

I dithered for an hour, till I panicked, pressed the call button and spoke the digits. I never heard the door open. She seemed to know exactly when to—*strike;* yes, that *is* the word I want. I sensed her there. She didn't even touch me. I let go the call button.

"Who were you calling?" Carla asked.

"Just a guy I used to pair with," I said, but it came out husky and gulped and quivering.

"Well, go ahead. Don't mind me."

Her maroon voice, bored and amused and indifferent to anything I might do, held me like a steel claw. And I discovered I had to turn around and face her. I had to stare into her eyes.

The scorn in them was killing. I wanted to shrivel and roll under the rug, but I couldn't look away.

"But if you're not going to call anyone, run my bath, darling," Carla said.

I ran her bath.

It was that easy. Of course.

She was magnetic. Irresistible.

I couldn't—

I could *not*—

Partly, it had all become incredible. I couldn't picture myself accusing Carla of house-plant-eating to the medics at the Institute. Who'd believe it? It was nuts. I mean, too nuts even for them. And presently, I left off quite believing it myself.

Nevertheless, somewhere in my brain I kept on replaying those sentences of the medic in charge: *the occasional lapse in the behavioral patterns . . . a mood, an aberration . . .* And against that, point counterpoint, there kept on playing that phrase the beautiful black medic had reeled off enigmatically as a cultural jest: *But what befalls a soul trapped for years, centuries, in a living yet statically frozen body?*

Meanwhile, by sheer will, by the force of her persona, she'd stopped me calling. And that same thing stopped me talking about her to anybody on the street, sent me tongue-tied to fetch groceries, sent me grovelling to conjure meals. It was almost as if it also shoved me asleep when she wanted and brought me awake ditto.

Doesn't time fly when you're having fun?

Twenty days, each more or less resembling each, hurried by. Carla didn't do anything else particularly weird, at least not that I saw or detected. But then, I never woke up nights any more. And I had an insane theory that the meters had been fiddled, because they weren't low, but they felt as if they should be. I hadn't got any more plants. I missed some packaged paper lingerie, but it turned up under Carla's bed, where I'd kicked it when the bed was mine. Twenty days, twenty-five. The month of Carla's post-resuscitation tests was nearly through. One morning, I was stumbling about like a zombie, cleaning the apartment because the dust-ease had jammed and Carla had spent five minutes in silent comment on the dust. I was moving in that combined sludge of terror, mindlessness and masochistic cringing she'd taught me, when the door signal went.

When I opened the door, there stood the black medic with a slim case of file-tapes. I felt transparent, and that was how he treated me. He gazed straight through me to the empty room where he had hoped my granny would be.

"I'm afraid your call doesn't seem to be working," he said. (Why had I the notion Carla had done something to the call?) "I'd be grateful to see Mz Brice, if she can spare me a few minutes. Just something we'd like to check for the files."

That instant, splendid on her cue, Carla manifested from the bathroom. The medic had seen her naked in the frosty box, but not a naked that was vaguely and fluently sheathed in a damp towel. It had the predictable effect. As he paused transfixed, Carla bestowed her most gracious smile.

"Sit down," she said. "What check is this? Tacey, darling, why not arrange some fresh coffee?"

Tacey darling went to the coffee cone. Over its bubbling, I heard him say to her, "It's simply that Doctor Something was a little worried by a possible amnesia. Certainly, none of the memory areas seem physically impaired. But you see, here and there on the tape—"

"Give me an example, please," drawled Carla.

The black medic lowered his lashes as if to sweep the tablotape.

"Some confusion over places, and names. Your second husband, Francis, for instance, who you named as Frederick. And there, the red mark—Doctor Something-Else mentioned the satellite disaster of '91, and it seems you did not recall—"

"You're referring to the malfunction of the Ixion 11, which broke up and crashed in the midwest, taking three hundred lives," said Carla. She sounded like a purring textbook. She leaned forward, and I could watch him tremble all the way across from the coffee cone. "Doctor Something and Doctor Something-Else," said Carla, "will have to make allowances for my excitement at rebirth. Now, I can't have you driving out this way for nothing. How about you come to dinner, the night before the great day. Tacey doesn't see nearly enough people her own age. As for me, let's say you'll make a two-hundred-year old lady very happy."

The air between them was electric enough to form sparks. By the "great day" she meant, patently, the five-channel Spatial event when her four thousand and ninety confrères got liberated from the sub-zero. But he plainly didn't care so much about defrostings any more.

The coffee cone boiled over. I noticed with a shock I was crying. Nobody else did.

What I wanted to do was program the ready-cook for the meal, get in some wine, and get the hell out of the apartment and leave the two of them alone. I'd pass the night at one of the all-night Populars, and creep in around 10 A.M. the next morning. That's the state I frankly acknowledged she had reduced me to. I'd have been honestly grateful to have done that. But Carla wouldn't let me.

"Out?" she inquired. "But this whole party is for you, darling."

There was nobody about. She didn't have to pretend. She and I knew I was the slave. She and I knew her long-refrigerated soul, returning in fire, had scalded me into a melty on the ground. So it could only be cruelty, this. She seemed to be experimenting, even, as she had with the gadgets. The psychological dissection of an inferior inhabitant of the future.

What I had to do, therefore, was to visit the ready-set hair parlor, and buy a dress with my bi-monthly second W-I check. Carla, though naturally she didn't go with me, somehow instigated and oversaw these ventures. Choosing the dress, she was oddly at my elbow. *That* one, her detached and omnipresent aura instructed me. It was expensive, and it was scarlet and gold. It would have looked wonderful on somebody else. But not me. That dress just sucked the little life I've got right out of me.

Come the big night (before the big day, for which the countdown must already have, in fact, begun), there I was, done up like a New Year parcel, and with my own problematical soul wizened within me. The door signal went, and the slave accordingly opened the door, and the dark angel entered, politely thanking me as he nearly walked straight through me.

He looked so marvelous, I practically bolted. But still the aura of Carla, and Carla's wishes, which were beginning to seem to be communicating themselves telepathically, held me put.

Then Carla appeared. I hadn't seen her before, that evening. The dress was lionskin, and it looked real, despite the anti-game-hunting laws. Her hair was a smooth auburn waterfall that left bare an ear with a gold star dependent from it. I just went into the cooking area and uncorked a bottle and drank most of it straight off.

They both had good appetites, though hers was better than his. She'd eaten a vast amount since she'd been with me, presumably ravenous after that long fast. I was the waitress, so I waited on them. When I reached my plate, the food had congealed because the warmer in the table on my side was faulty. Anyway, I wasn't hungry. There were two types of wine. I drank the cheap type. I was on the second bottle now, and sufficiently sad I could have howled, but I'd also grown uninvolved, viewing my sadness from a great height.

They danced together to the septophones. I drank some more wine. I was going to be very, very ill tomorrow. But that was tomorrow. Verily. When I looked up, they'd danced themselves into the bedroom and the panels were shut. Carla's cruelty had had its run and I wasn't prepared for any additions, such as ecstatic moans from the interior, to augment my frustration. Accordingly, garbed in my New Year parcel frock, hair in curlicues, and another bottle in my hand, I staggered forth into the night.

I might have met a thug, a rapist, a murderer, or even one of the numerous polipatrols that roam the city to prevent the activities of such. But I didn't meet anyone who took note of me. Nobody cared. Nobody was interested. Nobody wanted to be my friend, rob me, abuse me, give me a job or a goal, or make me happy, or make love to me. So if you thought I was a Judas, just you remember that. If one of you slobs had taken any notice of me that night—

I didn't have to wait for morning to be ill. There was a handsome washroom on Avenue East. I'll never forget it. I was there quite a while.

When the glamorous weather-control dawn irradiated the city, I was past the worst. And by 10 A.M. I was trudging home, queasy, embittered, hard-done-by, but sober. I was even able to register the tabloes everywhere and the holoid neons, telling us all that the great day was here. The day of the four thousand and ninety. Thawday. I wondered dimly if Carla and the Prince of Darkness were still celebrating it in my bed. She should have been cold. Joke. All right. It isn't.

The door to my apartment let me in. The place was as I'd abandoned it. The window-blinds were down, the table strewn with plates and glasses. The bedroom door firmly shut.

I pressed the switch to raise the blinds, and nothing happened, which didn't surprise me. That in itself should have proved to me how far the influence had gone and how there was no retreat. But I only had this random desultory urge to see what the apartment door would do now. What it did was not react. Not even when I put my hand on the panel, which method was generally reserved for guests. It had admitted me, but wouldn't let me out again. Carla had done something to it. As she had to the call, the meters, and to me. But how—personal power? Ridiculous. I was a spineless dope, that was why she'd been able to negate me. Yet—forty-one medics, with a bevy of tests and questions, some of which, apparently, she hadn't got right, ate from her hand. And maybe her psychic ability had increased. Practice makes perfect.

. . . *What befalls a soul trapped for years, centuries, in a living yet statically frozen body?*

It was dark in the room, with the blinds irreversibly staying down and the lights irreversibly staying off.

Then the bedroom door slid wide, and Carla slid out. Naked again, and glowing in the dark. She smiled at me, pityingly.

"Tacey, darling, now you've gotten over your sulks, there's something in here I'd like you to clear up for me."

Dichotomy once more. I wanted to take root where I was, but she had me walking to the bedroom. She truly was glowing. As if she'd lightly sprayed herself over with something mildly luminous. I guessed what would be in the bedroom, and I'd begun retching, but, already despoiled of filling, that didn't matter. Soon I was in the doorway and she said, "Stop that, Tacey." And I stopped retching and stood and looked at what remained of the beautiful black medic, wrapped up in the bloodstained lionskin.

Lions drink blood, not roses.

Something loosened inside me then. It was probably the final submission, the final surrender of the fight. Presumably I'd been fighting her subconsciously from the start, or I wouldn't have gained the ragged half-freedoms I had. But now I was limp and sodden, so I could ask humbly: "The plant was salad. But a man—what was he?"

"You don't quite get it, darling, do you?" Carla said. She stroked my hair friendlily. I didn't shudder any more. Cowed dog, I was relaxed under the contemptuous affection of my mistress. "One was green and vegetable. One was black, male, and meat. Different forms. Local dishes. I had no inclination to sample you, you comprehend, since you were approximate to my own appearance. But of course, others who find themselves to be black and male may wish to sample pale-skinned females. Don't worry, Tacey. You'll be safe. You entertain me. You're mine. Protected species."

"Still don't understand, Carla," I whispered meekly.

"Well, just clear up for me, and I'll explain."

I don't have to apologize to you for what I did then, because, of course, you know all about it, the will-less indifference of the absolute slave. I bundled up the relics of Carla's lover-breakfast, and dumped them in the waste-disposal, which dealt with them pretty efficiently.

Then I cleaned the bedroom, and had a shower, and fixed Carla some coffee and biscuits. It was almost noon, the hour when the four thousand and ninety were going to be roused, and to step from their frost boxes in front of seven-eighths of the world's Spatial-viewers. Carla wanted to see it too, so I switched on my set, minus the sound. Next Carla told me I might sit, and I sat on a pillow, and she explained.

For some reason, I don't remember her actual words. Perhaps she put it in a technical way and I got the gist but not the sentences. I'll put it in my own words here, despite the fact that a lot of you know now anyway. After all, under supervision, we still have babies sometimes. When they grow up they'll need to know. Know why they haven't got a chance, and why we hadn't. And, to level with you, know why I'm not a Judas, and that I didn't betray us, because I didn't have a chance either.

Laziness, optimism, and blind stupidity.

I suppose optimism more than anything.

Four thousand and ninety-one persons lying down in

frozen stasis, aware they didn't have souls and couldn't otherwise survive, dreaming of a future of cures, and of a re-awakening in that future. And the earth dreaming of benevolent visitors from other worlds, father-mother figures to guide and help us. Sending them buzz-whuzzes to bleep, over and over, *Here* we are. *Here. Here.*

I guess we do have souls. Or we have something that has nothing to do with the brain, or the nerve centers, or the spinal cord. Perhaps that dies too, when we die. Or perhaps it escapes. Whatever happens, that's the one thing you can't retain in Cryogenic Suspension. The body, all its valves and ducts and organs, lies pristine in limbo, and when you wake it up with the correct drugs, impulses, stimuli, it's live again, can be cured of its diseases, becoming a flawless vessel of—nothing. It's like an empty room, a vacant lot. The tenant's skipped.

Somewhere out in the starry night of space, one of the bleeping buzz-whuzzes was intercepted. Not by pater-mater figures, but by a predatory, bellicose alien race. It was simple to get to us—hadn't we given comprehensive directions? But on arrival they perceived a world totally unsuited to their fiery, gaseous, incorporeal forms. That was a blow, that was. But they didn't give up hope. Along with their superior technology they developed a process whereby they reckoned they could transfer inside of human bodies, and thereafter live off the fat of the Terrain. However, said process wouldn't work. Why not? The human consciousness (soul?) was too strong to overcome, it wouldn't let them through. Even asleep, they couldn't oust us. Dormant, the consciousness (soul?) is still present, or at least linked. As for dead bodies, no go. A man who had expired of old age, or with a mobile on top of him was no use. The body had to be a whole one, or there was no point. Up in their saucers, which were periodically spotted, they spat and swore. They gazed at the earth and drooled, pondering mastery of a globe, and entire races of slaves at their disposal. But there was no way they could achieve their aims until—until they learned of all those Cryogenic Suspensions in their frost boxes, all those soulless lumps of ice, waiting on the day when science would release and cure them and bring them forth healthy and *void*.

If you haven't got a tenant, advertise for a new tenant. We had. And they'd come.

Carla was the first. As her eyes opened under the crystal, something looked out of them. Not Carla Brice. Not any more. But something.

Curious, cruel, powerful, indomitable, alien, deadly.

Alone, she could handle hundreds of us humans, for her influence ascended virtually minute by minute. Soon there were going to be four thousand and ninety of her kind, opening their eyes, smiling their scornful thank-yous through the Spatials at the world they had come to conquer. The world they did conquer.

We gave them beautiful, healthy, movable houses to live in, and billions to serve them and be toyed with by them, and provide them with extra bodies to be frozen and made fit to house any leftover colleagues of theirs. And our green depolluted meadows wherein to rejoice.

As for Carla, she'd kept quiet and careful as long as she had to. Long enough for the tests to go through and for her to communicate back, telepathically, to her people, all the data they might require on earth, prior to their arrival.

And now she sat and considered me, meteoric fiery Carla-who-wasn't-Carla, her eyes, in the dark, gleaming topaz yellow through their copper irises, revealing her basic inflammable nature within the veil of a dead woman's living flesh.

They can make me do whatever they want, and they made me write this. Nothing utterly bad has been done to me, and maybe it never will. So I've been lucky there.

To them, I'm historically interesting, as Carla had been historically interesting to us, as a first. I'm the first Slave. Possibly, I can stay alive on the strength of that and not be killed for a whim.

Which, in a way, I suppose, means I'm sort of a success, after all.

In a Petri Dish Upstairs

George Turner

If space colonies are to survive, they'll have to prove their worth to the people on our planet who support them. Their greatest immediate value would seem to be in gathering solar energy and transmitting it to Earth, which could be a tremendous boon to those of us who will remain here. But colonies quickly become worlds unto themselves, wanting freedom.

What *is* the cost of freedom? Must it be blood, or might power, carefully guarded and carefully dispensed, be more effective? George Turner, who has garnered major literary awards in his native Australia, wrote this fascinating novelette as a "prequel" to his highly regarded novel *Beloved Son*, and it was published in a remarkable anthology of Australian science fiction titled *Rooms of Paradise*, edited by Lee Harding. Turner's space colony may not seem at first to be anything like Paradise, but then, we don't live there.

1

When, some fifty years after the Plagues and The Collapse, Alastair Dunwoodie put the first Solar Power

Station into synchronous orbit over Melbourne Town—that is, some 38,000 kilometers above it—no warning angel tapped his shoulder to whisper, "You have created a fresh culture and rung the knell of an old one."

It would have been told to mind its own celestial business. With solar power now gathered by the immense space mirrors and microbeamed to Earth for network distribution, the Golden Age was appreciably closer. With a Station in Heaven, all was right with the world.

Remarkably soon there were seventeen Power Stations in orbit above strategic distribution points around the world, sufficient for the needs of a planet no longer crawling with the famined, resource-consuming life of the Twentieth Century. The Plagues and The Collapse and yet less pleasant events had thinned the problem.

Dunwoodie was a builder, not a creator; his ideas had been mooted in the 1970s, some eight years before, but had not come to fruition when The Collapse intervened. It was, however, notable that even in those days, when social studies of crowding and isolation had been to the fore, nobody seemed to have considered what changes might occur among the first people to live out their lives in a steel cylinder in space.

And not for a further eighty years after the launching did the Custodian of Public Safety of Melbourne Town begin to consider it—when, for the first time in three generations, an Orbiter proposed to visit Earth. When he had arrived at the vagueness of a possible decision, he visited the Mayor.

"Do you mean to give a civic reception for this brat?"

The Mayor of Melbourne Town was unenthusiastic. "It's an event, of sorts. A reception will let Orbiter vanity preen while it keeps the Town's society belles from claiming they weren't allowed to meet him. I hear he's a good looking lad."

The Custodian seemed uninterested in that.

The Mayor asked at last, "But why? After three generations they send a youngster—nineteen, I believe—to visit. What do they want? Why a boy?"

"A boy on a man's errand, you think?"

The Mayor's expression asked, *Why are you wasting my time?* and he waited for explanation.

The Custodian went at it obliquely. "The Global Ethic," he said, "the Ethic of Non-Interference—do you ever question it?"

The Mayor was a very young man, the Custodian an old and dangerously experienced one. The Mayor went sharply on guard but his expression remained as bland as his answer: "Why should I? It works."

The Custodian's authority outweighed the Mayor's— Mayoral duties were social rather than gubernatorial— but he had no overt power to punish. But advancement could be blocked or privilege curtailed without open defiance of the Ethic as it operated on Departmental levels.

The Custodian surprised him. "You should, James; you should question continuously. Particularly morals, conventions, habits, regulations—and ethics. The older and more ingrained, the more questionable."

Stiffly, "Those are matters for Global League delegates."

The Custodian grinned like a friendly skull. "You needn't be so damned careful; I want your help, not your scalp. Review some facts." He flicked a raised finger. "First: the Power Stations as originally flown were rotated about the long axis to afford peripheral gravity." Another finger. "Second: when the final Stations were flown, the seventeen formed themselves into the Orbital League." Third finger. "Then they made unreasonable demands for luxuries, surplus wealth, cultural artifacts and civic privilege under threat of throttling down the power beams. That was seventy years back."

"School is a year or two behind me," said the Mayor coldly, "but basic history remains familiar."

"I'm selecting facts, not lecturing." Fourth finger. "So the Global Council of the time authorized use of a remote-action energy blind, a—call it a weapon— whose existence had not been publicly known. The Orbiters threatened our microbeams, so *we* blinded the internal power systems of Station One from a single projector in Melbourne Town. After a week of staling air, falling temperature and fouling water they cried quits and—" fifth finger "—the Orbital League has made no such further error since."

"So for once the Ethic was ignored."

"Oh, but it wasn't. We took suitable action, harming no one seriously, to preserve the status quo. That was all."

The Mayor said, "It was *not* all. The Stations had been earning extra revenue with their null-g factories—perfect ball bearings, perfectly formed crystals and so on. Earth stopped buying, limiting Orbiter income to the Power Charter allocation. That was reprisal and un-Ethical."

"Earth protected herself against wealthy Stations accumulating the means of further blackmail."

The Mayor was contemptuous. "Semantic drivel."

"It was a Council decision. Do you dispute it?"

"Yes," said the Mayor and waited for an axe to fall.

"Good, good, good! So you see, the bloody Ethic means whatever you need it to mean."

The Mayor retained caution. "Most realize that, privately. Still, it works."

"Because *laissez faire* has become part of our cultural mentality. But what of the cultural mentality Upstairs?"

"Well, we know they have developed non-Terrene conventions and behavior. There's been little physical contact since they cut themselves off."

"Quite so."

Silence dragged while the Mayor wondered had he said more than he knew. What the Orbiters had done was to stop the rotation of the Stations and give themselves over to a null-g existence. When you thought of it, why not? To live in utter physical freedom, to fly, to leap, to glide, to dispose for ever of the burden of the body . . . the wonder was that they had waited so long to grasp delight.

It followed that the first generation born in space was cut off from Earth. Once muscle structure and metabolism had settled into null-g conditions, exposure to gravity became inconceivable, possibly disastrous . . . ahh!

"This young man, this Peter Marrian—how will he deal with weight? Power-assist harness?"

"I must tell you about that," said the Custodian. "You'll be fascinated . . ."

The no-nonsense Orbiters preserved no fairy tales from their Earthly heritage but they had formulated a few austere anecdotes for the very young. One concerned a super-virile Orbiter who married a Terrene heiress and brought her home to live in orbit.

Peter heard the tale when he was not quite three and already absorbing Orbiter lore with a mind the commune nurses noted, in their giggly fashion, as destined for Upper Crust privilege.

"—then, when he'd defeated all the schemes of the rich girl's wicked father, he joined with her in a church as they do Downstairs. Then he brought her to the Station with all her riches and the Commune Fathers awarded him such extra privileges that he lived happily ever after."

It did not occur to him then (or later, for that matter) to ask how *she* lived ever after. His interest was in the early part of the story, which told how the young Orbiter became big and powerful in order to face the monstrous Terrene weapon, Gravity. Now, how was that accomplished?

He spat at the nurses who said he would understand when he was older. They had no idea, for they were only thirdwomen and not educated beyond their needs, and such rearing facilities did not then exist. But soon would.

Such facilities, *all* facilities, cost money. The Commune's only money-wealth was the cynically limited income derived from the Power Charter, kept at a "reasonable minimum." The Orbiters were welcome to pride and null-g freedom—at a suitably cheap rate.

The first generation had tried blackmail and learned a rapid lesson.

The second generation had reasoned that conditions were humiliating rather than unbearable—and in fact provided much which Earth could not—and could be endured until better opportunity offered. The important thing was to acquire money with which to buy—well, facilities.

By the third generation the Commune Fathers had grown longer sighted and the first cheese-paringly sequestered funds were being transformed into a huge centrifuge at about the time young Peter asked his question. Cutting gravity and so cutting culturally loose from Earth had been a fine gesture but there could be advantage in a squad of Orbiters who could move comfortably on Earth's surface. And recommencing rotation was out of the question for the older folk.

"I hate it!"—shrieked and repeated to exhaustion—was the reaction of Peter, aged four, to his first experience of the centrifuge. Even the fiddling 0.2 g was outrage to a physique which had come to terms with mass and inertia but knew nothing of weight, nor wished to.

On the second day, after a bout of desperate clinging to the doorgrip, he was allowed out after ten minutes, bellowing, while the thirdwomen giggled at his aggressiveness. It would be a useful trait in the future planned for him.

After a fortnight of systematic lengthening of his daily accustomization—allowing internal organs to realign gently to a vertically weighted structure—increase of the g factor began. His rages evolved into arrogant self-confidence as the psychlinicians worked with cold devotion on the boy's emotional fabric.

At age six he lived most of his day in the centrifuge, a series of belts round the internal circumference of the Station and large enough to accommodate a considerable cadre now that a method had been established. With his weight at 0.5 g (he was the only one as yet on the fastest belt) he looked forward, under psychological prodding, to greater conquests. Signs of muscular shape, as distinct from subcutaneous muscular structure, were discernible.

The Commune Fathers allotted him the personal name of "Marrian"—a joke of sorts, and their first mistake.

"Since the Orbiters set aside wedlock and the family system, second names have been allotted on a descriptive basis, focusing on job or personal attributes. What does Marrian describe?"

The Mayor had been, as promised, fascinated by the facts but more intrigued by the Custodian's possession of them. "I'm sure I don't know, and I know even less how you came by this knowledge. You have excellent informants."

"If you mean spies," the Custodian said comfortably, "say spies. I haven't any really. Only shuttle pilots and a few delivery agents visit the Stations, but their tattle and observations add up to this and that."

"So they penetrated the nurseries to learn bedtime stories and discovered the centrifuge nobody else knows about—and didn't, er, *tattle* even to their best friends?"

"Well, they told *me*."

"They thought bedtime stories worth a custodial report, these most unofficial agents?"

"Perhaps I should admit to some literary license in fleshing out the picture." The Mayor, played with, shrugged and was silent. "Am I so inept? Must I tell the truth?"

Administrative secrets can be slippery, but curiosity had carried the Mayor too far for retreat. "It would help," he said coldly and the Custodian's instant grin warned him that he shared the pool with a shark.

"The Power Stations talk to each other. I listen. I don't hear deadly secrets, for they aren't stupid. Only occasional indiscretions and errors come my way. It has taken fifteen years to form a picture from scraps."

"They talk in clear?"

"By line of sight laser."

The Mayor saw appalling involvements opening but the hook was in his jaws. "Transceivers would be shielded, and you can't tap into a laser beam undetected."

"Who can't?"

It was not really a shock, only one more privacy violated by nameless men. The Custodian offered a spinoff comment: "The intention of the Ethic is preserved by continuous distortion of the letter."

"Semantics!" But the repetition was half-hearted.

"The price of language. Now you know some secrets. There's a price on those also."

"Which I pay at once?"

"There is an action to be taken and I must not be implicated. Public Safety must not seem interested in Orbiter affairs. Less obvious people are needed—like those uniformless couriers of yours who fix giddy-gossipy eyes on Town affairs and keep you informed of the social fluxes you so gently do not seem to guide."

The Mayor said uncomfortably, "I rarely inter-fere—"

"But how could you? The Ethic, the Ethic! But I want to share your knowledge of everything Peter Marrian does on Earth and every word he speaks here."

"My boys aren't equipped—"

"They will be. Sensitized clothing and sound crystals at the roots of the hair. They'll be walking audio-cameras."

"This is all you want?"

"For the moment."

There it was, the—no, not "veiled threat," but . . . that phrase the pre-Collapsers had used . . . the "rain check" taken out on him. "Am I to know what we are looking for?"

"The reason for Peter Marrian's visit."

A part of the Mayor's very considerable intelligence had been worrying at the question since first mention of the name and had reached a conclusion. He thought, In for a credit in for a bust, and said, "But we know that, don't we?"

The Custodian smiled, at last like a man rather than a skull. "We do?"

"The Orbiters, if what formal communication we have with them is a reliable guide, have developed lazy habits of speech. They drop unnecessary final conso-nants, like *g* and *f* and *h*—sendin, mysel, strengt. Peter Marrian's name refers to his job, but has been misun-derstood. Peter Marrying."

The Custodian laughed like a madman. "Do you imagine they'd waste resources preparing a brat to come

Downstairs to get married? They don't even recognize marriage."

"But we do. And isn't that the whole point of the bedtime story?"

The Custodian calmed abruptly. "You'll do. It took me several years to realize that. The reason for it all?"

"Money. If you can't earn it, marry it. All Orbiter property is, I believe, communal."

"Good, good. And so?"

"This visit is, perhaps, exploratory, perhaps the opening move in an Orbiter campaign for . . ." He trailed off. "For what?"

The Custodian stood to go. "That is what I asked the Global Council to consider. They are still considering. Meanwhile it is up to you and me to see that Peter Marryin, however often best man, is never the groom."

2

It was unfortunately true that the Custodian's information derived mainly from Orbiter indiscretions and errors. Much escaped him entirely; much was filled in only after the affair was over.

He did not know, for instance, that Peter Marryin's face was not wholly his own. Orbiter technicians, observing the TV shows of Melbourne Town's entertainment idols (whom they despised utterly) with special attention to those who brought the young grovelling in ill-concealed sexual hysteria, spent two years designing the face; surgeons spent a further two creating it. The result was coldly calculated to turn the heads and raise the blood pressures of a prognosticated 90 per cent of Melbourne Town females between the ages of thirteen and thirty—a carnally desirable young lout with something for everybody and a dedication to its use.

Such thoroughness would have scared the Custodial wits out of him, more so if he had realized that the target had been narrowed to this one city on Earth.

Peter should have gone to Earth when he was eighteen, in that era an ideal age for a beginner at wiving, but the Commune Fathers were a committee and had fallen into the committee traps of indecision, vacillation

and name calling without in nearly twelve months selecting a plump enough fly for their spider.

There were too many possibilities. One of the more
disastrous outcomes of the planetary Ethic of Non-
Interference had seen economic expertise, enhanced by
psychelectronics, carve obese fortunes out of the re-
industrialized planet; young heiresses were available in
a wealthy world where small families were still the cautious habit of a species which had once already come
within an ace of starving itself to death.

The Commune bickerings had ended with the death
of old Festus Grant, right under their feet, in Melbourne Town. In wonderment they totaled the fabulous
holdings—Rare Metals Research, Lunar Constructions,
Ecological Rehabilitation and Exploitation, Monopole
Ramjets, Mini-Shuttles Corporation, Sol-Atmos Research and Reclamation and more, more, more— The
list rang louder bells for them than all the Jesus Cult
cathedrals in history.

And all—all—all went to Claire Grant, only child of
the dead widower.

The haste with which they groomed, briefed and
dispatched the casually confident Peter was worse
than indecent; it was comic and contemptible. And
thorough.

At nineteen the boy had all of the traditional Orbiter
contempt for Earthworms, amplified by the hundreds
of teleplays he had been forced to watch in order to
become familiar with customs, speech idioms and etiquette. (He still did not really understand their drama;
third generation Orbiters were unable to comprehend
the preoccupations and philosophies of people not
reared in a steel tube.) He had also an instilled awareness of being a cultural hero in embryo, the bedtime-
story-boy who lived happily ever after in a swagger of
privilege.

By Terrene standards he was paranoid (by Orbiter
standards arrogant) but had been coached in adapting
his responses to an Earthworm norm. The coaching,
brilliant in its fashion, allowed insufficiently for unpre-

dictable encounters (encounters were rarely unpredictable in an Orbiter tube) and the shuttle was scarcely spaceborne before his furies stirred to Earthworm insolence.

The pilot was a jokey type, all bonhomie and loud mouth, saying, "You'll find old Earth heavy going, feller," and laughing madly at his obscure pun based on an idiom not in use Upstairs—one which sounded to Peter like a mannerless criticism. And: "Watch the women, boy! They'll *weight* for you to *fall* for them. Get it? *Weight* for you to—"

"I get it, thank you. Now mind your own damn business and watch your disgustin tongue."

"Hey, now!"

The co-pilot dug him in the ribs to shut him up and grinned sympathetically at Peter, who interpreted the grin as zoological observation of the freak from Upstairs and returned a glare of rage. The co-pilot shrugged, adding fuel to a conviction of insulting pity.

The fool at the landing field, who mocked his strength by offering to carry his luggage, was saved from assault only by a memory of teleplays showing the planetary obsession with menialism—free intelligences actually *offering* service! He relinquished the bags with contempt and began to focus his accelerating dislike for things Terrene on the unfortunate girl he had been reared to meet. *She* was responsible for the shame and insult he must bear in the course of duty.

In his anger he forgot even his irrational fear that Earth gravity would be mysteriously different from his experience in the centrifuge—that "real" weight would be something else. By the time he noticed that it was not he had calmed sufficiently to go through the mental balancing routine laid down for him by the Orbiter psychlinicians.

It was an excellent routine, devised by men who knew more about his mind than he ever could. By evening he was ready—"debonair" was the word he favored—to face the Reception at the Town Hall, the first in line of the haunts of the rich bitches. The Grant had better be there; he was not in dawdling mood.

It was the Mayor, now, who sat in the Custodian's office; the audio-crystals and the transcripts Englished from them were politically too touchy to risk outside a secured area. The tape they had heard had been prepared from a crystal lodged at the root of a hair on the head of a shuttle co-pilot. How the Mayor had achieved that, far outside his sphere of authority, the Custodian had the good taste not to ask; he was certain that this young man would go far and successfully.

"An unpleasant little shit," he said.

The Mayor (who, if age were the only factor, could have been the Custodian's great-grandson) was beginning to feel at home with the old exhibitionist. "I think that the Orbiters are what we have made them."

"Yes. Be properly glum about it."

"If he looks like bringing off a marriage——"

The Custodian said harshly, "He won't."

"But if?"

"Very well—if?"

"We might engineer small events, derogatory to his self-esteem, to push him past his restraints, allow him to erupt in public scenes which will make him socially unacceptable. Then we could look down our official noses and send him back Upstairs with a complaint of his behavior."

The Custodian laughed and asked, "Are you ambitious?"

"In two years I will be thirty and no longer eligible for minor civil office. If I am not selected for a further Supervisory career I must fall back on commerce. The last Mayor of Melbourne Town is now a factory hand. This youth-decade in Social Administration can be a trap for the unprepared."

"I wouldn't worry too much."

They understood each other exactly.

But they did not understand Orbiters at all. Deny how they might, they shared in the recesses of their minds the common opinion that Oribiters were peculiar, backward and hardly to be taken seriously. In a perilously easygoing culture the problems of underdogs—their sense of grievance and drive, not for equality but for revenge—were little comprehended on realistic levels.

Nor did either understand the drive for achievement latent in a moneyed nonentity. They had thought, when assessing the field, that Peter would certainly be snatched up by the glamour crowd, and little Cinderella Claire lost in the crush.

3

The hall was crowded. Not, of course, that one cared a damn for the barbarian Orbiters or their peculiar tribalisms, but one was justified in observing a Social Curiosity.

Amongst the crowd Festus Grant's daughter was strung taut, breathless at her own projected daring, at what she intended to do tonight. When this ball was over she would be the envy of the smart set, even a center of scandal, but for once she would have shone as "the girl who dared."

She was a social nobody and knew it. She would, at age nineteen in a year's time, attain her majority and control of the greatest fortune in Australasia, but that meant nothing to the Pleasured Classes; after a certain number of millions money became an environment rather than a possession and simple quantity no ground for eminence.

That she was intelligent, good hearted and socially more willing than able counted not at all against her plain features, washed-out eyes and too-plump figure. The physical defects could have been surgically corrected but among the Pleasured Classes this was Not Done; the struggling masses might falsify and pretend but One Was Above That.

Worse, she lacked taste. She was wickedly overdressed—with too much jewelry, a too blatantly fantastic hair arrangement, a dress too brightly red and too ornate and—and without the subtlety of choice which could subtract and adjust and transform her into what she wished to be.

All she had was useless money. She was accustomed to the attentions of men who pursued her prospects rather than herself and, as one who could buy any number of husbands, despised men who could be bought.

She danced with one of them to pass the time. *He* would not appear until just before the Protocol Dance, the fourth. While the eager young man found her unresponsive, in her mind she rehearsed her move. As the richest heiress present (and this was a point of etiquette wherein money *did* count) she would automatically take place next to the Lady Mayoress and be the second person presented. If *He* had been married, some wealthy matron would have been in the place of opportunity; it paid to know the rules and to be prepared to use them.

Color and sound died as the orchestrator left the keyboard, and she rid herself of the eager young man.

When at last *He* arrived—he was anticlimactic.

Secretly she had hoped against common sense for something strange, exotic (so, secretly, had they all), an outworld fantastication of dress, an oddity of manner or unexpectedness of appearance—

—anything but the too-ordinary pale and slender young man, in commonplace Terrene attire, who hesitated at the door as if taken with yokel surprise at the spectacle of Melbourne Town's Pleasured Class frozen in the half-bow and half-curtsy of welcoming protocol, then came uncertainly down the hall, guided by the traditional Visitor's Escort of Police Controller and Aide, whose dress uniforms outshone him utterly.

He was a mistake, a nothing. Her scandalous resolution lapsed; he was not worth it.

Then he came close. The escort fell back as he halted the correct four paces from the Mayor. At least, she thought, he had been coached in the observances. The Mayor stepped forward and the Orbiter lifted his face to the light.

Disappointment vanished before the most vitally handsome man she had ever seen. He was the epitome, the gathering, the expression of every media star and public idol who had ever roused her fantasies. He was The Orbiter—unearthly.

She scarcely heard the formal exchange; she ached to

have done with it and with the visitor's formal round of the floor with the Lady Mayoress, so that she . . .

Peter bowed to the Lady Mayoress as the introduction was made, but the matron did not offer her arm.

They talked.

With the orchestrator's hands poised, waiting, over the keys—they talked.

Claire was furious. The woman was waiving the protocol of the first dance. Orbiters might be socially backward, but this was diplomatic insult.

Then the Mayoress took a pace back, terminating the exchange, and still the orchestrator waited on the Mayor's signal.

Claire saw a faint uncertainty in the Orbiter's fixed smile and knew that this was the moment. A public prank became an act of rescue.

She stepped quickly forward and he, perceiving the movement, half turned to her. She made the formal half-curtsy, knew she did it awkwardly and cared not a damn for that, and asked with a clarity that shivered to the doors of the hall,

"May I request the Protocol Dance?"

There was a stillness. She saw fury on the Mayor's face, instantly veiled. She sensed rather than heard an intake of half a thousand breaths—and realized the meaning of the disregarded dance, the substitution of formal chat. Gently the Protocol Dance had been passed over in consideration of a visitor who in a weightless community could never have learned the Viennese waltz.

Through the petrification of her shame she heard the voice that could have charmed demons: "Why, thank you," and felt the slender fingers take hers. Lifted from the curtsy, she gazed into the smile that had been sculpted for her to gaze into. He said, "I shall be charmed, Miss Grant." But it was she who was charmed that unbelievably he knew her name, and it was she who triumphed over Mayor and Mayoress, escort and orchestrator and all the Pleasured Class as he added, "I have taken delight in learnin your ballroom antics."

While he cursed the Freudian slip behind his plastic smile she treasured it as the needed oddity, the other-worldliness that made him truly a visitor to Earth.

If Claire Grant and Peter Marryin made a less than graceful couple, the swishing of tongues outmaneuvered was balm to the ugly duckling's waltzing ego.

Sensitized areas on the couriers' jackets did not make the best of cameras. Subject to crumpling and difficult to aim with accuracy, two of them yet caught Claire's expression at different times during the ball.

"She's in an enchantment," said the Mayor.

"She's on heat," said the Custodian, to whom romance had suddenly become a dirty word. "He's had brat's luck."

"Or good preparation."

"Meaning what?"

The Mayor ran back through the audio tapes. "This."

Peter's voice murmured in midair, "Ugly ducklin? What is that? You have charm."

"You don't mean that." She was coy, ecstatic, flirtatious and pleading all at once. ("Thank sanity we don't stay young," the Custodian muttered.)

Peter's ghostvoice said, "I do mean it. Men appreciate charm in a woman."

"They appreciate money in a woman."

"I don' understan you."

"You don't understand money?"

"Intellectually I do, but not as an attraction. We don' use money Upstairs."

Then he talked of other things as though money were of no interest.

"Neat," the Custodian agreed. "Made his point and left it at that. Even stuck to the truth."

"But not to the truth behind the truth. He has been very well prepared."

"Fortunately, so have we."

The Custodian was wrong about that. On his fourth day on Earth Peter Marryin proposed to the infatuated, richest girl in Melbourne Town, was accepted by her and married to her (with housekeeper and maid for witnesses) by public data-record plug-in, a terminal of which was, quite naturally, located in her late father's study.

Capture and consolidation took something under fifteen minutes, whereas the Custodian had relied on an Engagement, a Round of Gaiety and a Splendid Society Wedding for time in which to generate a dozen subtle interferences. Against Peter's precision and speed no bugging system could do more than record the outwitting of science and power.

The Mayor was silently amused at the old man's raging against defeat. The backward barbarians Upstairs had foreseen opposition and surveillance and designed a lightning campaign to outflank both. He began to respect the barbarians.

But the old man stamped and raved in gutter language that stripped away the cool superiority of his public persona. It was altogether too humanizing. Embarrassing.

The Mayor raised his voice to drown the performance. "She's under age. The marriage can be annulled."

The Custodian snarled at him, "Only if her guardians demand it. Do you think they give a damn while they control the money in trust?"

"There might be means to persuade one of them—"

The Custodian calmed suddenly. "All right, you're trying. But we can't do it. Undue influence? Try and prove it! Even the newscasts are squalling 'the starstruck love story' a bare hour after the event, telling the world romance is alive and throbbing. Public opinion will see interference as bias against Orbiters. Nobody gives a damn for Orbiters but everybody loves lovers, and bias will be elevated into accusations of racialism or exoticism or some bloody pejorative coinage. And if interference were traced to me—" He shuddered.

And certainly not to me, thought the Mayor, who now had an assured future to protect.

The "starstruck lovers" honeymooned brilliantly

around the Earth for a month before Mr. and Mrs. Peter Marryin left for the Power Station.

A structure two thousand meters long and five hundred in diameter, floating below a battery of thousand-meter solar mirrors, is immense by any standard, but nothing looks big in space until you are close enough to be dwarfed and awed. Dwarfed and awed Claire Marryin surely was, gasping at her beautiful husband's ambience of marvels.

She had never been in space. (After all, who had, save those whose work took them there? Nobody would *need* the stars for generations yet.) So she played with null-g, bruising herself a little and laughing at her own clumsiness, while Peter fumed and was darling enough not to show it. When the shuttle entered the vast lock in the Station's anal plate (they actually called it that, she found, with a smothered laugh) she calmed down and set herself to be a stately matron of eighteen, worthy of a wonderful man.

From the passage opening on the interior of the Station they came quite suddenly—he guiding her, at times a little roughly, because Orbiters made their topology connective at any angle instead of in terms of up and down—to a platform from which was displayed the whole panorama of the Power Station.

She looked along a huge tube whose walls were checkered with little square boxes which she only slowly recognized as dwellings, grouped around larger boxes which were community buildings and surrounded by neat squares and circles of lush green. In the gravitational center of the tube hung a great disk whose visible face seemed to be nearly all window glass and which occupied perhaps a third of the inner diameter. But it was nearly a thousand meters distant and did not at a glance seem so big, any more than the boxes two hundred meters below and above—*around, away*—seemed large enough for dwellings.

She clapped her hands and cried out, "It's like a toyland!"

"Toylan!" On his face an expression she had not seen there before—anger, revulsion, contempt—slipped into bleak control. He said stiffly, "Your toylan is the home of a fine an proud people," and led her to the conveyor belt while she held back tears for her stupidity. Then it seemed he remembered that these were new and fabulous sights for her and set himself to be kind, and within minutes she was asking shy questions, trying not to have them foolish ones.

"The disk? The factory, we call it. It's empty."

She asked timidly, "But why?" and thought he considered carefully before he answered.

"It was part of the original Station, a complex for the manufacture of artifacs which could be perfecly formed only in null-g conditions. But the Station grew too rich for the comfort of Earth an an embargo was placed on our goods. The factories have stood empty for more than seventy years."

"But that's unfair!"

"Yes!" The one word, with again the blank look of emotion repressed.

So there was a tiny cloud of resentment of her Earth. Best to ignore, allow it time to disperse. There was much to exclaim at here; for instance, she had not expected moving streetways, with railings. There were, in fact, railings everywhere. Strange for dwellers in free fall, free flight.

"There are free jump areas," he told her, "above roof level. There people may break their bones as they please. Once you take off you can' slow down or change direction, an in collision no weight doesn' mean no inertia. So in public places you ride an hang on, for the sake of others."

There was a touch of explanation-to-the-child-mind about that, and some impatience as he said, "I suppose you busy Terrenes don' think about such things."

Her loving tongue babbled, "Why should we, dear? It isn't our way of life."

She did not know she had just told a paranoid hero that Orbiter affairs were not considered interesting. Or that were it not for her nearing nineteenth birthday and the Grant industrial holdings he could have wished her dead. The stupid, yammering bitch!

The Station observed a twenty-four hour routine for metabolic stability, and that "night" Peter played host. Claire undersood that social customs must alter and evolve in a closed community and that personal contacts might come uneasily until she found her niche, but the function left her bewildered.

The "party" was held on the lawns surrounding their "house"—their living-box—like a green pool. The box itself existed for privacy; in the weatherless Station life was conducted in public.

There was nothing for her to do. A fleshy, shapeless woman appeared, requisitioned by Peter, to prepare snack dishes, and Claire's attempts to talk to her were balked upon grunted variations of "I'm only third-woman an don' know those things," making it plain that she was there to work and wanted only to get on with it.

What was a thirdwoman? A junior wife? But the Orbiters did not marry. They had some manner of temporary liaison for early child care but she, Claire, was uniquely the only *wife* on the Station. She could not question this clod but later must ask Peter.

At eight o'clock the major lights dimmed throughout the tube. Streetlamps remained and some freefloating clusters of colored globes and rods and planes that she found restful to watch. The Orbiters' artificial night had its own soft charm.

Nothing else did. The guests arrived in male and female groups, never mixed. They congratulated Peter on his bride—and hesitated over the word or pronounced it with a sly grin or could not recall it until reminded. They seemed to regard the marriage as a triumphant joke.

After they had congratulated Peter they stared uninhibitedly at her. When Peter introduced them, most seemed not to know what to say to her; the men in particular seemed resentful at being expected to make conversation at all.

Even the women, grouped together and apart from the men, seemed interested in her only as an exotic display piece. And well, she thought, might they stare! Plain on Earth, here she was a beauty. These shapeless females, all flesh and rounded tubes of muscleless limb, were like talking grubs. She swore she would exercise, go daily to the centrifuge and *never* let herself fall victim to null-g.

The men were as bad as their women, pipestem rolypolys; Peter alone looked like a real human being. And even he, she thought with a touch of dispirited spite, was no physical match for a real Terrene man.

Perhaps in her isolation and disappointment she had drunk too much, and had become afraid of vertigo in weightlessness, for she showed no more than a dumb resentment when a massive pudding of a woman dragged her into a disapproving group to hiss at her, "Stop tryin to talk to the men. Sexes mix in private!"

Even Peter seemed only occasionally to recall her presence. The "party" dragged interminably and she did not remember going to bed.

She woke to a hangover and a furious Peter dressing with compressed lips. She scarcely believed she heard him mutter, "Drunken bitch!"

Over coffee she gathered courage to ask what a thirdwoman might be and he snapped at her, "A bloody servan, trained for that an nothin else."

The words were plain but she did not understand the threat in his eyes.

He said, "I'm goin out. Stay here. Don' leave the house. I'll be an hour."

Desolate and uncomprehending, she drifted through the living-box, with its neatness, its compactness, its accessories to comfortable living. To efficient living, she amended; the Orbiters were not a comfortable people. She recalled the ill manners of last night, the resentment scarcely repressed, the smiles that were silent laughter.

And was suddenly afraid. And as suddenly more afraid that it was too late for that.

Peter returned within the hour, in more cheerful mood, ready to kiss and play. She responded with silly relief, as if a smile could cancel ill-will already delivered. He had "pulled strings," he told her, made an arrangement which only her special circumstances could justify.

"The Psychlinic will take you immediately."

She fled from his arms, too affronted for fear. "I'm not ill, Peter!"

"No, no!" He laughed, soothing and conciliating and as handsome as all hell and temptation. "It's a teachin group. It isn fair to toss you unprepared into our ways and customs so I've arranged an implant, a rundown of all the special social conditions, etiquettes, things you need to know so as not to stub a social toe every time you step out."

She cried a soft "O-oh!" for a gift without price. Much of her education had been by psycho-implant and she knew what was involved. He had given her a ticket to painless knowledge she would have been months in achieving.

And a man who could command the time of a Psychlinic was no mean husband.

The clinic was absurdly old fashioned, its "chair" a cocoon of electrodes and leads and handles to be gripped and precision clamps and heaven knew what else. On Earth the whole thing was done with a single helmet and a hypodermic.

Perhaps her amusement showed, for the Psychlinician explained, in a tone stiff with non-apology, that the Station used its original equipment, that there was no money for new models from Downstairs.

Claire said with her friendliest smile, "Then I shall buy it for you," and sat herself firmly in his ancient chair.

An unreadable expression came and went as he said, "Why, I'm sure you will."

It might be their mode of thanks, but it lacked gratitude. She felt a mild numbness in her thighs, shifted slightly to ease it and realized that the whole buttock was losing sensation.

In sudden, frightened anger she cried out, 'You've used a penetrant narcotic! In the chair seat!"

He said bluntly, "Yes," and winced as her voice rose to screaming pitch.

"That's treatment for dangerous criminals and violent lunatics. I'm not—I'm not—"

He said forcefully, "Sit back an shut up!"

And, since that was the nature of the drug, she obeyed. In the few minutes of mental freedom left her she peered into hellmouth.

What they did with her occupied several days. They fed her the acclimatization material, of course, since she was to dwell here permanently and not be a clumsy nuisance. Then came the establishing of submissive reactions, no simple job on a mind accustomed to freedoms which to the Orbiters seemed sheer anarchy. Only then could they begin the deep probing necessary to planning the personality split. When that was done they designed and imprinted the controlled schizophrenic balance that could be tipped either way with proper triggering. It was necessary that a superficially "normal" personality be available if Melbourne Town should send an envoy who would demand to talk with her when the inevitable questions came to be asked.

Aside from that, the Psychlinic found her a fascinating study; relaxation viewing of Terrene teleplays had not prepared them for the revealed truths of Earthworm culture.

"Effete and decaden," said the Chief, "floatin over realities and never seein them. Gravity or no gravity, it's we who are the strong. *We* are the human future."

4

On her nineteenth birthday a healthy and self-possessed, if unwontedly serious Claire Marryin contacted her guardians by visiphone and made her wishes known. They argued against the control of immense wealth being taken out of Terrene hands; they pleaded, stormed and stalled until she threatened to settle the matter by simple deed of transfer. She behaved throughout with polite but weary stubbornness.

The Commune Fathers of Power Station One became the administrators of the Grant interests.

"That," noted the Mayor, "makes them owners of just eight and one quarter per cent of Melbourne Town and unhealthily concerned in mining estate and development from Mars to the solar corona."

"It was expected," said the Custodian, "but what will they do with it? We know better now than to guess at Orbital thinking."

What they did was unexpected in its naïveté. They tried to play the market. They not only lost a great deal of money but wreaked some small havoc with those lesser Grant holdings they chose for their experiments in finance.

"Economic stability is threatened," said the Custodian, with a perfectly straight face. "It is time to return their visit."

<h2 style="text-align:center">5</h2>

The seventeen Spokesmen of the seventeen Station Commune Councils were in session on Station One when a delivery receivals clerk chattered over intercom that the Custodian of Public Safety of Melbourne Town was in the anal corridor and demanding entry.

"How large is his party?"

"He is alone, Alastair Father."

"Delay him five minutes, then escort him here yoursel."

"Yes, Alastair Father." The clerk returned to the corridor where the lean and lined and very patrician old man took his ease without benefit of handhold, as to the manner born. In a Terrene that seemed obscurely insolent, as did the silent waiting for the clerk to speak.

"I am to escort you to the Father, but firs there are matters I mus atten to. I won' be—"

The Custodian delivered arrogance with a polite smile. "I am sure you have nothing more important on your hands than my visit."

The clerk said, "That's as may be," and turned towards his office. *Snotty Downstairs bastard!* Orbiter insularity overcame him. "Stationhans don' take orders from Terrenes."

"Pity," said the Custodian equably. The clerk withdrew, wondering was that a subtle Terrene threat.

Alastair First Father, who had been Alastair Dunwoodie, swept them out of the room like children. Before his immense prestige the communards made no attempt to argue but sought invisibility in the nearest dwellings. All, that is, save the inevitable youngest-promoted, still inclined to display intransigence rather than sense.

"Refuse him! Sen him about his business!"

"He is about his business." The First Father urged him towards the door. "It is too soon to invite reprisals, an I am curious to see Charles again."

"Charles! You know him?"

"We were friens once. Now, go!"

The youngest-promoted went, bemusedly reckoning the Father's age.

Were friens? It was an uncommonly wistful thought for Alastair. And now? Loyalties had come between. He punched an intercom number and said, "There's a Terrene envoy here. Prepare Claire Thirdwoman."

The Chief Psychlinician dispatched his Physical Training Authority, Peter Marryin, to the hydroponic garden where the girl would be making the daily harvest of fruit and vegetables, a faintly stupid smile on her face. She was plump now, and losing shape, but seemed contented enough; it had been necessary to repress most of her emotional reaction-strength in order not to blur the edges between personalities by creating a too-obtrusive secondary.

The code phrase which brought her original persona to life was cruel to the point of obscenity but served its purpose of reaching deep into the preconscious. Peter, who had never conceived of her as more than a means to an end, gave no thought to brutality and outrage as he said distinctly into her ear, "Peter Marryin loves Claire Grant."

The young Charles had worked in space and knew the rules of null-g movement, and the old Charles had wisely spent fifty hours in the shuttles reconditioning himself before facing Alastair. He would not lose face through physical incompetence.

He even managed to inject a hint of swagger into his slide-and-shuffle entry into the Council Hall where the old man stood alone at the head of the long table with its—yes, seventeen chairs. All present and correct—then hurriedly got rid of while impudent clerk obstructed.

He said, "You're showing your age, Alastair," and gave his skull grin. "Old as God and no doubt twice as crafty."

Alastair flowed to greet him in a movement which seemed to glide him, upright, down the length of the room, making Charles's swagger mere bumptiousness, and held out his hand. "Well, ol frien!"

The Custodian returned the grip gently and allowed himself a bare sentence of old affection: "I have always remembered you, Alastair." Then, as they measured each other with uncertain and wary smiles, "I bring not peace but a sword."

Alastair, too, had been a Cultist in the old days. "To set man agains his father an daughter agains her mother? Not on the Stations, Charles. Our conception of relationships does not allow internecine frictions."

"Not Terrene against Orbiter, those brothers on Earth and in Heaven?"

"The chance of brotherhood is gone by."

As simply as that the lines of battle were drawn.

They sat at the table, using the bodybelts that allowed movement and gesture without reactive floating, and the Custodian launched his attack directly.

"The Governance of Australasia suggests—" he laid the lightest of stresses on the verb, "—that a Committee of Advice be appointed to guide your financial handling of the Grant holdings."

"There are no Grant holdins. I suppose you mean the Orbital League holdins brought to the Communes by Claire Thirdwoman."

So the whole League was in it; not really news. The final words penetrated less swiftly, then shockingly.

"Thirdwoman! Alastair, that's slavery!"

The First Father smiled thinly. "What could she be good for but manual labor an childbearin? Your children of wealth learn nothin useful to an Orbiter. I assure you she is not discontented."

"I want to see her!"

"You shall."

"Good." *Some double dealing there? Be watchful.* "Now, the holdings—"

"No Committee of Advice, Charles!"

"You're amateurs. You'll go broke."

"Our economists are learnin. We buy expert advice now from Earth. Terrene's have little that can' be bought, includin allegiance."

"I know damned well what you buy. I also know that your first attempts to deal in millions caused a minor recession in Melbourne Town. If you succeed in bringing down the whole Grant empire there'll be economic chaos."

"We aren' stupid."

"But you are inexperienced. We must protect ourselves."

"No Committee, Charles!"

"It is already set up."

"*Un*set it. We won' obey it." The Custodian's expression gave him pause. "The Ethic, Charles! You can' interfere." The skull grin threatened to engulf him. *"What have you done, Charles?"*

As the declaration of love unlocked the sleeping persona, Claire burst from within herself like an emerging butterfly. Life flooded her face; her lips parted and smiled, her spoiling body straightened and she looked into her lover's eyes with an instant's joy that faded into apprehension and loathing.

He had seen it all before, was turning away when she asked, "What do they want now?" and answered over his shoulder, "Firs Father wans you. There's a Terrene envoy here."

Envoy! Hope was immediately quenched. No envoy could free her. In a moment they would give her the injection and tell her what to say and do and there she would be, gabbling that she was happy and had no desire to leave the Station, that everyone was so kind and that she had fulfilment here such as Earth could never offer and more and more gushing, lying rubbish.

She asked, "Why should I bother?"

"What?"

"What's the use? I don't want to see him, to tell force-fed lies and build myself more unhappiness."

He faced her furiously. "Listen, girl! You're an Orbiter and what Firs Father says, you do."

In the rare periods of personality release, such as the visiphone communications with bankers and inquiring relatives, her hatred had been born in the schizophrenic hell of the submission drugs. During the long weeks of third woman regression her subconscious mind had been conjuring powers of viciousness the little Claire Grant could never have roused from her psyche. Now, in these moments of hyper-euphoria, between the awakening and the drugging, she was uniquely herself, undrugged and unregressed—a creature of misery and rage.

She said, with a menace he did not hear because in his thinking it could not be there, "Don't talk to me like that."

"Come on; don' waste my time."

She goaded, "Your time is nothing to me."

"Bitch!" He put out a grasping hand and she struck it away, hissing, "Don't touch me, you filth!"

It was stunning. No woman spoke to a man like that, *no* woman. Nor would a man dare use such words to Peter the Culture Hero. And she had struck his hand! Outraged self-love rose like a scald in the throat and his fingers hooked into claws.

She said, making sure of him, "If you touch me I'll kill you."

She needed to kill someone, and who better than the man who had married for her money the girl who despised fortune hunters? As his hands reached for her she casually took one in hers, dragged the arm straight and kicked him in the elbow, breaking it to the obbligato of his screaming. It was easy. Orbiters knew little about aggression or defense; both were difficult or embarrassingly ludicrous in null-g.

The screaming unleashed joy in her and she knew

that she *would* kill him. Others in the street had heard
him and heads were turning but they could not save
him. She, Claire Thirdwoman, slave, dupe and Earthworm, was about to murder the Culture Hero before
their eyes.

They could not realize how simple it was for her. A
year of null-g had made her competent in the leaps and
anglings of free fall, and her Earthworm musculature
made it possible for her to achieve take-off speeds and
endure landing collisions no Orbiter could match. Even
her centrifuge-reared "husband" was not her equal.

She caught his arm and he shrieked again, and
hooked her foot under the moving-way guide rail. Figures now leapt towards her, too late. Taking him by
wrist and smashed elbow she flung him, howling,
against the wall of a dwelling twenty meters away. He
hit it face forward, sprawling like a spider, and she
launched herself after him, turning in mid-air to strike
with her feet at his spine, and heard it crack.

She had her moment of murderer's ecstasy, sexual,
blood-deep, complete. Let the surgeons and bioche-
mists revive and rebuild him (as they would), but she
had cleansed herself of shame and hatred.

Then reaction set in and with a crippling weariness
of spirit she turned to defend herself . . .

"Done?" the Custodian echoed. "I have set up a
Committee of Advice. Nothing else."

"Unacceptable."

"But there are, of course, alternatives."

"Which are?"

"One is that you should re-assign the League holdings to Claire Grant and return her to Earth."

The First Father laughed, but uneasily because the
breath-taking impudence of the demand spoke of threat
behind threat. "You're out of your min."

"We can take the money from you, you know."

"Not by way of Claire. She gave it to us. I feel you
will have a record, verbal and written, of the whole
transaction."

"I have, Alastair. And an expert psychological report
on her speech and behavior patterns during the ex-

changes with her administrators, showing a ninety per cent certainty that she was under submission drugs. I can recommend that the Marketing Court freeze your assets while the transfer is re-examined."

"You can' prove druggin."

"You don't deny it?"

"Or admit it."

The Custodian felt less regret for that old friendship. Neither was the same man he had been eighty years ago, and both were centenarians, patterns of biochemistry and geriatric technique, with interests and loyalties eight decades divergent. He found himself caring not a damn for Alastair's needs so long as Melbourne Town survived. The perilous honesty of chauvinism at least left him unrepentant of hard hitting.

"You'd have to kill the girl to prevent me getting the truth. Would you do that, Alastair?"

The First Father's smile was deep winter. "No. I don' wan the Global Council puttin a military prize crew aboard my Station."

They came from all sides, angling up towards her. Almost lethargically she struck with her feet at the first comer, a squealing firstwoman spitting anti-Terrene rage, and used her mass to change direction and clutch at the jump-halting rail on a dwelling roof. The rest fell into a confusion of collisions and reachings for any anchored mass. Their babbling anger and shock sounded ridiculous; they lived such ordered lives that in emergency they flapped and fluttered. If they caught her they would kick and hit and pinch and threaten but in the end she would still be thirdwoman in the hydroponic garden. And Peter reconstructed. And nothing changed.

Then why not let them take her? There was no freedom.

For an instant, looking upward, she saw where, five hundred meters away across the diameter of the cylinder, final freedom lay, and reflexively launched herself towards it.

At once she knew she had been stupid, that it was

better to live. There could always be the unexpected, the reversal of fortune. In panic she began to struggle, but what Peter had told her was true: once in free fall you cannot stop or slow down or change direction.

Her launch had been deadly accurate, a simple straight line with no gravity-fed trajectory for miscalculation.

The end of Claire Thirdwoman, crying and clawing for the inaccessible sides, was entry into the twenty-meter maw of the Station disposal unit, the vast mouth that could swallow machine complexes or obsolescent building units without the need for laborious dismemberment. She died at once as the heat units sensed her, felt nothing as the grinders shredded her contemptuously in a spurt of gears and in seconds was a mist of molecules expanding into invisibility in pressureless space.

6

In a right little, tight little island in the sky there is small precedent for announcing the neo-death of a local hero and the dissolution of his killer. Inexperience blurted out the news breathlessly in front of the Earthworm stranger.

For the second time during the affair the Custodian exploded in ranting fury, cursing Orbiter and Terrene stupidity alike, reducing himself to manic gutter level, until he saw that the First Father watched him with the bleak care of a duelist who sees advantage.

He checked himself abruptly. In an access of intuition, even some residual affection, he pondered the needs and frustrations the Orbiters had brought on themselves when they sought the pastures of heaven by casting away weight.

He said, "We need truth, Alastair, both of us. Neither was ready to move; now we must."

The First Father bowed his head. Concealing a smile? At any event, he made no attempt to argue. In minutes the Custodian knew all he needed, including the business of the League meeting his advent had dispersed—the secret buying of weapons, offensive and defensive, from men on the five continents Downstairs who would sell honor, history and the future for money.

That was bad enough. Worse was that the First Father did not fear him.

Feeling all his years, he sat down with the other old man—friend, enemy and gameplayer—to plan a fresh tomorrow.

Emotion subsided; perspectives revived; Claire's death became a tactical weapon each sought to grasp. They circled, testing defenses, until a confident Alastair made the first lunge.

"Charles, you can no more risk investigation of this affair than I can."

The Custodian sighed inwardly. It had been, he supposed, inevitable that Alastair, despite his remoteness from the social psychology of the Earthworm, should recognize that.

Still, he must try. "*You* certainly cannot. Your League is no danger to Terrene culture yet, but this last year holds the proof that you will be. Some day. Even soon." He added easily, "You will be stopped, of course."

Too late; that hand was already lost. "How, Charles? How will Earth explain retributive action a secon time? Attemp it and I, *I*, will tell the story of how Claire Marryin died. I will tell the trut, all the trut. And your Earthworms will discover how their precious Ethic has created a poverty-stricken ghetto in the sky, but one that intens to kick the Ethic to pieces rather than continue as the unseen slaveys of some Victorian servan quarters in the attic Upstairs. Revenge on us may be swif but public scrutiny of the Ethic *and* of its manipulators will be pitiless. It will be the end of the Ethic."

The Custodian had seen from the beginning that he was caught. It was not easy even to go down fighting. He said lightly, "But everybody questions the Ethic in his heart. It is an elaboration of good manners, pointless in essence but providing a permanent framework of behavior for discussion without bloodshed."

Alastair laughed at him. "It mus be one of the great jokes of history that Earth has based its firs planetary culture on good manners, then created an offshoot with none. An a better joke that the collapse of a lie nobody believes in could plunge you into cultural anarchy. All your international relationships balance on it. You won' take the risk."

Of course he, and Earth, would not. Bluntness now would serve as well as anything. "What do you want?"

"To be rid of you."

That was unexpected; he said nothing at all but waited for Alastair to continue.

"You can' blow us out of the sky. Too un-Ethical and too revealin. But you can pay us to go away. And we'll go." He grinned with sudden savagery. "Like the classic barbarians on the Imperial borders."

That was staggering. The Custodian groped for words, any words to stall for thought. "The power supplies—"

"Automated platforms to replace the Stations. The plans are ready. Ten years from keel to full operation."

That was worth a sour laugh in return. "We've had automation plans of our own for the past twenty years. The problem has been what to do with you. Now you tell me you'll go away. Where to? Let me guess at your view of the matter."

He ruminated.

Alastair said, "There's somethin you should see. Come along."

They floated out of the hall to a moving-way which carried them up the curve of the hull, through little nests of the living-boxes and the lawns and gardens in their patterns of cultivated brilliance. All growing things were a passion of Orbiters. Their natural art form, perhaps? They could have chosen more coldly and worse.

He said, "I think I have it. The basic need was money. First for armaments in case Earth did indeed become provoked into violence by the demands you would some day make. Second for *material* to implement whatever design you have in mind. Behind this is a determination to cut loose from Earth once and for all. The cultures have diverged to the point where neither understands the other or needs the other. Cultures which don't understand each other despise each other, have no use for each other, no matter how they pretend otherwise. Am I doing well?"

"Very well."

They left the moving-way and Alastair opened a door. Inside was nothing at all, an empty room.

"Total isolation breeds its own neuroses, Charles. Our psychologists set up this room years ago. People come here to soothe their tensions, pacify their resentments, defuse their aggressions."

He touched switches; the room became black dark. A slit twenty meters wide glimmered faintly in the floor, opened like a vast eye, and gazed at the stars.

The Custodian understood only vaguely. "The galaxy means little to me, but for you it has come to have psychological significance. Is this where you will go?"

"Eventually. Not yet. It is a long dream."

"And now?"

"Firs, Jupiter. You can pay us to mine the satellites and the atmosphere."

The Custodian knew he should have foreseen it but the politician in him asked, "Why should we?"

"Because in a century or so you will have another population-an-resources crisis Downstairs, and you can use somebody to prepare the alternatives for you. By then we will be wealthy enough an self-sufficien to engage the universe on our own terms. There are eighty thousan people in the Stations now; we mus plan for a million. Ten Mother Islands and a hundred minin scows for a start. The resources out there will cover your nex dozen population explosions; you'll find us a good bargain. And what remains of the Ethic can seek virtue in Non-Interference with our cultural destiny."

"The impudence of it all is breathtaking. All I need do is lay the idea before the Global Council and they'll collapse like cards before your diplomatic acumen! It will need more than a silver tongue to sway them."

"Let the Ethic sway them!"

The Custodian swallowed a sound like a smothered laugh. "Blackmail, Alastair!"

"But mos Ethical, Charles, within the Terrene meanin of the word. By the way, did you know that the original twentieth century intention in suggestin space platforms was to establish free colonies in space?"

"Was it indeed?"

"Indeed. I have always said that we learned nothin from The Collapse. We've simply taken a little longer to arrive where they wished to go anyway."

Several hours later, when the Custodian was preparing to return home, the First Father glanced fortuitously overhead to where, across the diameter, a disposal gang loaded a day's garbage into the vent, and felt a twinge of guilt.

The Custodian, following his gaze, wondered aloud if everything was recycled.

"Not quite everythin."

"No? Oh, yes, of course, that— Tragic business; tragic . . ." He was busy formulating his approach to the Global Council.

7

The version retailed to the Mayor was perhaps a little slanted. He was impressed. "You know, we'll be well rid of them."

"For the time being."

The Mayor's eyebrows rose.

"Nothing ends, James. Alastair First Father is quite aware that as Lords of the Solar System one day they'll come home again—as barbarians at the ancient gates. But you and I won't be around to worry over that."

Recommended Reading—1979

POUL ANDERSON: "The Ways of Love," *Destinies*, January–February 1979.

ORSON SCOTT CARD: "Breaking the Game," *Analog*, January 1979.

ROBERT CHILSON: "Written in Sand," *Isaac Asimov's Science Fiction Magazine*, December 1979.

FELIX C. GOTSCHALK: "The Trip of Bradley Oesterhaus," *Fantasy and Science Fiction*, July 1979.

JOE HALDEMAN: "Blood Sisters," *Playboy*, July 1979.

LEE KILLOUGH: "Broken Stairways, Walls of Time," *Fantasy and Science Fiction*, March 1979.

RONALD R. LAMBERT: "More than Life," *Analog*, June 1979.

STEPHEN LEIGH: "Encounter," *Destinies*, April–June 1979.

KEITH MINNION: "Ghosts," *Asimov's SF Adventure Magazine*, March 1979.

PAUL NOVITSKI AND

FREDERIK POHL: "Mars Masked," *Isaac Asimov's Science Fiction Magazine*, March 1979.

FREDERIK POHL: "Mars Masked," *Isaac Asimov's Science Fiction Magazine*, March 1979.

MARTA RANDALL: "The Captain and the Kid," *Universe 9*; and "The View from Endless Scarp," *Fantasy and Science Fiction*, July 1979.

SHERRI ROTH: "The Fare," *Isaac Asimov's Science Fiction Magazine*, November 1979.

MARY H. SCHAUB: "Court of the Timesifters," *Galileo*, September 1979.

HILBERT SCHENCK: "The Battle of the Abaco Reefs," *Fantasy and Science Fiction*, June 1979.

BOB SHAW: "Frost Animals," *Universe 9*.

JOHN SHIRLEY: "Will the Chill," *Universe 9*.

ROBERT THURSTON: "Vibrations," *Chrysalis 4*; and "The Wanda Lake Number," *Analog*, January 1979.

RICHARD WILSON: "The Story Writer," *Destinies*, April–June 1979.

The Science-Fiction Year

Charles N. Brown

The predicted downturn in science-fiction publishing failed to develop once again, though sales throughout the book industry dropped ten to fifteen percent. Even the optimists are now beginning to predict a slump in the number of titles to be published in 1980. Nevertheless, over 1,000 sf books (both new and reprint) were published in North America during 1979. Final figures are not yet available, but the total might go over the record 1,189 titles published in 1978. If so, it will probably be a record which will stand for a while. Dell, Ace, Berkley and other publishers have fewer books scheduled for 1980. Gregg Press, the largest science-fiction hardcover reprint house, has also reduced its scheduled output for 1980.

Book prices continued to rise, with average paperback costs for lead titles hitting $2.25 to $2.50, and hardcover prices for average novels passing $10.00. The day when the average reader could afford to go to a bookstore and pick out a dozen new titles at one time is gone. Discretionary buying (and discretionary driving to bookstores) will be more pronounced in 1980.

The publishing industry continued to treat science fiction as commercially important. The annual national convention of the American Booksellers Association, the largest get-together in the publishing industry, featured sf prominently in both events and displays. Some of the most crowded autograph sessions were those for Anne McCaffrey, Frank Herbert and the Hildebrandt brothers. Bantam, Ballantine, Berkley, Pocket Books and Warner all sponsored sf-related events.

Advances for writers continued to set records. Robert A. Heinlein's new novel, *The Number of the Beast*, went to Fawcett for a half-million-dollar guarantee. The reprint rights to a fantasy fable, *The Book of the Dun Cow,* by Walter Wangerin, Jr., sold to Pocket Books for $280,000. Jack Vance, Gregory Benford, Janet Morris, Poul Anderson and Joan Vinge all received advances over $50,000.

The large advances brought a change in how science fiction and sf authors were treated by publishers. More books were promoted in general markets such as *Publishers Weekly* and *The New York Times Book Review.* There were TV and radio ads, author tours, etc. Ballantine has scheduled some heavy TV advertising for 1980, and other publishers will probably follow suit. Sf authors are gaining more recognition and prestige from the world at large: Brian Aldiss was part of a distinguished-persons delegation invited to China, Jack Williamson received the New Mexico Governor's Award for distinguished contributions to the arts, and many authors were invited to attend the Jupiter and Saturn fly-bys at the Jet Propulsion Laboratory in California.

Alien was the most successful science-fiction picture of the year and generated all the book tie-ins and paraphernalia which have become the hallmark of the big movie. I find it quite disturbing that the basic 1950 monster movie, no matter how well made, should be so popular. Blood and gore still seem to be the standard fare for a successful movie.

Ralph Bakshi's *Lord of the Rings* turned out to be a bomb, while *Superman,* despite some idiotic plotting, was fairly successful. While not exactly fantasy, a newly cut version of *The Wicker Man* appealed strongly to the fantasy audience.

Star Trek and *The Black Hole* have just opened to bad reviews but large audiences. Thanks to huge advertising budgets, both will probably be commercially successful. *Star Trek* is at least mediocre and has nostalgia for the series working for it. *The Black Hole,* a lowest-common-denominator committee version of *Star Wars,* has no redeeming qualities.

In 1980, we can look forward to the *Star Wars* sequel, *The Empire Strikes Back.* A movie of *Dune* and an animated version of *The Last Unicorn* are also in the works; both are being scripted by their original authors.

Two of the big books announced for 1979, *The Magic Labyrinth,* by Philip José Farmer, and *Last Dangerous Visions*, edited by Harlan Ellison, did not appear. Both have been rescheduled for 1980.

A number of general fantasy books, besides movie tie-ins, made the regular best-seller lists in 1979. Len Deighton's alternative world described in *SS-GB* (Knopf), a thriller set in Nazi-occupied Britain, was one of the top novels of the year. *The Dead Zone*, by Stephen King (Viking), is an excellent blending of science fiction, fantasy, and terror. *The Last Enchantment,* by Mary Stewart (Morrow), which completes the Arthurian cycle she started with *The Crystal Cave* and *The Hollow Hills*, reached the top of the list within a week of publication.

Although not strictly science fiction, two fascinating books of interest to sf readers are *Wasn't the Future Wonderful: A View of Trends and Technology from the 1930's,* edited by Tim Onosko (Dutton), and *The 80's: A Look Back at the Tumultuous Decade 1980–1989,* edited by Tony Hendra, Christopher Cerf, and Peter Elbling. The former is a straightforward compilation of what, forty years ago, we thought the future would be like. The latter, a satirical rendering of the next decade, probably contains more truth than we would like.

In general, it was another dull year for novels. I found it very difficult to pick ten favorites, and won't even attempt to guess what will be on the Hugo and Nebula ballots.

Arthur C. Clarke's announced final novel, *The Fountains of Paradise* (Harcourt), was well written and had some interesting ideas but lacked excitement and depth. Charles Sheffield, using the same basic plot, the building of a space elevator, in *The Web Between the Worlds* (Ace) erred too much the other way by trying to pack too many ideas and too much melodrama into a single book. Nevertheless, both novels are worth reading and complement each other.

Titan, by John Varley (Berkley/Putnam), *Kinsman,* by Ben Bova (Dial), and *Jem,* by Frederik Pohl (St. Martin's), were all impressive in different ways. Varley's spirited adventure story, using the fantasy-quest motif in a science-fiction setting, is fast-moving and fun to read. *Kinsman,* an episodic novelization of a group of short stories about our next twenty years in space, works very well. *Jem,* a *very* depressing book, is a well-written, frightening look at the future.

My personal favorite is *Catacomb Years,* by Michael Bishop (Berkley/Putnam), another episodic novel of the future. There is also some astonishingly fine writing in *On Wings of Song,* by Thomas M. Disch (St. Martin's), and *Juniper Time,* by Kate Wilhelm (Harper & Row).

Bandersnatch, by Kevin O'Donnell, Jr. (Bantam), was a very good first novel. His second, *Mayflies* (Berkley), was even better. Based on these two, I'd call O'Donnell the best new novelist of 1979. I missed another first novel, *Nightwatch,* by Andrew M. Stephenson, when it first appeared in England in 1977. The first American publication by Dell in 1979 shows the author as another name to watch for.

Disappointing novels of the year included *The Jesus Factor,* by Frank Herbert and Bill Ransom (incomprehensible), *Macrolife,* by George Zebrowski (dull), and *Dragondrums,* by Anne McCaffrey (a rehash of the two earlier juveniles in the series). The Herbert and McCaffrey volumes were big sellers.

Harpist in the Wind, by Patricia A. McKillip (Atheneum), struck me as the best fantasy novel of the year; it's a marvelous finale to a trilogy destined to become a classic. Other outstanding fantasy novels included *Watchtower* and *The Dancers of Arun,* by Elizabeth A. Lynn (Berkley/Putnam)—the first two volumes of a trilogy; *Kindred,* by Octavia E. Butler (Doubleday), a time-travel fantasy; *Death's Master,* by Tanith Lee (DAW), a sequel to *Night's Master*; *Daughter of the Bright Moon,* by Lynn Abbey (Ace) — very much a mixed bag, but a good start for a new author; *The Merman's Children,* by Poul Anderson (Berkley/Putnam), a novel based on Scandinavian folklore; *Castle Roogna*, by Piers Anthony (Del Rey); *The Dark Bright Water*, by Patricia Wrightson (Atheneum); and *The Palace*, by Chelsea Quinn Yarbro (St. Martin's).

Most-disappointing fantasy novels of the year were *Urshurak*, by The Brothers Hildebrandt and Jerry Nichols (Bantam), and *Dragonworld*, by Preiss, Reaves, and Zucker. The pictures were nice.

For the second year in a row, there was a slew of excellent collections. Outstanding examples are: *The Change War*, by Fritz Leiber (Gregg), *Fireflood and Other Stories*, by Vonda N. McIntyre (Houghton Mifflin), *The Science Fiction Stories of Walter M. Miller, Jr.* (Gregg), *An Infinite Summer*, by Christopher Priest (Scribner's), *The Star-Spangled Future*, by Norman Spinrad (Ace), and *Eyes of Amber and Other Stories*, by Joan D. Vinge (Signet).

The single most important science-fiction reference book of the year was *The Science Fiction Encyclopedia*, by Peter Nicholls (Doubleday), the first true encyclopedia of the field. Buy the hardcover if you can; it should be a major reference work for decades.

The science-fiction magazine field has changed drastically in the past few years. Sf magazines used to be easy to define. They were digest-size, printed only science-fiction stories, and had small, ever-decreasing circulations. Things have changed.

Omni, with an audience in the millions, publishes about four stories per issue. The audience is not the traditional sf reader, and the stories tend to be more general. Robert Sheckley has just taken over as the new Fiction Editor, and Ben Bova has moved up to Executive Editor.

Starlog and *Future Life* also have circulations higher than the usual sf top of 100,000. They don't print fiction but are of interest because of their features about science fiction and sf movies.

Heavy Metal, under its new Editor, Ted White, has just dropped straight fiction but still does articles and "graphic stories" of a science-fictional nature.

Analog, Fantasy and Science Fiction and *Isaac*

Asimov's Science Fiction Magazine raised their price to $1.50 recently but otherwise remained pretty much unchanged in 1979. *Galileo* went to newsstand sale and expanded its market. *Galileo*'s publishers also bought *Galaxy* and will redesign it for publication in 1980. Although *Galileo* seems to have constant production problems, it apparently had a very successful year.

Destinies, the paperback magazine put out by Ace Books, went from a bimonthly to a quarterly schedule, but it maintained its $2.25 cover price throughout the year.

Amazing and *Fantastic* have returned to original fiction and improved dramatically from the first tentative issues under the new management.

Asimov's SF Adventure Magazine and *Unearth* suspended publication during the year.

The American Book Awards, successor to the National Book Awards, will give two sf prizes in 1980—one for paperback and one for hardcover. The nominating and voting procedures seem cumbersome and open to various interpretations. These awards may or may not become important to the field.

The 1979 Nebula Awards were presented at the Nebula banquet in New York on April 21, 1979. Winners were: Best Novel—*Dreamsnake,* by Vonda N. McIntyre; Best Novella—"The Persistence of Vision," by John Varley; Best Novelette—"A Glow of Candles, A Unicorn's Eye," by Charles L. Grant; Best Short Story—"Stone," by Edward Bryant. The Grand Master Award was given to L. Sprague de Camp. A special award was presented to Joe Schuster and Jerome Siegel for their creation of "Superman."

The 1979 Hugo Awards were presented on August 26, 1979 at the 37th World Science Fiction Convention in England. Winners were: Best Novel—*Dreamsnake,* by Vonda N. McIntyre; Best Novella—"The Persistence of Vision," by John Varley; Best Novelette—"Hunter's Moon," by Poul Anderson; Best Short Story—"Cassandra," by C. J. Cherryh; Best Dramatic Presentation—*Superman*; Best Professional Artist—Vincent DiFate; Best Editor—Ben Bova; Best Fanzine—*Science Fiction Review*; Best Fan Artist—William Rotsler; Best Fan Writer—Bob Shaw. The John W. Campbell Award was won by Stephen R. Donaldson.

The 1979 *Locus* Fiction Awards were announced on July 8, 1979 at the Westercon in San Francisco. Winners were: Best Novel—*Dreamsnake,* by Vonda N. McIntyre; Best Novella—"The Persistence of Vision," by John Varley; Best Novelette—"The Barbie Murders," by John Varley; Best Short Story—"Count the Clock that Tells the Time," by Harlan Ellison.

The 1979 John W. Campbell Memorial Award was announced in July 1979 at the University of Kansas. The winning novel was *Gloriana,* by Michael Moorcock.

The 1979 World Fantasy Awards were presented on October 14, 1979 at the World Fantasy Convention in Providence, Rhode Island. Winners were: Life Achievement—Jorge Luis Borges; Best Novel—*Gloriana,* by Michael Moorcock; Best Short Fiction—"Naples," by Avram Davidson; Best Collection/Anthology—*Shadows,* edited by Charles L. Grant; Best Artist—Alicia Austin and Dale Enzenbacher (tie); Special Award/Professional—Edward L. Ferman; Special Award/Non-Professional—Donald H. Tuck.

The Prometheus Award, a new prize, was presented at the National Libertarian Convention in Los Angeles on September 8, 1979. The award, $2,500 in gold, given for the best sf novel expressing libertarian principles, was won by F. Paul Wilson for *Wheels Within Wheels*. A marvelous hedge against inflation, the award has doubled in value since its presentation.

There were many other minor awards presented last year. It seems to be the thing to do for any group larger than two.

Seacon '79, the 37th World Science Fiction Convention held in Brighton, England August 23–27, 1979, brought 3,244 attendees together in a horizontal Tower of Babel. Fans and professionals communicated in nearly every known tongue. When all else failed, body and sign language spanned the gap. There were sizable contingents from France, Germany, Sweden, Norway, Finland, Japan, Australia, The Netherlands, Beverly Hills, Spain, Russia, Portugal, Iceland, Yugoslavia, and our famous representative from Sri Lanka—Arthur C. Clarke, making his announced last appearance (maybe) outside his adopted country. The truly international aspects of the convention created an incredible feeling of good will between people who had met before only through the printed word. These conventions remind us that science fiction is more than a clutch of new book releases each month; it's an expanding community of shared ideas.

The 38th World Science Fiction Convention will be held in Boston August 29–September 1, 1980. Guests of Honor include Damon Knight and Kate Wilhelm. For information on membership, write Noreascon Two, Post Office Box 46, MIT Branch Post Office, Cambridge, MA 02139.

The 39th World Science Fiction Convention will be held in Denver September 2–7, 1981. Guests of Honor include Clifford Simak and C. L. Moore. For information on membership, write: Denvention 2, P.O. Box 11545, Denver, CO 80211.

Membership, supporting or attending, in the world convention is the only prerequisite for nominating and voting for the Hugo Awards.

Charles N. Brown is the editor of Locus, *the Newspaper of the Science Fiction Field. Copies are $1.25 each. Subscriptions in North America are $12.00/ year (2nd class), $18.00/year (1st class); overseas, $13.50/year (sea mail), $21.00/year (air mail). All subscriptions are payable only in U.S. funds to Locus Publications, P.O. Box 3938, San Francisco CA 94119.*

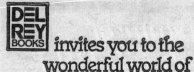